T0002456

THE
WRONG
BRiDESMAID

Irresistible Bachelor Series

Anaconda
Mr. Fiancé
Heartstopper
Stud Muffin
Mr. Fixit
Matchmaker
Motorhead
Baby Daddy
Untamed

Get Dirty Series

Dirty Talk
Dirty Laundry
Dirty Deeds
Dirty Secrets

Dirty Fairy Tales

Beauty and the Billionaire
Not So Prince Charming
Happily Never After

The Virgin Diaries

Satin and Pearls
Leather and Lace
Silk and Shadows

THE
WRONG
BRIDESMAID

LAUREN
LANDISH

 Montlake

This is a work of fiction. Names, characters, organizations, places, events, and incidents are either products of the author's imagination or are used fictitiously. Otherwise, any resemblance to actual persons, living or dead, is purely coincidental.

Text copyright © 2022 by Lauren Landish
All rights reserved.

No part of this book may be reproduced, or stored in a retrieval system, or transmitted in any form or by any means, electronic, mechanical, photocopying, recording, or otherwise, without express written permission of the publisher.

Published by Montlake, Seattle

www.apub.com

Amazon, the Amazon logo, and Montlake are trademarks of Amazon.com, Inc., or its affiliates.

ISBN-13: 9781662507410 (paperback)
ISBN-13: 9781662507403 (digital)

Cover design by Letitia Hasser

Cover photography by Wander Aguiar

Cover image: © MG Drachal / Shutterstock

Printed in the United States of America

THE
WRONG
BRIDESMAID

Chapter 1

Wyatt

Welcome to Cold Springs!!
HOME of Friendly Faces and Scenic Vistas!!!

A lot of people ask the universe for "a sign" when they've got a decision to make. What I don't think they expect is for it to be a five-foot-wide by three-foot-tall green-and-white reflective chunk of metal with questionable punctuation and capitalization. I certainly didn't. Though the extra exclamation points and overly emphatic capitalization do make me snort a little.

The sign is the doing of the one and only Francine Lockewood, Cold Springs' librarian and self-proclaimed historian. When the oldest elder in town declares the city council is being old fuddy-duddies and that she'll haunt the entirety of city hall if the winner of her slogan competition isn't honored, it's hard to disagree. Of course, the fact that no one had condoned a contest to begin with, and Francine had taken it entirely upon herself to run one, meant nothing.

I remember hearing my dad bitch about it, but in the end, Francine won. The city council ponied up $1,000 for that sign just to stop her from whispering to every school kid, soccer mom, and library visitor about the council members. They were protecting their jobs, what with an election coming up. Besides, it is sort of friendly and quaint, so maybe it is a little bit of a good sign?

Better than the one that actually drew me home, at least: the wedding invitation in the passenger seat of my truck. That one hit me like a bolt from the blue—literally, since my mailbox is blue. It's the universe telling me to handle my shit like a grown-ass man. Point taken, albeit reluctantly. Coming up to a red light, I glance at the ivory, heavyweight cardstock with fancy gold embossed script for the dozenth time.

> *The pleasure of your company is requested at the marriage of*
> *Miss Avery Singleton*
> *and*
> *Mr. Winston Ford*
> *Ford Family Home*
> *Saturday, May 21, 6:00 p.m.*
> *RSVP*

The words alone are shocking, but I still might've ignored the invitation despite the fact that my younger, perpetual-bachelor brother is apparently getting married. The accompanying handwritten postscript hadn't been as easily dismissed.

> *Come to the wedding, Wyatt. I want you by my side.*
> *Please. —Winston*

Even then, if he'd left it at the first two sentences alone, I would've skipped and claimed my invite was lost in the mail if anyone ever called me on it. Not that they've called me in the years I've been gone. But that last little bit, the *please*, had been my undoing.

Once upon a time, Winston and I were close. He and I were united, allies in a struggle of behavioral appropriateness and familial expectations that eventually had me leaving town. And despite our relationship growing distant since I left, our bond is still strong. If I were getting married—which I'm never going to do—I would want him by my side. Hell, I'd even go so far as to admit that I've missed him, and some other members of my family, but not enough to go back. Until now.

So here I am, drawing closer to the town that never did anything for me but expect my sweat and tears simply because of my blood. Cold Springs, the city that is both kingdom and prison to my family.

My father isn't simply on the city council that argued with Francine; he's been on it for most of my lifetime, and is currently the mayor.

My mother? President of the Junior League, former head of the parent-teacher association, and back in the day, Miss Cold Springs herself, who took first runner-up at the state contest.

My uncle? The largest developer and contractor in the county. At least 60 percent of the houses here were either built by Ford Contractors or have had repairs done by Ford Contractors.

The Fords *are* Cold Springs. For a lot of people, it'd be enough. I could've set myself up as a small-town prince.

Except I don't want any part of it. I didn't when I was younger, and I still don't now.

Francine was right about one thing—this town does have scenic vistas, but there will be few to no friendly faces for me on this visit. Thankfully, the rolling green hills and bright blue skies are beautiful enough to make up for it.

Almost.

I roll my window down, calling out to the trees, "Home sweet home. You miss me?"

The wind carries my words off, the trees ignoring my question as they focus on photosynthesis, and I suck in a deep breath of fresh, crisp air. As my lungs expand, my gut turns, souring the sensation.

This is going to be a clusterfuck of epic proportions. There's no way around it. I've found peace and enjoy a life where I'm not judged on my last name, except by car lovers. I've settled into a routine of my own making, but returning to my hometown automatically dredges up all the reasons I left.

I won't be able to avoid them when they're standing proudly at Winston's wedding like Dad of the Year and Uncle of the Century. It's going to hit me like a baseball bat to the balls.

Speak of the devil, or even think of him, and he shall appear. A larger-than-life billboard looms tall beside the road with my Uncle Jed's face beaming from its vinyl surface. It's been photoshopped, his teeth bleach white, his skin tanned, his hair perfect. Next to his face is the text.

TRANSFORMING WITH THE TIMES
SPRINGDALE RANCH SUBDIVISION
* LUXURY HOMES * NEW SCHOOLS * PRIVATE TECH HUB
COMING SOON—THE NEW AND IMPROVED COLD SPRINGS

The boring lack of extraneous punctuation tells me that Francine had nothing to do with the billboard, but it's the overall tone that furrows my brows. New and improved?

What in the hell is Uncle Jed up to now?

Luxury homes in Cold Springs? I mean, Mom and Dad's place is definitely nothing to sneeze at, but a whole new subdivision of them seems aggressive for what's always been a place that can't quite decide if it's a tiny city or a town.

And new schools? As in plural? I'm not sure there's even a need for that. I'm not that old, and Cold Springs High wasn't crowded back when I was there.

Most of all, what the hell is a private tech hub? Sounds like an overpriced copy machine that'll make espresso while you wait for your shit to print out.

The billboard version of my uncle doesn't answer. He stands silently with his arms crossed and a shit-eating grin on his face, khakis perfectly pressed and light blue shirt screaming his "rich guy pretending to be a working man" image.

"Plans, boy. I've got big plans."

He told me that once, and though I never doubted that he did, I didn't quite think he meant . . . this. Maybe it's a good thing I'm coming back when I am. For the wedding and to find out what the hell is going on.

As I drive through downtown, I see signs in the windows of businesses and the historical homes surrounding the old-fashioned square that's still the center of town.

McMansions = Higher Taxes for You and Me! Say NO to REZONING!

And the most vehement and blatant one . . .

Fuck Jed Ford!

The tone of the last one is a little bit scary, especially given that it's got a pitchfork poking a cartoon version of Uncle Jed's crotch and devil's horns sprouting out of his ubiquitous cowboy hat. But it's outside the local bar and grill, which is run by a woman who has a sordid history with Uncle Jed, so maybe it's saying more about her than him? I'd like to hope so, but a little voice in my head whispers, "I doubt it."

I finish making my way through downtown and get into the part of Cold Springs where my family and family friends live, and the signs change to ones that are more supportive of whatever Jed is up to. Or at least supportive by default . . .

Bill Ford
Cold Springs Mayor
Rezoning for the Future

The plain lawn signs may have my dad's name on them, but he's always been the "one" of the one-two punch that is Bill and Jed, no jokes about "excellent adventures" necessary. So anything supportive of one is in favor of the other. That means I'll need to have a talk with both of them to catch up on what's happening in Cold Springs.

I grunt in displeasure at the very thought. This is why I left. Or at least one of many reasons. I don't want to be involved in all this "politics interlaced with business and all connected by family" bullshit. It's shady as fuck and driven as much by greed as by progress.

But those thoughts dissolve into the breeze as I see my childhood home. It's a large, historical house that's been kept in meticulous condition for over a hundred and fifty years. The two-story white columns and black shutters surrounding every window look freshly painted, and the manicured green lawn is dotted with pristine flower beds pruned into submission. Dandelions are afraid to even land on that dirt.

The double-wide driveway of stamped concrete is clear of even a speck of dirt or grass, and I wouldn't be surprised if Mom has it swept every morning.

I used to play on the lawn as a child. Me, Winston, and our sister, Wren, would run amok, play hide-and-seek, and create entire fantasy worlds with our "castle" as a backdrop. I didn't realize how true that was until much later, though, when school became a study in classism, the haves and the have-nots naturally dividing into groups. Membership was declared through a hundred subtle signs, from what brand and type of shoes you wore to how worn or fashionable your jeans were.

As the wealthiest of the haves, I was treated as either the fabled prince who could do no wrong—despite my considerable list of wrongdoings—or the spoiled rich boy who couldn't be bothered to actually *do* anything.

The truth lay somewhere in the middle back then. It wasn't like I sat around waiting for life to be handed to me on a silver platter . . . but I definitely ignored more than a few rules, confident I wouldn't catch hell for it.

It was, in ways that a lot of people don't understand, miserable. A lot of my acting out was simply rebellion, asking someone to actually make me pay for my bullshit. And it kept getting excused. Which of course just led to more bullshit.

However, it did teach me an important lesson. Sometimes people will have preconceived ideas about you, and regardless of their accuracy, they will not be swayed, no matter the proof to the contrary. People liking or disliking me, using or dismissing me, without knowing anything other than my last name was a hard pill to swallow. Even now, living in a city where my name means nothing, I find it difficult to trust people's intentions.

Shutting off my engine, I relish in the moment of silence, taking one last breath of freedom, and wishing I could reverse out of here and never look back. But I can't.

All because Winston fucking said *please*.

I step out of my black Tundra, my boots barely touching the ground before the tall glass double doors swing open and a yellow bomb of fluff blurs toward me. Before I have a chance to react, it launches at me like a heat-seeking missile, hitting me flat in the chest and knocking me to the ground to be attacked by wet, sloppy kisses.

"Mr. Puddles! Hey, buddy! I missed you too," I tell the goldendoodle, who is nipping at my stubble as though trying to figure out what weird animal is currently living on my face. Mr. Puddles whines, his butt wiggling happily as I pet him. "That's my stubble, not an intruder," I tell him laughingly as I press my forehead to his. I did miss Mr. Puddles.

There's the click of heels on concrete, and another voice calls out, "Well, I'll be a damned liar! I told Winston there was no way you'd come back, not even for a wedding. Way to surprise even me."

My sister's voice is sharp and sarcastic but doesn't hide the thread of hurt beneath the venom. Knowing her, she meant for it to show so she could twist the knife a little. Pretty much every rock or country singer's epitome of that small-town girl who can turn his heart inside out and go dancing off into the sunset without a single fuck given, Wren is smart as a whip and more skilled at verbal warfare than anyone I've ever met.

Thankfully, I know how to deflect her a little. "I missed you, too, Wren."

She blinks, not giving in. In fact, her chin rises another inch, her nose haughtily in the air.

"And I'm sorry?" I hope it's enough because it's all I have to give her. There's no big story to tell, no tears of remorse, and no promises that I'll stay for good this time, because I'm not sorry I left.

Though I am sorry I hurt her by leaving.

"It'll do," she tells me, the ice slightly melting in her emerald eyes. "For now."

In a rapid switch of blondes from goldendoodle to human sister, she's crouched down beside me, hugging me tight. The smell of sunflowers and vanilla wafts up from her hair, and I realize that I'd forgotten what her signature perfume smells like. It's more of a gut punch than anything else has been today.

Mr. Puddles takes the opportunity of having two of his favorite people on his level to dive back in for more cuddles, and squirms his way between Wren and me, his belly up as he lets us know exactly where to pet.

I give in, rubbing his soft fur before shifting over and getting up. I offer Wren a hand up as well, and she follows it in for another hug. She's tiny next to me, barely five foot but full of confidence that makes her seem ten feet tall and bulletproof, another one of her traits that seems to be pure Wren. Of course, the Ford name doesn't hurt. Neither does the trademark Ford beauty, which she puts to good use.

Early on, Wren learned from Mom how to make the most of her green eyes, hair with natural highlights most women pay for, and feminine figure. I'm pretty sure that during her time at Cold Springs High, just about every guy had at least a passing crush on her, but that's mostly a guess since I was already gone for the majority of those years.

But just as importantly, she learned how to put her brain to use by watching Dad, though she likes to play the dumb-blonde act to her advantage when it suits her.

"Wy, I can't breathe," she grunts, laughing despite her lack of oxygen. I squeeze a little tighter, and she thumps me on the back hard enough to take my breath away too.

"Oh, sorry. Just happy to see you," I tell her, surprised at the honesty in my own words.

"You could've come visit anytime," she reminds me. Her perfectly filled-in brow arches as she experiments with delicately calling me out.

"You could've come visit me anytime too," I echo, not taking the bait.

"Psshaw, and leave all this." Her smile is bright and as fake as a twenty-five-cent diamond from a gumball machine as she throws her hands out, indicating the house behind her.

"You'd like Newport, Wren. City shopping, for one. And there's less . . ."—I search for the right word, but find only one—"*Ford* there." Somehow, she knows exactly what I mean when I use our last name to describe the difference between Cold Springs and Newport.

Her nod is resigned. She understands better than anyone, I suspect. "There's a lot going on here at the homestead, Wyatt. I didn't feel like there was ever a good time to leave."

"There never is." The truth sits heavily between us. My leaving went over about as well as a stink bomb in Sunday school, but I still feel like it couldn't have gone over any better regardless of the timing. "Well, let's get this over with."

I take a step toward the front door, following Mr. Puddles, but Wren makes a sound of uncertainty. She clears her throat, and I look down at her. "There are things you should know. About Winston, about Dad and Uncle Jed."

I don't stop my progress, on a mission now that I've started it. "I figured as much. Let me see what the hell they've gotten into now."

I burst through the front door and into the grand foyer as my mother, Pamela Ford, comes rushing down the stairs. She's wearing one of the typical uniforms she rotates through, a white tennis skirt with matching tank top. Objectively, my mom is still a knockout, even if there hasn't been a Miss Cold Springs pageant in at least a generation. She's diligent about taking care of herself with visits to the tennis courts, the salon, and I suspect, the doctor.

Her eyes go wide as she gasps at the sight of me. "Oh my goodness! Wyatt! Are you really here?" Her hands flatten against her chest dramatically. *And the Best Actress Award goes to . . .*

"Flesh and blood, Mom."

"My baby!" she exclaims, running toward me. Her arms go around my waist, and I crouch slightly to wrap my arms around her shoulders, careful not to squeeze her too hard.

"I'm not a baby," I growl, fighting a smile.

She pulls back, looking up to remind me, "Thirty-six hours of painful labor to push that big head out gives me the right to call you my baby for your entire life."

Yeah, I've been hearing that one awhile. "Disagree. But I'll agree to *your* life. Deal?"

In answer, she hugs me again. I take that as agreement and call it a win.

From somewhere behind me, Wren adds on, "Sounds like you're assuming you'll outlive Mom. That remains to be seen with the upcoming festivities. I'm predicting Mom'll be wailing at your funeral within the week."

"Oh, Wren! Don't be like that," Mom scolds her. Abandoning whatever plans she had, Mom starts dragging me toward the living room, talking a mile a minute and hitting me with rapid-fire questions. "I'm so glad you came for the wedding. Have you seen Winston yet? He'll be so pleased to see you. How long are you staying? You'll stay upstairs in your room, of course. Did you bring a date? You know she'll have to stay in a different room so things are proper."

"Mom." The tone of exasperation is obvious and does at least make her pause to take a breath. "I haven't seen anyone but you and Wren yet, but this is strictly a visit. I'm going home after the wedding." She didn't ask that, but I know it's the one thing she wants to know, and I've got to stop that train long before it can even start to leave the station. "And I'm alone. I wouldn't dream of subjecting someone I actually care for to this circus shitshow."

Harsh, but true. And while my mother may not like it, Wren snorts and then mutters under her breath, "True that."

"Wyatt," Mom gasps again, this time more in horror than excitement at my presence. I *dare* to call my family situation a circus shitshow? Oh, the humanity.

A sudden shout brings us all up short, tension shooting through all three of us.

"William? Is that really you?"

Mom and Wren meet eyes, matching worry blooming faster than a hothouse flower. Their reaction worries me, and a moment later I can see why as my father, William Ford II (never Junior), stumbles into the room with a glass of amber liquid in his hand. From here, I can smell that it's scotch.

It's early for a drink, definitely not an after-work cocktail, but maybe he had a rough day? He looks as though that's a possibility, his expensive black slacks wrinkled and his white dress shirt rolled up to his elbows. He squints at me through bleary eyes, and I begin to suspect this isn't his first scotch.

"William? That you?" he repeats. It sounds like he's forgotten that he already asked, and my concern ticks up a notch.

"It's Wyatt, dear," Mom corrects him, touching his arm gently. I might be William Wyatt Ford III, but I've always gone by my middle name, the same way my dad has always gone by Bill.

What the hell? I think, alarmed. *Is this what Wren wanted to talk about?*

In all my years, I've never seen my usually meticulously steady and stoic father sloppy drunk. I think I've only seen him tipsy at a party once or twice, and those were usually events like New Year's or a birthday.

After all, he prides himself on his standing in the community as mayor and city council representative. He wouldn't want to tarnish his reputation by being seen as something as mundane as a drunkard.

For a moment, I'm too shocked to even respond, but eventually words come. "Hey, Dad. Cutting out of work a bit early today?"

This a skill set us Fords learn at a very young age—the ability to say something without actually saying it. It's all in the delivery, the tone, the subtle eyebrow lift.

"Wyatt," Mom starts, her worry morphing into embarrassment. "Don't make it worse. Your father has been hard at work."

"Don't need you to make excuses for me," Dad snarls, jerking his arm away from Mom, who looks stricken.

Wren sighs heavily before calling out, "Leo, code D-A-D in the living room."

Leo, one half of the couple who has cared for our home and us for decades, pops in immediately. He looks the same as the day I left, his dark hair still blacker than night and his eyes full of a degree of kindness I only ever received from him and his wife, Maria. "Oh, Mr. Ford, let me escort you to your office. You can have a minute to gather yourself."

Leo wraps a gentle but strong arm around Dad's shoulders, urging him toward the hall, but Dad's feet don't budge. "I don't need to gather myself. Don't you see my son here? Back from running away to do God knows what, only God knows where."

I grit my teeth at being likened to a runaway throwing a temper tantrum when I left for valid reasons. But my anger morphs as I observe the power struggle, and I watch Leo subtly glance to Mom for approval, and she nods slightly. It appears to be a routine of "control the drunk" they've done before, and I'm left with a sour, bitter twisting feeling in my stomach.

What the fuck is going on here?

"Mr. Ford, I must insist. I believe there's a call for you. Something about the council meeting?" Leo suggests more firmly, grasping Dad's arm. I'm certain there's no phone call and it's simply a ploy to get Dad to agree to a moment out of sight.

"Leggo of me!" he snaps, not willing to play along, it seems. "I'm perfectly fine!"

Dad might be drunk, but he's still strong. He jerks out of Leo's reach, and the sudden movement knocks the glass out of his hand. It falls, shattering loudly on the floor. The sound's like a hand grenade, shocking everyone in the room, and we all freeze.

"Okaaay," Wren says firmly, the first to gather her wits. With a note of resigned frustration in her voice, she directs, "Leo, I got *this*." She gestures to Dad with a look of disgust. "Can you get Maria to clean this up and then grab Wyatt's bags from his truck?" She motions to Mom, cutting me a look so hard that she doesn't have to tell me to stay out of this. "Mom, can you help me with Dad?"

He's standing on his own, at least, a forlorn look of confusion on his face as he frowns at the mess of glass at his feet. It's like he honestly doesn't understand how the hard material in his hand suddenly got to the floor, droplets of scotch soaking into the cuffs of his pants.

Wren walks over and wraps Dad's right arm around her shoulder, and Mom takes his left. "Dear, I think you were working so hard that you forgot to eat lunch again." Still making excuses, or maybe finding ways to make Dad more agreeable, they manage to help him from the room.

"S-s-sorry, son," Dad slurs, "I should've had lunch. Get Maria to make you a plate." His voice fades as they go upstairs, heading toward not his office but my parents' bedroom. I suspect he'll be passed out, snoring obnoxiously, within moments.

"How long has he been like that?" I demand from Leo as soon as they're out of sight, my eyes still locked on the now-empty stairs.

Leo hums thoughtfully, but he's not counting days or weeks or months. He's counting something that doesn't apply to a lot of people any longer . . . loyalty. "Not my place to say."

I turn to look at him, realizing he doesn't look exactly the same. The grooves on the corners of his mouth are deeper than I remember, as though he's frowned more than he used to, and there's a tiredness in his eyes that wasn't there before. But this is one that I can't let slide. "Leo?"

He licks his lips and replies in almost a sigh. "You should talk to your brother. Things haven't been the same since you've been gone."

The statement shouldn't surprise me. I knew leaving would have consequences, but I mostly thought of them in terms of what I'd be gaining—freedom, a fresh start, control of my own destiny.

It's a heavy feeling to be reminded of what my leaving might have cost back here at home. And that a lot of those costs were going to be paid by the people I love.

"Where is Winston?"

"In your father's office. Getting Bill around Winston is usually helpful in these situations. That's why I told him there was a phone call," Leo explains.

I nod, and walk quickly down the hallway to Dad's office. I stop short, though, when I see Winston propped up in Dad's chair with his feet on the desk, phone pressed to his ear. His hair is longer than I've seen it before, with flips of length falling over his ears and into his eyes. His nose crinkles as he says, "I don't care about champagne brands or colors, Cara. Cristal, Dom, Moët . . . don't care. Ivory, pink, or neon orange like Cheetos . . . I don't. Give. A fuck." He's silent for a second, listening. "Whatever Uncle Jed said is fine unless Avery wants something different."

I clear my throat and he looks up, half in shock, half in worry he just got caught out doing something wrong. When he sees me in the doorway, he shouts, "Wyatt? Holy shit, bro! You came."

That sounds like my brother, eloquent as always. Where Wren got the skills to verbally slice and dice at will, Winston is more of a smash-and-trash sort. I'm somewhere in the middle, I guess.

Winston hangs up the phone without another word and rushes at me, grabbing me in a fierce bear hug and slapping me on the back. "You came."

"Of course I did," I say when he lets me go. "Not every day my little brother gets married."

There's more question there than there should be, but this is Winston we're talking about. He once proclaimed that he was never going to get married when there were so many women to sample. Of course, he was a mouthy fourteen-year-old virgin who'd just been shot down by his crush at the time, but I thought he'd held on to the sentiment.

"Nope. I'm a fucking goner of the one-and-done variety. Avery owns me—dick, heart, and soul."

"Romantic," I summarize with a raised brow. "I want to hear all about this Avery who's managing to get you down the aisle, but first, what the hell is up with Dad? He came sloshing through the living room like a squirrel who'd been noshing on old grapes off the vine."

Winston groans, and takes a step back to rub at his forehead. "Again?"

Before I can question that, Wren barrels into the room, her eyes tight and her jaw clenched. "Incoming—Mom's looking for you both. I'll hold her off as best as possible. Get out while you can."

Winston and I look at her in surprise, our brains still computing what she just spit out in one rapid-fire sentence.

"Go!" she hisses.

That's enough to get us moving, and we hustle through the foyer and out the front door like so many times before. We never had to "sneak out," exactly. That was part of being a Ford: if you wanted to leave, you did, walking out with your head held high and your shoulders back. Anything less was weakness, and Fords do not show that to anyone, especially family.

You just have to make sure you walk your ass out the door at the proper time. Thankfully, my keys are in the cup holder, right where Leo left them when he grabbed my suitcase from the back seat. I start the truck and pull out at a reasonable speed—to punch it and spin out would only call attention to our departure.

"Wren's the best," Winston says from the passenger seat.

"Always was, always will be," I agree. "Now . . . we talk."

Chapter 2

WYATT

"Are you sure about this?" I ask uncertainly as I pull into the lot Winston directs me to. "There's a sign right there that says 'Fuck Jed Ford,' and this is Uncle Jed's ex's place. Pretty sure we're not welcome here."

"Here" is the Puss N Boots bar and grill. It's a long, skinny building, cinder block and clapboard with a tin roof just outside downtown, with the aforementioned sign and a ten-foot-tall neon cartoon Puss in Boots, complete with hat, boots, and swishing sword.

"Yeah, I come here all the time," Winston says dismissively, as if that's supposed to be reassuring. "It's kind of an escape, because Jed and Dad wouldn't dream of setting foot inside these four walls. Mostly because Etta would personally chop them to bits and Tay Tay would fry them up and serve them with a side of his homemade fancy ketchup. He does a killer one, by the way."

"What?" I ask, not clear on half of what Winston said. But *escape* I understand, so I park and follow Winston's lead inside. It's not that pleasant of a walk: my guts are still roiling from what happened at the house, and a potential ambush doesn't help things, to be honest. I haven't been in town in years, and I'm not expecting a warm welcome or any of those supposedly friendly faces at my return. My hackles are up, my skin uncomfortably tight, and I'm ready to throw down at a moment's notice.

When the door closes, I look around, alert for any incoming friends or foes. Honestly, I don't want either one right now. But I can see why this is a popular spot. Regardless of the exterior architecture, the bar feels spacious but warm at the same time, with enough room for a bunch of tables, a bar, and an area with pool tables and a few arcade games. The wood paneling and hardwood floors are well worn but look cared for, and despite the midafternoon hour, there's quite a crowd in here.

There's absolutely no pretentiousness to it. It's a bar with a "take it or leave it" vibe. And right now, I think I want to take it. Especially if it offers that escape Winston promised.

Three hours in town and already looking for an out doesn't bode well for this visit, man.

"Order up," a voice calls as a bell dings. "Come get your shit or I'mma eat this good-looking, finger-licking basket of fries myself, Charlene."

"That's chicken, not fries, Tay Tay. Chicken is good-looking and finger-licking," another voice answers.

From the kitchen, there's a bark of laughter. "Girl, everything I make is good-looking and finger-licking. And by everything, I mean *everything.*"

I see a blonde woman approach a large cutout in the paneling that shows the kitchen beyond. A guy in a black, silky do-rag peeks out with a smirk of satisfaction. I'm going to assume that's the cook, and the blonde snaps some gum as she gives him a look. "I know what you're implying, Tay Tay, and ain't nobody sucking on your"—she cleared her throat—"straw to give a Yelp review."

I snort in surprise, nearly choking on my own spit. Holy shit, there are levels, and then there's this place.

"Have to take my word for it, baby. Five stars, every time," the guy—Tay Tay, I guess—quips, flashing five fingers through the air repeatedly.

"If you say so," she tells him, grabbing the basket of fries and speed-walking across the room. As she passes by the door, she sees Winston and me and I hold my breath, ready for another bomb. "Seat yourself anywhere. I'll be with ya in a jiffy."

Without a second glance she's off, doing business. Huh, no evil looks, accusations, or punches thrown my way. I'm more surprised than I'd like to admit.

"See?" Winston says, reading my thoughts. "We're fine here. And we can talk without Dad interrupting. Or trying to drunk dial council members." He rolls his eyes.

"No way. He did that?" I ask, somewhere between horrified and delighted. There're a few members of the city council who need an unfiltered verbal smackdown, in my opinion, though it surprises me that it came from Dad.

"More than once," Winston informs me, pulling out a stool and perching at a table I suspect might be his usual. There are pictures of Etta all over the place, mixed in with newspaper articles about Cold Springs, but the photo by this table is of Hyde Hill, one of Winston's favorite places to go when we were teens.

Before I can ask anything else, the blonde reappears at the side of the table. "Hey, honey-babies, what can I getcha?"

"Draft beer and a burger, please, Charlene," Winston says automatically.

There are no menus to speak of, so I go for the sure bet and echo Winston's order. "Same for me, please."

The woman's eyes narrow as she looks up from her notepad. "Who's your tall-drink-o'-water friend, Winston? Gonna introduce me?"

Winston chuckles and slaps me on the back. "Charlene, this is my brother, Wyatt. Wyatt, this is Charlene, who is way, way, way out of your league."

Charlene tuts. "Now don't you go telling tales. You don't know, maybe I'm looking for something a bit different this go-round." She's talking to Winston, but her eyes are drinking me in like I'm fresh spring water on a hot day in the desert. "Hi there, Wyatt. Pleased to meetcha."

She slides her pen behind her ear and offers her hand, which I take, shaking politely. "Nice to meet you too, Charlene. I'm afraid my brother's right, though. I'm not looking for a . . . go-round, sorry to say." Her pink-glossed lips pout, and I rush to correct the harsh brush-off. I lean to the side, scanning her head to toe to take in her blue cutoff denim shorts, white shirt knotted above her slim waistline, glittery nails, and eyes surrounded by liner and long, fake lashes. "As beautiful as she might be."

"Hmmph," she answers.

"Woman, your Fat Pussy is ready. You planning on handling it yourself, or you want me to take it to table nine?" the disembodied voice calls out from the kitchen before I can reply to Charlene's self-confident taunt.

Charlene rolls her eyes and huffs, leaning in. "He means my burger, not *my* fat pussy. I don't have one of those. Mine's pretty as a porno."

"Um . . . okay?" I stutter. I thought I could handle a conversation. Apparently not.

She whirls in place, leaning back against the table like she hasn't got anywhere better to be or anything else to do. I can see a small tattoo on the back of each arm with a name and date.

"Tay Tay, can you give a girl a minute to see if she can get laid, please? Marcus, go get your burger real quick. Mama's busy making friends." A guy across the room nods agreeably and gets up to grab his own burger. "Thank you, honey-baby." Whirling back, she smiles in my direction. "Now, where were we?"

I blink. Winston grins, and I'm beginning to think he chose this place specifically to set me up for whatever *this* is.

"Oh, that's right," she says, snapping her fingers. "Pretty pussy. Now, my hair extensions cost me a penny, my nails cost me a dollar, and my makeup was free. Got these lashes done over at the beauty college by a student," she confides to Winston. Laser locking me in her gaze once more, Charlene adds, "But I'm not one of those high-maintenance types. You ain't never seen something look this good that costs so little, I guar-on-tee you that, Mr. Wyatt. And don't get me wrong, I ain't looking for no baby daddy—got two of those already—or a ring on my finger. It's just that sometimes a girl likes a dick with a heartbeat instead of a pulse mode, know what I mean?"

Somewhere along her crazy line of propositioning, I find surer footing. She's half playing. Her signals are clear: If I want a ride, she'll let me play cowboy. But it's no skin off her ass if I don't. "That's definitely understandable. But I'm afraid my heart quit beating a long time ago, if you catch my drift. You'd be better off with machine-gun mode on your nightstand friend."

Telling a woman that I've got a case of the no-rise dick disease is definitely not a move I'd usually pull from my playbook, but in this case, fighting fire with fire seems like a safe choice.

And it works, as Charlene cackles loudly and then slaps Winston's bicep. "Honey-baby, you did not tell me your kinfolk was funnier than a hyena on laughing gas. Big-ass liar too. I'mma bet you've got an engine like a Harley. Steel hard and thrums all night. I like this one. Keep him around." Then to us both, she says, "I'll be back with those beers and Fat Pussies."

She lifts and lowers her eyebrows quickly, still suggesting more than a mere burger meal. As she sways her hips and struts away, I turn to glare at Winston. "A little warning would've been nice."

He chuckles. "Oh, Charlene and Tayvious—that's the mouthy cook back there—are fine, and entertaining as fuck. Besides, you should've seen yourself . . ." He lets his eyes go wide and his jaw drop open dumbly, his voice picking up a drawl. "Um . . . what? I uh . . . don't want to sex you up despite your free-and-clear offer, ma'am."

"Fucker, that's not what I sounded like," I growl. He purses his lips thoughtfully, tilting his head. "Shit, was it that bad?"

"You did save it with the limp-dick comment, but yeah. Preeetty bad, Golden Boy. Kinda nice to see you fall off your pedestal a bit, though."

Why does that sound like he's talking about a lot more than my crash-and-burn attempt at not hurting Charlene's feelings? Still, I scoff. "Pedestal? I smashed that thing to fucking ruins a long time ago. You know that."

Winston sighs. "Yeah, guess you did."

Charlene runs by, dropping off our beers and blowing me a kiss as she scoots on her way, catching up on serving her other tables after hanging out at ours for so long.

I take a big swig, not even tasting it as I swallow but needing the liquid courage. "Alright, back to business. What the hell is going on around here?"

Winston takes a healthy drink of his own before asking, "You want the good, the bad, or the ugly first?"

I shrug. Doesn't matter, I need all of it. Let Winston tell it however the hell he wants.

He hums, and takes another sip. "Let's go chronological, I guess, starting when you left. After that, I went to school, got my architecture degree. Did my internships with Uncle Jed, of course."

"Of course," I agree, not surprised.

"While I was at school, I met Avery. She's actually from Cold Springs, but she's a little younger than me, more Wren's age, so we'd never met before, though she knew exactly who I was. She was taking nursing classes and wouldn't give me the time of day, no matter how hard I tried. But eventually, I won her over. Fuck, it was hard, but she's worth it."

I'm surprised at the soft tone in my brother's voice and the sparkle in his eyes. "So she's the one?"

The very idea is foreign, especially for the Winston I know. That Winston tried to fuck his way through the girls' soccer team, or at least date his way through them. But maybe I don't know him so well anymore, I realize.

The idea is uncomfortable. I've certainly changed while I've been gone, but in my mind, everyone else stayed exactly the same, frozen in time. But maybe we've all changed?

"The one and only," he says emphatically. "We're getting married, rain or shine, hell or high water." His eyes go wide, as if he's being hit by the idea for the first time. "Fuck. I'm getting married, Wyatt."

I reach over to place a hand on his shoulder, patting him comfortingly. "It sounds like she's either a psycho or an angel. I'm betting the second. Especially if she's putting up with you, so don't fuck it up, bro," I tease. He answers with a big grin, and I consider whether maybe he's not surprised so much as he is excited about the idea of marrying Avery.

"I can't wait to meet the magical woman who's turned you into a blubbering romantic, waxing poetic about her awesomeness and admitting your unworthiness."

He ignores the playful jab. "I can't wait for you to meet her. You're going to love her. She's . . . different than us, Wyatt. That's what I love about her."

He glances down to his still-empty ring finger as though imagining the wedding band that will soon be there. "Funny thing is, the day I met her, I was talking shit like usual, and then she walked in the room. I was blown away, but knew she'd smell the douchery on me. I had to grow up a fuckton before she'd even give me a chance, but I'm so glad she did. So fucking glad." His eyes clear as his mind returns to the here and now, and our discussion of me meeting Avery. "We'll have to see when we can get that to happen because she's really busy with wedding stuff, plus she takes care of her grandpa."

"Shit. That's a lot to handle," I say, stating the obvious because I don't know what else to say.

Thankfully, Charlene drops off our burgers, saving me. "I put a little extra sweetness in yours, honey-baby." That sounds sketchy, so I hesitate to taste my food, but Winston does so easily. Slowly, I pick up the delicious-looking burger and take a tentative bite.

"Damn, this is good," I tell Winston. "Whatever 'extra sweetness' Charlene added to mine, do *not* tell me, please, because I really want to keep eating this."

My brother laughs, choking on his mouthful of burger, which serves him right. Looking to turn the conversation back toward more productive avenues, I ask, "So Avery takes care of her family?"

"Yeah, and she does it with a smile. Her grandpa lives with her, but he has an aide come in to help with some of his personal care. He says he doesn't want Avery seeing his frank 'n' beans—that's what he calls them." Winston laughs and I chuckle along. "And she works shifts at the nursing home when they need her. PRN, they call it, but basically it means that when someone calls in sick or needs a vacation day, they call her. So she might work days on end or not at all for weeks. Could be day shift or night shift, or even a long weekend double."

"That's tough," I comment. "You know, the unpredictability of hours or money."

"Yeah . . . but that's Avery. She's amazing."

"You ever think that's why she hasn't realized yet that you're . . . you?" I tease.

"It's definitely crossed my mind," Winston admits. "But I'm different than before too. Or as much as I can be." A shadow crosses over his face, and his bright smile fades into a frown in a matter of seconds. Back to the hard shit, it seems.

"Sounds like we're moving into the bad? Or the ugly?" I prompt, not tiptoeing into it. I'd rather rip the Band-Aid off and take the scab with it.

Winston scoffs. "Yeah. So after school, I came home and started working for Uncle Jed full-time. Avery was still in school, so I went balls to the wall for the company, getting in on every project they'd let me in on and learning everything I could. It was good at first. The other people accepted me, saw that I was trying to work hard and listening more than talking. I felt like I was growing, putting my degree to use, and I advanced up the chain quickly. Not because of my name, though it didn't hurt," he says sardonically, "but because I'm damn good. I am, Wyatt."

It sounds like he's trying to convince me. What he doesn't realize is that in the past few years, I've learned a few things myself. "I don't doubt that, Winston. You were always smart, you just fucked off. And yet somehow managed to still get As and Bs."

He nods appreciatively at the compliment.

"This latest project is a bitch, though." He shakes his head. "It's years in the making. Research, politics, plans, contracts. It's big, bigger than anything Jed's done. He says it's going to be his crown jewel."

"Are you talking about the subdivision thing? I saw a big billboard on my way into town and then a bunch of signs saying to vote no to rezoning. Along with the Fuck Jed sign, though I guess I'm not sure if that's about the subdivision thing or in general from Etta."

Winston nods, his face serious. "I don't think any of us expected there to be so much pushback. Fuck, I think Jed thought everyone would see him as the savior messiah, bringing us out of the dark ages into the bright light of the future. But there's a lot of outrage, from more than half the town. And Dad's taking the brunt of it, having to walk the line carefully between his roles for the city and his relationship with Jed. He started drinking a while ago, stressed out and exhausted. It's not constant, or at least I don't think it is, and we all watch closely, but it's too often. He's falling apart in front of my eyes, and I don't know how to help him or what to do. I thought the wedding might help, give him a happier focus, you know, but even that went wonky."

"How so?" I ask.

The sigh that passes Winston's lips is one of full surrender. "Jed. As soon as Avery and I announced the wedding and started making plans, Jed pulled me into his office. He offered to pay for the wedding."

"Please, for the love of all fucks past, present, and future, tell me that you told him no," I beg. I know my Uncle Jed and how he works, and what Winston just said has *danger* written all over it.

"I tried, but you know how he is," Winston says forlornly. "Avery and I wanted something small. She'd have been content with the two of us at City Hall. She didn't grow up this way, Wyatt. When I asked her for her wildest wedding fantasy, she talked about a cake from the local bakery, flowers from a farm out in the country, and a dress that made her feel beautiful. She wants everyone to smile and dance, eat, and have a good time. That's it."

"And now that Jed's involved?" I ask, already knowing the answer.

"It's become this cable-channel fucking monstrosity of a wedding, with everyone from work, and I don't mean the people I actually see. I'm talking vendors and business associates. He acts like my wedding is a networking event, for fuck's sake," he huffs. "It's still at the house, I made sure of that because I want to get married in the garden out back, but that's about the only thing the same. There's going to be big white tents, a live band, and ten thousand dollars' worth of champagne. Avery doesn't even like champagne! She'll probably have a white wine and call it good."

"What else?" I prompt him, leading him to a big reveal I can feel beneath his fretting about drinks and tents.

"It's a lot, Wyatt. We're over a hundred grand at least. And rising . . . daily."

My jaw drops. "Holy shit, man! For a wedding? You should've just run off to Vegas or Hawaii or something."

"I wish we had," he agrees gloomily. "This is going to haunt me, but it got so out of control so fast. I didn't know what Mom and the wedding planner were doing, or what Jed was adding to the list because it . . . it . . ."

"It was easier to not know," I finish for him. "Been there, done that. I understand how that goes better than anyone." He looks at me sadly. "You're going to be beholden to him now. He won't give you a contract, but . . . it'll be there. A big fuckin' debt sheet, your balls listed as the collateral. That's his game, and he led you right into the trap like leading a pig to slaughter."

"A really fancy slaughter," he corrects. "With a *band*."

"Just like the *Titanic*. They'll play while you sink into Jed's control." Winston presses his lips together in agreement. "Does Dad know? About Jed paying?" I'm honestly scared of the answer. Has Dad learned nothing from what happened with us?

Winston shrugs. "I don't think so. He probably figures Mom has it under control because he's been too worried about the optics of the wedding to worry about who's paying for it. I mean, with the whole town split down the middle about this subdivision and bringing in fresh blood—and money—it's a really shitty time to have a big blowout bash of epic proportions. People are already gossiping about the cost, the guest list, the whole thing."

"And you just want to marry the woman who straightened out your shit, and live your happily ever after?" I summarize.

"Yeah," Winston sighs. "So . . . welcome home, big brother."

I scoff, and take a bite of my burger. "I wish I could say it's good to be back, but that'd be a lie. The only reason I'm here is because you said *please*, you damn fucker."

Winston laughs darkly. "Thanks, Wyatt."

"Anytime."

We fall into silence, digging into our meals. My mind turns all the information over and over, looking for angles and strategies, for Winston, Dad, and even Jed. Not because I'd ever help Jed, but because by thinking the way he does, maybe I can figure out what the hell he's up to. Because he's always up to something. He only does things that benefit him. That's a sure thing.

"How've you been?" Winston asks after a bit, probably looking for some good news in the day.

I shrug, trying to encourage my brother without making my plain, normal life seem like a victory to lord over him. "Good. I work, I go home, I work, I go home. It's . . . peaceful, I guess is the right word? I like earning a dollar with the sweat of my own brow and the work of my own hands."

I look down at my once soft and smooth hands, noting that they're covered in scars and rough calluses now. I consider each mark a badge of honor. My honor. Here's my education, my lessons taught and left on my flesh forever.

"Never would've guessed you'd end up the hard-labor type," Winston says around a mouthful. "Mom and Dad would shit themselves if they knew."

He's probably right. I do custom woodworking, using centuries-old methods of joinery and responsibly sourced heritage woods. It was slow going at first, but I've made a name for myself in certain circles, ones that have nothing to do with my family.

My brow furrows at Winston's last comment. "They don't know? I figured Jed told them years ago."

"He knows? I had to hire a damn investigator to track you down!"

Of fucking course. When I left, determined to strike out on my own, Jed hunted me down, trying to guilt-trip me into coming home, but I refused. He even tried to throw me some pity contracts, saying he wanted to support my "little business," but I turned them down.

"He tried to play his games with me too," I explain simply. "I thought I'd gotten away scot-free, but I guess he's holding that card for another day."

"Sounds about right," Winston says with an eye roll. I'm sorry that he's getting to know firsthand how convoluted this family can be. I really hoped that wouldn't be the case.

You knew. You just had to save yourself.

It's an ugly truth to admit, even silently. But it's a little like putting on your own oxygen mask before helping anyone else in an airplane. I had to escape for my own well-being. I meant to come back and save Winston and Wren someday, but it never seemed like the right time, and I told myself that they could've walked away on their own too.

They didn't have to wait for me.

But maybe that's all bullshit to excuse my guilt, because they got trapped. And my leaving made the trap that much stickier for them to get out of.

I have to own that.

The sound of shattering glass snaps my attention away, and I see Charlene standing in a pile of glass by the bar, a river of orange-red liquid around her heels as the bartender rushes to get a broom. Despite the initial flash of imagery, it's not blood . . . It's something else.

"Etta's gonna be pissed!" Charlene whines, wringing her long-nailed fingers in distress. "We have too much overflow!" Turning toward the pool tables, she raises her voice over the din of the bar: "Would be nice if the other waitress, who's still in the building, having fun playing pool, would stop for a bit to help out."

I'm not sure who she's talking to, but I hear a sexy, sultry voice float right back from over by the pool tables: "One, ask for what you want, not all this 'would be nice' suggestion shit. Ain't nobody got time for that. Two, my shift is over, Charlene. If you wanted me to work overtime to help out, you should've asked before I clocked out. Three, this is my *me* time. Four, your tap's overflowing your pitcher."

Charlene grumbles something I can't hear under her breath in response, but she runs over to shut off the beer tap and set aside the overflowing pitcher. I scan the crowd over at the pool tables, looking for the owner of the voice.

When I see her, my mouth goes completely dry.

Bent over one of the pool tables, holding a pink cue, is one of the most stunning women I've ever seen. Dressed in denim cutoff shorts, a red-and-white plaid shirt that's tied in a knot above her belly button, and caramel cowboy boots that have seen better days, she looks like your classic country girl next door.

Except she's not some country music video starlet. She's 100 percent real, a knockout in the flesh.

Without even worrying about Charlene's situation, she flicks her long, dark waves over a shoulder as she lines up a shot. From here, I can tell she's got a waist I'd like to grab and a round peach ass I'd like to smack.

For the first time in a while, I feel something stir. And not just my cock, though it's perking up as she slides the pool cue between her fingers smoothly. There's something about her confidence in telling Charlene off and the suggestiveness of the way she's stroking her cue.

"Holy fucking shit."

I don't even realize I've said that out loud until I hear Winston lean over and say, "That's Hazel Sullivan."

He could have said she was the queen of England, or any other name in the world. I barely notice with so much of my attention caught up in her movements. "Who?"

"Avery's best friend. She was in the same grade as Wren, so you might not know her, but let's just say she grew up *good*." I nod dumbly, agreeing wholeheartedly even though I have no idea what she looked like before. "Before you get too invested in your eye-fuck situation, she's also Etta's niece."

Two words . . . and a tsunami wave of cold water on my burgeoning interest.

"Of course she is. Fucking Uncle Jed." I pick up my beer, telling myself I've struck out even before getting to the plate, but I can't take my eyes off her.

I realize that the blond man behind her is her opponent in her current pool match, and a quick scan of the table tells me there are eleven balls left—five solid, five striped, and the eight.

I watch as Hazel walks around, positions herself, and steadies her cue. Following her gaze, I see the ball she's trying to hit. Three ball, center right pocket. It's an extreme cut shot, one that some semipro players might struggle with.

"No fucking way you're making that," I whisper to myself, but sense Winston turning around to see what I'm looking at so intently.

"She will," he says nonchalantly. "She always does."

I watch, hypnotized, holding my breath, as Hazel goes still as a statue. All time seems to stop. Then she pulls her arm back and pushes her cue forward with a graceful and precise motion.

My eyes follow the cue ball as it hits the red ball with a clean, muted click, sending it sailing cleanly into the center right pocket. Not too hard, not too soft . . . just right.

Impressed, I let out a low whistle as a triumphant smile spreads across Hazel's face. In contrast, her opponent's face turns a dark shade of red. But Hazel doesn't pay him any mind, strutting around the table to take her next shots. She makes each of them easily, and her opponent only seems to get madder with each successful shot.

On a run, she hits the last solid in and pauses. The eight ball is at the top left pocket, shielded by two of her opponent's balls. There's no way to hit the ball without hitting those. Depending on the table rules, she could be out of luck.

But that doesn't seem to concern Hazel as she positions herself again, her hair falling over her shoulders and down her side like a dark, silky veil as she stretches her body out over the pool table, angling her cue to line up her shot.

Despite his frustration, Hazel's opponent runs his eyes over her body appreciatively before returning his attention to the balls on the table, and I have to remind myself that it's just a game.

Pop!

Hazel hits the bottom of the cue ball, and it jumps over her opponent's balls, tapping the eight ball into the pocket before safely caroming off and coming to a rest.

"Whooo!" Hazel cheers loudly, waving her pink pool cue above her head. "That'a girl, Joannie!"

Who's Joannie?

Strutting, Hazel walks over to the blond guy and sticks out her palm expectantly. "Alright, Roddy. Pay up."

Roddy looks like he's on the verge of explosion, his face red and his lip curled in a snarl. I'm paying close attention, but even if I weren't, I'd be able to hear his rebuttal. "I'm not paying you shit. You're a fucking cheater, Hazel Sullivan."

Hazel's grin melts into a sneer of her own. "One, you owe me for that eye fuck you just gave my ass. And two, I am not a cheater. You're just salty that I beat you fair and square."

Roddy laughs bitterly. "Fair? Your aunt owns this place, so who knows what kind of booby traps you got under these damn tables to help you win. There's probably magnets and shit."

"Booby traps and magnets? Really?" Hazel rolls her eyes. "Do you know how incredibly stupid you sound right now?"

"I dunno, I sound pretty smart to me, because I'm keeping my two hundred in my pocket." He pats his chest pocket as he looks over his shoulder at two guys perched on nearby stools. They grin at Roddy like that comeback was actually a solid burn.

Hazel licks her lips slowly, and I can practically see the wheels turning in her mind. After what she said to Charlene, I almost can't wait. Part of me wants to get involved . . . but not quite yet. We're still at the talking stage, and Hazel doesn't seem to need or want any help in that department.

Loud and clear, she says, "I get it, Roddy. You've been talking shit for weeks about how you were gonna wipe the floor with me, only to find out that not only is my dick—oh, I mean, *stick*—bigger than yours, but I've got better skills with it too. So your choices are to hold up your end of the bet, pay up, and live to play another day, or . . ."

Hazel doesn't threaten him out loud, but she does hold her pink pool cue in front of her, tapping the thicker end against her palm. The intention is pretty fucking clear.

"Fuck off. You're not gonna hit me with that stick of yours. We all know what it means to you." Roddy eyes the pool cue in question as he takes a small step toward Hazel, who holds her ground.

The move alone is aggressive, but partnered with the threat, it's crossing a line. I've seen and heard enough. I'm out of my seat before Winston can stop me, heading straight for Roddy. And Hazel.

Chapter 3

HAZEL

Holy fuckballs! Is Roddy actually gonna make me smack him around?

I don't want to. He's right—it would probably fuck up Joannie. But that doesn't mean I won't give him a swift kick in the ass if I have to. I'm a waitress in a place that serves Fat Pussy burgers, so I have thick skin by default and a mouth that would shock a sailor. My spine and smack talk are usually enough to get me through almost any situation.

But Roddy is in an extra-pissy mood, not that I blame him after losing so epically. He should just suck it up like the buttercup he is and move along. If he weren't making such a big deal out of this, his buddies wouldn't either. But they smell blood in the water . . . Roddy's. And he's deflecting big-time, hoping to sic them on me instead.

I bend my knees slightly, getting my weight centered, and flick an angry scowl Roddy's way. He's so close, I can smell the cheap beer on his breath and the sweat from a day's work on his skin. I tighten my grip on Joan of Arc, a.k.a. Joannie, my pink pool cue that I saved up to buy. This maple cue has seen me through some tough games over the years. She's my baby, and if Roddy ends up making me defend myself with her, I will make him pay for a proper funeral service for my best girl, and a replacement Joan of Arc 2.0 that's bigger and better. Or at least lighter, my personal preference.

Roddy doesn't seem the least bit frightened by my stance or scowl, though, probably too hyped on liquid courage and testosterone-fueled desperation. His balls are on the line, at least in his mind. He doesn't make a move to reach for the cash I know he has stashed in his chest pocket.

As shitty as his refusal to pay is, it's not the first time this has happened to me. In fact, it's why I try to not play strangers on my home turf. They see the cute waitress, flirt a little, and think they're going to "teach" me to play. By the time I've wiped the table with them, their wounded pride rears up, and more than once, I've had to get a bit tough with them. But they always pay up . . . eventually.

I thought I was safe playing Roddy, though. He's a regular, after all, drinking and having a good time with his buddies here at least once a week. He damn well knows I'm good. Hell, he's been watching me play, studying my moves for weeks. He should've known this would be the outcome.

"Pay up, Roddy," I grit through clenched teeth, only loud enough for him to hear, though we've gotten quite an audience now. He doesn't acknowledge it, but it's not only two hundred bucks at risk here. Both our reputations are on the line.

For fuck's sake, man, just do it. Reach in your pocket, take out the money, and hand it over. I'll even let you make a few comments to salvage yourself, let you play it off if you want to save face with your buddies. I'll save my rebuttal for after you stomp out the door like a pissed-off pit bull.

His hand moves toward his chest, and though I'm tempted to let out a sigh of relief, I hold my breath steady, staying ready. It's a wise decision, because while Roddy is giving in, it's on his own terms.

"Fucking take it, bitch." He pulls out the wad of cash he flashed when we bet and throws it at me. The green bills smack me in the chest and then flutter to the floor. In a different environment, people might scurry to grab up the money like squirrels gobbling nuts.

Ha, nut-loving critters! The phrasing makes me laugh even at a time like this, but only on the inside.

But not here. Not right now.

Nobody rushes to grab a single bill because they're mine and everyone knows it. Especially Roddy. There's saving his rep . . . and then there's this.

I don't move, don't drop a single inch toward picking up the cash, because I won't tolerate this kind of disrespect. Pool is a game of rules, and even in a barroom match, I won't be disrespected. And I for damn sure am not getting my head anywhere near his dick level. "Pick it up. You don't have to hand it to me if it hurts your *wittle feewings*, but at least put it on the table so everyone can see you're a man of your word."

Okay, so maybe poking the drunk, angry bear isn't the wisest thing I've ever done, but it's definitely not the dumbest, either, despite what happens next.

Roddy knocks Joan of Arc out of my hands, and she clatters to the floor. "Pick it up yourself. It'd do you some good to spend a few minutes on your knees. I'm out of here."

Oh, hell to the nah nah nah.

He spins, already throwing a hand up at his buddies to signal it's time to leave. His arrogance gives me the perfect opportunity. With a primal scream that draws from an ancestry of women who don't put up with anyone's shit, I jump onto Roddy's back like the worst piggy ever, gripping him with my knees and clawing at his wide shoulders.

"Pick it up!" I shout over and over. "Pick it up, pick it up!"

Roddy pitches forward but catches himself, thankfully not throwing me ass over his head. "Get offa me, you crazy bitch!"

We tussle, him trying to get me off his back and me using my weight to get him closer to the ground so he'll pick up the money. Around us, cheers and shouts ring out, mostly on my side.

"You show him, Hazel!"

"Ride that bastard, cowgirl!"

"That ain't no way to treat a lady!"

"You call *that* a lady?"

Okay, so that last one might not've been in my favor, but if defending myself makes me unladylike, then un-fucking-ladylike I'll be.

I'm making progress, or at least I think I am, when a booming voice orders, "Enough!"

Viselike arms wrap around my waist, pulling me from Roddy. Thinking one of Roddy's friends has suddenly grown a pair and intervened, I flail and fight back.

I drive back with an elbow, but the contact is weak, glancing off the thick shoulder behind me. I kick my feet, aiming for shins, and connect with a knee, judging by the grunt behind me.

I will take this to my deathbed, and never even whisper this secret to my best friend, but wrestling around with the thick-bodied, hard-muscled man behind me is the most excitement I've had in ages. I can't see his face, but the feel of his strength is sexy in a dominant, powerful way.

And that's enough of that nonsense, Hazel Sullivan. You ain't that type of girl.

"Put me down!" I bite out, also considering biting my captor. Maybe on that bicep I can feel flexing as he holds me securely.

"Only if you calm down. Both of you."

I hear a snort from our audience as they get their comments in. "That one ain't too bright, is he? Everyone knows not to tell a woman to calm down unless you want her to go nuclear." *Nuclear* is said like *newk-eww-lerr*, with long drawls on each syllable.

At least that one's right. I give it all I've got, wiggling for my life. Fine, and also maybe to see if I can feel abs behind me . . . or something more. But I'm not admitting that, even to myself. But before I can do more than wriggle, my feet find the floor. Instantly, I step away, whirling to face my captor.

"What the fuck do you think you're doing?" I spit out, the accusation fortunately preformed by my brain and already sent to my mouth, because as soon as I see him, my brain turns into complete static.

A tall, broad-shouldered, trim-waisted, sexy model stands before me. Seriously, he looks like he just walked off the pages of *Modern Logging*. Is that even a thing? If not, it should be, and this asshole should grace the cover of the premier edition. His blond hair is stylishly messy in that way that should take forever but, since he's a guy, is likely actual bedhead. His jawline is chiseled and shaded by day-old stubble that makes him look rugged instead of pretty. And his eyes, blue diamonds that are sparkling with delight.

"Helping you," he explains with a healthy dose of "duh" woven through the words.

Ah, there it is.

He's one of *those* types. White knights. The saviors who want to rush in to save the little damsel in distress, all the while laughing at her inability to take care of herself. He's nothing but trouble with a bonus side dish of asshole.

"I don't need your help. Or anyone else's," I return, waving my hand to urge him back to his beer or whatever. "So skedaddle along back to wherever it is you came from, Prince Charming. I've got this handled."

"Wyatt?" Roddy says behind me.

Hell, I'd almost forgotten about that particular jerkwad.

"The one and only," the walking sex god says dryly. "I'd shake your hand, but I think we have another issue to take care of first." He glances down at the cash on the floor pointedly. "Why don't we all pick it up together, put it on the table, and call it good?"

Roddy looks at me and shrugs, suddenly willing to give in now that another guy is running the show.

That pisses me off anew, but I try to not cut my nose off to spite my face. "I get the two hundred either way."

Okay, maybe just a tiny slice.

The three of us slowly bend down, gathering up the scattered bills. To his credit, Roddy shoves the wad he's collected into my hand instead of dropping it on the table. As I put the bills into my pocket, Roddy picks up Joannie, laying her on the table and rolling her forward and backward to make sure she's still good. My breath catches in my throat, both from his hands being on my prized pool cue and in hope that she rolls cleanly.

"Looks okay, but lemme know if not." It's all the apology Roddy offers, so all the acceptance I give is a dip of my chin. He looks past me and startles. "Think I better call it a night, I guess."

I lift a brow and glare over my shoulder. Sex God Wyatt is standing like a bodyguard, feet firmly planted to the floor, arms crossed over his chest, and a hard look on his face. Turning back to Roddy, I say, "Probably for the best. Looks like I have a line forming of assholes to deal with."

Roddy's lips twitch. "You saying stuff like that makes me want to stick around and see someone else get his ass handed to him." Still fighting off a grin, he holds his hand out to Wyatt. "Good luck with this one, man. Glad to see ya."

I have no idea what Roddy's talking about. I'm perfectly pleasant when I'm not being disrespected.

Wyatt shakes Roddy's hand, and then Roddy heads out with his two friends in tow. They're already teasing him about both losing the game and getting beat down by me, which serves him right.

I turn back to Wyatt, ready to handle whatever his business is fast and quick. Cold and hard, I inform him, "I didn't need your help. I had it perfectly under control."

"Roddy's a big guy," Wyatt replies easily, seeming not offended in the least by my ungratefulness. "Looked like he was about to walk away from the bet to me. Or worse."

I roll my eyes. Roddy might know this hunk, but this hunk definitely does not know me. "Puh-leeze. Roddy wouldn't have laid a finger on me. He's been a regular for years. He gets a little hotheaded sometimes, but nothing I can't handle. Especially with Joan of Arc backing me up." I pick up my cue, brandishing the pink maple like a lightsaber, complete with sound effects, causing a few nearby people to step out of the way of my swinging arc. Wyatt chuckles at my antics, and the deep, full rumble tickles something within my core, making the fine hairs on the back of my neck rise.

My body's traitorous response to his voice annoys me. I'm not exactly celibate, not even close to it. I get hit on by people here at Puss N Boots so often that I could easily get laid more than a hooker working Main Street during a parade. But the flip side of that is that I see too many no-good cheaters walk through these doors and have seen the fallout of a betrayal firsthand, because Aunt Etta hasn't been the same since she swore off men after catching her fiancé cheating on her on the eve of their wedding. And that was so many years ago, we measure it in decades at this point.

So I make it a habit to be selective. To the point of . . . wait, how long has it been? I try to think back, but when I start counting months in the double digits, I decide to examine that later. Much later. And alone.

"Your pool cue is named Joan of Arc?"

"Nope, we're not doing this," I reply to his question, holding up a palm to stop his get-to-know-you small talk.

His smile blooms, white and bright. He's not just lumberjack-magazine sexy; he's a toothpaste commercial too. "We're not? It kinda seems like we are . . . I'm here, you're here, we're talking." He shrugs one shoulder, daring me to disagree with the obvious.

Point taken, I spin in place. Game. Over. "Bye."

My plan is to beeline to another pool table, play a stress-free, no-stakes game to relax and forget about Mr. Modern Logging–Sex God–Prince Charming–Asshole.

"You forgot something." The deep voice behind me stops me in my tracks, and I groan in annoyance. So help me if I turn around and he says something stupid like "saying thank you" or "your phone number." I will have to teach him a lesson the same way I was willing to teach Roddy one.

But when I look over my shoulder, Wyatt is holding up a ten-dollar bill. I grit my teeth and trace the few steps back. When I grab at the money, he lifts it high, using his height against me. "Let's play a game. Double or nothing."

I jump, snatching the money from his hand. Fuck, I hate it when tall guys do that. I know it's just to make my boobs bounce. "Except this is already my money."

The jump puts me even closer to him, though, and a waft of his cologne works its way into my nose and lights up my brain. It's woodsy and spicy, reminding me of leather and pine trees, a combination that suddenly seems sexy as fuck. My nipples perk up and my ovaries stretch from their long slumber, hopping up like a pair of joyful jelly beans, both of them demanding a little extra attention.

What the hell is wrong with me? Am I ovulating or something? I've heard that can make you hornier. Or maybe Wyatt has some megawatt pheromones that are wreaking havoc on me?

"Then let's play for bragging rights," he suggests, which is honestly a bigger gamble than a few bucks. My reputation's worth more than money around Puss N Boots.

"Let's don't and say we did. Besides, I don't play newcomers," I explain, adding, "for your protection. Grumpy losers are bad for business." I gesture toward the door, where Roddy stomped out moments ago.

"Newcomers?" he echoes, his brows pulling together. And then he grins. "You don't know who I am, do you?"

"Should I?" I scan him again, making note of the thick thighs, narrow waist, broad shoulders, tanned skin, and gorgeous face. There is something vaguely familiar about him, but if I'd seen him before, I definitely wouldn't have forgotten him.

Instead of answering, he repeats, "Let's play."

Nope, no way, nuh-uh. These are all the responses that run through my mind, but my mouth doesn't get the memo, and to my surprise, I hear myself say, "Okay."

Shit, why did I say that? Now I'm going to have to actually spend more time with the devil, and dancing is not what's on my mind, unless you count the horizontal mambo. Trying to save a little face, I quickly sputter, "Your funeral. Don't say I didn't warn you."

"Pretty sure you warned me, Roddy warned me, and Charlene over there is currently warning me too." He hooks a thumb through the air, and I follow it to see Charlene still busting ass with the rush but keeping one eye on Wyatt and me. It's the stink eye she reserves for the worst of customers.

I hold off from going straight into my "I was right" victory dance, taking the time to ask, "You know Charlene?"

There's the tiniest bit of disappointment in my gut, and it's threaded through my voice. She's like an irresistible force of nature. She wants a man, she gets a man. That's it. Like gravity, or taxes, or death, she just is.

"Nope. In fact, I just met her when she took my order. Though she did offer a go-round." He laughs lightly, and I can imagine what Charlene offered.

"And you said?"

"Thank you, but no thank you?" he says, though there's a hint of confusion in his answer. I guess he's not used to being questioned boldly about another woman. But I don't want to step on Charlene's toes. Sisters before misters and all. Not that she's my literal sister, but she's like one.

"Alright then." I shouldn't agree to play with him. I know it from my fingertips to my toes, but I've never claimed to make the right decisions 100 percent of the time. I don't claim it for even 50 percent of the time! I aim for a solid 33 percent responsible, another 33 dumb, and one more 33 percent fun. The last 1 percent? That's for absolute, purely ridiculous outrageousness. It's what I call balance.

We wait for the next available table, then get set up. I'll give Wyatt credit, he racks like a newbie should, but at the same time nice and tight. He knows what he's doing as he selects a cue, and I pat Joannie. "I'm good. You need a breakdown of the rules or anything? I don't want you bitchin' and moanin' about me cheating when I win," I tell him, referring to Roddy's hissy fit.

Wyatt shakes his head, taking chalk and rubbing it on the tip of his cue. The movement is practiced and experienced. Curiously, I ask, "Are you sharkin' me?"

"Nope," he says, "but do you mind if I break?"

I swear to God if he pockets the eight ball and I lose outright, I will slam his face to the felt. But I gesture with one hand, giving him not the floor but the table.

He positions himself where he wants and takes a strong stance behind the cue ball, and my eyes go to his butt as he leans down. *Total dump truck of an ass,* I think. In fact, I'm so focused on it, I almost miss him pumping his cue forward to strike the ball.

Crack!

The cue ball slams into the ball set with incredible force, sending balls all over the table. Two of them find their way into pockets. Luckily, one is a stripe while the other is solid. It's still anyone's table to run.

Wyatt takes another shot successfully, sinking the one and claiming solids, and then one more before missing.

Good game so far, Wyatt. But it's all over now. You won't get another shot. With the balls or me.

I try to quell my giddiness as I size up my shot and quickly weigh my options.

I'm lined up on the nine ball, aiming straight for the left corner pocket. It's an easy shot, one that I could make with my eyes closed.

I'll have to make sure I use the right English to set my next shot up, though.

I get into position, angling myself, but I pause, my skin prickling. Out of the corner of my eye, I see Wyatt looming off to the side, like a giant sentinel watching me. I don't know why, but it's *so* very distracting the way he's staring at me, which is particularly frustrating because I'm usually good at canceling out any distractions when playing, no matter *who* I'm playing.

But there's something about Wyatt that is throwing me off my game.

"Good form," I vaguely hear him say.

Focus, Hazel, focus! He's trying to distract you to get in your head.

Putting my eyes straight on my target and leveling my gaze, I hit the cue ball, and it flies forward, hitting the yellow-and-white ball toward the pocket . . . but double-bangs off the corners before rolling away, missing.

I stare in disbelief, hot embarrassment burning my cheeks. How could I miss that? I could've made that shot when I was ten years old! The fact that I obviously screwed up only because of Wyatt eye fucking me has me shook.

Serves you right for being so cocky, I tell myself angrily.

"Sorry to interrupt y'all's lovely game," a voice says from behind me, and I turn to see my best friend's fiancé, Winston, walking up to clamp a hand on Wyatt's shoulder, "but I have to steal my big brother away, I'm afraid."

"Give us a few, we're in a match," Wyatt growls. "And it was just starting to get good."

Brother? It hits me like a ton of bricks.

Wyatt. Ford. As in, of the Ford family. Jed and Bill Ford.

That's why he looks vaguely familiar. I can see the similarities between them now.

"Winston, did you say this guy is your brother?" I want to be sure before I go off half-cocked again. I like Winston . . . now. At first, when Avery came back from school, talking my head off about this guy she was dating, I was happy for her. Then she told me his name, and my happiness for my friend evaporated into thin air. In fact, it led to the biggest fight we've ever had. But Winston has proven himself to be completely different from his uncle. He loves Avery and is totally gone for her—hook, line, and sinker. And if he loves her that much, then I'll give him a pass on his shitty family. He didn't choose them, after all.

But Wyatt?

I feel duped for some reason. It's not like we exchanged last names, phone numbers, preferred positions, and post-fuck snack recipes, but c'mon, he knows the weight his name carries around here. Hell, I'm surprised he didn't lead with that since those four little letters are probably enough to get him a legs-open invitation from some women.

"Guilty as charged. He's home for the wedding," Winston tells me. To Wyatt, he says, "As I was trying to tell you before you charged off, Hazel is Avery's best friend and she's in the wedding, so you'll see her there."

"You're in the wedding?" Wyatt repeats, sounding just as surprised as I feel.

"Yeah," I drawl out, not liking his tone. "Don't worry, I clean up real purdy and won't embarrass your kinfolk by leaving my POS car on the front lawn or picking my teeth with a shrimp fork." I have no idea if a shrimp fork is even small enough to get between my teeth, but the point stands. I'm not in the same class as these two. Not in the same world.

And if there was ever a man for me, his last name would not be Ford, because he would not be related to the man who is turning my hometown into a battleground and who broke my Aunt Etta's heart.

"The little plastic swords from the appetizers are better toothpick substitutes," Wyatt suggests casually, almost sounding . . . amused?

I scowl, not liking this back-and-forth. Why can't he just take the burn and slink away like most guys do? Is that so damn hard?

Winston looks from Wyatt to me. "Uh, okay . . . so there's that. But we do need to leave, Wyatt. Avery wants me to bring her dinner."

That's enough to stop the mental formulation of my next attack plan. "Is she okay? Why hasn't she already had dinner? It's late."

Avery is a giver through and through, and if she's asking for dinner, it means she's at the end of her rope.

"She's fine. Grandpa just wanted Tayvious's chili, so I offered to take him a bowl. And I can't very well take him dinner without taking Avery some, right? So I got her a big burger. I'm gonna have Wyatt drop me off, and I'll stay over to make sure she eats." He pauses, then corrects himself: "Make sure they *both* eat."

Avery's grandpa is still a lively, slick one. His mind's sharp as Tay Tay's favorite knife, but without the nastiness a lot of old folks get when their bodies start to betray them. But he needs a lot of care, enough that Avery spends the majority of her time supervising him. It sounds like she's got Winston to help with that now too.

"Yeah, of course. Tell her to call me if she needs anything." It's a safer conversation than the one Wyatt's eyes are trying to have with me—one filled with confusion at my whiplash cold shoulder. "Bye!"

I try to make it sound breezy and casual, but I'm pretty sure I fail.

The brothers turn and make their way out. And though I try to fight it, I can't help but watch Wyatt as he walks away, his stride strong and powerful, his well-defined ass looking magnificent in those jeans of his.

More than one woman in the room has her eye on him, too, some of them literally looking like they're in heat with their tongues hanging out. Charlene herself looks like she's about to pull the seltzer hose from underneath the bar and start hosing people down, starting with herself.

It's at that moment I make a firm decision.

Whatever happens, and whatever I do, I'll be sure to keep far, far away from Wyatt Ford. No matter what, I have to avoid him at all costs . . . wedding or otherwise.

Chapter 4

HAZEL

I bump the front door with my hip, trying to open it without dropping the precious bag of goodies I'm balancing in my hands, all the while knowing the highest-value item is the to-go cup of white wine I had the bartender pour. Thankfully I'm successful, but my inner celebration is cut short by a siren followed by a loud automated voice . . .

Woo-ee-woo-ee

Intruder alert! Intruder alert! Call 9-1-1!

Police have been notified.

Woo-ee-woo-ee

This would be concerning . . . if I actually had an alarm system. But I don't. What I have is a loudmouthed gray parrot, who is currently perched on the back of one of my dinette chairs and giving me an evil glare.

"Lester! Shut up! You better not have called the cops again." The *or else* is heavily implied.

"Bawk! Bitch! Bawk!"

There are times I really wish that bird couldn't talk. Meanwhile, I beeline for the kitchen, setting the bag of food and Styrofoam cup on the counter to grab the phone from the wall. I listen to see if there's an open line anywhere in the house but thankfully get only a dial tone.

The 9-1-1 operators know Lester well, considering the number of times he's actually called them. But that was mostly when he was my Gran's companion, and she did occasionally need help, so we were thankful for that particular party trick of his. Since she passed a few years ago and I inherited Lester, the operators have taken to double-checking before sending anyone out, mostly because of an incident involving me, Deputy Milson, and a baseball bat. In my defense, he peeked in my bedroom window while I was changing clothes and I thought he was a Peeping Tom. I was well within my rights to swing that Louisville Slugger. The first time.

"Bwahahawk!" It's Lester's version of *gotcha* as he laughs, his big feathery head bobbing like he's really proud of himself.

"I oughta pluck your feathers and cook you up for Sunday dinner," I threaten, not meaning a word of it. Truth be told, Lester and I are buds. But sometimes, the best friends are the ones who give each other shit.

"Lester too salty." And now my bird is talking about himself in the third person. Great. "But he's a pretty bird. Bawk! Pretty bird!"

I can't argue with that. He is a beautiful specimen, gray with a white mask around his eyes and a shock of deep red feathers as a tail. "You are a pretty bird. And do you know what pretty—and *well-behaved*—birds get to do?" His beady black eyes flick around, then focus on me intently. "Go visit Aunt Etta. You wanna go for a visit?"

Aunt Etta's little cottage is visible through the window over the kitchen sink. Back when she had the pink house with white trim and shutters built, it was a compromise with Gran, who needed some careful supervision but refused to have anyone, strangers or family, living with her. Independent until the end, she did things her way and left a legacy of strength, boldness, and take-no-prisoners sass. All of which means Aunt Etta, Mom, and I are peas in a very small pod.

After Gran's death, Aunt Etta didn't have any interest in moving into Gran's house with her own so close by. Mom also refused, wanting to keep her space above her downtown bakery so that she could go between work and home at the drop of a hat. We also didn't want it to be sold. I mean, the house meant a lot to us.

So it seemed only natural for the house—and Lester—to go to me. I happily moved into the small ranch house that held so many of my childhood memories.

"Bawk! Let's go, bitch!" Lester flies over, perching on my shoulder. His claws dig into my skin a little bit, but I'm mostly used to it and he's exceedingly careful to be gentle.

I should do something about his foul language, but it's too late now. He learned from Gran, Aunt Etta, Mom, and me. And there's no telling what my brother, Jesse, has taught him. Hell, he probably has old Lester spying on me and reporting back details of my actions. I wouldn't put something like that past Jesse. He's my brother and I love him, but he forgets that I can handle myself sometimes and acts like he's the only thing keeping me from a shallow grave or prison, which is ironic considering he had the chance to move into Gran's house, too, but he laughed his ass off at the idea of bringing a woman out here: *"I'd be lucky to live long enough to date. More likely, Aunt Etta would call me a 'typical dick-led asshole' if I tried to get laid and bury me in the back forty after running off anyone I tried to spend time with."*

Trusting Lester to not fly off, I grab the food and wine and head out to walk the one hundred feet to Aunt Etta's.

This is a walk I've done hundreds of times. Anytime Jesse and I would come to see Gran, we'd inevitably end up at Aunt Etta's, a double whammy of fun and spoiling we fully enjoyed. Jesse and I would chase each other around the big yard, then chase fireflies after dark. Aunt Etta taught us how to shoot bows and arrows, ride horses, and of course, shoot pool. And then Gran would cook us a delicious dinner topped off with a melt-in-your-mouth sweet potato pie.

I miss you so much, Gran.

The lights are off in the front of Etta's house, but I'm not surprised. I know where Aunt Etta is. The barn behind her home is her sanctuary, and where she spends all her time if she's not at Puss N Boots. I slide open the door as quietly as I can and make my way down the center aisle to Nala's stall. Lester hops off to explore on his own, and probably hunt down one of the horse's oat cookies to snatch.

"How's she doing?" I ask softly, scanning the sorrel quarter horse, who's watching me with interest.

Aunt Etta doesn't move from her place, sitting in the soft hay and leaning back against the wooden wall. She's wearing well-worn jeans, a snap-front plaid shirt, and boots covered in various shades of brown staining. Her dark hair hangs in one long braid over her right shoulder, and her eyes never stray from Nala, who might as well be her child.

"Better. Another day or two and she'll be good as new." She says it as though declaring it will make it so. Actually, she might be able to—I bet even God wouldn't risk pissing off Aunt Etta. "Chiropractor came by earlier and did an alignment. Made a big difference."

Nala snorts as though she's agreeing with Aunt Etta.

"Good. I brought you some grub, and some wine." I slow step toward her and Aunt Etta reaches up to take the offered bag and cup. Hands now free, I sit down next to her in the hay.

"Bless you, girl. I need this." Aunt Etta pops the lid off the cup first and takes a sip. She smacks her lips. "Yep, needed that. What's in the bag?" she asks, already opening it and thrusting a hand inside. "Ooh, is this one of Tay's famous fried-catfish po'boys? You are too good to me, Hazel."

She takes a second bite before swallowing the first, obviously hungry but unwilling to leave Nala alone for even a moment.

"I'll stay with her if you want to walk around a bit to stretch your legs or go to the bathroom." I make the offer even though I already know the answer. Nala's her baby; she isn't going anywhere.

Aunt Etta snorts her reply, sounding vaguely like her beloved horse did a moment ago, and then adds a fry to the mouthful of sandwich she's working on. We fall quiet, both of us watching Nala while Etta eats. After a few minutes, she says, "You gonna tell me about tonight or not?"

I huff out a wry laugh, not surprised that she's already heard about the fiasco with Roddy. This town gets bigger every day, but not so fast that the small-town grapevine can't keep pace. For folks like us, Cold Springs natives, that grapevine works faster than Twitter. "Roddy finally decided to man up and play me. I won, of course, which made him totally forget himself. Tried to stiff me on the bet, but he paid up in the end and stomped his way out like a pissed-off possum, hissing and snapping his teeth."

Aunt Etta takes another drink. "Not what I meant. Everyone knew you were gonna wipe the floor with that boy. Only question was how big the margin was going to be. You've been a better player than him since you were twelve years old." I preen at the praise from the woman who taught me how to play pool, although I will admit that I did have a bit of "home table advantage," considering how well I know every square inch of that surface. "I mean, you gonna tell me about *after* that?"

She leans my way a bit, pinning me with her dark eyes, which are hard as marbles right now.

Play dumb, my brain shouts, though I'm not sure why exactly. I didn't do anything wrong.

"After?" Aunt Etta's glare somehow gets harder and icier. "Oh, you mean *aaafter*. Well, there was a guy that butted in to the deal with Roddy, and I played him. Said his name was Wyatt, and then I found out what he should've said was his name's William Wyatt Ford III."

I leave out my body's reaction to him and all the filthy thoughts I was fighting. Etta doesn't need to know any of that for damn sure.

"Bill's oldest. That's what I heard." Etta nods emphatically as her lips turn down. "You'd best watch out for that boy. He's got that Ford blood, and he's a runner. Double whammy."

I don't understand why, but my gut reaction is to defend Wyatt. I know next to nothing about him. Name? Definitely in the negative column. Stepping in between Roddy and me? Annoying and unneeded, but maybe a bit sweet. All the banter? As much as I hate to admit it, I enjoyed it. I don't often meet people who can go toe to toe with me. My rough edges are a little too abrasive for most folks.

"Oh no. He's already seduced you, hasn't he?" Aunt Etta scoffs, her eyes not missing a moment of whatever expressions crossed my face. "Figures."

"No. He has not," I argue petulantly. But a second later, I quietly ask, "Do you know anything about him specifically, though? Or just the Fords in general."

"Knew it." She shakes her head but sighs as her attention returns to Nala. "Not a lot. He left town a while back and doesn't visit, but nobody knows what that's all about. Could be that Daddy told him no about a flashy car or could be because he thinks his dad's a horse's behind. No telling. But he's fruit of the poisonous tree, so he can't be all that great."

She's got a point, but . . . "Winston's great. He interrupted my game with Wyatt because he wanted to drop off dinner for Avery and Grandpa Joe."

Etta snorts again. "Winston wasn't always great. The love of a good woman can help a man see a different path. If his eyes are open and his heart's willing." She sounds like a wise old hippie more than the country woman she is. "I think we'd both agree that Avery's about the best woman any of us know."

The implication that I'm not isn't some big shocker of a revelation. Avery is truly one of a kind, and we definitely follow the friendship rule—one is nice and boring; one is crude and crazy. She says I keep her life interesting, and she makes me think before reacting.

Sometimes.

"Avery had her work cut out with Winston. I think it was worth it, though. The wedding is going to be beautiful."

"As long as the marriage is too," Aunt Etta adds thoughtfully. "Too many people thinking all about one day, when you've got to think about thousands of others."

Relationships are a touchy subject for her. She was once a soon-to-be bride, innocently thinking her fiancé was as impatient and excited for their wedding and marriage as she was. She was floating on cloud nine.

But walking in on him balls deep in her best friend was the shock of her lifetime and altered the trajectory of everything she thought her future would be. It doesn't help Aunt Etta's opinion of Winston and Wyatt that her fiancé was the one and only Jed Ford.

"You think it won't be?" I question, concerned that she sees an issue with Avery and Winston that I don't.

She jolts as if coming out of a trance and pats my hand reassuringly. "I'm sure it'll be fine, just fine. You're right, Avery has changed that man."

I wish she sounded as sure as those words would make it seem. Then again, Aunt Etta lets Winston into her bar, so she's got to have some confidence in him. Though that was a process in itself, requiring Winston to prove himself through a labyrinth of hazing and insults before being officially welcomed at Puss N Boots.

Lester flies into Nala's stall, landing high on one of the wooden walls dividing it from the next. "Bawk! Lester good bird. Want cookie."

Aunt Etta points a finger at the bird. "You've been in the tack room eating cookies this whole time and we both know it. Greedy bird, you're going to be so fat, you won't be able to fly."

I hiss, "Don't tell him that! You'll give him a complex." I hold out my hand and Lester hops down to me, settling in my lap. I pet his feathers gently. "You're perfect just the way you are."

"Lester know. Perfect bird." Apparently, he doesn't have a complex, unless it's a superiority one.

I let out a dramatic sigh and look over to Aunt Etta, who looks back at me with approximately zero sympathy. She's not always Lester's biggest fan, often calling him "the devil bird from the deepest pits of hell." But that's a leftover from the time Lester pooped in her freshly done hair. It was an accident—he's fully paper trained—but Etta doesn't forgive or forget easily. She does sneak him cookies, though, so I know she's not too hate-filled.

"I think I know a bird who needs to go to bed," I tell him. I get up from the hay, dusting off my butt. "You need anything else?" I ask Aunt Etta, knowing she'll be out here all night, probably sleeping here so she can keep an eye on Nala.

"No, I'm okay, honey. Thank you again," she says, holding up the Styrofoam cup.

As I walk out of the stall, she calls, "Hazel . . ." I look back and she glances down before meeting my eyes deliberately. "Be careful. I don't know Wyatt, but I know what he comes from. It's not about whether you're enough to change him like Avery did Winston. It's about . . ." She licks her lips, thinking. "Just be careful. I don't want you to get hurt."

I hate that one man hurt her bad enough to sour her on them all, but touched at her care, I dip my chin, placing a hand on my heart. "I will be, Aunt Etta. I promise."

She nods once, accepting my words. "Good, because if he hurts you, I'll kill him. And then I'll go to jail. It'll be a whole messy thing." She waves a hand around like there's mess all over the freshly cleaned stall. "And who'd take care of Nala then?"

"They'd never catch you anyway," I tease, but I understand what she's telling me.

Lester and I head back home. I know his sleep habits like the back of my hand, and he needs at least ten hours a night of sleep and darkness. So after changing out his paper and his water, I pet the feathers on top of his head, making little calming sounds until Lester steps onto his perch in his cage. "Bedtime, Lester."

"Bawk!" Lester agrees. I give him a smile and slowly close the blinds on his cage, drawing them around and doing the Velcro so he can relax in the darkness.

I retreat to the doorway and click the light. "Good night, Lester."

"Lester sleepy bird!" He begins making fake snoring sounds that do sound vaguely like Gran sleeping in the living room recliner she used to love. It's long gone now, but I can still see her laid out on it like it was her favorite place to be.

I retreat to my room and start my own night routine, showering and scrubbing my face with Noxzema before using cocoa butter to prevent wrinkles. After that I lie in bed, but instead of a Netflix show or two, my thoughts return to tonight . . . and Wyatt.

What was it about him that set me on edge so readily? I mean, yeah, he's hotter than a jalapeño-flavored lollipop, but that's usually not enough to catch my attention the way he did. But there's no denying it—I wanted him. I'm just smart enough to not let that happen. At least not in real life.

There's no harm in fantasies, I tell myself with a sly smile in the dark. *They're what makes life interesting . . . or tolerable.*

I take a deep breath, feeling my chest scrape along the weight of the blankets on top of me. My nipples perk up, remembering how close Wyatt was and how good he smelled. I clench my hands, trying to fight it, but heat is already pooling down low in my belly.

Aunt Etta's voice echoes in my head: *Be careful with a Ford.* I heard it tonight, I've heard it before, and the whole town knows it. The Fords are power here in Cold Springs. But power can run your toaster . . . or stop your heart.

"No," I chide myself, "Hazel Ann Sullivan, you are not jilling off to some guy who was possibly sharking you at pool, and definitely lied by omission by not telling you his last name. Which is fucking *Ford.*"

Saying his name aloud is enough to mostly dash my fantasies. With a growl, I flip over to my side, curling in on myself and willing my body to fall asleep. Now.

Chapter 5

WYATT

Why did I agree to put up with this?

It's a good question. I have a perfectly good black suit that fits like a glove and is completely appropriate for a garden wedding. I've worn it maybe a dozen times since I got it, all for formal occasions.

But for some reason beyond my comprehension, "appropriate" isn't good enough, and Mom says I need a dove-gray suit to fit the theme of the wedding. I'm annoyed but doing my best to hide it.

"Quit fidgeting and be still," the woman kneeling in front of me hisses, and I look down at the seamstress. I'm pretty sure her last job was sewing suits for funerals, the way she handles adjustments.

"I'm trying," I growl.

She glares up at me from behind half glasses that are perched low on her nose, and dryly orders, "Try. Harder."

I clear my throat and straighten my spine.

"That'a boy, Wyatt. Let the poor woman work, for fuck's sake," Wren says with a vacant smile as she carelessly flips through the same magazine she's been looking at for thirty minutes. But I'm quite certain she isn't reading the articles about upcoming car prototypes and synthetic oil brand comparisons.

I consider lunging her way threateningly because if it'd been only Mom guilting me into this, I could've gotten out of it, but Wren took her side, and the two of them together wore me down. I'm out of practice, I guess, but Wren was the extra push that got me here.

I've had dozens of suit fittings over my life, but this one is by far the most unusual. Mrs. Hinsley—or as Wren calls her, "the Duchess"—has a no-nonsense attitude and a silver-streaked bun, and every time I shift in the slightest, she stabs me with a pin. I suspect she rather enjoys that part of her job. But for all her harsh seriousness, she is humming off-key theme songs from children's movies. It took me a while to recognize "Pure Imagination" from *Willy Wonka & the Chocolate Factory* because her version is somehow slowed down and off beat.

Mrs. Hinsley wraps her red tape measure around my right thigh . . . again. She's measured me all over, checking and double-checking her numbers and scribbling them in a notebook in sharp, old-school cursive.

"I know I'm a big guy, but are we almost done?" I ask.

She stops her humming in an instant and rises to her full height, which puts her at my chest level. Ripping her glasses off, she pins me with a glowering sneer. "It will take however long it takes. Normally, I'd be done already," she says acidly, "but most of my clients are not as large as you are, nor do they fidget like an eight-year-old child hyped up on sugar."

I'm going to ignore the comparison to a squirmy child, and typically, a woman calling me "large" would be a compliment, but I can tell by her tone that it most definitely isn't. Especially since she's talking about my thigh and not my other "leg."

Wren snorts but covers her mouth and turns it into a cough. When both me and Mrs. Hinsley turn fiery eyes her way, she says, "I think I'll step out for a minute. Let you two wrap this up."

She twirls a delicate finger through the air at Mrs. Hinsley and me, and for the first time, I feel more than frustration. I feel desperation. "No! Don't—"

It's too late. Wren steps out of the large private dressing room, closing the door behind her and leaving me alone with the female version of Edward Stabbyhands.

Realizing that pissing off the woman who could easily stab me in the balls and sell it as an accident isn't my smartest move, I try to backpedal. Slightly. "I appreciate you helping on such short notice. I want everything to be perfect for my brother."

Her sigh is one of long-term suffering. Maybe it is. She probably does shit like this all the time. "I understand. Let's cut to the chase here: I need accurate measurements so I can begin making your suit, and you want to be done with me." She pauses and I nod agreeably. "Good, then strip."

"*What?*" I exclaim.

"Oh, pishposh, boy. Don't act so scandalized. You don't have anything I haven't seen before. Not like I'm asking to see your pecker anyway. Just to your skivvies, so I can get the best measurements with minimum of fuss," she explains as though it's no big deal and completely normal. She glances at her watch and taps the dial. "Strip and let's get this over with."

Her gesture toward her watch is the only thing that makes me do it. I want to be done so I can follow up with Winston about what the hell's been going on around here while I've been gone. I need more than the cursory version he shared at the bar. I want the details.

And Mrs. Hinsley's right—I'm sure she's seen and done worse as a custom seamstress.

I sigh, resigned but still grumbling. "This is madness, you know?" I pull my T-shirt over my head, tossing it to the chair in the corner. My hands go to my belt and freeze for a moment, but I ultimately make quick work of losing my pants too. Standing in my boxer briefs and my sock feet, I tell Mrs. Hinsley, "Let's get on with it."

Her face stays neutral as she bows her chin deferentially, but I swear I see the smallest uptilt of her lips as she steps behind me to climb back onto her step stool. Stretching her tape measure across my shoulders once more, she triple-checks her numbers and makes more notes.

She does the same down my right arm and then left, before encircling each bicep.

"No tattoos?" she asks conversationally. "That's unusual these days."

I grunt, not wanting to make half-naked small talk.

She follows the same progression she did earlier, ending up kneeling in front of me again. The tape measure stretching from my ankle up my inseam feels especially invasive. Thankfully, nothing "moves."

"Ah, a leftie," she says, and yup . . . she got the lay of my land.

At that exact moment, the door opens again and Wren shouts, "Wyatt!"

Looking in the mirror's reflection, I see behind me, and a pit of horrified shock slices through my gut, leaving me wide open. Wren stands in the doorway, her hand still on the knob, which wouldn't be so bad except that with her are two other women.

One is a middle-aged blonde wearing a pastel print pantsuit, a chunky necklace, and large round pink frames over heavy eye makeup that makes her lashes look a mile long. At first, she's looking at the tablet in her hand, but when she looks up to see me, her eyes go wide. The other woman is Avery. I recognize her from the pictures Winston showed me, telling me how gorgeous she is, but also how kind and smart. Her mouth drops open before she covers her eyes politely.

"Um, excuse us," Avery says, but the other woman just keeps getting herself an eyeful as if that's all I'm here for. And Wren's looking amused as hell, as if her brother looking foolish is just good TV.

"What the hell, Wren? Get out!" I order, cupping my hands over my dick as if that will hide my state of undress.

"No time for that, my boy. There's work to be done," the middle-aged blonde woman with Wren says as she barrels into the room, waving my privacy away. "I'm Cara DeMornay, the wedding planner."

She holds out a hand, offering a shake that I refuse with a lift of my brow. I am not shaking hands while standing in my underwear. I don't do that with my doctor, so I'm sure as hell not doing it with some random woman who shouldn't be in here to begin with.

"Uh, Wyatt?" Wren says again, more questioning than shocked this time.

Red faced, I grumble, "Don't start. This is all her idea." I point at Mrs. Hinsley, who promptly pokes me with a pin.

"Stop moving."

"I wasn't moving," I insist.

She gripes under her breath and then begins humming again. I've never heard "Spoonful of Sugar" sound so aggressive as it does in her off-tune, off-beat growl through clenched teeth.

Cara snaps her fingers in front of my face, being flat-out disrespectful. "Good, now that we've settled that, we have things to discuss. You're the best man, correct?"

I look at Wren in surprise and see Avery beside her, nodding politely while still averting her eyes. Winston hasn't said anything about that. I mean, if I'd thought about it, I probably would've assumed simply because we're brothers, but I haven't had a chance to even consider it.

Wren obviously has, because she rolls her eyes and says on a sigh, "Don't act so shocked, Wyatt. Of course you're the best man—you're Winston's brother. It's expected."

Oh. Any warm fuzzies about the wedding trying to bubble up inside me dissipate. It's not that Winston wants me to stand by his side; it's that I'm a box to check off the list. I'm simply another rule to follow. Winston has always been good at that, better than me, at least. "Wow," I deadpan, "I can feel the love. Such an honor."

"Wah wah wah," Wren whines mockingly, and I have to admit it hurts a little. "Poor Wyatt wants to be wanted for who he is, and not because he's the firstborn male heir."

She's being playful, but there's a thread of bitterness in her teasing. If there's time, maybe she and I need to do some relationship repair. I wish I could put it higher on my priority list, but right now I can't. Not when I'm naked, and not with the wedding looming. Instead, I give her a look. "Wren?"

"No worries, big bro. Winston's not all Miss Manners approved. I'm a groomswoman." The absolute delight is vibrantly bright in her eyes, and I think it's both because she's getting the honor and because it is a bit of a middle finger to the rule book. Women are bridesmaids; men are groomsmen. It's tradition, but it's the twenty-first century, and if Winston wants his sister at his side, then that's exactly where she's going to fucking be.

That's what I like to hear. I hold up my hand and Wren high-fives me. We switch to a fist bump and then wrap our forearms around each other and high-five again, backward this time. It's automatic, though we haven't done it in years. It feels like some of that relationship repair I was just thinking about. But now I'm somehow standing here in my boxer briefs again with no hands to hide behind. It's oddly more comfortable since no one else is acting like it's a big deal. Slightly so, at least.

Mrs. Hinsley pokes me again, but I ignore it this time. "I like it," I tell Wren, "though maybe you should be best woman, and I'll be a groomsman."

She shrugs. "I'll take what I can get. Want to hear the best part?" She keeps rolling, not waiting for my answer. "I'm wearing a suit! Pants, collared shirt, tie, and all. Though mine is slim-fit thanks to Mrs. Hinsley's magic."

"It'll look amazing," Avery agrees, offering Wren a warm smile. But when she turns back to me, her smile melts incrementally, making me wonder what Winston has told her about me. Or maybe it's that I'm still more naked than dressed.

"You're welcome," Mrs. Hinsley answers Wren's compliment, never stopping her measuring and now getting dangerously close to my junk on the other leg as she checks my inseam. "Hmm."

Cara looks down, checking to see what's wrong—which is *nothing*, because there's nothing wrong with my legs or my dick. "Oh my! Is that real? Can you allot room for that?" She's talking to Mrs. Hinsley as though I'm not standing right here and she's not talking about my dick.

"It's real alright. Been staring me in the face for the last ten minutes," Mrs. Hinsley replies.

Are they really talking about my dick size? I mean, I'm not monstrous like some porn star, but I'm bigger than the average man, I guess. Never tried to compare.

I eye the door, looking for an escape route out of this awkwardness. But find only Wren fighting off a severe case of the giggles.

"Don't even think about it. This is important and you damn well know it," she warns, reading my intentions.

"Yes, dear. It's fine," Mrs. Hinsley says, patting my thigh comfortingly, as though it's not weird as fuck. "You heard Wren. I'm a magician and I'll make your slacks fit you to perfection." She kisses the air, putting her thumb and fingers together and then popping them apart in a chef's kiss motion.

I try to cover back up, but Mrs. Hinsley slaps my hand out of the way. "Seriously, dear. Be mature, please. I don't give a rat's ass about your penis. I simply need to dress you properly because everyone knows I'm the tailor for the Ford nuptials."

My eyes roll back in my head as I stare unseeingly at the ceiling and try to breathe away the mortification.

It can't get any worse, Wyatt. Let her finish and get out of here. We'll threaten Wren that if she ever mentions this again, I'll tell everyone about the time she peed her pants at school. Be cool, man.

The pep talk is working. A little. Right up until the door opens . . . again.

What the hell? Is this a fucking train station? It might as well be because it's as busy as Grand Central!

"Oh! My! Heavens! Why . . . hello there." A feminine voice of surprise turns to a purr.

Only able to look in the mirror, I see Hazel. She's wearing jeans and a faded red T-shirt with a graphic so washed out that I can't tell what it once was. Her face is different from last night, clear of any makeup, and her dark hair is piled on top of her head carelessly, leaving tendrils loose around her face.

She's standing beside another woman, who has perfectly curled blonde hair and pristine makeup, and is wearing a modest skirt-and-blouse combo with heels. It's the not-Hazel woman who's spoken. She looks like she's just stuck her tongue onto a nine volt battery.

I should be utterly mortified, or feel like a piece of meat, and I do. For a moment. But then I see Hazel's eyes track down my body and back up, faster than a blink, and her cheeks pinken ever so slightly. That is all the influx of courage and confidence I need.

I take a deep breath, letting it swell my chest and spread my shoulders. I tighten my abs and widen my stance a tiny bit, making myself look as good as possible. I'm attractive, I know that. But even though I'm not a model, I know there are certain tricks to show your best features.

Dropping my voice and letting it go rough, I say, "Hello, ladies." I greet both the newcomers, but my eyes are locked on Hazel's in the mirror.

"Didn't know you were the bachelorette-party entertainment. I would've skipped if I'd known," Hazel answers bluntly, clearly putting up a shield.

"Hazel!" Avery squeals, aghast at the insult. "This is Wyatt, Winston's brother. I'm afraid we've invaded his appointment. But Mrs. Hinsley will be done in a jiffy, and then she can do your final fittings."

Hazel flicks her eyes to Avery, and I watch as her hard look softens for her friend. Oh, so there is a soul inside that tough exterior. I just don't get that version of Hazel. Lucky me. "We've met," she says. "He tried to shark me last night and then bailed when he realized I was better than him."

"That is not what happened and you know it," I taunt, giving her a smirk.

"I'll play pool with you," the other woman offers, twirling a curl around her finger.

"Oh! Rachel, this is Wyatt. Wyatt, Rachel. She's a friend from college and a bridesmaid, along with Hazel, who I guess you've already met," Avery says, playing hostess with the mostest, which is odd considering that I'm still mostly naked.

"Very nice to meet you, Wyatt," Rachel says. She seems a little lost, like she wants to shake hands but knows that's awkward, so instead, she kinda curtsies a bit, which is also weird. But her smile is good-natured.

"You too," I say, barely looking her way before locking my eyes on Hazel once more. "So, you want to finish the game? Name the day and time."

"Pass." Hazel's answer is no-nonsense and all business, but I see her thick swallow and know she's not as unaffected as she's playing things.

Avery makes a sound of delight and claps her hands excitedly. "Oh! That's a great idea! We could all get together and play a game or two, eat dinner, and have fun. That sounds perfect since Winston and I don't want to do bachelor/bachelorette parties."

Cara jumps in before I can disagree with the idea. "If you'd like to do that, it will be on your own. I don't have the bandwidth to add it to my already long list of duties." She taps her tablet, highlighting her busy-busy-busy self.

I try not to roll my eyes too hard at her self-justification of whatever fees she's charging as I remember Winston's estimate of the total wedding cost. "I'm sure we can handle feeding ourselves and playing a game. Tomorrow night?"

Avery looks at her phone and, in an instant, says, "Done! I have someone on standby to stay with Grandpa Joe all week so I won't go crazy with the plans and last-minute prep. Just like this!" She throws her hands out, looking from Hazel to me to Wren to Rachel, and beaming the whole time.

I can see what Winston sees in her. She's bright and smiley in an infectious, joyful way, and is someone you want to be around and make happy. Why? Because she wants to make the rest of the world happy too. Or at least that's what Winston says. I get the feeling Hazel feels the same way about her friend.

I smirk at Hazel, letting the ball fall slowly into her court with all the impact of a mic drop. Is she going to disappoint her friend just because she's mad at me for some reason? Or is she going to step up and play ball?

"Fine. Tomorrow night. *For Avery.*" Her reluctant give-in is clearly in spite of me, not because of me, which is fascinating. Is she really that worked up or pissed off at me, or is it something else?

On the other hand, Rachel's eyes are flashing like neon lights, and her smile is filled with anticipation. "Tomorrow night, for sure. I'm not very good at pool, I'm afraid. Wyatt, do you think you'll be able to *teach me*?"

"Hmm, well, I could. But I think Hazel is the real pro, so she'd probably be your best bet to learn," I say, brushing her off gently. I don't want to piss off Avery's friend, but I have zero intention of doing the whole arms-around-her, ass-against-my-crotch deal that "teaching someone to play pool" implies.

Now if Hazel wants a little help with a shot, I'd be down for that.

"Hazel really is the best. She's been playing since she was a kid," Avery tells us all.

Hazel shifts from foot to foot, fidgeting uncomfortably at the praise. "You don't have to brag on me, Avery. Nobody cares."

"I care. I like to know who I'm going up against." I smirk her way, enjoying the banter once more. "Like any good sportsman, I'm never going to look down my nose at a little scouting report."

"Is that so?" Hazel volleys back, looking me up and down, deliberately slow and obvious about it. When she makes her way back to my face, she shrugs as though unimpressed. "Well, I can see exactly what and who I'm up against."

Now *that's* a full mic-drop moment, and it's followed by shocked silence. I don't think I've ever felt so dismissed, but instead of melting under Hazel's words, I mostly want to laugh. I have the urge to chase after her as she spins on her booted heel and heads out of the too-small room, which feels empty without her energy, despite the abundance of women standing around my still mostly naked self.

"I'm gonna make a call. Let me know when you're ready for me, Mrs. Hinsley," Hazel says, already out the door.

"Of course, dear," Mrs. Hinsley says from somewhere down by my feet. With the back-and-forth with Hazel, I'd kinda forgotten about her down there, especially when she quit measuring and was basically just watching the show.

"Are you finished?" I chide, and she blushes a little at being called out.

"Huh? Oh . . . oh yes. I've got everything I need," Mrs. Hinsley says. I feel like she's not talking about my measurements.

Great. I'll be the talk of the gossip vine before I get in my truck. That's just what I need.

Cara snaps her fingers, annoying me. "We're on a timetable here, I'm afraid. Wyatt, if you're done, can you step out so we can get on with the ladies' fittings?"

"Sure. You all get to stand around and ogle me, but you want me to get out for yours."

It's not that I want to stay, but the double standard is sort of irksome.

Cara places a hand on her chest, and though they're not pearls, she's gripping the beads of her necklace as though they are. "Of course. I'm a woman of the times, and certainly like to keep things fresh and exciting. However, that does not include having the best man lolly-gagging around like a pervert while we do the fittings for the bride, bridesmaids, and groomswoman."

I'm not surprised. Like I said, I don't want to be here for this anyway, and the whole point of stripping down was to get my appointment with Mrs. Hinsley over with sooner so I can track down Winston.

"Fresh and exciting? I'm sure," I say doubtfully as I pull my jeans and shirt back on. I shove a foot into my boot, not bothering to lace it up. I don't really need to at the moment.

Wren snorts. "Actually, you'd be surprised. Or well . . . you *will* be."

That gets my attention, and I cut my eyes to Wren quickly. "What does that mean?"

"Oh, nothing . . ." Her voice trails off playfully. Great . . . she's cooking something up in her head. FML.

"Okay, okay . . . excuse my French, Wyatt, but get out, please," Cara says, not cussing in the slightest. But I guess talking to the groom's family harshly is likely frowned upon.

Meanwhile, I have questions, dozens of questions, like . . .

What is Wren talking about?

What does a sweet girl like Avery see in my brother?

What is Hazel's deal, and why does she seem to hate me on sight?

What is going on with my dad? My uncle? And this town?

And so many more. But now is not the time apparently, because Cara is literally shoving me out the door. Normally I could plant myself like a boulder, but I'm hopping on one foot, with my other boot still in my hand. She closes the door, and it bounces in its frame as though she fell back against it after the strenuous workout of moving me. I swear I hear her say, "Whoo, he is solid as a rock. I thought as much, but it doesn't hurt to confirm, now does it?" And then she laughs airily before saying, "Rachel, you're up first, dear."

I shake off the shivers that run down my spine at Cara's declaration, feeling dirty and grossed out by a woman old enough to be my mother making that kind of comment.

But I know one thing that will make me feel better. I look around the small outer retail space of Mrs. Hinsley's shop, hoping to see Hazel, but find it empty.

Where did she go?

I step outside, my head swiveling left and right as I scan the sidewalk. *Aha! There she is!* Hazel is standing a few stores down, leaning against the building with her back to me, but I'd recognize that ass anywhere.

I stride quickly toward her, eager to continue whatever verbal sparring match we've started, but a few feet away, her voice floats to me on the breeze.

"Yes, Mom. I know he's a Ford."

Is she talking about me? Or maybe Winston? Unashamed, I eavesdrop.

"Aunt Etta already warned me. And I don't know if he's just here for the wedding or for the hearing. It's not like I can ask. He'd probably lie."

Hearing? What hearing?

"I promise. I'll come by the bakery later today, 'kay?" She's quiet for a moment and then says, "Love you too. Bye."

I should ask her outright what the hell she's talking about, but I think the wise move is to ask Winston first. A conversation with him has been my objective all day, and I want some information before I blindly walk into something with Hazel because she will no doubt eviscerate me if I go in at a disadvantage.

Instead, I step back into the shadow of the doorway between us, turning my back her way in hopes that she won't notice me. I watch her in the glass's reflection and breathe a sigh of relief when she passes by without a glance. Right up until I realize the store window has photo canvases of boudoir photography on display and it looks like I'm staring at them intently.

"Shit!" I hiss, jumping back and whirling to make sure no one's noticed me.

But right inside the door is a woman looking at me with raised brows. She waves her hand, gesturing for me to come on in, and flashes a friendly smile.

Fuck! This will definitely be more fodder for the town grapevine.

I wave back but shake my head and mouth, "No, thanks."

I need to find Winston and find out what the hell's going on before I make even more of a fool of myself around town. But even in my haste, I peek down the street where Hazel disappeared, hoping for one more sighting. When I see the empty sidewalk, I growl at myself and my disappointment. "Enough of that shit, Wyatt. Get your head on right."

And with that order to myself, I get in my truck and roar off to find Winston.

It's easier than I expect, considering he's set up at the kitchen table at home, with a laptop open in front of him and a spread of papers covering the glass surface.

"Hey, man," I say. "Got my suit fitted, but you could've warned me about the Duchess's grabby, stabby hands."

Winston looks up in surprise, echoing, "Grabby, stabby hands?"

I mimic her cupping my ass a little more exaggeratedly than actually happened, and Winston grins.

"A little birdie also told me something," I start, using our (not so) codename for Wren from when we were kids.

"No telling what she's got up her sleeve now," Winston says wryly.

"She said she's a groomswoman, and you want me to be your best man?" It's not that I doubt Wren, or more accurately Avery, but I need to hear it from Winston firsthand.

He leans back in the chair, crossing his arms. "And if I do?"

It's more of a challenge than an invitation, but I guess I deserve that. "I would be honored to stand by your side. But I'd also understand if you wanted someone more . . . present." It's as close as I can get to acknowledging how long I've been gone and how out of touch I've become. I'm working on fixing that, at least for now, but I don't have the right to expect a place of honor like best man.

Winston stands, coming around the table to offer his hand. "I wouldn't have anyone else, man."

I bypass his hand and grab him in a manly bear hug, patting his back as he slaps mine. So much is healed between us in this moment, and I'm struck with how much I've missed him.

As we sit down, I tell him, "I met your girl. She's just as pretty as you said. Also, side note . . . she saw my junk."

The bomb drops the way I thought it would, with Winston's eyes going wide and then narrowing sharply. "Explain," he orders.

I laugh. "Kidding. Sort of . . ." But as I tell him about my morning standing half-naked in a roomful of women, he's the one laughing at my embarrassment.

Chapter 6

HAZEL

The bell above the entrance to Mrs. Hinsley's shop tinkles when I come back in, and it somewhat snaps me back on task as I go to the back. Opening the door, I find Rachel and Wren already in their wedding attire. Rachel's in her bridesmaid dress, an empire-waisted, silver-gray, sleeveless shift that's absolutely the complete opposite of a stereotypical ugly bridesmaid dress, and Wren wears a slim pantsuit, gray tuxedo-style pants expertly cropped to show off her sky-high stilettos and ankles, a white silk shirt, and a vest that somehow covers and accentuates her figure at the same time, her jacket carried over her forearm.

"Damn, looks like we've got Victor *and* Victoria all at once," I joke, and Wren grins as she strikes a model-worthy pose.

Before she can say anything, though, Cara snaps her fingers, a habit of hers I really don't like. It feels like she's snapping for a dog to obey or something. "Lovely ladies. Hazel, get changed quickly so I can see you all together. I need to make sure that the drape works with both of your figures."

Apparently, we're all stripping in the small room today, because Rachel's and Wren's clothes are on hangers on the wall. I'm glad Wyatt is gone. Despite his arrogant confidence at being nearly naked in a roomful of women, I would not strip down in front of him.

No way, no how.

Cara is still being a taskmaster, checking things on her tablet. "Wren, you're wearing the necklace the bridesmaids are wearing, correct? To ahem, *soften* your look."

"Soften?" Wren echoes with a bit of attitude, lifting an eyebrow. She's as girly-girl as they come, the quintessential debutante, but she's got an edge to her, and is more than willing to fuck with people's heads just for shits and giggles. "Uh-huh. That's me, soft as a lamb." She examines her nails, which are filed to a respectable length but painted red with black french tips.

Pulling my own dress on with Mrs. Hinsley's help, I hide a giggle. I know the wedding planner isn't all too keen on having a groomswoman, despite her constantly saying that she wants Avery's wedding to be "unique" and a "one-of-a-kind statement" for the memory books— a.k.a. Cara's work portfolio.

Still, for a wedding pulled together in a matter of a few months, Avery has been more than pleased with the things the planner has come up with. Then again, Avery would've been happy with just her and Winston and an officiant and zero muss or fuss.

She doesn't need all the bells and whistles, but that doesn't mean she's not enjoying them. She's getting to be a princess for a day, and to be honest, I want her to enjoy the hell out of it. Besides, she looks amazing in her luxe dress and fancy heels.

Wren's still being Wren, though, and while she's definitely on board with Avery being a princess, she's not going to make it easy for Cara. "Yes, I brought the necklace with me *as instructed*," Wren bites out, "but I was thinking a bow tie would be better."

A bow tie. Fucking . . . awesome. Seriously, when I met her, I thought Wren was going to be a full-fledged, spoiled-rotten diva princess. I mean, we went to school together, and she was basically the queen of every dance, sweetheart of the football quarterback, and able to get away with murder with a flutter of her lashes.

Instead, in the times we've spent together, she's been bold and blunt, and though I never would've guessed it, I think we'd be great friends . . . if her last name were anything else.

Avery seems to like her, too, and Wren has been fully supportive of my best friend's "pulling my brother's head out of his ass," as Wren described Winston. Maybe that's what it is. Maybe it's only the Ford men who are the way they are . . . like it has something to do with their testicles.

Completely ignoring Wren's suggestion, Cara and Mrs. Hinsley go about pinning here and discussing there, making me feel like a piece of meat in my dress. Though it is pretty, I'm not used to wearing fancy shifts or frocks or whatever they call this style. But for Avery, my bestest bestie in the whole wide world? I'd dress up as the Cold Springs High School Falcon, complete with floppy-beaked feathered head if she asked me to, and smile politely in the pictures. Thankfully, she didn't ask for that. Though the idea of "flying" down the aisle, yelling "caw caw," would be quite the memory.

"Wren, tell me more about Wyatt," Rachel says when she can breathe and Mrs. Hinsley isn't fussing over her. "Other than how cute and sexy he is. I could see that for myself."

I hold back a groan, but luckily Wren delivers one loud enough for the both of us. "Cute? I suppose. But he's an asshole too," she warns. "My biggest brother's nobody's prize."

I snort and mumble under my breath, "Shocker."

Too late, I realize Avery is looking from Rachel to me curiously. "What'd you think of him?" Avery asks. "You know, the other night, since you'd already met him first."

The second bit is deliberately emphasized, like she's reminding Rachel of girl code. Funny, considering I was just telling myself the same thing last night when it came to Charlene. "Not calling dibs like we're kids, Avery."

Rachel cackles gleefully, rubbing her hands together like a Disney villain. "Good, because I am!" she announces. "No shame in my game! That man looks good enough to sop up with a biscuit."

"You're welcome to him. He's a Ford, after all, and you know what that means," I declare automatically, sounding eerily like Aunt Etta, and it's only after the words are out of my mouth that I realize what I just said . . . and who's in the room with me. I flick apologetic eyes to Wren, who shrugs, unoffended, and then to Avery. "I didn't mean Winston . . . sorry."

Avery waves it off, and it seems I've ducked a bullet for now. "It's okay. I know Winston, and know his heart. He's mine—heart, soul, mind, and body. He might work for his uncle, but he's nothing like him."

I hope, for Avery's sake, she's right. And for myself, too, because if Winston hurts her, I'm going to kill him, slowly and painfully, and the life in prison will be worth it in honor of my BFF's heart.

⚜

After the fittings are done, I tag along as Avery and Cara go to the bakery to check on the cake. The bakery is right on Main Street in downtown, with a well-cared-for kelly-green canvas awning over the front door and a pink-and-white sign overhead that shows years of weathered age. I remember when Mom showed it to me the first time, though . . .

"This is our future, Hazel. We'll do it together, you and me."

She was right. Mom has run the Bakery Box for years, mostly doing it on her own. I help out as much as possible, going from Aunt Etta's place to the bakery as many days a week as I can. But this is Mom's baby, her pride and joy.

Lauren Landish

Inside, the pine floors gleam, though their history is apparent, with nicks in the wood and visible nails at the corners of the boards. The glass display cases are new, purchased used only a few years ago, and fitted with daylight LED lights that make the pastries inside glow with warmth.

The menu board on the wall was hand-drawn in chalk pens by the local art teacher, listing things like Creamy Box Pie, Mom's take on a lemonade icebox pie. Between Mom and Aunt Etta, they've got the inappropriate-food-name market cornered.

Working between the two places, I talk about pussies and boxes more than any reasonable person should, and definitely more than someone whose pussy box is getting zero action should.

Cara and Avery sit down at one of the little café tables, and I step into the back. "Mom! We're here!"

Mom steps out of the walk-in freezer, wiping freshly washed hands on her white apron, which is streaked with red.

"Uh, Mom? Anything we need to discuss? You know I'll alibi you for anything, but you can't keep the bodies in the freezer. Health Department."

Her face wrinkles in confusion for a moment, then clears as she shakes her head and swats at me. "Oh, you. This is icing, not blood, and you know it. I just finished the Thompsons' red velvet anniversary cake with fifteen red roses, one for every year." Her smile is bright, though I know she's thinking of my dad. He died when I was a kid, one of those tragic accidents that always seem to hit the wrong people, and Mom still misses him. I do too. "You here with Avery for her final tasting?"

I nod, then warn her, "Yeah, Cara's here too."

Mom shrugs. "She's a big personality, but I know the type. She's got to be able to handle bridezillas, groomzillas, momzillas, and all the other 'zillas. I don't envy her, that's for sure. I'll stay back here in my kitchen, where the only arguments I get are from Helga."

Helga is Mom's huge, industrial, heavy-duty mixer with a mind of its own. Every handyman in town has taken that bitch apart to poke

76

and prod her, and she still won't stay fixed. Mom puts up with it and treats the machine like a good-luck charm at this point. "Alright, let me get a fresh apron on, and I'll grab Avery's samples."

"Want help?" I offer, heading to the case, where I see the mini cupcakes for Avery. Just minis today, though the reception's going to have full-size creations straight out of Avery's dreams and Mom's imagination.

"I've got it, honey. You go sit with your friend and be a bridesmaid today, not a worker bee." Mom shoos me off from the case, pulling her red-streaked apron off and tossing it into a bag of laundry, before grabbing a pristine white one.

She pulls it over her dark ponytail and settles it around her neck, tying it around her thin waist quickly. I'm struck suddenly by how pretty she is. I mean, she's my mom, so I know she's amazing, but I forget that she's growing older the same way I am.

There are faint lines around her eyes and small parentheses around her mouth that I don't remember being there, even though I see her damn near every day. She's still as beautiful as she's always been, but I can see the toll life has taken on her in a way I never have before. Maybe I'm more aware, or maybe she's more exhausted from the long hours she keeps, but I feel like I need to freeze this moment and take a mental snapshot.

"Thanks, Mom," I tell her, a little choked up. "I'll grab some waters for everyone. It's the least I can do." I want the busywork as a chance to hide my out-of-the-blue reaction.

As I step back into the café, I hear Cara asking Avery, "And you're sure about this place? I mean, we could have someone come into town and make your wedding cake. Anyone you want. The *Cake Boss* guy? Or a fancy French baker? Or even Martha Stewart! I've been told that nothing is out of reach, so reach for the stars, Avery. It's your special day."

I freeze, not wanting to put pressure on my friend. I do want her to have a special day, and will move hell and high water to make it happen if needed, but these are Mom's cakes we're talking about. I've never had anything Martha Stewart made, but I've had my mom's baking and I can't imagine anything better.

"I want one of Daisy's cakes. It's what I've dreamed of since I was a little girl," Avery tells Cara, and I breathe a sigh of relief.

"Here's some waters," I say brightly, coming in with a tray of drinks. "Mom is grabbing the samples."

Avery beams. Cara's brow lifts snootily, but I ignore it and set the glasses down neatly before taking the tray back up to the counter.

Barely a minute later, Mom comes out with her own tray, a full array of mini cupcake samples ready to go for Avery's approval. "This is my famous sweet cream cake," she says as she hands everyone a mini cupcake on mismatched china plates. Cara takes a dainty bite, as though expecting it to taste like shit. Avery and I know better and stuff the whole thing in our mouths in one bite, chewing and moaning loudly in tongue-gasmic pleasure. "I see it meets the mark?"

"If I die now," Avery says, "I'll have no food regrets."

Cara looks at the remaining three-fourths of a mini cupcake on her plate, then takes it in one big bite. "Oh my, that is tasty. So moist and creamy."

"That's what he said," I jest, and Avery has to clap her hand over her mouth to prevent crumbs spraying everywhere.

Mom, of course, is aghast. "Hazel! Behave yourself."

I try to laugh, but choke and, unlike Avery, end up coughing cake crumbs everywhere. I slap my hands over my mouth and mumble, "Sorry."

Cara stabs another mini cake with her fork and eats the whole thing in one mouthful, as if afraid I'm going to yank it from her despite my ability to get these anytime I want.

I'm calling that a win for Mom.

"Mmm. Divine. I stand corrected, Avery," Cara says as she finishes the second sample. "Is this your choice for your wedding cake?"

"It's my preference, but Miss Daisy's cakes are all good," Avery says. "Unless you think the Red Wedding strawberry cake would be better?"

"No, no. I think you've chosen wisely. Now, let's confirm the decorations."

Mom and Cara start chatting about fresh-flower inserts and Swiss dots versus polka dots on the five-tiered cake they have planned while Avery and I sneak another sample. Cara may be dumb enough to turn down Mom's Red Wedding strawberry, but we sure as hell aren't.

Cara hrrmphs when she realizes that Avery and I are four samples deep. "Ladies, ladies . . . keep that up, and I shall have to schedule another visit with the seamstress."

Avery sets the small cupcake in her hand down like the good girl she is. I, however, shove mine into my mouth once more, not caring about Cara's look of disapproval. I narrow my eyes and glare back, daring her to say one word about it.

Suddenly, Cara's eyes go bright and a light bulb basically dings over her head. "Oh my! I have the best idea ever! Daisy, how many of these mini cupcakes can you make by Saturday night?"

Mom is a consummate businesswoman who knows the correct answer to a question like that. "However many you need."

Cara takes Avery's hands in her own and meets her eyes. "Midnight. Madness."

She seems to think that her brilliance is apparent, but we're all still just as confused as before she spoke. Avery gives me a glance, and I shrug, and Avery turns her eyes to Cara. "What?"

Cara gets up and starts pacing around the room, seeing her vision before her eyes instead of Mom's bakery, but somehow not running into any errant chair legs. "Picture it, everyone has had dinner, we've cut the cake, and the dance floor is starting to wane. But we want to send people home with a bang, one last memorable hurrah with the wedding-night send-off. Midnight Madness."

Something is starting to take shape in my mind, but it's mostly that Cara isn't quite right, not anything wedding related.

"We'll draw everyone outside, and it will be like a second cocktail hour of passed snacks and sweets to keep everyone in good spirits. Like the mini cupcakes in flavors completely different from the wedding cake. Something fun and boozy maybe? Chocolate bourbon pecan?" she asks Mom, who nods excitedly. "Strawberry champagne surprise?" Another nod. "And there will be a fireworks show!"

Avery was feeling the additional sweets, but fireworks make her balk. "Fireworks? Isn't that a bit . . . excessive?"

Cara gives Avery a condescending look that irks me, but I bite my cheeks instead of telling Cara that I hope she steps in manure when she gets off her high horse. Instead, Cara planner-splains her ass off. Yup, I just made that up. "Dearie, you're marrying into one of the wealthiest, most influential families in the area. Fireworks are completely appropriate."

As though the matter is already decided, Cara sits and types on her tablet, making sound effects to go with her movements: "Beep-bop-bum-bum-bum, and voilà!" She finishes with a flourish of her hand. "I'll follow up with the fire department for permits and source a professional. Daisy, let's do three passed sweets, your choice on flavor combinations. Something that'll knock their socks off." She glances at the plate of mini cupcakes as though they're proof enough that Mom can handle some freedom with her assignment. "What do you think about four hundred total servings, or thereabout? Decide what feels appropriate and send me another quote, in addition to the updates we made to the cake design today, m'kay?"

Cara is buzzing with excitement, nearly bouncing in her chair, as though she can't wait to get out of here and begin making the fireworks arrangements. Meanwhile, in my head, I'm thinking of the amount of work Mom is going to have to do on top of the wedding cake and running the bakery to get another four hundred mini cupcakes done.

But of course she's going to do her best. "Of course. Also, if I may be so bold, you mentioned snack food too. I'll get with Etta—she's the owner of the best café in town with the best cook in town. We can do small fry baskets and cheeseburger meatball bites, some good old-fashioned deliciousness to keep people partying."

Cara snaps her fingers and points at Mom. *Here, Rover, good dog.* "Yes! Perfect! Do it all as one quote and send it to me."

And with that, Cara stands again, effectively ending the meeting. "This all sounds great, everyone! Let's get to it!"

She claps her hands and then she's off, leaving Avery, me, and Mom at the table feeling like we've lived through a tornado of whirlwinds and debris. I look around and take a deep breath. "Anybody else feel like a cow just flew by? Mooo," I deadpan. Mom and Avery look at me in confusion. "You know, *Twister* Cara? She's a lot."

"I know, and I resisted at first, but I couldn't have done this without her," Avery says, sighing a little bit. "She's right, Winston has all this family and they have expectations. I think if I'd organized the wedding myself, we'd have ended up as laughingstocks."

I don't like that, not one bit. My friend might not know how to throw some black-tie cotillion or anything like that, but any wedding she'd plan is one I'd have a blast at. "You stop that right now. Like any of this matters. It's pageantry and appearances, not the real stuff," I reassure Avery, patting her on the shoulder. "This is one day. The important thing is that you and Winston have a life together."

"There's value in pageantry too. There's a tradition, a shared experience, in something like this. For the wedding," Mom says as she turns to Avery, "there's a foundation being built by going through this with Winston, but also, a woman's wedding day is something she talks about forever. Don't wave it off like it's nothing, Hazel."

Mom's eyes are sad and glittery, as she likely remembers her own wedding. I've misstepped and hurt her unintentionally. "I'm sorry, Mom. I didn't mean it like that."

Mom shakes her head, waving me off. "It's okay, baby. I know you're focusing on the forever for Avery, not the one day. And you're right there too. Just don't overlook that forever is built one experience at a time. None of them are unimportant."

She makes me sound noble and puts my feelings into words better than I ever could.

I nod, telling Avery, "That's what I'm trying to say. Badly. I want you to be happy, and if Winston makes you happy, then I'm on board. But I know you, and all this fanfare isn't your style. That's all I meant."

Avery smiles and throws her arms around me in a tight hug. "It's not, but can I let you in on a secret?" I meet her eyes questioningly. "It's so much fun! I mean, can you imagine . . . fireworks at a wedding? That's like Hollywood movie–level stuff, and it's going to happen at my wedding. Me, Avery Dawn Singleton! Who'd have thunk it?"

She throws her voice into a heavy accent for the last bit, making herself sound more country than she is, but I get her point. Things like this don't happen to people like her and me. We're just small-town girls, not Zendaya or something. "I really am happy for you, girl."

Avery grins. "Thanks."

We hug again and Avery excuses herself to go check on Grandpa Joe. Before she leaves, Mom gives her a bag of muffins, danish, and a loaf of bread. "Tell Joe to let me know what he thinks of these muffins. It's a new recipe I'm trying out."

Avery smiles gratefully, promises a no-holds-barred Grandpa Joe review, and leaves with the goodies.

Alone again, Mom looks at me with worry in her narrowed eyes. "I truly hope that boy doesn't hurt her. I think he loves her, but she is so kind and good-hearted, and that whole family is ugly to the roots of their family tree. Makes me scared for her spirit."

Mom doesn't talk bad about folks usually. But Jed Ford's business dealings have left the downtown retailers hurting, especially with him owning most of the commercial buildings, including Mom's, and she's bitter and fearful about his next project and the effect it'll likely have on Cold Springs. And while Bill Ford has been a good, even great, mayor in the past, his brotherly support of the rezoning has turned folks against him now too.

"Everything okay for now?" I ask, turning to Mom's business. "Nothing new with Jed Ford, is there? Or the development?"

Moms shrugs. "Nothing new, just the same people saying the same things. He's lying through those fake white teeth of his, reassuring us all that the development's going to be beautiful and bring new blood to our stores. And the whole town is threatening to hang him at sundown for betraying Cold Springs by selling out to people who don't care about our town and its traditions."

There's that word again . . . *tradition*. It's the biggest battle around here—the townsfolk desire to honor it, respect it, and keep things the same as they've been. And Jed's desire for progress, not for a noble reason like growth, or to keep Cold Springs vibrant and alive, but for the oldest reason in the books: money.

"Well, if anything changes, or there's going to be riots in the streets, let me know so I can get my ass-kicking boots on, 'kay?"

Mom laughs, reasonably sure that I'm kidding.

To be honest, though, I'm not. Jed Ford scares the bejesus out of me, not because of the man himself, but because of the power he holds. My mom, aunt, brother, and me all live and breathe Cold Springs, and if Jed fucks that up, we're done for.

The same as so many others.

"As for Winston and Avery, if he does hurt her, I'm going to need to borrow your freezer and have you give me an alibi."

I smile when I say it, pretending I'm joking.

Plausible deniability, you know.

Mom frowns slightly, knowing I'm not. "You can't put the bodies in the freezer, baby. They always get found there. Now the old, dried-up well behind your place . . ."

Dark humor for sure, but we both laugh, all the while hoping it never comes to that.

Chapter 7

WYATT

"Where is everyone?" I ask Maria as I finish the breakfast taco she made for me this morning. It's not my usual start to a day—I'm normally a simple eggs-and-coffee type of man. But I would never turn down anything Maria makes, both because it's always delicious and because I wouldn't want to hurt her feelings.

"Waiting for you," she says quietly. She jerks her chin toward the hallway that leads to Dad's office, and her eyes deliberately cut to the left and then back, so quick I almost think I imagined it. "Be careful, *mijo*. You've been gone a long time. Things are different now."

"What do you mean?" I whisper, following her lead. Maria is an incredibly wise woman, and more than once growing up, I trusted her advice more than that of my own parents.

She shrugs as she scrubs a nonexistent spot on the island. "Mr. Bill . . . he is worried all the time."

I remember Dad's midafternoon drunken stupor earlier this week. I don't know if *worried* is the word I'd use to describe it. *Out of control,* maybe? But I don't want to argue semantics, so instead I say, "About what?"

"Mmm," she hums. "Mostly about Mr. Jed. He is . . ." She pauses as though searching for a word to describe my uncle.

"A *pendejo?*" I suggest.

"No, you awful boy," she scolds playfully, swinging the towel at me. I laugh and duck away, and she smiles softly. I've missed her. Always taking care of us and kind, but also firm when a situation calls for it, especially with us "kids." "He is not well liked in this town. That's what worries Mr. Bill."

"I think 'not well liked' is your sweet soul speaking. He's downright hated from what I can tell, and that's going by the signs around town."

Her dark eyes pierce deeply into mine, saying so much that she won't let pass her lips. After a moment, she resumes wiping the counter. "You want another taco? I've got enough for one more."

She's told me all she's going to, and though I'd like to push for more, I won't do it with Maria. When she shuts her mouth, it's sealed tighter than a bank vault. It's time to find out what's going on from the source. "No, thanks. This was delicious, but I'm stuffed."

I get up and automatically rinse my plate before putting it in the dishwasher. It's a new habit, one that's developed since I left Cold Springs, and doesn't go unnoticed. Maria leans back on the counter, her arms crossed over her middle. "Ah, *mijo*. You are different too. Living on your own has been good for you."

I chuckle, and though my cheeks flush, I wink at her teasingly. "Growing up has been good for me. If I stayed here, I think I would've only grown out." I pat my belly, full of her good food. "And then what?"

She laughs happily, enjoying the compliment. "You'd best get in there," she says, glancing toward Dad's office once more. "Just remember . . . *tranquilo.*"

I nod, but I'm still gritting my teeth as I steel my spine. Squaring my shoulders, I purposefully blank out my face before I go down the hall and knock on Dad's office door.

I fucking hate this. Shit like this is why I left in the first place.

I don't wait for permission to enter. I'm not a kid anymore, and this family meeting has been a long time coming. We all know it. I open the door to see Dad sitting behind his desk in his leather chair and Winston in one of the club chairs in front of it.

Dad looks like he's ready for the office, wearing a white collared shirt and patterned gold tie, likely part of his usual suit, but he's removed his jacket and his sleeves are rolled up his forearms as he steeples his hands and stares at Winston.

Thankfully, Dad's eyes seem clear and bright this morning, so at least he's sober. I shiver inside, thinking, *When did that become a thing to be thankful for?*

Winston is dressed more casually, though still professionally, in khakis and a polo embroidered with Uncle Jed's business logo on the chest.

"Morning," I say, not as a greeting but more as a way to get this ball rolling. "You ready to ream me out for leaving, Dad?"

My distaste and, to be honest, lack of a single fuck is obvious in my dry delivery. I hear Winston's sharp breath, but my attention is focused on Dad's reaction as I casually take a seat in the other club chair and get comfortable. His eyes narrow and his cheeks go a bit ruddy, which I take a bit of twisted delight in.

So many times before, I shrank beneath this same glare, but that was when I was a boy. Now, living on my own, proving myself to myself and the world, has made me strong enough to stare back, prepared for whatever he throws at me. Years of imagining this moment have let me anticipate every possible move he'll make.

He sighs, resigned. "I deserve that, but no, I'm just glad you're here." There's a small pause before he adds, "For the wedding."

The fire I'm holding at the ready to unleash in a verbal smackdown cools at his quiet concession. This is not the powerhouse giant of a man in my memories. Has he become weaker, or have I grown that much stronger? Or maybe the distance and time have done both of us some good?

"I wouldn't miss Winston's vows." I leave off that it was that damn *please* in his letter that got me back.

Winston butts in: "You say that, but we weren't sure. I'm glad our doubts were misplaced." He holds out a fist, and I bump it with one of my own.

"How are you feeling about the wedding?" I ask my brother. I already know the answer, but this is a conversational directive to get us where I'd like to go. Winston's equally aware and plays along as though we haven't had this conversation already over beers and burgers.

"The wedding? Fine. The marriage to Avery? Fucking ecstatic. She's everything, more than I deserve for sure." Winston's smile is brighter than I've ever seen, and that alone is worth facing my dad and uncle for.

Dad snorts. "You deserve anything and everything, son."

Aaand there it is.

It's the same entitled attitude I grew up with as a guiding force, the one I came to realize was nothing more than bullshit and illusion. Shedding it was both freeing and terrifying, and without it, the world feels grossly unbalanced but also as though anything is possible.

"You don't *deserve* anything, Winston. You've earned Avery's love, the same way she's earned yours," I state flatly, only partially talking about Winston and Avery's relationship.

"Is that what life out there has taught you?" Dad demands, laughing bitterly.

"Yeah, it's too bad you haven't learned that lesson." I look around Dad's fancy office, the same one I used to sneak into and sit in front of the fireplace, imagining the room was mine and I was a businessman.

Dad sneers, driving a fingertip into the surface of his desk. "You think I haven't *earned* every bit of this? That I haven't worked myself to the bone for this city? For you?" He points at me with a slightly trembling finger. "You come back all self-righteous, like you haven't benefited from being a Ford since the day you were born. Easy to piss on that from your place on high, son. But at least I recognize it and take on the responsibility it comes with. I don't run away from it. So excuse me if I take a bit of appreciation in the luxuries I've worked for."

He holds his hands out, encompassing his office in appreciation, not in judgment like I did. Keeping my cool, I throw back, "I hear you've been 'appreciating the luxuries' quite a bit recently."

I glance down at the mug on his desk, questioning whether there's a bit extra in his coffee. Dad flinches before picking it up and taking a long, deep drink. "Pure Colombian dark roast, if you must know. I wasn't expecting you the other day and had a liquid lunch because I was working, something you know very little about."

"You don't know anything about how hard I work," I scoff, quickly remembering the hours of sweat and aching muscles I get from my woodworking. "You don't know anything about me, Dad."

"Whose fault is that?" he accuses, then shakes his head sadly. "It breaks your mother's heart."

"Guilt trip? That's what you're going with?" I toss back. "If Mom wants to say something to me, she's certainly strong enough and capable enough to do it for herself."

Whatever his next strike was going to be is cut off by the door opening.

"Hey there, boys! How's it going?" Uncle Jed bursts in with his trademark Colgate-approved smile as he pulls his cowboy hat from atop his head. The very air changes, feeling thick and heavy with his sliminess. He's a good-looking man, I can allow that, with his full head of blond hair, blue eyes, and tanned skin. Age has given him some wrinkles, but they serve only to lend him a sense of weathered ruggedness. If you saw him in passing at a party, you'd be impressed by his gregariousness and romanced by his charm. It's only deeper that his true ugliness lies.

I see the moment he realizes I'm here. His eyes widen slightly, but he's quick to play it off. "Wyatt! Well, I'll be damned, boy. It's been a while."

He comes in closer, holding his hand out for a shake. I hesitantly glance at his hand for an instant, but shake it, not wanting to start off at worse odds than I'm already facing. That won't serve me in finding out what's happening around here. "Jed."

"What the hell you been up to?" Jed asks as he perches on the side of Dad's desk. It looks casual, a logical solution to there being no available chairs, but distance and time have allowed me to see that it's so much more than that. It's a calculated move that permits him to loom over all three of us, making him seem like the man in charge, though he's in someone else's space.

I purposefully smile as though we're friends. "Little of this, little of that. But I'm sure you already know that, don't ya?"

Jed chuckles, nodding. "Gotta take care of family, you know. Glad to hear your little woodworking business is doing well in Newport."

Dad's eyes cut to me in surprise, but he doesn't speak. *So Uncle Jed didn't tell Dad about coming to see me. Interesting.* Winston didn't know where I was until he did some investigating, but Jed not telling his own brother about his kid is another level of shitty. I wonder if he was holding that card for play against Dad at just the right time too.

"How about you? I hear you're up to big things in Cold Springs."

"Oh, little of this, little of that," Jed replies, throwing my own words back at me.

I do the same: "Yeah, gotta take care of . . . Cold Springs, you know." His eyes narrow, so I dig a little deeper, at the same time lightening the mood strategically with a laugh as I ask, "What the hell is a private tech hub, anyway?"

"Damned if I know!" He slaps his leg, laughing at his own unfunny joke. "But I hear it's all the rage, something about work-from-home folks wanting flex offices, fiber optic cables, and some other techy shit too convoluted for me to understand."

He's lying through his whitened, straightened smile, making himself seem like a good ol' boy who doesn't know a thing. Truth is, he knows each and every line item on his balance sheets at his company. But it's a time-old trick so people will underestimate him. I won't make that mistake. Not again.

"Gotta give the people what they want, I guess," I hedge carefully. I want to get him talking about one of his favorite subjects—the first one being himself, the second being his work—but I can't be too direct or he'll be suspicious. "That the big seller for the new subdivision?"

Jed stands, helping himself to a cup of coffee from the pot on the side table. As he stirs a bit of creamer into the mug, he brags, "Yep. Tech hub, new schools, and some of the most beautiful homes I've ever built."

Well, he's talking, but that's not new information. I gathered that much from the damn billboard on the edge of town. "That an actual compliment to the architects?" I ask, looking at Winston with a practiced smile.

Winston shakes his head, while Jed's smile dims at my backhanded compliment. "Not me. I'm working on the overall development. We tasked a private firm with the floor-plan designs, and will offer a few different options for customization. But the feel of the entire development is my responsibility."

"Yeah, this one does a good job making things happen. He turns my crazy ideas into reality," Jed says. I'm sure he means it to be a compliment to Winston and a dig at me, but I think Winston is learning quickly that if Jed thinks you're doing well, you're probably on the wrong path and heading toward nothing good. Jed likes you as long as he can use you, or until you become a potential threat.

I nod agreeably, letting him have that one. Jed takes the win as he settles back onto Dad's desk and sips at his coffee. "That's actually what I was stopping by for." He looks to Dad. "How's the zoning progress going? We should be a sure thing by now."

This is more like it—the real dirt I want to hear.

Dad lifts one shoulder, not quite agreeing or disagreeing. "Still have a few holdouts. The city protests aren't helping either."

"Psshaw"—Jed makes a noise of dismissal—"they ain't doing nothing but arguing with the wind. When they see the money start flowing in, they'll be singing a different tune. Won't they?" Jed looks to Winston for backup and he nods dutifully, but I see the look of uncertainty in his eyes.

"Protests?" I question, giving Jed the floor to bitch and moan in the hopes of learning something useful. Sometimes, the best way is to just open the door and set out the mat . . . and Jed walks his way right in.

"Damn people so stuck in the past, they can't see the future or how it's leaving them behind. Did you know that Cold Springs' population has been steadily decreasing for the last forty years?" he says, and I wonder who's playing the politician game now. "If we maintain this rate, we'll be completely obsolete in the next thirty years. But does anyone want to listen to reason? Of fucking course not. They want to stay in their same house, with the same neighbor, shop at the same store, and don't give a damn if they die with the city. We're not going to let that happen. Ain't that right, Bill?"

Dad's obviously heard Jed's elevator pitch on all the things wrong with Cold Springs, because he jumps right in with part two. "Yeah, it's hard to be the voice of progress because it's uncomfortable and scary sometimes. But it's a necessary growing pain if we want to be successful as a town." Just for me, he adds, "Leading means doing the hard stuff no one else wants to do because you know it's for the best. It's a big responsibility and not always kissing babies and shaking hands."

Zing! He aimed that right at me because of my earlier accusations.

"It doesn't hurt if doing those things makes you a little richer in the process, though, does it?" Cynicism isn't a character trait I'm proud of, but it's hard to ignore it when Dad and Uncle Jed are talking as though they're the self-sacrificing saviors of a town too stupid to know what's good for them. I don't even know all the ins and outs of the subdivision project, but I know that if people don't want it, there's got to be a good reason.

Dad growls, but Jed holds out a staying hand. To my disgust, Dad honors it and lets Jed handle things . . . handle me. "Of course we profit from it. You think we're doing things out of the goodness of our hearts? Naive boy, money is what makes the world go round. Always has and always will. But that doesn't make what we're trying to do here any less right."

Having said his piece, Jed stands. He takes one long drink of his cooled coffee and then sets the mug on Dad's desk. "Let me know when you handle the holdouts, Bill. And, Winston, hope everything's going well with the wedding plans. You let me know if there's anything I can do to help. As for you, Wyatt . . . always good to see you, boy."

He moves toward the door and Dad stands too. "I'll walk you out."

When both Dad and Uncle Jed are gone, I look to Winston and deadpan, "That went well."

He shakes his head in disbelief. "You are something else, man. I don't know how you're sitting in that fucking chair with balls that big."

I huff a laugh, surprised at his good-natured ribbing. I expected him to give me a hard time too. "Just gotta swing 'em forward as you sit down so they have room. It's easier than hauling them around everywhere." I mime carrying two bowling ball–size testicles in the circle of my arms, swinging them left and right and grunting at their weight.

"You're an asshole," Winston says, laughing. "Come on, let's get out of here before Dad comes back and starts in again on how hard he works."

We get up and peek out the door—me looking left and Winston looking right—and seeing that the coast is clear, we escape together like when we were kids. Walking right out the back door like ice couldn't melt in our mouths, we're so chill.

Chapter 8

HAZEL

To a lot of folks, tonight might seem weird. A bachelorette party that's combined with the bachelor party? I mean, where's the fun in that? No strippers, no craziness, and nobody gets to suck on a dick-shaped lollipop or drink creamy Jell-O shots that are slightly salty from a waitress's belly button.

But with all the insanity that's going to come over the next few days with the rehearsal dinner and wedding, tonight's party is about the most normal, Avery-like thing I can imagine. Still, it's not perfect.

"Did he *have* to bring his brother?" I grumble as I park my car in front of Puss N Boots. "I mean, really?"

"He is the best man," Avery points out, then grins.

"Ugh, don't remind me," I groan, looking across the parking lot as a big black truck pulls up. "You ready?"

"Duh," Avery says, getting out and beelining for Winston, who is basically running toward her. They meet in the middle, and he wraps his arms around her waist, spinning her in a joyful circle. They act like they haven't seen each other in months, not hours.

Sickening. And sweet as hell.

Another car pulls up and I see that Rachel's joined us as well, completing tonight's party attendance. I get out and cross over to the assembled group, feeling a little bit of something I won't give a name to when Wyatt immediately ignores Rachel's already pretty blatant looks to give me a once-over.

"Miss Hazel," he says with all that country charm that I know works . . . but can't be real.

"Wyatt," I reply evenly, promising myself that I'm not going to be rattled by him.

Wren seems to notice my voice, though, and lifts an eyebrow, like she hears something I don't mean to say. "So how about we see what's going on inside?" she offers, grinning. "I want to see my brother get his ego checked, and I think Hazel's the woman to do it."

"Can we have some fun first?" Winston asks hopefully, and Wren laughs. "Come on, let's have fun."

The bar's lively but not too busy, probably because of the sign that Aunt Etta posted on the door: **Wedding Party Tonight—They Come First, You Come Second. If that's a problem, go fuck yourself somewhere else!**

I grin, thinking that even Etta's notices have semi-intended, slightly sexual overtones. I'm guessing it turned a few folks away at the door, but Charlene looks happy about it as she gives us a wave. "Hey, Etta! Kin's here!" she hollers.

I'm a little nervous, to be honest, as Aunt Etta comes out from the kitchen, wiping her hands on a bar towel. There's no telling what's about to come out of her mouth. "Well, y'all are right on time," she says, giving us all polite smiles. "Shame Hazel can't manage that for her shifts." Etta cuts her eyes my way with the dig, and I stick my tongue out at her, both of us aware that I get here early, stay late, and cover shifts often. "Now, Avery, you and Hazel know the rules, but I'm gonna say 'em anyway so there's no confusion. Have fun tonight, but keep things on this side of the crazy line. You wanna act up some, I gotcha. But don't make me tell you twice to keep to the orderly side of disorderly. Got it?"

"We're clear, Miss Etta," Avery says, and Etta gives me a meaningful look. She knows that everyone's all good intentions and manners now, but I'm the one who's going to need to step in if necessary so she doesn't have to. For once, I'm the good cop, and she's the bad one.

I'm cool with that.

I hold my breath when she looks Wyatt's way, afraid she's going to throw him out or give him shit on my behalf. Wyatt looks back at her boldly, but I'm glad when he decides not to get into a stare off, ultimately giving her a polite, deferential nod and offering his hand. "Nice to finally meet you, Etta. I've heard a lot about you."

Aunt Etta ignores the hand but gives him a returning nod. "Yeah, I was home with my horse the other night when you came in, but I heard all about it. It's too bad I missed you."

She sounds vaguely threatening, like if she'd been here, she would've run him over with her truck. Truth is . . . maybe she would have. Wyatt doesn't miss a thing, but instead of reacting, he gives her a soft look. "How's your horse now? Better, I hope?"

Don't know how he knows it, but Nala is one of Etta's few weak points, and I swear she softens the tiniest bit at the question about her baby.

"She's fine now, all better," Etta assures him. "Just needed some babying."

"Don't we all?" I ask, grateful at the positive turn in conversation.

At least I am until Etta adds, "Which means I can focus on y'all tonight."

She glances around the group, but puts V'd fingers to her eyes and then turns them around toward Wyatt before giving me an eyebrow lift of warning. Without another word, she goes back behind the bar like nothing happened.

"I think that's our cue to find a table and relax?" Winston says, and after a moment of deciding, we find ourselves at one of Puss's bigger tables. Charlene brings over a pitcher of margaritas to start things off.

"This one's on Tay Tay," she says with a wink to me. "He knows you like it salty."

"Thanks, but I think I like things a little sweet," Rachel purrs, winking at Wyatt.

Unexpectedly, I feel a bit of cattiness inside.

Wait . . . what? No, no chance in hell. Can't be.

Charlene begins pouring glasses of margarita, but Wyatt holds up a hand. "Charlene, I'm the DD. Would you mind getting me something virgin?"

Wren leans forward. "Me too, actually." When Charlene looks at her in surprise, Wren explains, "I don't drink much." She glances at Winston, and something passes between them that I don't understand.

"Virgin?" Charlene repeats to Wyatt, ignoring Wren's odd statement. "I bet you've had a few of those in your day. Poor things never quite know what they're doing. You won't have to worry about that with me later tonight. I know *exactly* what I'm doing."

"The only thing I'm doing tonight is making sure my brother gets to the altar in one piece so Avery can tear him up afterward," Wyatt deadpans, and his humor is so out of left field and unexpected that everyone stops, gawking at him for a moment before we all explode in laughter.

"Hooo boy, I like the way you think!" Charlene says, grinning as she fans herself with her order pad. "Don't worry, honey-baby. I'll get something for you and Birdie in just a moment."

Charlene leaves, while Wren stews. "Birdie? You told her about calling me that?"

"Of course not, but it's kinda obvious, you know? Could be worse," Winston says. "I spent months being called nothing but 'ya bastard.' I knew Charlene accepted me when I actually got called by my name."

"I'll take the hit for that one," I volunteer to Winston, who raises an eyebrow. "Well, she was going to call you 'motherfucker,' but I told her to be more imaginative."

Winston lifts his glass my way, letting me know there are no hard feelings.

Charlene drops off a couple of drinks for Wyatt and Wren, and Wyatt climbs to his feet. "A toast," he says, his voice rising above the muted din of the room. Almost everyone quiets, but Wyatt ignores the rest of the room to look at his brother and Avery. "To Winston and Avery. I'll save the real emotional stuff, and the blackmail material, for the reception. For now"—he pauses dramatically—"may every day see you grow in love, in happiness, and in closeness. To the newlyweds to be."

"I'll drink to that!" Winston says, and we all lift a glass to the happy couple.

We relax, talking and getting to know each other better.

Well, Rachel's definitely taking the opportunity to get to know Wyatt better. "So, Wyatt, now that Avery's got Winston, what sort of woman revs the engine in your Ford?" She giggles like that's cute and funny.

"Well, I'm kind of particular," Wyatt says, leaning back in his chair.

I take a sip of my margarita and glance over to the pool tables, definitely *not* hoping that Wyatt gives me a peek into those pants of his.

I mean, brain.

I mean, I don't care in the slightest.

"Oh really?" Rachel asks, batting her eyes. "Particular how? Like brains and beauty? Because I qualify for that." Her smile says she's teasing, but her eyes are completely serious. She looks at Avery, hoping for an assist. "Isn't that right, Avery?"

Gotta give the girl credit. She's definitely got brains and beauty, but she forgot one more thing she's got in spades . . . balls. She's flirting hard.

"Definitely," Avery says, cutting her eyes to me, "but I'm lucky like that. All my friends are amazing. You, Hazel . . ."

"Don't forget me," Charlene jokes as she brings over another pitcher of margaritas and hears the end of Avery's sidestep, "because right here's the best of the best of the best . . . with honors."

"And what honors are those, Charlene?" Wren asks wryly, getting Charlene back for the nickname. "And are they available online?"

Char laughs. "You've got no idea to the tricks and skills I've got, little Birdie."

"I'm sure," Rachel says, laughing along as she tries to rejoin the conversation and gain Wyatt's attention.

I've been watching the women volley back and forth, but risk a glance at Wyatt, only to find him already looking at me. I roll my eyes and sit back, enjoying my drink and trying to stay as removed from this as possible because I'm not in this battle for Wyatt's attention.

Because the truth is . . . nearly every woman in Puss N Boots, except for Avery and Wren, wants him. And the harder truth is, I'm included. But I'm smart enough to hide it and not throw myself at him.

Nothing but trouble messing with a Ford.

"You know, Hazel, you've been pretty quiet," Wyatt says at one point, raising his glass of what looks like ginger ale toward me. "Don't tell me you don't have anything to add to the conversation?"

I lick my lips, tasting the sour lime and alcohol there, and enjoy the way Wyatt's eyes zero in on the movement. "I have plenty to say, but Avery made me promise to play nice tonight."

"You know how to behave?" Winston asks me disbelievingly.

"There's a time to behave," Wyatt tells his brother before zeroing back in on me, "and a time to misbehave."

"What do you mean by that?" I ask, and Wyatt raises an eyebrow. "Oh, me jumping on Roddy's back? That was nothing."

"I bet Roddy would beg to differ," Wyatt argues. "In fact, I bet once sober, he was kicking himself for not enjoying the moment more fully."

"Enjoying me attacking him?" I ask, confused.

Wyatt's eyes brighten, and I realize I've stepped directly into a trap. I'm usually better than this, used to all sorts of setups for cheesy come-ons from customers. But that's not what Wyatt offers . . .

"Attacking him? With your knees locked around his waist, your chest pressed to him, and your breath on his neck while you screamed?"

He makes my banshee-yelling piggyback ride on Roddy's back sound like something completely different.

It's like that for hours. On and off, he and I spar verbally. Sometimes he's tossing me some pretty blatant comments, other times he's almost subtle with his come-ons. Meanwhile, I've found that trying to irritate Wyatt Ford is fun. He doesn't show it easily; in fact, the best way I can tell that I've gotten one in on him is when he literally doesn't change his reaction one bit from my last comment. That straight face, hiding his emotions, is more revealing than any of the flirty smiles, deep laughs, or long looks.

But with each round of stories or comments or jokes, I find myself more and more distracted. He's not perfect, like some movie producer's wet dream of a hero. No, he's too cocky, too zero fucks given, for that. But that means the good things I see are all the more real. Like his affection for his brother and sister. Whatever there is between them, and I think those three have more layers than an onion going on there, he's got a big heart for them both.

"Are we going to see this pool face-off?" Rachel asks eventually. "Because I'm ready to see you play with your balls, Wyatt!"

"I'm going to need therapy for that one," Wren says, wincing.

I look over at Wyatt, and the sudden image of him bent over the table, his tight bubble butt filling out his jeans, his big biceps stretching the sleeves of his shirt as he strokes his cue has me dry mouthed, and I have to swallow the rest of the margarita in my glass. "Yeah . . . let's do this."

"Let's not," Wyatt says, and I gape at him in surprise.

"You're chickening out on me?" I ask, and Wyatt shakes his head. "Sounds like it to me. Bawk! Bawk! Bawk!" My impression sounds a bit like Lester mimicking a chicken, but it gets the point across.

"When we play, Hazel, we're going to do it when we're on equal level," Wyatt says. "You're getting tipsy. I won't take advantage."

"I could beat you falling down drunk!" I protest, and Wyatt laughs.

Getting up, he comes over to my seat, one hand on the back and one on the table to whisper in my ear, "When we play again, I want you sober so that you *know* without a doubt that I'm the one man good enough to handle you." I look up at him, searching his face for the lie, but he smiles easily. "Or maybe I need a little liquid courage before I try again."

It's sexy, so sexy I can feel a sudden flash of heat between my thighs. Confidence, praise, and some self-deprecating humor all in two sentences? It's a headier mix than the drinks that are not making me tipsy in the slightest.

"If you want to play, Rachel, go ahead and grab a table. I'm sure Wren will play. I think I'll get some mushy love songs playing on that jukebox over there. Set the mood for this party." Wyatt saunters off, going over to the big Seeburg that Etta bought almost at the same time she opened Puss N Boots.

Rachel and Wren look at each other, shrugging and not making a move to claim a table.

"I think I'll make sure he isn't loading up a bunch of Carly Rae Jepsen or something," I mumble, getting up to follow Wyatt, my eyes locked on his broad back and tight buns as he looks at the selections on the digital screen.

He doesn't look my way when I walk up beside him, as though he knew I'd follow. That irks me. I'm not one of these lovesick, or horny, women he can lead around like a puppy on a leash.

"I'm surprised," he says as he pushes a button and the screen changes. "I thought you'd have an old-school box here, not digital."

I ignore his comment and lean in. "You're wasting your time."

"Hmmm?" he asks, dropping a quarter in and punching in a code. A few seconds later, Pink's "Raise Your Glass" starts playing, and Wyatt moves on.

I try again. "You're flirting with the wrong bridesmaid, Wyatt. That one over there is an easy bet," I tell him, pointing over at Rachel. "I'm not going to play with your balls anytime soon, but you could probably have her in a bathroom stall with a crook of your finger. No shame in that," I clarify. "Rachel's a sweetheart, and a bathroom romp with a hot stranger would be one of those naughty stories she looks back on fondly for the rest of her life."

Wyatt chuckles and cuts his eyes to me, smirking. With him leaned over the jukebox, he knows it's just him and me here, and there's nobody's feelings to protect other than our own. "Maybe I don't want easy," he says. "Maybe easy is boring, even if it is a quickie in a bar bathroom with a hot stranger." He pauses, looking me up and down. "Maybe I want something more than that."

I blink, surprised.

So quiet I almost miss it, he says, "Or maybe I don't know what the hell I'm doing here." Before I can question that, he punches in another code on the jukebox, then another. "Okay," he says, stepping back. "So in about ten minutes, you can blame 'I Want It That Way' on Winston."

"You're kidding . . . That's on the jukebox?" I ask, and he nods. "Fuck."

We go back to the table, and true to his word, the Backstreet Boys' song does play. To my surprise, Winston cheers, singing along as he serenades Avery, who laughs along with him. I get the feeling this isn't the first time they've done this together, and I smile at the mental image of them singing and dancing around together at home to old boy band songs.

By the chorus, Wyatt joins in, the two brothers harmonizing at various points, and I'm half expecting them to break out into a choreographed dance routine. As the bar realizes what's happening, they start singing backup for Winston, and it becomes an entire concert with Winston and Avery as the center stage stars.

But Wyatt's eyes aren't on Avery, or Rachel, or Charlene. And they're definitely not on his brother, who's kneeling and holding Avery's hand now. Wyatt's eyes stay on me as he sings, and heat fills my chest. I find myself fighting the urge to meet his eyes, and I know I'm probably blushing, even if I should be weirded out that Wyatt Ford's singing an old love song to me while staring at me like a creeper.

But it's powerful, knowing I'm the sole focus of his attention. It's like I'm driving him crazy, and I decide to lean into it, giving him a wink and playing with the straw on my drink. It's subtle, but he seems to respond to that more than having it thrown in his face. Or he just responds to me . . . regardless of what I'm offering.

I decide to test that.

While I'm figuring out my next move, the Backstreet Boys song ends and Wren runs to the jukebox, shouting, "Our turn!"

The next song starts, and I catch Wren's suggestion that we do a performance in answer to the one Winston and Wyatt, and most of the bar, just gave.

Game. On.

I know how to work my assets—I'm a waitress, after all—so I run with Wren's idea.

"On the bar!" I call, and Charlene and Aunt Etta both give me raised eyebrows, but when a soon-to-be bride wants to dance for her man to "Side To Side," there really isn't anyplace better than on top of the bar, or on top of the table.

Since we can't fit more than one person on the table, the bar's the place to do it. Wren pulls Avery up, and I join them a moment later, dancing along with the other two. Rachel defers, shaking her head when Avery waves her up, but Charlene joins in to the hoots and hollers of the entire bar.

But even as the four of us do some halfway decent hip shaking and even a coordinated booty drop that leaves quite a few tongues wagging when we bring it up slow, I'm not dancing for the crowd.

I'm teasing one person, and one person only. So when I look over my shoulder, it's Wyatt's eyes I look into first, letting the heat there inspire my next few moves, before I intentionally look over to some other random dude and flash him a wink.

This is the sexiest I've felt in a very, very long time. And that it's because of a Ford is an extra naughty thrill.

Afterward, Aunt Etta slows down the pace at which the pitchers flow to our table, which is probably a good thing. Even as I slow down, I feel a bit tipsy, and I'm glad for the cool night air when we all leave.

Somehow Wren manages to volunteer herself as the driver for Rachel, Winston, and Avery. "I'll drop Rachel off at the hotel, and then take Winston and Avery to Avery's house. I'm good to drive home after that."

Wren lifts questioning brows at Wyatt, waiting to see if he'll say anything to change those plans. I keep my mouth shut, knowing she's leaving the two of us here alone together, but not sure how I feel about that yet.

Wyatt says nothing, and a moment later, Wren's herding her passengers away.

Almost afraid of myself, or maybe what could happen, I turn without a word and start walking toward my car. Wyatt follows, catching up quickly. "What are you doing?" I ask.

"Walking you to your car," he says, his voice a deep rumble in the quiet night. "You shouldn't be driving."

"I'm fine."

I am not fine. Not to drive and not to be alone with him.

"I wouldn't play you in pool. You think I'm going to let you drive? No," Wyatt says in a no-nonsense tone. "Not a chance, Hazel."

No one talks to me this way, least of all guys. They're usually begging for scraps of my attention. But not Wyatt. No, he demands it, but gives it back just as powerfully. The fire inside me roars, liking his confidence, even enjoying his bossiness, and the ache in my body for more than flirting grows uncomfortable.

"Fine."

We reach my car and he leans in. For a panicked moment, I think he's going for a surprise kiss.

Nuts him in the knee! I mean, knee him in the nuts!

My automatic response screams across my brain, but I refrain this time. I don't want to imagine his balls all swollen and purple later. That's a definite mood killer, and I'm going to have to take care of this fire inside me.

Dammit. I meant to make him hot and bothered, and ended up doing it to myself too.

But instead of the kiss that I've decided to allow, he gently plucks my keys from my hand, and steps back, pressing the unlock button on the fob before holding out a hand. I blink stupidly, then realize he's walking me around to the passenger side. Tipsy me is a sucker for gentlemanly manners.

With my filters down, I tell him, "You're nice sometimes."

He doesn't gloat, thankfully, but I think he chuckles under his breath. He covers it with a cough, so I'm not 100 percent sure—more like 97.3 percent.

"Where to?" he asks as we walk around the back of the car, his voice gentle. "I don't know where you live." Ugh. I'm letting him put me in the shotgun seat of my own car.

"Not going home," I answer unexpectedly. Not sure where that came from because I was totally thinking about going home and using the muscle-blaster setting on my showerhead to blast my clit. Hard and fast, it'd get me off like a rocket, and probably knock me out for the rest of the night.

"Okay," Wyatt says agreeably. "Where to, then?"

I turn to lean against the passenger door. "Mom's bakery."

Wyatt gives me a very suspicious look. "Where?"

"The Bakery Box," I explain, being very careful to enunciate each word. "I work there, helping out as much as I can, and she's extra busy this week with the wedding prep."

"You want to bake? Now?"

"No, I want to clean," I retort sarcastically. "Of course I want to bake. It's a bakery. That's what you do there. Or are you too good to get your hands dirty?"

"I clean my workshop every day," Wyatt scoffs. "But you work for Etta and your mom? At the same time?"

"Yep," I reply with pride. "It's a family affair. Twenty-four seven, three hundred and sixty-five. It's what we do."

Wyatt shivers. "That sounds awful."

Maybe that's true for his own family. I think it speaks volumes about the Fords, and gives me a bit more insight into why Wyatt left town. Maybe I can find out why? "Depends on the family."

"Ain't that the truth?" he says almost wistfully. Suddenly, he gives me a smile. "Think you could use some help?"

"At the bakery?" I ask incredulously. "I was joking about your hands, Wyatt."

"I know. And why not?" Wyatt offers. "I promise, despite me being a Ford, I do know how to scrub a pot or use a mop. I can help."

"Do you bake?" I ask, and he winces.

"Noooo," he says hesitantly, "but I can follow orders."

I snort. "Yeah . . . I'm sure that's not true in the slightest."

Wyatt shrugs. "Let's say I can follow orders when I want to, when they make some sense and are given by someone I want to please."

I'm pretty sure we're not talking about cupcakes or mopping floors any longer, but I'm almost eager to find out exactly what we are talking about. "Okay, let's test that theory."

Chapter 9

Wyatt

For most people, going to work half-tipsy at half past midnight isn't the best idea.

But Hazel seems to feel this is perfectly normal. Judging from her 24/7/365 comment, maybe for her, it is? She's getting more clearheaded by the minute, not having any alcohol in more than an hour and putting away a basket of cheese fries by herself, so I'm not in doubt of her decision-making skills. And it's not like we're breaking and entering. She has a key.

Honestly, even if we were committing a little light B and E, I'd probably go along with it to spend time with her and get to know what makes her tick better.

As Hazel flips on the lights, I'm surprised at the charming bakery before me. After seeing Etta's version of Puss N Boots, and hearing that her mom's business is called the Bakery Box, I was worried it would be sexy red velvet fabrics and black lights. For Cold Springs, it'd seem apropos in the craziness. Instead, it's bright and clean, with pink-and-white striped walls, a trio of four-seater tables, and chrome display cases that are currently empty.

Hazel looks at me expectantly, awaiting my verdict or a snappy comment. But I'm enjoying surprising her as much as possible.

"This is cute. Your mom must be an amazing baker," I say kindly.

"She's the best," Hazel agrees, and I can sense the indecision in her. Under the eyes of her watchful aunt at the bar, she was flirty but knew she had a solid safety net that would keep her from taking things too far. She could tease and torment me, all the while telling me that I didn't have a chance with her because of one thing. My name.

But now? Alone, with only herself to stop her, I can feel her wavering. She wants me, she just doesn't want to want me. It's a situation I've never been in, and I suspect she hasn't either. As for me? I certainly wasn't expecting to find something, or someone, to make this trip home bearable, but Hazel has more than done so.

The kitchen is different from the front of the shop. Gone are the cutesy decorations and soft pastels, replaced with commercial-grade stainless-steel worktables, an industrial mixer that looks like it could handle cake batter or concrete with equal ease, a huge refrigerator, and a trio of big ovens that could bake a whole wedding cake at once.

Oh, and a microwave. It looks out of place, the only black thing in the entire bakery, with a twist dial and a huge scuff on top. "What's with this old thing?" I ask, running my hand over the surface. It's clean, just scarred.

Hazel looks my way and flips the switches on the wall with practiced ease. "Mom only uses that for two things."

"What's that?"

"Rewarming coffee and melting butter," she says, pointing at the big industrial sink. "You. Hands. To the elbows."

I sense this is my first test—to see if I actually will follow directions. I scrub up to my elbows like a surgeon getting ready for open-heart surgery, with every intention of acing this test. "Now what?"

Her reply is to toss an apron in my face, and I'm tempted to protest. It's . . . cutesy.

But without a word I slip the baby-blue gingham strap over my head, fiddling with the ties to get something approaching a bow knot going behind my back. I feel like I look stupid, but Hazel gives me an appreciative look. Though it's possible that's because she's tying her own plain white apron on.

"Cara had this crazy midnight-madness idea," Hazel explains, giving me flashbacks of the awful wedding planner barging into my suit fitting like she owned the place, "which is actually brilliant, but I will kill you if you tell her I said that." She points a sharp finger at me, and I hold my hands up, promising that I'll do no such thing. "Good, because it basically means that, in addition to Mom making the wedding cake, she now has to make four hundred desserts."

"Four hundred?" I ask incredulously. "Holy shit, that's a lot."

"Exactly," Hazel says. "Now we can't bake it all tonight, and Mom's already started on some of the goodies, but we can help out by getting a few batches of cupcakes done and in the cooler for her."

It makes sense, and I'm even more impressed as Hazel looks up at a big whiteboard on the wall. It's covered in a mess of scribbled notes in a rainbow of colors that looks about as decipherable as the walls of an Egyptian pyramid. But she clearly understands it.

"Okay, what's first?" I ask, and Hazel points. "The flour?"

"Yeah, the one marked 'all purpose,'" she says. "Use the baker's scale there, and get me two pounds of it."

I find a large plastic tub and do as she says, putting in two pounds of white flour. "Now what?"

Hazel, who's in the fridge, looks over her shoulder. "Do the same thing with fourteen ounces of sugar, but put that in the bowl when you're done. It's a wet."

"A wet?" I ask. "But it's sugar. Dry."

Hazel flashes me an amused look. "It dissolves so quickly with liquids, sugar's considered a wet ingredient for our purposes."

I peer into the bin of apparently "wet" sugar that looks completely dry to me. "If you say so."

"I do," Hazel says, bringing her own ingredients over. Dropping what looks like an obscene amount of butter into the big metal bowl on the mixer, she starts the mixer up at a slow speed. "C'mon, Helga. I know it's early, but you can do it, girl," she purrs to the mixer in a sweet, cajoling voice. To me, she simply orders, "Get me a fresh gallon of milk."

I grab her the milk, and as she pours it in without measuring, she asks, "What do you do now that you've run away from home and are apparently the black sheep of the Ford family?"

"Is that the rumor? Hard to believe I'm the black sheep." She gives me a wry look, and I shrug. "I'm a woodworker, own my own shop making heirloom furniture and period-appropriate reproduction millwork."

"Blah blah . . . wood . . . blah blah . . . furniture. That's about all I understood," she teases, cracking eggs into the bowl.

I laugh, charmed by her "no big deal" attitude. But I want her to know me, as much as I want to know her, so I explain. "When people are renovating historical homes and need trim moldings, you can't just go down to Home Depot and pick it up. The pieces are special, unique, and though we could machine-mill them with the technology we have now, creating them by hand, carving them the same way they were centuries ago, is . . . important." I realize Hazel has stopped what she's doing, listening to me attentively, and I fear I've revealed more than I intended. "The heirloom furniture is my cake and pie, though," I joke, pointing at the bowl she's holding. "Custom pieces using turn-of-the-century methods to make furniture your great-great-grandkids will sell at an estate sale one day."

Hazel laughs, letting me lighten things. "So you have a bunch of big *tools* and *machines*?"

"I do, but most of my work is done with my hands," I reply suggestively.

"You must be good with them then," Hazel says. I hold my hands up, letting her see for herself. She smiles her approval before jumping subjects. "Where do you live now?"

"Newport. I've got a little house that's smaller than my shop, which was the garage at one point. It's enough for me." She slows down the mixer before adding the dry ingredients, and I ask a question of my own. "Who's the better baker, you or your mom?"

"Mom, no doubt. She's a better baker than most of those idiots on TV," Hazel says immediately, "but I'm learning what I can."

"I bet," I say appreciatively, not only of her but of her various skills. Her confidence in the kitchen is almost as sexy as her cockiness at the pool table.

She turns the mixer back up. "Okay, give that a minute to mix, and we'll get the bacon and candied pecans going."

"Bacon *and* pecans?" I groan, my mouth watering. "Damn, that's like seduction in a cupcake for me."

Hazel's eyes sparkle. "Good to know your stomach is the way to your . . ." I wait for her to finish the phrase as expected, but I should've known better because she leans my way to say, "Dick. I picked out that combination. A little salty, a little sweet. Pure sinful decadence."

I shift on my feet, feeling some sins of my own coming up, and though the move is subtle, Hazel misses nothing. With a coy smile, she scoops cupcake batter into the paper baking cups of a large tray. She pops the tray into the oven, asking, "Why did you leave Cold Springs?"

"It's a long story." I don't add that it's one I don't particularly want to get into. I figure Winston will want an explanation, and I probably owe him and Wren one, but it's not a topic I like to dig out and showcase.

"We have twenty minutes until that batch comes out of the oven," Hazel says as she goes back over to the fridge and pulls out four packets of bacon. "Try me. And you can peel bacon while you're talking."

I grab a big cookie sheet from a pile I see on a rack, deciding whether I'm going to share. And if so, how?

"Okay, let's see. First off, I grew up with opportunities, obviously. I won't deny that."

"That's good, very self-aware of you," Hazel teases, grabbing a bag of pecans and scooping brown sugar into a bowl.

"But there was also an expectation of who I'd be, what I'd be," I explain carefully, and she lifts an eyebrow. "I know, I know. Poor little rich boy, right? But it was there, just the same. Like my whole life was laid out for me, planned out . . . where I'd go to school, what I'd major in, what I'd do after graduation, who I'd marry, and what I'd do from there. It felt a little like being told the world was your oyster, but then realizing that you don't like oysters, and that there's a whole ocean of other options out there. And land. And air."

"So you wanted to sink or swim with the fishies?" Hazel says as she pours the pecans into a big industrial food processor. "You sure you moved to Newport and not New York?"

I laugh, shaking my head. "I'm sure. I guess what I mean is . . . I just wanted freedom. Rise or fall, it'd be closer to being by my own hands."

"Closer?"

"Regardless of how much I might have given up moving out of Cold Springs, I still started life with a lot of advantages," I admit. "But I tried to leave as much behind as I could. I took my truck, same truck I've got now, and started driving. Didn't know where I was going or what I was going to do. I just wanted to figure things out on my own without the family static."

"But you took the money, right?" Hazel asks, a bit accusatory, and I get it. Like I said, I had advantages that I'm well aware of. Even so, I feel like I should say no, as if the money is going to be a sticking point for Hazel that lets her discount anything unexpected I might've done. But if I'm telling Hazel about leaving, I'm going with the truth.

"Yes and no. I took what was in my accounts and lived on that for a bit while I figured myself out. And you could say I used my family resources to take out a zero-interest startup loan for my shop," I explain. "But once I had some success, I stopped. I've been putting money back into the savings accounts my parents set up when I was a kid, paying on my business loan, and living on my own income. I've got a budget all set up for it."

To my surprise, Hazel smiles. "Idiot. No sense leaving money on the table. Take what you can get when you run. If it's in your name, it's yours."

"Well, I guess I can see your point. I just want to make sure at some point I'm doing it on my own, even if it's only in my own head." I laugh, what she said registering fully. "I figured you'd be all 'rich-boy runaway on Daddy's dime.' That's what I think most people hear when I tell them about leaving."

Hazel looks thoughtful. "I think you'd be surprised. Do you know how many people have those thoughts? Getting out of Cold Springs or whatever town they're in? Getting away from some bullshit in their past? People do just about anything for a fresh start."

In three seconds, she's making me feel less guilty about taking the money than I've been able to do for myself in years. "Most people don't have the opportunity to start over."

"Hopefully, they stay because the reasons to stay are better than the ones to go," Hazel says optimistically.

But I've seen Winston's and Wren's situations, and their balance sheets definitely tilt in favor of getting the hell out of Cold Springs. Yet here they stay. "Hmmph," I grunt.

"You tell many people about why you left?"

I freeze. I have to think hard, just to be sure, but in the end, I look up at her, her with her pecans and brown sugar, me with my tray of bacon slices. "Honestly? Just you." When she lifts an eyebrow, I nod. "It's the truth. I have friends in Newport, but I haven't exactly told them where I come from. I'm not ashamed of it, but it doesn't seem relevant, either, because it's not who I am anymore. They don't care about my last name, or associate it with the way . . . well, folks here do."

"Ah," Hazel says as if she's discovered something exceptional. "So it's not what they think, it's what you think. You're the one who thinks you're a 'rich-boy runaway on Daddy's dime.'"

"Shit. You don't mince words, do you?" I ask, stepping back.

Hazel shrugs. "Why bother? If people can't handle my mouth, they can't handle me. It's easier to filter people out from the jump. Door's over there," she offers as though she expects me to be one of the ones who limp away from her sharp tongue.

Except other than backing away from the raw bacon and wiping my hands on my apron, I'm not going anywhere. "What's next? More bacon?"

Hazel turns to check the oven, trying to hide her pleased smile from me, but I see it clear as day in the reflection of the glass. I think I just passed one of Hazel Sullivan's tests with flying colors.

By staying. Something that's not my usual strong suit.

"What about you?" I ask. "What's your story?"

She opens the oven and pulls out the cupcakes, setting them aside as she pops the tray of pecans and brown sugar down low, my bacon up high. "Not so different than yours but without the money. My family has run Puss N Boots and the Bakery Box for years, and I grew up helping Mom and Aunt Etta. I never really considered doing anything else. Guess you could say I was in that big middle."

"Big middle?" I echo, and she nods.

"Sure. Lots of folks around Cold Springs would say our family is doing pretty well for itself. Maybe we are. I mean, Aunt Etta's got her own horse, and that's all she wants in the world. Same with Mom and this bakery. And I've got my home. But we're not so rich that we don't clip coupons, do without sometimes, and we work hard to keep the businesses running right."

I nod, knowing what she means. I don't say it, but I remember the man who came into my shop one time with an antique Scottish hutch he wanted to sell. It was in serious need of restoration, but even still, tears were in his eyes when I asked why he wanted to part with it.

The reason? Medical bills. So I paid what he asked, even if I took a small loss on the resale when I added in the costs of the restoration. I even offered the hutch back to the man, but he refused. It taught me a tough lesson, because I would've happily eaten the cost to bring a smile to his face, but he said the hutch had painful memories now. It was only my determination to live on my own work that forced me to eventually sell the hutch.

"You want to take over one or both businesses someday?" I ask. "You know, sling cakes by morning, beers by night?"

Hazel shrugs. "Don't really think about it. I mostly put one foot in front of the other and keep everything from going off the rails as best I can."

She opens the oven door, stirring the pecans before closing it up once again.

"Do you ever go off the rails? Let loose a bit?" I challenge, stepping in front of her once she's clear of the hot ovens.

I'm truly curious. She's a hard worker, dedicated to her family, staunchly loyal to her friends, and though I think she'd consider herself a bit of a wild child, the truth is, even when she lets loose, like dancing on the bar or playing pool, she's in complete control.

Every move she makes may not be calculated for pros and cons, but the bets she makes are ones she knows she can win, and her rowdy behavior isn't all that rebellious in a bar where she feels safe and knows that everyone there would help her if she needed backup.

I lean in closer, my breath on her cheek. I can feel the heat coming off her body, both from the oven's blast and the work she's been doing. Anticipation fills the small space between us, and I wait, not moving to see if she'll make that crazy leap into uncertainty.

114

A test of my own, if you will.

I want her to kiss me. I want to feel the savageness of her soul because I bet Hazel Sullivan is a sight to behold when she unleashes. She licks her lips and I'm on edge, barely holding on to the end of my rope. I think this is going to be a pivot point, the time before Hazel kissed me, and after.

Inside my boots, I'm clenching my toes so I don't step between her feet to get even closer. My hands curl into fists as I fight my desire to touch her. I work my jaw, trying to look calm and patient, as inside I'm anything but. I tilt my head slightly and part my lips, so fucking ready for her.

Her breath catches, her breasts rising a scant inch, as her eyes dip to my mouth.

Kiss me, I will her with my mind. She's going to do it, I can see it in her eyes.

But at the last moment, instead of a kiss, she steps back, her voice hardening. "Fuck you, Ford."

"What?" I growl, feeling like I just got slapped in the face. Ice dumps through my veins at the loss of her heat when she moves away. I hate every single inch she's added between us, not only physically, but with her words.

"You heard me," she says, now sounding pissed off. "Fuck you, Ford."

I plant one hand on the metal workbench, my knuckles whitening as I grab the edge for balance. "Why are you calling me that?"

"What?"

"Ford," I hiss. "You're using my last name against me. Like it's a curse or something."

"Isn't it?" she asks bluntly.

"I thought we'd gotten beyond that," I say angrily. "My family has flaws. I'm well aware of that. I fucking laid them out in black and white for you."

She snorts. "You laid out *your* issues. You forgot a few. Like Jed breaking Etta's heart. And don't forget what your dear old dad is pulling with the zoning. I love the way you can make ramrodding the town sound like y'all get a little too competitive playing Monopoly. Like real people's lives aren't being affected."

"I don't know what the hell you're talking about with the zoning," I tell her honestly. "I'm just figuring that shit out myself. And Jed and Etta's thing was almost thirty years ago. It sure as fuck shouldn't determine what you or I do. But maybe it does for you?"

Though I shouldn't be, I'm disappointed. In the situation, at my family, and even in Hazel. I thought she'd see beyond my last name, especially after I told her everything I did.

She's right—I haven't shared that with anyone.

But maybe that doesn't mean as much to her as it does to me. Maybe she's playing me the same way Jed wanted to, as a pawn in whatever game they're trying to win.

The timer on the pecans goes off, and I turn to grab it this time, giving Hazel my back as I put my walls up. Lost in Hazel's beauty and fiery personality, I dropped my guard too easily, too quickly.

I won't make that mistake again.

But I am a man of my word, despite whatever she might think.

So we're going to get these goddamn trays of bacon and candied pecans finished so Hazel's mom can have a head start for whatever Cara's Midnight Madness shit is. Silently, I stare into the last oven, waiting for it to ding too.

She says nothing, and it's only once the last batch of goodies is out and cooling that I look her in the eyes again. I can see the glitter of moisture there and take no joy in her tears, especially since it's colored with confusion and so many other warring emotions that I can't label them all.

"You seem sober enough to drive home," I tell her, setting the keys to her car on the table. "Good night, Hazel."

Without waiting for a reply, I leave, tugging my apron off and putting it on a hook before I simply walk out into the cool morning air.

The walk back to Puss N Boots is long, but it goes by in a flash as my mind whirls, replaying the entire night. When I get to the parking lot, I get in my truck, turning on the heater for a few moments, warming not my body but my heart.

It's a longer drive than it should be, going back home to fall into bed just as the sun starts to rise. The last thought I have before sleep takes me is . . .

Tomorrow is the wedding rehearsal. Gonna be a fucking nightmare.

Chapter 10

HAZEL

I stifle a yawn, but after a bachelor(ette) party and working at the bakery until three in the morning, I'm exhausted. I just hope I don't look it, dressed in the gray-and-white checkered dress and pink heels with a matching pink belt that Cara sent home with me after the final fittings with Mrs. Hinsley. Though this dress is off the rack, Mrs. Hinsley did a few alterations to make it fit perfectly.

Thankfully, the Ford family paid for that service along with the dress itself because, for some reason, Cara insisted Rachel and I wear matching dresses for the rehearsal and then our actual bridesmaid dresses tomorrow for the wedding too.

That was a new one for me. But I'm also not going to argue with Cara . . . or a free dress that twirls like a ballerina onstage. And yes, of course I checked that, spinning in the living room and putting on a fashion show for Lester. He told me I looked like a "pretty bird," which is high praise from him.

I run my hand along my thigh nervously, smoothing an invisible wrinkle. This dress seems out of place in my old Nissan, but Nessa serves me well and will get me to the Ford estate.

Once there, of course, Nessa will be the one out of place on their fancy driveway. I pat the dash, urging her, "Please don't leak oil, 'kay, girl?"

Nessa shifts into the next gear seamlessly, and I take that as a good sign. Actually, there are a lot of good signs today. Driving out to the Ford estate, it's a beautiful day. The sun is out, with just enough fluffy cotton-candy clouds to cut the heat a little bit, and a gentle breeze stirs the leaves on the trees and makes everything smell fresh and clean.

Almost everyone is out and about, enjoying the weather. As I pass the elementary school, I see one group of boys playing basketball on the court, while in the baseball field, there's another group doing what looks like Little League practice.

I drive past Mom's bakery and smile at the small line I see inside. Even if she's got to be busting her hump, she's handling business, and I'm sure she's got the rest of her crew helping her out, running the register and more.

My smile dims some when I hit the center of downtown and see the city courthouse and a few protesters outside. It must be their break, because they're sitting in folding lawn chairs, drinking Cokes, and their **No Rezoning** signs are leaning against a nearby tree. They're not taking it easy, though. They've likely been out here all day, making sure everyone knows the risks of the rezoning proposal that will be discussed at the hearing next week.

As I pass by, I toot my horn and offer a thumbs-up of encouragement, which is returned with smiles and fists thrown in the air. Sure, I feel a little guilty going out to Bad Guy Central today, but that's about Avery. Even the most militant of the protesters would understand that.

Arriving at the Ford estate, I gawk at the manicured lawn, which is literally a single shade of vibrant green. I don't think even the Cold Springs High football stadium's field is this consistently lush.

The house is impressive, too, and while I'll admit it's nowhere near as gob-smacking as that ninth-grade class trip to Washington, DC, to see the White House, it certainly feels like the giant home has similar aspirations. For a small-town mayor's house, it's definitely got the grandeur and the fanciness, right down to the big double front doors and the columns holding up the second-floor walkway.

Monogrammed signs direct me where to park, and I remind Nessa again of our deal about holding her oil while on the fancy concrete drive.

Tucking my key into my purse, I swallow my nerves and approach the front doors. I feel small, insignificant, and part of me wonders whether I should have brought my ID along just in case they ask. Or maybe a twenty to tip the bouncer?

Before I can turn around, an older man opens the door. Immaculately dressed in pressed black tropical-weight slacks and a white dress shirt, his lack of tie, even though his collar is buttoned, tells me that he's definitely not one of the Fords.

"Hello," I greet him, trying to sound relaxed. "I'm—"

"Miss Hazel Sullivan," the man says, surprising me. "A pleasure. I'm Leo."

I laugh in shock, cocking my head. "How'd you know?"

For some reason, my thought is to wonder whether Wyatt told him. But that ridiculousness is dashed when he whispers, as though confiding to me, "Ms. DeMornay gave me pictures of the wedding party. She even gave me a picture of Winston, as if I wouldn't know who he is."

The man laughs and I instantly like him. There's something warm and real about his dark eyes. Maybe it's the web of crinkles on the edges of those eyes, ones that come from lots of similar expressions of mirth.

"Well, I appreciate it," I tell him. "I was waiting for someone to unleash the hounds and run me off the property."

Leo shakes his head with a widening smile. "Please, come in. The ladies are upstairs in one of the guest rooms, getting ready."

Leo escorts me through the house, which is very much a historical home. The rooms are majestic, with soaring ceilings, fancy furniture, and art that looks museum-worthy. Actually, that's exactly what this feels like—a museum. I try to imagine being a kid here, running cars along the wooden floors, or doing messy crafts at the fancy dining table I see, and I can't picture it. It makes me somewhat sad for Wyatt, Winston, and Wren. Almost.

But the narrow hallways are thickly carpeted, and my heels don't make a sound as Leo leads me upstairs to a bedroom that's bigger than my living room, dining room, and kitchen combined.

"Miss Sullivan," Leo announces me even as Avery, Rachel, and Wren get up excitedly. Cara's here too, her outfit flawlessly put together, but her face looking quite pinched. Vaguely, I wonder if I should suggest one of Tayvious's Big Daddy footlongs to her. They've been known to clear up constipation in a matter of hours. Probably because of the amount of horseradish he puts on them.

But I don't care about Cara or what's made her look so stressed. My eyes are on my bestie, who looks absolutely beautiful in the white wraparound silk cocktail dress that hugs her figure while still being light and airy. It's the opposite type of fit from my fuller circle skirt, making her look sleek and sexy in a sophisticated way. It's perfect for today's events, and I gawk. I've seen her top-secret wedding gown, but haven't seen this before. "Avery, you look *hot!*" I gush, hugging her and then leading her in a spin so I can see the full effect. "Winston's going to be stiffer than the front columns on this place when he sees you in this!" I mime Winston's rock-hard dick falling out of his pants, using my forearm as the dick in question. "Thwak!" I say, adding a sound effect to the tasteless motion.

Avery blushes, but grins. "Thank you! I wanted something very different from my wedding dress so that Winston wouldn't be underwhelmed tomorrow."

I scoff, but I have to grin as Wren, behind her, rolls her eyes, twirling her finger around her ear to express her silent opinion on Avery's concerns. "Honey, there is no way he could be underwhelmed. You could be wearing a potato sack, and he'd still think you're the most beautiful thing he's ever seen," I tell her honestly. "Actually, that might be a good thing, because this? Oh, honey, he's going to want to skip tomorrow and drag you to bed *tonight* in this thing." I swat her ass playfully.

"That would be highly inappropriate!" Cara blusters, her nostrils flaring. "And please get your hands off her. If you wrinkle her or get her dirty, I will be forced to kill you."

I'm almost sure she'd try it at this point. Cara looks stern and no nonsense, even for her, today. "Chill, Cara," I tell her as I move a few inches away from Avery. "I'm pretty sure that Avery is washable."

"Perhaps," a regal voice says from behind me, "but white is a dirt magnet that will show every speck and spot in the photos we'll be taking later."

I turn, seeing a face I've seen a few times in the newspapers, and of course around town whenever Bill Ford's stumping for reelection. But we've never actually met before. "Pamela Ford," she says.

She's just as elegant as she looks on her husband's campaign posters, but her smile's warmer than I expected as she shakes my hand.

"Hazel Sullivan," I greet her, and she nods. But an instant later, her eyes flash in recognition of my name, and I swear she's about to say something when a much more familiar face sticks *his* head in the door.

"Girl, you'd best get over here and hug my neck or I'll whip your behind."

I'm laughing before Pamela Ford can turn around, sidestepping past her to get to the only man I love unconditionally. I lean over his walker to pull him in for a hug. "Grandpa Joe! Didn't they tell you this is the ladies' dressing room? You should be in the other room with the guys," I tell him as I squeeze him carefully around the shoulders. "It's been a dog's age since I've seen you!"

"Well, that's cuz of my kidneys," Avery's grandfather says, grinning. "Can't hang out at a bar when three sips has me high-steppin' to the whizzer! So I do what any self-respecting old man does, and do my drinkin' at home! Hell, every once in a while, they give me one of them catheters, and I race my kidneys, seeing if I can drink faster than I can piss it out. That's more entertaining than half the shit they put on the boob tube these days. Have you seen they got some show where they drop people off in the woods, naked as the day they's born? Ridiculous! I mean, I wouldn't mind checking a few of the ladies for ticks, but the fellas are on their own."

I laugh, partially at his crude conversation and partially at the way Cara is grasping at invisible pearls around her neck with every word Grandpa Joe says.

Avery comes over to assist her grandfather to a chair. As always, she takes care of Grandpa Joe, but there's a big part of me that thinks he takes care of her too. In his own way, he looks out for her, and having a responsibility like Joe has run off many a lesser man Avery tried to date.

The fact that Winston not only stuck around but gets along with Joe so well is testament to how far Avery's fiancé has come. Because Joe definitely will test your fortitude.

"Now, as for the stags," Grandpa Joe says as he settles comfortably into a huge wingback leather chair, "why would I want to be in there with the lot of them? Swinging dicks here and there, talking about golf scores and yachts. Or whatever richy-rich folks jibber jabber about. I'd much rather be in here with the beautiful ladies. This is where you hear the good stuff anyway." He wiggles his bushy white brows at me. "Carry on with the chitchat like I ain't even here."

Pamela Ford looks surprised but, at the same time, charmed.

I shake my head. "You are incorrigible, old man."

"That'd only be true if I wanted to change," Grandpa Joe says with a grin. "No time for that nonsense at my age."

"Are you saying you can't teach an old dog new tricks?" Wren asks.

Grandpa Joe shrugs, folding his gnarled, arthritic, and knotted fingers together. "I'm saying if a dog is perfectly content lying on the porch in the sunshine, eating a good meal, and enjoying the company of a kind woman now and again, there ain't no need for him to learn nothing new."

Avery gasps. "Grandpa Joe, you can't be talking about women like that."

Grandpa Joe rolls his eyes, shushing her. "Little girl, you might be all grown up, but you ain't gonna tell me what I can and can't say. One of the benefits of being old is that I don't have to use what little filter God gave me. I can get away with anything. Watch this . . ."

He smiles, and the charming young man he used to be flashes for a moment. "Ma'am, could you c'mere, please?"

He waves at Cara, and though she looks at the tablet in her hands longingly, she does hustle over to Joe's side. "Yes?"

"After all this hustle and bustle is over with, do you think maybe an old fella could walk you home?"

Cara's eyes go wide, and her overly pink mouth circles into an O. "What?"

"Grandpa!" Avery scolds her grandfather even though she's grinning. "Do not piss off the wedding planner before the wedding!"

But he's not done. Instead, Grandpa Joe's smile becomes even more salacious. "Don't you worry about this gadget, doll." He pats his walker affectionately. "My legs work just fine, and the rest of me's just fine too." He pumps his arms, wiggling his hips to hump the air. "I promise you that life has taught me one very good skill . . . patience."

He licks his pale lips and winks at Cara, and I have to admit that might be going too far.

Avery's also reached her limit. "I'm going to die of mortification right here and now. I am so sorry, Cara. Please ignore my apparently horny grandfather." She points a perfectly french-manicured nail at Joe. "And you . . . we're having a conversation with Dr. Yung next week about how you're losing your marbles."

Cara sighs dramatically, pushing her hair behind her ear. She is in no mood for Joe's teasing and flirting, that's for sure. "We really need to get serious here. As for you," she snaps at Joe, "don't interfere with this wedding. I've worked too hard to let the likes of you mess it up now."

We all look at each other in surprise at her sharp tone. Cara is going cutthroat, take-no-prisoners style. She's definitely got a big job on her plate—or tablet, I suppose—but is being nice to the bride's family that much to ask? Joe's a big goofball, and is known to say some crazy things for sure, but he was obviously kidding, considering that he walks with either a cane or a full-on walker, complete with tennis balls on the feet, and it's going to damn near kill him to walk Avery down the aisle. But it's important to them both, considering that they are all the family they have.

Avery turns pink, and I can see she's not happy. *You can snap at her all you want, Cara. But go for Grandpa Joe? Oh, you done went too far, and you're likely to catch my bestie's hands.* She's not nearly as good at making bad choices as I am, but she's protective of Grandpa Joe in a honey-badger, vicious sort of way. So I step forward, sacrificing myself so that Avery can save face with her new in-laws. If anyone needs to piss off the wedding planner, it's me. I've got no problem pissing people off.

But before I can put her in her place, Cara thankfully moves on, clapping her hands lightly. "Okay, ladies, line up for inspection."

Mrs. Ford leans over to us, and quietly asks, "Is she always like this?"

Avery hums back, "Mm-hmm."

Mrs. Ford looks unimpressed. "Guess that's why Jed said she's the best?" she whispers back questioningly.

Cara whips her head toward us, her eyes blazing. "Quiet! No chitchat!"

Dayum, I thought Cara was a bit controlling before. Now? She's turned it up to eleven.

"Yes, Drill Sergeant DeMornay!" I snap back, my jaw clenched and communicating that my next snap might just be her neck. Cara glares back at me, but since we're all gathered together, she doesn't press the issue.

Instead she looks us over, going down the checklist on her tablet . . .

"Hair?" Cara looks up, scanning each of our heads. I apparently pass muster, but she stops in front of Wren, shaking her head. "Bit of spray there."

Wren starts to step out of line, but an assistant appears out of nowhere and sprays where Cara indicated. The same basic thing happens for makeup checks, teeth-brushing and lipstick-on-teeth checks, dress checks, shoes checks, lotion checks, and so on. She even gives Joe a once-over, though it's cursory at best.

"Last but not least," Cara says after she's satisfied, "who needs to visit the ladies' room before I go check on the men?"

Avery raises her hand like a kid in school. Cara looks annoyed, as if peeing is somehow unnatural or wrong or, in the least, an unnecessary annoyance.

"You have ten minutes and then meet me downstairs. Please make sure your dress isn't stuck in your underwear afterward."

"Considering what I'm wearing, I don't think anything could get stuck without me knowing. I'd feel the breeze on my ass," Avery mumbles under her breath as Cara disappears out the door, her assistant quick stepping along behind her.

I snort, shaking my head. "You think she's going to pull that act with the guys?"

"Considering my brother," Wren says, "I'd pay big money to see her try."

Mrs. Ford laughs lightly, as though Wren is joking. I don't think she is. I'm just not sure which brother she's talking about. Although part of me suspects she means Wyatt . . . who I'm still trying not to think about after this morning.

Avery disappears into the adjoining bathroom and then steps back out. "I checked in the mirror to make sure my dress is okay, but can someone else check too? Cara has me all paranoid about flashing my undies to the whole world now."

Avery twirls, and we reassure her that she looks perfect.

"Okay," she says with a deep breath, "let's do this."

Mrs. Ford opens the door a crack. "Are we good to come out?"

Leo answers, "Yes, Ms. Cara said for you to wait at the bottom of the stairs. Except for Wren, who is to go ahead out back to meet with her brothers."

We dutifully trudge down the stairs, Leo helping Grandpa Joe, and Wren disappears. Soon, Cara's assistant, whose name I didn't get, waves us forward. She leads us to a formal living room with a long set of windows that overlook the garden. The transformation has already begun, and we gather at the window to check it out.

"Oh my gosh! It looks amazing!" Avery whispers, even as workers go hurrying past with their armloads of materials for setting up. Inwardly, I envy them. They might be working hard, but they look comfortable in their jeans and T-shirts.

But the garden does look good. Off to the far right, we can see the white tents in place, the flaps secured back as vendors carry decorations inside. In the middle of the garden, the rows of white chairs are set up and the archway is up but minus the flowers.

"Can we skip tomorrow and just do this now?" Avery says suddenly. "It looks so beautiful and we're all here. Winston is all I need."

"Just one more day, dear," Mrs. Ford says. "Besides, if we do that, we're really, really going to have to have a good story for the caterers and other guests."

"I guess."

The guys are taking their places beneath the archway in front of the officiant, who looks a bit pale, making me wonder what Cara said to him. Winston is in the middle, with Wyatt and Wren by his side. She looks a bit out of place wearing a dress, but I know tomorrow she's going to be rocking her suit and looking right at home.

I look over to find Avery's eyes focused on Winston and getting glittery with tears.

"Oh! Don't cry," I whisper to her. "You're going to melt if you do!"

The assistant jumps into action, dabbing at Avery's eyes and telling her to look up and think about flamingos wearing leg warmers. Maybe not my choice, or anyone's really, as Mrs. Ford asks, "Flamingos? In leg warmers?"

"It's a proven fact, thinking about random idiosyncrasies short-circuits your brain, and focusing on making sense of that turns off emotional responses," the assistant says.

"Is that true?" Rachel wonders aloud.

I nudge Rachel, indicating for her to look at Avery, who does somehow seem better. "It's working, so I'm not gonna argue with it."

We smile at each other and let Avery compose herself in peace. In the garden Cara seems to be content with the setup, because she points to us like a symphony conductor.

"Here we go!" the assistant says, opening the back doors.

Cara, who is standing halfway between the door and the altar with a megaphone, kicks into narrator mode. "Okay, here's how this is going to go: everyone is seated, the groom processional begins, you three walk out in order." She points to Wren, then Wyatt, then Winston, all three of whom nod.

"Good. Mother of the groom and father of the groom walk out." Mrs. Ford steps through the doorway and Bill Ford joins her, escorting her to the altar. Winston and his father shake hands, he kisses his mother's cheek, and then they sit down.

"Perfect. Then my bridesmaids walk this way."

I wait for Rachel to go, ready to follow in her footsteps as maid of honor. But she freezes, so I nudge her. "Psst! Go, before she pulls out a Taser!"

Rachel bites her lip and looks at Avery in a panic. "Avery, I have an awful, horrible, no-good request that I'm begging of you."

"What?" Avery asks, her own panic returning as the assistant looks like she's about to faint at this disruption.

"Remember the favor you owe me? The really big one that we vowed to never, ever discuss again?"

Avery nods slowly.

Rachel takes a deep breath. "Let me walk with Wyatt." Rachel looks over her shoulder, toward the archway, and then back to Avery. "I think I've got a chance. He just needs a bit more time with me."

In my head, I'm laughing my ass off. Rachel thinks she has a chance with Wyatt?

Good luck, girl. He damn near never took his eyes off me last night, walked me to my car, and nearly kissed me at the bakery. And *any* man who'll put on an apron and do bad "makin' bacon" jokes at two in the morning isn't available.

But no one knows that. I haven't even had a chance to tell Avery, considering she has much bigger things on her mind today.

But also . . . last night ended poorly, and I'm not exactly looking forward to awkwardly hooking elbows with Wyatt while he gives me the cold shoulder the way he did last night as he finished up our baking. I mean, my baking.

"Rachel, I . . . uh . . . that's not . . ." Avery stammers, looking to me for help. I don't know what to say, though. This isn't my place.

Finally the assistant hisses, "I don't care who it is, but one of you needs to walk out there right now. She's coming."

We look back to see Cara stomping this way, megaphone in hand.

I make the call, hoping it's the right one. "It's fine, Avery. I don't care. I'm honored to be by your side today, tomorrow, and for the rest of our lives as friends. It's not about where we stand, it's about who we are to each other."

Avery tears up again, and the assistant growls a curse under her breath, grabbing another tissue. But Rachel's almost giddy. "Thanks, Hazel. Thanks, Avery."

Without another word, the assistant shoves me out the door. I stumble, nearly tripping over my own feet, but recover as quickly as I can and begin high kneeing it toward the archway. I feel like I'm back in my soccer days, except that I'm in a dress and heels.

Cara lifts her megaphone, calling out, "No, no, no. That's the wrong bridesmaid! Go back. Everyone go back and start over."

I make my way to Cara as fast as I can, still feeling like I'm in some sort of bad TV commercial. "It's okay. Rachel and I are switching places. It's fine. Keep going."

Cara sighs dramatically, rolling her eyes to the sky. I think she mumbles something about being done with crazy brides, but if she's talking about Avery, she's the least crazy bride ever. "Fine, fine. Keep going, everyone stay in place where you are. Next!"

I drop into a walk, as behind me, I trust that Rachel is following along with this new plan. At least, I don't hear any more screaming as I approach the arch, and Wren gives me an amused but questioning look.

"Okay," Cara says once Rachel's at the archway, "the music will change to the bride's processional, everyone stands up, Grandpa to the right of the door, and . . . cue Avery."

The first notes of the song Avery and Winston chose begin, a recording today, but tomorrow, it will be a cello-performed instrumental of "Can't Help Falling In Love." It was one of the few things Avery put her foot down about. It was Grandpa Joe's and her grandmother's favorite song when Elvis did it, and her parents loved the UB40 version at their reception.

As the classic instrumental Elvis version starts playing, Avery steps through the doorway, takes Grandpa Joe's elbow, and begins her walk.

"Perfect. Slow steps, don't rush it. He'll be there waiting whenever you get there," Cara calls, and I swear I can see Grandpa Joe muttering something under his breath. I can guess it has something to do with the fact he can't rush it anyway, and he doesn't need his hearing aid for this damn thing.

Either way, once we're all under the archway, my eyes drift to Wyatt. I find him looking at me, his blue eyes hard as marbles and swirling with thoughts I can't decipher.

I try to focus on what Cara is saying, knowing she's going to want perfection and probably give a multiple-choice test after this practice before she's satisfied. But now that I know he's looking at me, I can feel the weight of Wyatt's gaze. It somehow makes me both hot and cold, irritated and relieved.

Whatever last night was, Wyatt isn't giving me the cold shoulder anymore. His eyes are virtually screaming at me with unsaid things.

We go through the rehearsal, skipping certain parts out of tradition, such as the actual vows themselves and the final kiss. Still, Winston and Avery's joy, though premature, is real as they go back down the aisle arm in arm, rings on their fingers, only to be collected by Cara's assistant for tomorrow.

Now it's our turn. Wyatt steps forward and Rachel nearly runs into him in her excitement to get close to him. "Hello again," she gushes. "Imagine meeting you here. Do these often?"

Wyatt smiles politely at her, but as soon as Rachel looks forward, his eyes find me again. Still he says nothing, and he and Rachel depart. I meet Wren in the middle and she holds out her elbow, which I take, and together we walk down the aisle.

"You and Wyatt okay?" she whispers under the instrumental sounds of "All The Stars." That was apparently Winston's choice.

Me? I would have chosen "Come and Get Your Love," but I guess that's too funky and sexual for Cara DeMornay.

"Yeah, fine," I whisper back to Wren. "Why?"

"Because he was giving you the look, and he was your driver last night," Wren points out. "And he didn't get back until after I was asleep."

"It's fine," I whisper. "Just . . . not now."

Back by the house doors, we congregate as Cara directs the Fords and Grandpa Joe on how to exit the ceremony space. Once the whole wedding party is together, Cara finally unclenches herself a millimeter. "That was good. As long as everything goes *exactly* as it did today, everything will be perfect. There can be no changes. Understand?"

She looks at me and Rachel accusingly, and I resist the urge to ask whether that means I should still sprint across half the garden, instead flashing a thumbs-up. "We're all good. Promise."

Cara nods. "Good. Questions, anyone?"

There's a murmur of noes, and I'm sure everyone's ready for this part to be over with. Seriously, it's not the halftime show at the Super Bowl.

"Then please see your way into the dining room, where Mr. and Mrs. Ford have graciously offered to host you for dinner. After that, go home, dance the night away, or whatever," Cara says, relaxing some more and showing that, yes, she actually is a human being under the bitchiness. "Hell, play musical chairs and charades for all I care. There are only two rules . . . one, no getting drunk the night before the wedding. Nobody is pulling a *My Fair Lady* and coming in singing 'I'm gettin' married in the mornin'.' And two, go to bed at a reasonable hour. None of you are going to get a wink of sleep anyway, worrying about things I've already handled, but at least pretend like you're going to rest so the makeup artists don't have to cover your undereye circles. Understood?"

We all murmur again, agreeing this time. Although I'm sure I'm flat out lying, because I need to help Mom at the bakery again. I'm probably going to be flying high at the wedding with the assistance of caffeine and sugar, to be honest.

Declarations made, Cara and her assistant head toward the tent, megaphone at the ready and Boss Mode already reengaged. I feel bad for the vendors out there who are finishing their setup and hope Mom, or one of her assistants, isn't one of them.

Mrs. Ford, though, takes over with a much gentler hand. "Won't you all come in and sit down? I'm sure Maria is ready for us, and I for one could use some iced tea."

Chapter 11

WYATT

The Ford home has two dining rooms. One I don't like, and one I despise.

The "family dining room" is a relatively typical, although large, room with a six-person table. It's the one we used most often when Winston, Wren, and I were kids, for meals, homework, and craft projects. That table has a small spot from Wren's fourth-grade volcano diorama, which she insisted on building bigger than anyone else's because nothing but the best would do. Back then, I loved this room, hearing about Dad's day especially. As I got older, though, those family dinners became a bit more awkward, with Mom and Dad questioning me on my future, discussing my grades. Like most teenagers, I wanted to relax through the end of my high school years.

The other dining room is the formal one, with a table that's held up to twenty people for business dinners and political committee meetings. When I had to sit there, it was with the expectation that I would be seen and not heard, support Dad no matter what, and play the part of the perfect son. As a boy, I was proud to do so. Later, not so much.

But though we're in the formal dining room, tonight's no business reception or political thing. Tonight's about celebrating Winston and

Avery privately, intimately. This is the real celebration, in my opinion. Tomorrow's about appearances, at least for half my family and probably a good chunk of the guests.

Somehow Rachel manages to sit by my side, even scooting her chair a bit closer and flashing me a flirty smile. I'm trying my best to be polite, but damn! And what is up with the bridesmaid-order switch? I was looking forward to walking with Hazel, even after last night.

I spent most of the night thinking about her and what happened. She's skittish, understandably so, and I got impatient. I let what is basically her fear and established prejudice strike out at me and hit.

But I think she'll be worth it if I can go slow.

You're only here for a few more days.

Okay, not *that* slow, then.

"Well, I'd like to start with a toast," Dad says, standing up. He's got a drink in his hand, but I'm reasonably sure that this is his first. I've been watching like a hawk, because I won't let Dad fuck things up for Winston, and at this point, I don't trust him to make good choices. "Winston, I have watched as you've become a man, and I'm so proud of you. Now tomorrow, you're taking another step, and I couldn't be happier for you. Avery, from the minute Winston brought you home, we could see how special you are. The two of you deserve nothing but the best, and I think you've found that in each other."

Cheers go around, and I prepare to drink, but then Avery's Grandpa Joe stands up, his own glass in hand. "Well . . . since I'm sort of standing in as father of the bride, I'm going to take the privilege to say a few words. I know her parents would be very happy today if they were here."

The celebratory vibe dims, and I know we're all thinking about Avery's past. That her parents were taken from her so tragically . . . it's just wrong.

"Now, Avery's mother was the one with the words," Grandpa Joe says after clearing his throat, "and thankfully, she was also the one with the good looks, which she passed on to Avery. Lord knows what would have happened if you'd come out looking like me or your father!"

There are laughs all around, and Grandpa Joe continues, "You've been amazing in everything from the moment you were born, and look at you now. I changed your diapers when you were a baby, and now, you've had to change one or two of mine, but that's how things go . . . life comes around full circle." He gets quiet for a moment, his eyes going unfocused. He shakes his head, smiling. "Uh, what was I saying? Oh yeah, full circle . . . like your love for each other."

I don't know, but I think I like the old guy. He's funny, and Avery is smiling at him lovingly. Even Winston is smiling at the old man.

"Yeah anyway, that full circle, think of it like a wheel . . . it's going to keep rolling along," Grandpa Joe says, "so hang on to each other. Because soon enough, it'll be you two standing up here feeling foolish while trying to make some damn sense, when all you really want to say is 'I love you both, and I want you both to be happy.' Love hard, kids."

Now *that* I can understand, and my eyes flick across the table to Hazel, and find her looking back at me.

Slow, man. Remember that?

But slow is not what's on my mind as I stare into her eyes.

The dinner starts, and it's as delicious as I expect, but it's also a five-course meal. I've been through all this before; I know what to do. But as dinner progresses, it's pretty clear that Hazel doesn't.

Not that Hazel Sullivan cares, really. She relishes the food, from the pomegranate and feta salad to the poached trout appetizer. She might look around for clues about which fork to use and have no idea about fancy table manners, but I could watch her eat every day for the rest of my life and never get bored.

She examines the food, inhaling deeply as each new plate is delivered, and then takes joy in the food itself, moaning and groaning quietly as she samples each new thing. Some of it's familiar, and I'm sure some of it's brand new.

But whatever it is, she enjoys every bit.

"Now that the fathers have had their say," Mom says after the second course is cleared away, "would anyone else like to speak?"

"Yes, that would be nice," Dad adds, giving me a look. "I'm sure Wyatt has plenty of zingers for his brother. Maybe a few tonight and save the rest for tomorrow? What do you say?"

Before I can make a move, Hazel clears her throat, and I see she's rising to speak. I sit forward to listen carefully.

"When we were kids, Avery and I would talk about *the one*," she says, chuckling a little. "Probably because we were too into those *Matrix* movies. And when you told me you'd met *the one*, I was so happy for you. And then I heard who he is."

Uh-oh, is she going to do this at my parents' dining table? Really? I'm part horrified and part intrigued with what's going to come out of her mouth next, which is exciting. She's not one to bow down to Dad because of his position as mayor. If anything, she'll tell him exactly what she thinks of him and where he can stick it.

But instead, Hazel smiles. "Much to my surprise, your happily ever after is coming with a man I would've never expected. But you've shown, not just me, but everyone"—she looks around the table— "what love can do, what love can be, and how it can change you for the better."

Wren lifts her glass. "Hear, hear."

But Hazel isn't done. She narrows her eyes, pinning Winston like a bug under a microscope.

"But let me be clear that if you hurt her, I will absolutely destroy you. Not murder . . . that's too easy and not nearly painful enough. I will drag you out to the woods, tie you to a tree, and cover your body in Tayvious's fancy ketchup so that everything that creeps, bounds, and slithers along the ground will want to have a bite." She goes as far as clacking her teeth Winston's way, but he raises his glass good-naturedly.

I don't know if it's karma or if she was listening, but it's then that Leo and Maria come in, pushing the big serving cart. "Our main course . . . roast leg of lamb."

"Appropriate," I quip, and Winston laughs at least. Dinner continues, my own toast forgotten or perhaps delayed. After all, if Hazel's willing to throw down, what is the Ford black-sheep brother willing to do?

After dinner, Dad guides everyone to the living room, and I worry he's going to forget his promise about not getting drunk. But he pours himself a club soda with lime, giving Mom a pointed look, and then offers Grandpa Joe a cognac. Mom assists by pouring a few glasses of wine and dispensing them to Wren, Rachel, and Avery.

She offers Hazel one, but she declines and instead asks Wren, "Excuse me, where's the restroom?"

Wren points to the guest bath. "Down the front hall, second door on the right."

Hazel disappears, and a moment later, I make a quiet exit. I head toward the front hall, but hear voices in the dining room, and something tells me to go that way instead.

"No, Hazel. I've got this."

"How many times have you pre-bused a table for me when you come into Puss N Boots?"

I stand in the hallway, out of sight, and use the mirror's reflection to see into the dining room. To my surprise, Hazel is helping Maria clean off the table from tonight's dinner. Maria smiles. "Habit."

"Same here." They work together, chatting while everyone else is talking about the wedding in the other room. Hazel puts a plate on the cart, and looks over. "Is that your Leonardo that opened the door earlier?"

"It is. We've been with the Fords for years now."

Hazel lifts an eyebrow. "I didn't know that."

"Well, when I come in to eat, it's with my ladies' group from church."

"One margarita each, Tayvious's dinner specials, and a to-go burger and fries," Hazel quotes from memory. "For Leo?"

Maria smiles softly. "Yes. He is a good man . . . but a terrible cook."

Hazel laughs quietly before sobering. "Do y'all like working here?"

Maria nods, which warms me inside. "The Fords are good people, treat us well."

Hazel looks around suspiciously, and I duck back, making sure she can't see or hear me. Thinking she's clear, she leans toward Maria. "Let me guess . . . the walls have ears?"

Maria laughs. "It wouldn't matter if they do or don't. We're happy here."

"What about Wyatt?"

My ears perk up at that, and I lean closer to make sure I can hear every word.

Maria looks into the mirror, her eyes meeting mine. She knows all the tricks us kids used to use around here. She winks after making sure that Hazel is looking down at the stack of dishes in her hands.

"Wyatt? Oh yeah, he's a good-looking one, isn't he?" she teases.

Hazel blushes but nods.

More seriously, Maria says, "He's an interesting man. He was a good boy, always happy. But when he got older, something happened. I don't know what, but it changed him. He was never the same after that, more . . . angry? No, that's not it . . . He was jaded."

Her sad eyes glance up to mine, but fall immediately. She doesn't know why, but she does know how I reacted. "He left, and I hope he has found his happiness again. He deserves that."

"We all do."

Maria hears something in her answer, because she stops clearing the table, giving Hazel her full attention. "Are you happy, Hazel?"

Hazel sighs heavily. "I was. Or I thought I was. But maybe it's not happiness, so much as . . . content? Or stagnation?" Maria hums and Hazel rushes to add, "I don't know, I've just been thinking."

"Thinking is good. Sometimes, when opportunities come, we are not ready for them, but we have to get ready really fast. Like your Avery and my Winston," Maria says. "I know he was a boy when they met, but he grew up fast for her. And she adjusted what she thought her idea of perfect is. Because the truth is . . . no one is perfect. Not even my Leo. He farts like he has died and been resurrected in the devil's image whenever he has greasy french fries."

Hazel laughs. "I'm gonna tell Tay Tay."

Maria laughs heartily, making the cross motion over herself. "Go ahead. Because do I bring the fries? Of course I do. Because he enjoys them."

"Not sure this is the same thing as killer farts," Hazel says dryly.

Maria waves it off. "You'd be surprised what can be the thing that drives you crazy," she says wisely. "Now, you'd best get back to the party, where you belong. Let me do this."

"Okay, but you know I'm going to give you an extra-large serving of fries next time you come in, right?" Hazel asks, and Maria grins.

"Of course you are, and Leo will eat every last one while I curse your name."

I should run back to the party before Hazel sees me eavesdropping. She's likely to think this is another one of my character flaws. But I don't move, despite Maria's warning.

Instead I stay right where I am, and when Hazel walks into the foyer, she jumps when I say, "Hey."

Hazel puts a hand on her chest, gasping, "Wyatt! You scared the shit out of me." Her eyes narrow as she realizes where I am and how close to the dining room that is. "Could you hear us?"

I nod, completely unapologetic, ready for her fire to return. And it does. "You know that's a jerk move. That was a private conversation."

I shrug, keeping my voice low. "It's my house."

She turns to walk off dismissively, obviously ready to brand me a "fucking Ford" again.

"Wait."

"What?" she snaps.

I don't know what I was going to say, or what I should say. All I can see is the pink of Hazel's lips and fire in her dark eyes. There's a moment where my brain tries to function, to come up with something to make her stay, but in the end, I go with my gut, not my mind. "Fuck it."

I lean in, catching her jaw in my hand, cradling it firmly but gently enough that she could easily pull away from me. I'm giving her a chance.

She doesn't take it.

Instead, her mouth opens in surprise, and though I don't think she realizes it, she leans into my touch. It takes less than a single heartbeat before I'm kissing Hazel Sullivan.

Her lips are soft, that's my first thought. Softer than silk, softer than the downiest feathers, but pressing back into me. And taste of the last course's mint custard as I draw her breath into my mouth, relishing her.

She resists me for a moment, then melts into me, her body pressing against mine. Relief flows through me as I surrender the tight rein I've been holding myself under, but it's followed by sheer heat that's building fast. I cup her neck, my thumbs tracing her jaw, and she responds by teasing her tongue along my upper lip. I meet her with my own, groaning as we admit the truth. We want each other.

I want to explore her, every lush curve and creamy inch of her skin, map out what makes her writhe and brings her pleasure, but the need for oxygen forces us apart. "You want to get out of here?"

I can see in her eyes she considers it, but only for a moment. "No, I have to get back to the party. Avery's party."

I'm disappointed but not surprised. I told myself slow and then smashed that to fucking smithereens, but the least I can do is give her a second to play nice.

The least you could do is get her to a room with a lock before fucking us both to exhaustion. Not here in the hallway.

But she's right, and it makes me sigh. "Okay, but this isn't over. I'll go back in first while you pull yourself together."

Her brows pull together and she straightens her back, smoothing her dress. "What's wrong?"

I smirk, wiping my lip with my thumb and feeling the trace of gloss she marked me with, the same one that's currently a little bit smeared on her own lips. "You look like someone who just had the shit kissed out of them."

With that, I spin and hurry back to the living room, loving that she's growling like a pissed-off kitten behind me. When I enter, Wren looks at me with narrowed eyes, one perfectly drawn brow arched questioningly.

When Hazel walks in a few moments later, Wren's lips purse as she fights a laugh. She thinks Hazel and I sneaked off together. Little does she know how far from the truth that is, nor how much I wish she were right.

Now I just have to figure out how to get rid of Rachel without hurting her feelings or spilling the tea about what Hazel and I just did to anyone else. I trust that Wren can keep her mouth shut.

Next? Continue what Hazel and I started.

Except we did promise to get some sleep tonight in preparation for the wedding. But damned if I'm going to get any rest when I'm thinking of that kiss.

But I'm a man of my word. For tonight.

Chapter 12

Wyatt

The dawn breaks, and I roll out of bed having caught maybe an hour of sleep, two if you count that half-asleep, half-awake state you get into where you know you can hear the wind blowing outside your window, but at the same time, an hour feels like five minutes, and five minutes feels like an hour behind your closed eyelids.

I'm a little surprised to find Hazel in the kitchen, setting up cakes and small cupcakes on trays. I smile when I recognize the ones I helped with and feel a sense of pride until I see a guy helping her. He's a few years younger than me, with dark hair and eyes, and his short-sleeve shirt must be different from his usual because the tan line around his muscled bicep flashes as he moves the cakes.

Jealousy burns hot in an instant at their camaraderie and Hazel's easy laugh with him when he wipes icing on her nose.

I go in to introduce myself, and interrupt them. "Hey, guys, you two look busy. Can I offer you a hand?"

The guy gives me a once-over and grins as he holds his hand up, showing a glob of icing and then pointedly licking his finger salaciously. "Don't you have something to do? Like play a round of golf or get your hair done?"

Hazel glares at him, communicating something I don't understand, and he grins. "Jesse. Pleasure to meet you."

He didn't give a last name. Smart man, but in a town this size, I could find him.

"Wyatt. Nice to meet you too." Both of us are lying through our teeth about that one. "Seriously, can I do anything? I helped make these cupcakes, so the least I can do is help set them out."

Jesse's eyes narrow. And for whatever reason, I feel like we're now in a dick-measuring contest. "You helped make them?" he echoes.

"Yeah," I reply evenly. "That a problem?"

"When was that?"

I grin. "When Hazel took me to the bakery after hours one night."

Jesse looks from me to Hazel, accusation in his eyes. I can't help but feel a bit smug. "You took him to the bakery?"

"We got all the toppings and half the cupcakes ready for the Candied Nut Cups," she argues back.

Jesse looks unimpressed. "Mom know you had a Ford in there?"

The fuck? Is my family that hated in this town?

But then something else he said registers.

"Mom?" I ask, and Hazel backhands Jesse's arm.

"Way to go, jerk," she snaps as Jesse shrugs, uncaring. She sighs and points at him. "Wyatt, this is my clueless brother, Jesse."

I laugh softly, and offer a real handshake this time. "Gotta admit, it's better to meet you now that I know you're Hazel's brother."

Jesse's laugh is a little darker. "See if you feel that way after I tell Mom you were in her baby."

My eyes jump open and Hazel hisses. "Jesse!"

Jesse smirks triumphantly. "I meant the bakery, not you, but thanks for the confirmation."

Hazel's slap this time is more like a punch in the chest, and she puts some pop on it too. "I haven't fucked him! And even if I did, it's none of your business."

"Seriously? A Ford, and you think I wouldn't care?" Jesse asks. "Or Mom or Aunt Etta?"

"Aunt Etta and Mom know. And while you're all Ford-this and Ford-that, do I need to remind you who signs your paychecks?" She pauses, then steamrolls ahead: "Jed Ford. Remember that?"

I feel like my brain's in a blender with all this new information. "Wait. You work for my uncle?"

Jesse scoffs. "Most of the town works for him in one way or another. Might as well rename this fucking place Jedburg. Or Fordville."

I grunt, unable to argue with his assessment.

"Don't mean we like the fucker, if that's what you're thinking."

"Well, we can agree on that, at least," I tell him. There's a short silence, an acknowledged truce, and I decide to push my luck, willing to risk Jed hearing about my snooping for insight from a new source outside my family. "What're your thoughts on the new-subdivision thing?"

"Hard to say. It's above my pay grade, and it'll keep us all working, which is a good thing," Jesse says. "But to get it started, it's going to fuck over the residents out there now. And once it's done, it's probably gonna fuck up the whole town."

"How so?" I ask, surprised by his frankness.

Jesse shrugs. "One hand, it'll drive up rents. You think I can handle my rent being doubled because some hipster from out of town wants to overpay? And there'd be lots of folks moving in, not caring about the way we do things or how things have always been."

"You mentioned the people there now?" I ask, and Jesse nods.

"That's what the rezoning hearing is for," Jesse says, looking at me like I should already know this.

"I've been gone for a long time," I explain, "out of touch with my family and what's been happening here. I feel like I'm playing catch-up."

"Look, there are about five homesteads out there where Jed wants to build the subdivision. They're all zoned farming because those folks have worked the small plots for decades. For the subdivision to break ground, it has to be rezoned for single-family use and permits for development of the amenities center."

Damn. "What happens to the people and their farms?"

"They'll be forced out for their land," Jesse says, giving me a strange look. "Sure, they'll be compensated, but some of them would rather keep their land. Not to mention I figure they won't get the amount they deserve. The surrounding folks will end up moving out soon enough, too, because the property taxes for the whole area will go up once the subdivision is built. Expanding out will probably be phase two or something. Really will be Jedburg at that point, because let's be real, he ain't gonna let the town be named Ford-anything. Folks might get confused and think it's to honor your dad or some shit on account of him being the beloved mayor up till now. Jed'd want his name front and center."

"Well, shit," I mutter, not knowing what else to say. Jesse is joking about it, but I wouldn't put something like that past Uncle Jed. Nor am I surprised at what else he's been up to.

We're silent for a few minutes, all of us putting desserts on the trays. For my part, I'm mulling this new information over. Uncle Jed really is going big and might fuck over the whole town. Or at least change the town's feel.

"I'm gonna check in with Mom. See if she needs any help out in the tent," Jesse says when the tray he's been working on is full.

He leaves and Hazel looks at me thoughtfully. "You really didn't know?"

"First I knew about the subdivision was driving back into town."

Hazel tilts her head, examining me for any untruth. "I believe you. Is there anything you can do to help?"

"I don't know," I admit. "I need to talk to Winston, but today isn't the day for that."

We finish the rest of the trays, and as Jesse takes the last one out, Hazel checks the clock on the oven. "It's a busy day and we need to go get ready."

"Just one thing," I interject, stepping close enough to feel her heat and inhale the faint smell of vanilla on her. Before she can argue, I press my lips to hers in a quick kiss. A tiny, teasing taste for both of us. I pull back, grinning. "I'll see you at the end of the aisle."

Her answering shuddered breath lets me know that she's just as affected by my closeness as I am by hers. But that reassurance turns to laughter when she growls, "Asshole," as I leave the kitchen.

I go upstairs and take a shower, thinking about what Hazel and Jesse told me. I know Uncle Jed has big plans, he always does. But throwing people off their land, out of their homes, is taking it too far, even for him. The protest signs make a lot more sense now.

What is Jed thinking? Money, I'm sure. If I had to make a bet, he's only thinking about the money.

But Cold Springs is so much more than that. Dad's worries make a lot more sense now too.

If he's the mayor who leads the city-council vote to rezone land, which results in constituents being essentially kicked off their properties, he'll be booted out of office in the next election for sure.

Being mayor means everything to Dad, and losing that would destroy him.

I think back to before everything went wrong, back to when Dad was always smiling at ribbon-cutting ceremonies and giving speeches at Francine Lockewood's library events about city history. I may not know what's going on now, but I know one thing . . . Dad loves this town, which is why this is so confusing. He has personally supported Little League teams, delivered warm soup and blankets to elderly citizens during snowstorms, and planted trees in the city park to honor a guy who died overseas. He bleeds Cold Springs. Jesse called him "the beloved mayor," which isn't an exaggeration. Until now.

But if there's one thing that we've been taught, it's that family comes first. And while Dad might be the older of the two brothers, Jed has always been the more powerful and more conniving of the two.

With age, I can see that Dad and Jed have always been day and night. I replay stories I've heard of their younger days . . . of Dad serving on student council and Jed leading a coup against the teachers, arguing that homework was unconstitutional, of Dad being prom king and Jed being the football quarterback, of Dad shaking hands after a quiet entrance and Jed strutting into every room like he owned the place. One, studious, kind, and well liked. The other, a charming, manipulative life of the party. The perfect yin and yang, a complementary team. But they diverged—Dad into public service and Jed into self-service. Until Jed's big plan of rezoning. And I wonder again: *How did he rope Dad into this?*

I'm lucky that my younger brother is nothing like Jed, especially given that he's been under his influence these last few years. I don't know what I'd do if Winston were remotely like Jed. But I'm guessing drinking a little too much to cope would be the least of it.

I get ready, dressed in my suit from Mrs. Hinsley. I'm still not sure it was worth all the awkward measuring in my underwear, but I can give it to her. It's fitted to perfection.

⁂

Downstairs again, I find Dad, Winston, and Uncle Jed in the living room, all three with a glass of scotch. "A little early for celebrating, isn't it? Or are we squashing nerves?"

Winston turns to me, holding his glass up. "No second thoughts here. I'm ready to do this before Avery starts thinking with 'the good brain God gave her,' as Grandpa Joe says."

Jed guffaws. "That pretty little thing is lucky you're marrying her, not the other way around."

"Jed!" Dad protests. "For fuck's sake, the boy's about to walk down the aisle."

Interesting. Dad was telling Winston he deserved everything, and now he's calling out Jed for basically saying the same thing, albeit a bit more crudely. I guess even Dad has limits.

Jed takes a sip of his drink, unflustered. "Just speaking the truth, and we all know it."

Winston shakes his head. "I'm the lucky one. That's what I know."

It's the smallest disagreement, but it's telling about where Winston's loyalties lie. He's solidly with Avery, first and foremost. I'm glad because that's exactly where they should be.

"Good for you, boy," Jed says sarcastically, on the verge of condescending. "Guess I'd better get out there before the fun starts."

He swallows the rest of his scotch in one gulp and heads out the back door. Dad, Winston, and I silently watch as he walks toward the crowd of people already sitting in the rows of white chairs. Jed waves at everyone like he's the guest of honor, shaking hands and smiling wide as he makes his way toward the front of the groom's-side seating.

"Does he know what an asshole he is, or is he truly oblivious?" I ask. Dad sighs heavily, but Winston raises his brows, letting me silently know his answer.

Cara's assistant pops her head around the corner. "Gentlemen, are you ready? The photographer has done all the photos of the ladies and wants to do yours before we set up for first looks."

Winston smiles dreamily and I tease, "You imagining Avery in her dress or out of it?"

He throws a quick backhand to my chest. "Watch it. That's my wife you're talking about, asshole."

"Wife to be," I correct, though I'm smiling now, too, glad that I'm here to see Winston marry Avery.

"We really need to hurry," the assistant says, bidding us to follow her quick footsteps to the front door.

Outside, we find Cara bossing the photographer around. "You have ten minutes to get the shots on the list. If they're not listening, you let me know and I'll handle them."

I look to Winston and Dad, who are wearing matching expressions of surprise. I suspect my brows are equally high on my forehead. Out of the side of his mouth, Dad says quietly, "Don't get me wrong, I'm not scared of her, but I'm gonna say cheese and stand where I'm told. I suggest you two do the same so she doesn't tell your mother that we were difficult."

"You scared of Mom?" I question.

Dad glances at me before nodding. "Hell yes." To Winston, he adds, "And if you're half as smart as I think you are, you'll pay Avery the same respect. A little fear can be a healthy thing."

Before I can question what else Dad might be afraid of, Cara directs us to stand on the front steps and Wren appears from somewhere, joining us as the photographer begins snapping away. We've taken a few shots when I hear a voice call out, "Hey, Mayor Bill, you got a minute?"

Our eyes follow the sound, and I see a small group of people standing outside the closed gate.

"Seriously?" Dad mutters. "Right now?"

Cara snarls, "I'll take care of this."

"No, let me." Dad sighs. "Better for me to handle it before Jed gets wind that they're here." And with that decided, he straightens his back and heads over to the fence. I see him greet the men outside the fence with handshakes and begin talking. It doesn't look friendly exactly, but it seems civil at least.

Winston whispers, "Protesters at my wedding better not be a bad omen."

"Could be worse. It could be a pitchfork-carrying mob, out for your head." I place a heavy hand on his shoulder, reassuring him, a moment before Cara snaps her fingers.

"Perfect! Tell me you got that." Turning to the photographer, I see that he's been snapping away at our brotherly conversation and is nodding at Cara. "Good. Let's set up for the first look."

The assistant squeaks and runs for the side door, presumably to get Avery.

"You two. Best man and groomswoman . . . wait in the foyer for further instruction."

I wait until Cara spins before throwing her a haphazard salute. Winston snorts at my antics, but covers it with a cough. I offer him two thumbs-up of good luck—not with his bride, but with his wedding planner—and then go inside with Wren as ordered.

A few moments later, Dad joins us. "Everything okay out there?" I venture hopefully.

Dad clenches his jaw and pinches the bridge of his nose. "Yeah, I'm trying to . . ." He drifts off, shaking his head. "Hey, Maria?" he calls.

"Sí?" she answers, appearing instantly.

"Can you take a few snacks and coffee out front? Quietly and discreetly."

Dad's feeding the protesters? What the hell?

I don't get to question it because the door opens and Winston comes inside with Cara's assistant. "You're looking a little red-eyed there, man," I tease gently. "Avery call the whole thing off?"

Winston swipes at his eyes, laughing lightly as I'd hoped. "Shut up, fucker. She looks . . . I don't know . . . just . . . wow," he breathes.

"I think that's exactly the reaction Avery was hoping for," Wren says with delight.

Dad hands Winston a handkerchief, and along with it, a warm look passes between them.

"It's time," Cara's assistant says, directing us to follow her once again.

The garden looks a lot like it did yesterday, but with the volume turned up to eleven. The normally emerald rich bluegrass is now playing second fiddle to rows of white wooden folding chairs, the central aisle bedecked in white roses and silk that stretch all the way to the front row.

The wooden arch, which was empty before, is now covered in gobs of flowers, so many they must've emptied entire fields of roses just for the archway alone, adding that final touch of over-the-top fanciness to the whole damn thing.

Walking up the aisle ahead of Winston, I see that the crowd's ready. But to be honest, I barely pay attention until the bridesmaids start their procession.

"Down, big brother," Wren murmurs when it's Hazel's turn, and I can see exactly what she means. I thought she looked pretty yesterday? Today she's the most beautiful woman I've ever seen. Her dress caresses and highlights her voluptuous body, her hair is pinned up to show her graceful neck, and delicate drop earrings make me long to kiss her ears. I have to subtly pinch my thigh to keep myself from crossing the aisle to claim her right here in front of the entire crowd.

Hazel sees my reaction, and gives me a self-satisfied smirk before turning to take her place at the altar. Rachel follows, blocking part of my view as she takes the maid of honor position . . . and then I'm even more frustrated when Avery hogs up the entire view in her big white dress. *Okay, okay, you're the bride and I'm sure Winston's pitching a tent for you . . . but you're not the woman I want to see.*

"We ah gaathaaaad," the minister says, and I do a double take.

"What the hell?" I whisper to Wren, who's standing next to me. "This isn't the guy from yesterday."

"Slipped at home last night," she whispers back. "Broke his leg. Cara almost blew a gasket this morning."

"So she hired . . . this guy?"

"Actually, I found him," Wren corrects with a wicked smile, but she shushes me before I can ask what she was thinking.

Actually, once I get used to his accent, it's a sweet, emotional ceremony. Although hearing Pentatonix's "Rose Gold," the song that was playing on their first date, is even more ridiculous when a middle-aged man with a thick Boston accent starts talking about true legends never dying and standing the test of time.

Everything's pretty, but there's some stuff that's definitely Cara, I'm guessing. Like the rosemary and lavender woven into the wooden arch. It's a pretty detail, smells nice, and the herbs are old-school good-luck wedding symbols.

All good, but then there's the woo-woo stuff too. Like passing the rings around to the entire audience to have them "warm them with positive vibes and thoughts," which seems like a security risk given the rock Winston bought Avery, but Avery looks near tears as she watches each person close their eyes and whisper over the rings.

"I give yah Mistah and Missus Winstahn and Avery Faaahd!" the minister declares at the end, and even Wren has to bite her tongue hard at that one. Winston and Avery don't care, though. They're joyous as they kiss deeply. And when they start their recession, they're almost dancing down the aisle.

Now it's time for me to offer my elbow and walk down the aisle with the maid of honor. It's what I'm expected to do. Rachel's looking at me with a big smile on her face, but I can't. I don't want to.

"Follow my lead," I whisper quickly to Wren.

Of course she's confused. "What?"

I don't explain. I don't repeat myself.

Instead, I take the few steps across to the middle of the archway, feeling Rachel's eyes light up as she steps forward. But I move past her, my eyes locked on Hazel, and offer her my elbow.

Chapter 13

Hazel

"What are you doing?" I hiss while trying to smile and play off whatever the hell this is. "I'm the wrong bridesmaid."

Wyatt doesn't smile in the slightest. He looks at me with burning intensity, his face completely serious. "You're the right one for me."

I grit my teeth, glaring at him. "Trust me, I am not the one to be fucking with, especially not today."

At her position, Rachel looks confused, surprised . . . and maybe hurt, too, as she repeats my question, whispering, "What are you doing?"

Is she talking to me or Wyatt? I don't know, but it's not helping with the shitshow we're putting on. I look past Wyatt, seeing that the entirety of the guest list is looking at Wyatt and me with curiosity and beginning to murmur.

All except for Cara, who is bright red and seething, her eyes virtually screaming at us . . . *Follow. The. Plan.*

I'm trying to, lady! But it only gets more awkward the longer I stand there. So I do the only thing I can . . . I take Wyatt's elbow and walk down the aisle with my head held high and my shoulders back, daring anyone to say a word.

I even keep a big, fake smile on my face all the way back inside, waiting until I'm in the shadows before I turn and shove him in the chest. "What the hell? Are you trying to make me look like an idiot in front of the whole town?"

Wyatt looks back at me with absolutely no apologies. Just that same heat, that same confidence that has me pissed off . . . and burning inside. "Not even half those people are from Cold Springs, and even if they were, you don't care about what they think anyway and you know it."

I hate when he's right. "Fine, I'll concede that. But why are you fucking up your brother's wedding? It'd seem like *that* would be important to you."

He nods. "It is."

"Doesn't seem like it." I point over Wyatt's shoulder and he turns, seeing people start to file out of the white chairs and wander toward the tent for cocktail hour, but they're all getting close enough to get themselves an eyeful of us and our discussion.

Wyatt grabs my elbow and tries to steer me away so we can have some privacy, but I jerk my arm out of his grasp. "No," I growl. "Today is about Avery and Winston, and maybe my mom's desserts because this wedding is a big fucking deal for her. It is not about whatever *this* is."

I move my hand from my chest to his, because I can't deny that there's something between us now. Still, I'm pissed, and I stomp off to the reception.

I think Wyatt got my message loud and clear until I get to the tent and see him rearranging the place cards at the bridal party table . . . putting us side by side.

"You can't do that," I growl, grabbing his elbow this time.

Wyatt holds his hands out wide, gesturing at the tablescape I know Avery spent hours selecting. "Already did."

I want to argue, but out of the corner of my eye, I see Cara heading this way. I'll let her handle the evisceration. "You're gonna get it. Wedding Planner Drill Sergeant is on the warpath."

Wyatt looks around and sees Cara too. "I can handle her."

I gawk at him, trying to decide whether he's truly that brave or actually that stupid. Deciding that I can figure that out later, I grab his hand. "C'mon. If you don't have any self-preservation instincts, I guess it'll fall to me to keep the bloodshed to a minimum. For Avery's sake."

I pull him into the crowd, disappearing among the throngs of people. For the next ten minutes, I feel like Wyatt and I are playing hide-and-go-seek with Cara, popping into groups and ducking behind decorations to avoid her wrath.

The whole time, Wyatt's grin grows. "Whoopsie!" he whispers as he pirouettes gracefully around a waiter, snagging two flutes of champagne as he does. He hands me one, his smile wide as he pretends to check the pulse in his neck. "Here. To keep our hydration levels up."

I gape at him in awe, considering checking his pulse myself . . . and choking the hell outa him in the process. "Is this a joke to you?" I snap. "She's going to skin you alive!"

"She just . . . Here!" he whispers, grabbing my arm and pulling me behind a real tree that's been brought into the tent in a big pot. He ducks down, guiding me to do the same so we're not seen.

"Hmmph. Guess it's a good thing this tree was here," I say begrudgingly.

"Shrub. It's an arborvitae."

"Whatever. I'm just glad it's big enough to hide us both. How'd they get this thing in here anyway? A forklift?"

Do I care about the tree—er, shrub—or how it got here? No, not at all. But I'm staring at the pot and greenery so I don't have to look at Wyatt or risk Cara feeling my eyes on her. I get the feeling she has a sixth sense about those things.

"It's fake. A good one, but fake, so lighter than a real one because it doesn't need dirt," Wyatt explains.

"Will you please shut up?" I growl. "This is all your fucking fault. All you had to do was play nice for one minute and walk Rachel down the aisle, but did you do that? Noooo, of course not. Because that would be too easy for a fucking Ford."

"I—" he starts, but I'm in full-on rant mode.

"I'm a Ford," I interrupt, dropping my voice into a deep tone that is the best imitation of Wyatt's sexy rumble I can do. "I do whatever the hell I want and don't care what anyone else feels about it. Hur hur hur."

If I had my head on straight, I'd be embarrassed at my piss-poor impression of him, but I'm too mad to care right now.

I expect him to get mad at my mockery, but instead Wyatt touches my face, and the whirling tangent in my head stops instantly. "Hey, hey . . . it's okay. The only people I care about are Winston and Avery . . . and you. And look . . ."

He turns my head, directing my eyes across the tent to where Avery and Winston are whispering to each other, their foreheads pressed together and big smiles on their faces. They look like they're on a greeting card, they're so adorable.

They're happy, and Wyatt knows it.

"They don't care," he whispers to me. "So the only question is . . . do you?"

He doesn't wait for my answer. Instead he steps out from behind the tree slowly, his eyes locked on mine. Whoever sees him . . . sees him.

And like clockwork, from somewhere in the crowd, I hear a voice say firmly, "Mr. Ford. Wyatt Ford, a word, please."

Cara has found us.

But Wyatt shields me, turning to face Cara himself. "Yes, Ms. DeMornay." Behind his back, he points to his right, telling me to get out of here, protecting me from Cara.

I should step up to help him, but like a coward, I follow his order and scoot out of the line of Cara's fire. But as karma would have it, I get out of the fire and into the frying pan, nearly running smack into Rachel. And she's pissed. And hurt.

"If you were already involved with Wyatt, why didn't you just say so?"

"I'm not involved with him," I argue.

Rachel laughs bitterly. "Does he know that? Because it sure looked like you two are involved in something. He was eye fucking you all ceremony."

It's hard to debate that. But I can't explain it either. Not because I don't want to, but because I have no idea what would lead Wyatt Ford to pull a very public stunt like that.

Sure, a stolen kiss here or there, totally believable. But a display in front of all the wedding guests, including his family?

He might as well stick a target on my head as a person of interest to the Ford family. "Rachel, I'm sorry," I tell her quietly, trying to keep things calm. "I didn't mean to hurt you. You said you were interested, and I didn't want to get in the way. I was trying . . ."

Rachel sighs, looking off to where Cara is still talking to Wyatt. If nothing had gone wonky today, it might look like a friendly conversation, but the smile on Cara's face is basically a baring of her teeth and her eyes look a bit wild. I'm betting Wyatt's getting a wedding-planner ass chewing.

"It's fine. Any man willing to go to those lengths just to have you hold his elbow for a few seconds deserves a chance, Hazel," she says. "Lucky you."

That hurts. "Rachel—"

She cuts me off, holding up a hand. "It's fine, really," she says, although there's a trace of bitterness in her voice. "But if you'll excuse me, I think I'll mingle a bit before we sit down to dinner."

With that, she walks off, joining a conversation with a group of young professionals who seem particularly comfortable at the swanky affair, as though it's just a normal Saturday for them.

After checking in with Avery for any maid of honor–slash–bridesmaid duties and being assured that she wants me to enjoy the party and leave her alone to celebrate with her "adorable, sweet, sexy, new husband," I do my best to mingle, too, although I feel totally out of place in the crowd of rich folks, especially considering conversations tend to stop when I come up and begin again with one topic and one topic only—the return of Wyatt Ford to Cold Springs and what I know about it. And despite the ceremony chairs being laid out half and half for the bride and the groom, it's pretty clear that it was more like one-quarter for Winston, one-quarter for Avery . . . and about half for Bill and Jed Ford.

It doesn't get any easier when dinner starts. I'm a little surprised when Wyatt's still sitting next to me, but there are clear thunderclouds in his eyes when he takes his seat.

"Is everything okay?" I whisper. "You know, with—"

"It's fine," he says, cutting me off. Total bullshit, but I won't push the point. For now.

"Just remember, it's Winston and Avery's day," I whisper back, cutting my eyes to them as they come in for their formal entrance. Wyatt looks at the happy couple and nods, his face clearing most of the way as he plasters on what's clearly a manufactured nonchalant smile.

Damn. Must take a lot of years of dealing with Ford-type bullshit to get that good.

I do my best as well, and when the newlyweds sit down, they're so happy that they don't notice, and nobody else is willing to call us out on it.

"Whoo, this reception dress is *a lot* more comfortable," Avery says, looking dynamite again in her second dress of the evening.

During dinner, most of the conversation focuses on praising Winston and Avery for their ceremony, and the toasts are full of well-wishes for the couple.

Thankfully, up next is the cake cutting, and while the cake smooshing is a little cliché, Winston is grinning as Mom's Italian buttercream frosting drips off his nose and chin, flashing a thumbs-up for the photographer as Avery gives him a full puckered-lip kiss on the cheek.

Through it all, Wyatt doesn't say a word to me. Or to anyone, for that matter, other than to congratulate his brother and new sister-in-law.

The fancy cellos from earlier give way to a DJ, who elegantly plays Avery and Winston through their first dance on the monogrammed, lit wooden dance floor. And then the party starts. I'll hand it to the DJ: he keeps the music bumping and the laser light show flashing, keeping people on the floor with every song.

We work our way through the first slow dance, then the classic boogie of Earth, Wind & Fire's "September," and even an "Electric Slide" before we start stage four of dancing, with everyone doing the "Wobble" and wiggling their butts, even in their fancy attire.

A few of those young professionals have their ties looped around their heads, and Grandpa Joe is sitting in a chair, shimmying his shoulders and singing along, though I doubt he knows the words.

Me? I'm going with it, grooving to the next song, "Do the Lasso," working my ass up and down as instructed by the lyrics, but when I move back, I accidentally step on the toes of the person behind me. I cry out in surprise, but strong hands land on my hips to steady me before I can fall.

"I got you," a deep voice says in my ear, and I shiver. Of course . . . it's Wyatt. And I swear it just got hotter in this tent.

Suddenly, we're not following the repetitive moves of the dance like everyone around us. We're moving together, swaying with him at my back, his breath hot on my neck and hands firm on my hips, feeling my movements.

I want to turn around, slap him stupid, and walk off. He's been ignoring me, probably the smartest move for us both, but now he's drawing attention to us again. But Rachel's words echo in my mind—does he deserve a chance? Maybe more importantly, do I?

So I continue swaying with Wyatt, ignoring the onlookers, pretending we are in a bubble of our own making, and enjoying every moment of him.

Suddenly, the DJ announces that it's time to go outside for a very special send-off for the bride and groom. Damn, the time! "Midnight madness! The fireworks!"

"What?"

"Remember, the mini cupcakes?" I ask. "Cara set up a whole-ass fireworks show with snacks, ending with the happy couple's big send-off. Midnight madness."

Wyatt looks around for a quick moment, seeing where Cara is directing people. He takes my hand, pulling me toward the opposite side of the tent. "Come on."

"Where are we going?" I ask in surprise. And though he doesn't answer, I let him lead me away. He snags a few cupcakes from a passing waiter and then we're free, into the cool darkness of the night.

Chapter 14

WYATT

We make our way around the side of the house, through the side entrance that I know nobody's using. I lead her up the back steps and into my mother's atrium, and then out onto the rooftop deck. Finally, Hazel finds her voice. "What are we doing? We're going to miss everything."

"Watching the fireworks. We'll have a great view from here." I don't look at the dark sky above us, not caring about perfectly controlled fiery chemical reactions. No, that's not the fire I want to see. I want to see Hazel let her guard back down, quit playing polite with the other wedding guests. I want her, the real Hazel—unfiltered and relaxed.

I want to be myself too. Not the returning prodigal son, not a Ford, but just . . . Wyatt.

I throw the lock on the door and lead Hazel over to the big chaise lounge my father gave my mother for her birthday years ago. "Come on," I encourage her, setting the cupcakes down on a small side table to shrug off my jacket. "Get comfortable."

She gives me a long look but comes closer. She bends down, reaching for her high-heeled shoe, and I step in to help her with the strappy latch and slip the shoes off. I guide her onto the lounge, getting us arranged beneath a blanket, where Hazel curls into me.

"To Avery and Winston," I tell Hazel, offering her one of the mini cupcakes. "May their marriage be as sweet as these cakes, and not blow up like the fireworks."

"Hear, hear," Hazel says, tapping her cupcake to mine. "That was better than your reception toast. Seriously, you suck at best-man toasts."

I laugh softly, admitting, "Yeah . . . yeah, I should have practiced it a bit more. All those eyes staring at me made me nervous." It's only because of the moonlight that I see her look of doubt. But it's the truth. "And when I tried to picture people in their underwear, that was a mental image I did not need." I shake my head, and fake a shiver.

When Hazel laughs, I feel like a fucking god.

We take a bite of our cupcakes, and I moan at the flavor. I know I helped . . . but damn, the Sullivan family is better than the Keebler Elves when it comes to putting magic into baking.

"I don't know who made these, but this might be the best cupcake I've ever had," I comment, and Hazel's smile tells me which Sullivan it was.

"Yeah, I hear the chef is a total hard-ass. Or maybe it's that her assistants drive her crazy." She arches a brow, implying that I'm the one who made her crazy that night at the bakery.

I laugh, and appreciate that we're back to some banter. I never thought I'd miss her teasing me, but I have. "Maybe."

As we finish our cupcakes, a whistling sound fills the air. A moment later, the first firework explodes overhead, a big pink starburst that fills the sky. A second later, two more starbursts explode, white ones that make the whole thing look almost like a Mickey Mouse outline.

We sit back, watching the show. It's no little backyard show, but a full professional display, with music from the DJ filtering up in time with the explosions. We watch as crackling sparkle-flashers go off in time with Cascada's "Evacuate the Dancefloor," then big multicolored flowers for Beyoncé's "Love on Top," and a widespread display to the soaring lyrics of "I Will Always Love You."

The whole time, I don't focus on the fireworks as much as the feel of Hazel's arm under my fingers, the warmth of her body curled against mine. I feel like it's my chance to explore with my fingers what my eyes have feasted on.

I take my time, getting to know her body and what she likes. I caress her fingers, the ones I watched gracefully stroke her pool cue that first night she captured my attention. I trace along her arm, feeling goose bumps rise along her skin in response to my touch. Teasing along her collarbone, I dip into the gentle hollow there and her breath catches.

She shifts against me, not able to keep her hips still, and I know she can feel my cock getting thicker and harder.

She's practically humming with desire and breathing hard as the big finale starts, the music stopping as the sky is overwhelmed with explosions, all ending with a monogram of Avery and Winston's name in laser lights against the dark sky.

"Wow," Hazel whispers, her voice failing. I reach around, cupping her breast through her bridesmaid gown, and feel her nipple pebble against my finger.

I kiss the silky-soft skin of her neck before moving up to nuzzle her earlobe, tracing the shell with my tongue. "I want you," I whisper into her ear, and she moans quietly. "But if you tell me to stop . . . I'll stop."

Instead of saying anything, to answer me, she brings her hand to cover mine, pressing it harder against her breast.

I shift us on the lounge so that she's lying on her back and I have full access to pleasure her. I throw the blanket off, our own rising body heat keeping us warm now. Without the brightness of the fireworks, the dark night surrounds us, broken by only the moon's light as it illuminates Hazel.

We kiss, her mouth opening and her tongue wrapping around mine eagerly, eliciting a groan from deep in my throat. I stroke her body, sliding my hand up her leg, pushing the hem of her dress higher as I kiss down her neck to her chest, using my teeth to tug the cup of her dress down.

Touching my tongue to her nipple is like an explosion in itself as Hazel's back arches, her knees spreading wantonly. "Fuck!" she gasps, panting as I start to suck on the stiff nub. "Fuck, Wyatt!"

"I plan to," I growl against her breast as I run my hand up the inside of her thigh. Her panties are soaked, the thin, silky material clinging to her. I slip them out of my way and find her warm, wet center.

I explore her, letting her juices coat my fingers as I feel along her lips up to the pearl of her clit.

She groans, running her fingers into my hair. "This . . . means . . . nothing."

I hum, not agreeing or disagreeing as I slide a finger inside her. She cries out softly, gorgeous, glorious when she surrenders to the pleasure. "Of course it doesn't."

I'm not going to argue with her, not when she's letting her walls down, allowing me into her warm center. But this means something . . . to me, and to her. Even if she won't admit it.

I pump my finger slowly in and out of her, my thumb tracing up her cleft to find her clit.

Her cries get louder, and I kiss her fiercely, swallowing the sounds so they don't drift down to the wedding guests below as they cheer Winston and Avery off and slowly begin making their way to their own cars. Finding the pace she needs, I stroke both her inner walls and her clit until she's quivering, her hips lifting to meet my touch.

I can feel her spasms as she gets closer and closer, and I take her right to the edge. "Yes . . ." she whispers.

"Not yet," I answer, slowly withdrawing my hand. "Together."

She whimpers as she comes back from being so close, but nods.

It's a flurry of movement as she shoves her panties off and hikes her dress up to her waist. I jerk my shirt out of my slacks and undo my belt, freeing my aching cock as I climb between her legs.

We both gasp as I take myself in hand, running the head of my cock between her lips to cover myself in her slick wetness, and then tapping it lightly on her clit.

"Dammit, Wyatt . . . fuck me!"

Her growled demand almost makes me lose control and slam into her, but I squeeze the base of my cock tightly between my thumb and finger. "Fuck, Haze . . . that mouth of yours is so damn sexy."

I notch myself at her entrance and push in slowly, knowing I'm a lot to take, but she melts around me, her body drawing me in as we both moan at the tight pleasure. I go easy, pausing at times to half draw back and push in again, listening to her sounds for guidance. When she's ready, I go deeper.

And she takes me deep . . . all the way deep. When I'm pressed against her, root to center with our bodies joined, I kiss her again, giving her a moment. Hell, giving myself a moment so I don't come too soon after promising her we'd do it together.

Hazel puts her arms around my neck as I lift up and thrust in again, both of us gasping at the feeling. It's been a long time since I've felt a woman's touch, and I suspect she's not felt a man inside her in a while either. Not many get past our defenses and prickly exteriors.

So I know we can't last long. But I devote myself fully to giving Hazel her release, alternating powerful strokes with swirls of my thumb over her clit.

I feel Hazel tighten, and I know she's close. I kiss her fiercely, hammering with deep, hard thrusts into her eager pussy until she falls apart, her fingernails digging into my shoulders. The power of her pleasure equals her sass and fire. She doesn't do anything halfway, her passion full throttle at all times.

Her clenching, quivering orgasm pushes me higher, and I chase her, thrusting harder and harder until I'm on the edge myself, and she locks her legs around my waist. With a final stroke, I find my release, pumping thick, heavy pulses of my cream into her.

Still panting, I kiss her, wanting this moment to go on.

Afterward, lying in the chaise lounge side by side, my arms around her and the blanket pulled up to ward off the late-night chill, Hazel purrs happily. "Thank you."

I chuckle softly, and kiss the tip of her nose. "Uh, thank you."

Without warning, she moves, straightening her dress. "I guess I'd better get out of here before people realize Nessa is leaking on the driveway."

I'm confused. "Who?"

Hazel looks over her shoulder. In this moment, there is something so beautiful about her—an unguarded softness, an easy peace that is in such contrast to her usual fiery sass. Both are completely intoxicating. "My car."

Nope, I won't let her go. I reach out, pulling her back to the lounge with me, and she plops down again. "Stay," I tell her quietly before she can wriggle or protest. "Stay with me. Tonight at least."

She pauses, but shakes her head. "I can't."

"Why?" I ask, and I can see her wheels turning as she racks her brain for an answer. For me . . . or for herself? "Hazel—"

"I have an early shift at Puss N Boots tomorrow," she says quickly, though it sounds potentially made-up, "and because even if the valet and cleanup crew don't realize there's a weird car still here, your family most certainly will."

"So?" I counter with a shrug, knowing Hazel doesn't actually give a shit what my family thinks. "They won't say anything to you. Even if they wanted to, it's not their style."

"What is their style?" Hazel asks after a second's hesitation, a second I want to encourage to bloom into a night.

I pause. I want tonight . . . but I want more than tonight too. Which means honesty. "With outsiders? Manipulation and half truths. With family?" I pause again, then sigh. "Actually more of the same. Except Wren. She's a straight shooter."

Hazel chuckles quietly. "Charming. You're really selling me on them. But I actually do need to go."

She leans down and kisses me goodbye, but I grab around the back of her neck, kissing her deeply. In that kiss, I tell her the truth.

This isn't just tonight. Not by a long shot.

"I'll walk you down."

Once we've both got our clothes straightened and Hazel runs her fingers through my hair, I take her hand and silently lead her through the dark house, thankful for the map in my head and that all the craziness of the wedding seems to be over and cleared out.

"Skip the third step," I tell her as we descend the staircase, carefully taking a long step myself.

Hazel laughs in a whisper. "You snuck out a time or two?"

"Eh, a time or two."

The truth is, I didn't have to. I could stroll out the front door and no one would stop me, but they'd ask questions, tell me to be careful, and remind me that I'm a Ford, and sometimes, I just needed to get away from the expectations of home.

Outside, her car is the only one remaining. Carefully, I help her in, stealing another kiss when I do. She smiles, and I trace it in the moonlight. "I really do want you to stay."

"I know," she says.

Back inside, I lean against the door, my smile matching hers. It's wistful, a little dreamy . . . a good smile.

"Wyatt?" a voice calls from the living room, shattering my fantasy. I freeze. *Shit. That's Dad. How much did he see?*

I walk into the dark living room, but there's enough moonlight coming through the windows that I can see him sitting on the couch, holding a tumbler with a heavy pour of scotch. "Dad?"

He looks up, a little bleary eyed. "Wondered where you disappeared to. Should've guessed."

I tilt my head, immediately defensive. "Is that supposed to be an insult?"

Dad drops his tumbler to the side table heavily, sighing bitterly. "Why do you do that? Take everything I say in the worst possible way?"

My voice hardens. "Experience?"

Dad looks like he wants to argue, but his eyes are full of pain . . . and maybe defeat. Or maybe that's the scotch. "You know, when you were a kid, you used to be proud of me. Of what I do for Cold Springs. I don't know when you decided I was so awful."

I don't know either. He used to be my dad, a powerhouse of strength, goodness, and a role model I admired. But as I got older and realized that he wasn't infallible, and learned that some of the good he'd done came with a big price tag, I lost respect for him. With the passage of time, I can see that some of that was really me losing my innocence as I realized how the world worked and that my superhero dad was a mere human, with all the requisite flaws. And if it were only that, we could've been okay.

No, the real line we crossed was when I tried to go to him, to tell him about the issues I was having with Jed, thinking he would help me, but he dismissed me out of hand, essentially taking my uncle's side. That ship sailed long ago, though, and there are more pressing issues that need to be brought to light.

"Hard to with what you and Jed are doing with this subdivision thing," I tell him honestly. "Forcing people off their land so Jed can make a buck? How can I be proud of that, Dad?"

The accusation is bitter, but it's a shit move, even for Jed.

Dad shakes his head. "Is that what you heard?"

I shrug, not confirming. I won't rat out anyone, and besides, it's not like he doesn't know what the people of Cold Springs are saying. They're lined up around downtown, shouting it to the city council members' faces. And his. Not to mention, camped out on the front lawn.

After a moment, Dad pushes on. "There is so much more to it than that. But it sounds like you've already made up your mind." He swallows the rest of his scotch and gets up, setting the empty glass back on the side table. "It's been a long day and I don't want either of us to say something we can't take back, so good night."

He leaves, and I'm left in the empty living room, torn in half. One part of me wants to relish the memories of a chaise lounge, a beautiful Hazel, and the things we did. The other half of me wants to drink in the bitterness of my short conversation with my father, and twist my stomach on the acid.

With a heavy heart, I go upstairs. I've slept six hours in the past two days. Maybe a good eight hours will help clear my damn head, although I wish I had Hazel here to usher me off to dreamland.

Chapter 15

HAZEL

"You have achieved greatness," the talking panda in lederhosen says, his paw over his heart. "In protecting the realm, you've become a legend among all peoples. No longer will cake threaten the land."

I wipe the last of the pink frosting from my lips, shrugging. "Wah no problem." Oops, a cascade of cake crumbs spills out with the words, and the panda recoils a bit.

Okay, maybe the panda should have waited until I washed my mouth out with milk. I mean, it was a twenty-foot-tall cake. Give me a chance to clear the tract.

"For your bravery, we, the people of the realm, award you with a prize worthy of an adventurer as noble as yourself . . . the Cuirass of Penbron!"

The panda waves his hand—er, paw—and in the shimmering air, a golden breastplate appears.

"Oooh, gimme gimme gimme," I say, reaching out grabby hands.

I look down at what I'm currently wearing, a simple leather piece that exposes my stomach and arms, so different from what the panda is offering. I can't wait to don the fancy gear. No longer will I be leered at in the tavern, treated more like a wench than a sword maiden. No longer will I have to depend on "magical distraction" to avoid being gutted by enemies. No, with *the Cuirass of Penbron, I can be a proper warrior, admired for my skills and not my figure.*

I reach out, smiling, and with more befitting appreciation, I say, "Thank you. As for you, Cuirass—"

My fingers touch the scalloped edges of the armhole, and suddenly the entire piece shimmers. It's not real! The beautiful armor is nothing more than a floating hologram. I whirl, or I try to, but my overfilled cake-belly won't let me move that quickly right now. I manage to weeble-wobble around to face the panda, though, and he throws his hands out wide, unapologetic. "The cake was good, though, right?"

"Dammit!"

"Don't you be cursing when I call your name! Getchur ass outa bed, girl!" Mom's voice rouses me from my dream, but it's far away and I'm fuzzy enough that I ignore it, roll over, and pull the covers over my head.

"Nooo," I mumble. "I want real armor, Mom."

"Armor?" Mom laughs. "Must be some dream."

I grumble, waking enough to realize that was a weird-ass fucking dream. "Don't work until noon. Lemme sleep."

Yeah, like that's going to happen in this house.

The blankets are unceremoniously ripped from my body, and I hiss like a vampire whose crypt has been opened into the sun. Jerking into a fetal position, I hide my face beneath my hands and growl, "What the fuck?"

When I was younger, I wouldn't have dared speak to her that way, but I'm a full-grown-ass woman, with two—count them, two—jobs; a home—granted, I inherited it, but I pay the taxes and insurance like a responsible homeowner; and a foul-mouthed pet that will probably outlive me given my proclivity for mouthing off.

Doesn't matter to Mom as she repeats, "Getchur ass outa bed. Family meeting in sixty seconds at the kitchen table. Preferably with pants on. Already making coffee."

I don't see her leave, my face still buried in my hands, but I sense that I'm alone. And wearing only panties because I fell into bed after getting home from the wedding. Part of me is shocked I even got my dress off.

So yeah, my mom just saw me mostly naked.

Not a stellar start to my day.

I groan and rub the sleep from my eyes but realize that I hear voices in the kitchen. As in, plural. Not only Mom, but Aunt Etta, Jesse, and Lester too.

"Great, the gang's all here."

I lift my legs in the air, swinging myself up to a semi-vertical position. Getting up, I yank on a pair of sweats, a sports bra, and a T-shirt, and though I know I won't find one, I still look around for a suit of armor because nothing good has ever come from an impromptu eight a.m. family meeting.

Regardless, I need a massive dose of caffeine for this. Thankfully, I can smell the rich brew that Mom promised. In the kitchen, she's made herself at home with the coffeepot and the stove, slapping sausage and eggs into a large skillet. "Sit down. We've got some stuff to talk about."

I look at Jesse, hopeful for a clue, but he grins and touches the tip of his nose. "Not it," he mouths.

Fucker.

"Bawk! Trouble, I smell T-R-O-U-B-L-E!" Lester sings to the tune of the old Travis Tritt song. I'd yell at him, but I'm afraid he's right and I don't want any extra attention.

Aunt Etta sets her half-empty mug down. "How was the wedding, Hazel?"

A seemingly innocuous question the morning after the biggest wedding this town's ever seen, but I don't think it has anything to do with fancy events or my BFF's big day.

Nope, she's the *opener*. Which makes Mom the *closer* this morning.

At least that lets me know the game plan, because they've been using the same moves on Jesse and me since we were kids too stupid to know better. Probably did the same thing when they were kids to Gran.

But that means I know the countermoves too. "It was gorgeous, fancier than anything this town's seen before or will ever see again. And Avery was really happy, shockingly so, considering the groom."

I laugh lightly at my own sarcastic joke, but no one laughs along. Dammit.

I look from Aunt Etta to Mom, who's stirring the eggs around thoughtfully. Whatever this is, it's an old game being played at a whole new level.

So maybe it's time to break the rule book.

I ignore my coffee and lay my hands flat on the table. "How about we skip all this shit and get down to whatever led to me getting dragged out of bed at sun-thirty? Hit me with it, let's go."

Mom's eyes jump to me as quickly as her free hand pops to her hip. "Excuse me, young lady?"

Once upon a time, that would've scared the piss out of me. But I'm a big girl with a big mouth who's short on sleep today, so I double down. "What's going on? If you're here, the bakery's closed"—I point at Mom, then swing my finger to Etta—"and you're working the late shift today, so you should be asleep too." I look at Jesse. "And you should be doing community service hours to clear up your probation."

"What probation?" Mom snaps, horrified.

Jesse glares at me, but says to Mom, "She's fucking with you. I ain't on probation."

He's not, but it worked to my satisfaction, so I smile as though we're having a perfectly pleasant conversation. "Good, so now that we've established that we all have better things to do, can we get down to what this family meeting's about?"

Finished with the food, Mom sets filled plates in front of Jesse and me, then turns around to get hers and Etta's.

Jesse manages to say, "Looks goo—" before stuffing a forkful into his mouth.

Mom and Etta share a look that has my fork pausing halfway to my mouth. At least by the way Jesse's eating, it's not that Mom spiked the eggs with ghost peppers. But beyond that, I have zero guesses.

Mom says, "Well, I've got good news and bad."

Around a fourth mouthful in half as many seconds, Jesse murmurs, "Good."

I think he means good news first and isn't continuing to praise Mom. Then again, he really needs to get more home cooking, based off what I normally see him stuffing in his mouth. I know he works hard, but I've seen him put away an entire family pack of Hot Pockets for dinner and then look for dessert.

"The good news is, the wedding cake and midnight desserts were huge hits," Mom says, getting to business. "Like *huge*. The planner, that crazy woman, actually called me last night. Said she'd been worried I couldn't handle it, had tried to talk Avery out of using me to the point that she'd actually contacted a backup baker, *just in case, you know.*" Mom does air quotes with her fingers along with a decent impression of Cara. "Can you believe that nonsense!"

Etta interrupts with a confused look as she asks, "This is the good news?"

Mom shushes her and continues, "But apparently, she worried for nothing because the cake was elegant and delicious—her words, obviously. And the cupcakes, pudding shooters, and stuffed strawberries were, and I quote, the most orgasmically delicious things she's ever had. She actually ordered some of the strawberries to take back to Newport with her. And . . ." Mom pauses dramatically and we all freeze. Even Jesse stops with his fork midway to his mouth. "She wants to add me to her list of approved vendors for all her weddings."

Mom's smile is brighter than the noonday sun in summer, her excitement obvious, but . . . I don't get it. I'm not the only one either.

"So she's putting you on a list?" Etta asks. "That's the good news?"

Mom gives us a patient look. "Not a list. *The list.* She's big-time, like hundreds of weddings each year, so for her to recommend me, a nonbridal bakery, for her events is basically like winning blackout bingo on your first night at the lodge."

"*Bawk!* BINGO! Bingo! B-I-N-G-O, and Bingo was his name-o," Lester adds in his infinite wisdom.

I can't help but laugh at Lester and at Mom. "Why are you surprised, Mom? You're amazing, so of course she wants your cakes."

"Yeah, congrats, Mom!" Jesse adds.

Etta's caught on as well and gives Mom a smile. "Good job, sis. Did she say anything about the burger bites and fries? You know Tayvious is gonna pitch a hissy fit if she didn't."

Mom shrugs, chagrined. "She didn't say anything, but it'd be hard to travel to Newport with fresh fries and burgers. Cold cakes are a lot better than cold fries. And you know, maybe nothing will even come of this. There might never be another bride that wants one of my cakes, but the compliment was unexpected."

She's trying to soften the blow, but there's no need. We all know Tayvious is a magician in the kitchen, so if Cara didn't recognize that, it just means we'll get our dinner a little faster and keep Tayvious to ourselves.

Mom does a little happy wiggle in her chair, eating a few small nibbles of food, and I can see how truly excited she is. Her bakery is her baby, just as much as Jesse and I are, and she's worked hard to make her dream a reality. Some validation from someone in the biz with lots of experience is a big fluffy peacock feather in Mom's hat.

"Well, I hate to ask," Etta says as she takes another bite, "but what's the bad news?"

Oh yeah. There was more. And Etta's leading the opening into act 2, scene 1.

"Yes, about that," Mom says, her eyes shifting to pin me in place.

Shiiit.

I was afraid it was about me.

But I haven't done anything wrong.

Does casual sex with a Ford on the rooftop during the fireworks finale of your best friend's wedding ring any bells?

Okay, at least nothing she'd *know* about. Why can't it be Jesse this time? I'm sure he's done something stupid recently.

But like the good sister, and future blackmailer, I am, I don't throw him under the bus.

I sit up straight and meet Mom's eyes directly.

"Yesss?" I ask, innocently batting my lashes like I've never done anything bad in my entire life.

"You can stop with the innocent act, missy," Mom says. "The whole town's jawing about you and Wyatt."

"They are not," I argue, though I have no idea whether that's true. I've been in a sort of postsexual coma.

At the same time, Jesse and Etta talk over each other, eager to drink up the spilled tea. "Tell us what they're saying!"

Mom flashes me one of her infamous Mom Glares that used to get me to spill my guts in two seconds flat, but I'm stronger than that now and press my lips together. *My mouth's Fort Knox, Mom.*

"Fine, I'll tell them," Mom says after a moment. "Apparently, Miss Thang over there has been playing hide the hot dog with Wyatt Ford. Rumor has it, he's quite smitten with her, going so far as escorting her down the aisle instead of the maid of honor, and then disappearing with her while the newly wedded couple made their post-fireworks escape off to their honeymoon."

Etta turns to me, confused. "I thought you were the maid of honor?"

I duck my head. "I was. But Rachel really wanted to walk with Wyatt, so I switched with her so she could."

"But he wasn't having none of that, now was he?" Mom summarizes, and I have to shake my head. She adds judgmentally, "Bet he does whatever he wants most of the time."

The desire to defend Wyatt is strong in my chest. He came to my aid at the bar, helped make those amazing cupcakes, and sacrificed himself to rampaging Cara, so he can't be all bad.

And he definitely doesn't like Jed Ford. But singing his praises seems like a surefire way to piss off my family, so I try . . . "What was I supposed to do? He was standing there with his elbow out right in front of me! It would've been more of a scene if I'd snubbed him."

Mom hums in agreement, but I can tell she doesn't agree one bit.

"And I bet nobody even noticed us missing with literal fireworks going off and Avery and Winston making their getaway. Besides, at least half the people there weren't even from town."

Mom raises an eyebrow, noticing I didn't deny our disappearance.

Jesse snorts. "Winston invited the whole company. Basically, everyone from the crews up to the head honchos. I'm sure a few guys got cleaned up for a free dinner and open bar. I would've, but I didn't want Mom to put me to work as her bakery bitch."

Shit. "Okay, even so, what business is it of theirs who I'm spending time with?"

"You mean fucking?" Jesse asks. "I think a lot of people around town would be damned interested in that, especially considering you're you and he's a Ford."

"Fuck a Ford!" Lester adds in to the tune of the classic goofy children's song "Kiss A Cow." "Fuck a Ford! Fuck a Ford, fuck a Ford, fuck a—"

Mom, Aunt Etta, and I all yell simultaneously, "Shut up, Lester!"

"Bawk!" With that declaration, he flies off to the living room to pout. I'll have to give him a treat before I leave for work or he'll peck at the corner of the TV stand while I'm gone as retaliation. I've already had to sand and revarnish that damn spot twice due to him.

I sigh, setting my fork down because I'm not going to eat another bite this morning, and get ready to throw down the gauntlet. "Fine. Let's be blunt. I fucked Wyatt Ford. It was awesome." Jesse makes a disgusted face but quickly begins turning red and gritting his teeth, like I've got some honor he's supposed to protect. "And very, *very* consensual. And casual. It didn't mean anything. He's here for the wedding, and now that it's over, he'll be leaving. No big deal."

"And the hearing?" Aunt Etta asks. "He gonna be here for that?"

I shrug. "I don't know. It didn't come up when I had his dick in my mouth."

Mom frowns. "Hazel."

But Etta smirks. "I'm just saying . . . it might be good to have an inside track on what they're planning for the hearing."

I look at her in surprise. "I am not asking Wyatt to spy on his family!"

To my surprise, Jesse agrees with me. "She's right. When I met him before the wedding, he didn't have a clue about the subdivision thing. Honestly, I think he was pumping me for information. And he definitely didn't act like he gave two shits for his Uncle Jed."

"Two points for him in my book then," Aunt Etta says. "One for the 'awesome fuck' and one for hating that asshole, Jed."

Oh no. I do not want to get Aunt Etta off on a tangent about her younger days and how Jed Ford did her wrong right before their wedding day. It's bad enough to listen to her rant about how he's screwing up the town now, which he is, but old stories where he's the bad guy, which he also was, were a soundtrack to my childhood that I don't care to repeat.

"Good," I declare in a voice that says this chapter of our conversation is over. "Now that that's settled, I think I'll get ready for work a bit early. I bet Charlene would appreciate a few extra hours with her kids today since we're both working all evening."

Etta nods. "I'm sure she would. She works so hard for those babies."

I get up, grabbing my plate, but Jesse snatches the sausage from it before I can scrape it into the trash. I put the last bits of scrambled eggs into a shallow dish and call Lester. "Hey, birdbrain, you feeling cannibalistic?"

Lester flies to my shoulder. "Lester likes eggs. Baby bird yummy."

He mimics a robotic, zombielike voice that I taught him after learning that eggs are good for birds and keep their feathers healthy. I gesture to the dish, and he hops down to the counter, pecking away to eat the few bites.

Mom makes a disgusted face. "That's so wrong, Hazel."

Etta laughs, disagreeing with her sister. "He's not eating parrot eggs, so waste not, want not. You think the pigs care about eating ham?"

I leave the two discussing the animals Gran used to have on the land when she was alive and how she fed and cared for them. I'm also abandoning Jesse to the hens, because now that they're through with me, Etta and Mom are sure to zero in on him shortly. But he can use a little grilling, in my opinion.

I hop in the shower, washing my face and body quickly, but noting the pleasant soreness between my legs. It had been a while, and Wyatt stretched me in that way that hurts so good.

The replay of last night flashes through my head, and despite what Mom said about everyone gossiping, I don't regret it. Wyatt Ford isn't what I expected, and I'm glad he took the time to show me that. I just hope that after he's gone, Cold Springs can deal with the Jed shitshow.

⁂

No rest for the wicked, I muse as I cross the busy floor at Puss N Boots. Especially not tonight, where it seems that my newfound temporary infamy has brought in a lot more lookie-loos.

And just think . . . I wanted to let Char come in late just to face this. Thankfully she shot me down, probably in expectation of this.

"Listen here, Pork and Beans," I tell the two guys in sweat-stained shirts that are ripped to show off their hairy armpits, one Metallica, the other Red Sox, somehow making the nicknames I came up with on the spot seem appropriate, "either you order or get the fuck off my table. This isn't a spectator-sport situation. It's my bread and butter."

"Yeah, I heard you like a bit of butter on your bread," Pork says, already chuckling at his own joke so much that he barely gets it out. They've been sitting here taking up space in the place for about an hour, just leering and eating peanuts without ordering anything, and I'm tired of it.

"Ford-brand butter," Beans adds needlessly, not making a lick of sense. Still, it pisses me off some more.

I cut my eyes left and right, taking their measure. "Is that supposed to be some sort of commentary on me and Wyatt fucking after the wedding? Were you hoping to get all the dirty, filthy, nasty details? You wanna know how many times he made me come? Or skip straight to how big his dick is?"

Their mouths gape open in shock, definitely not expecting me to go on the offensive or be so . . . *loud* about it. Loud enough that I've gotten the attention of just about everyone in Puss N Boots, and considering we're mid-dinner rush, that's a fair number of people, all of whom have been eyeing me and gossiping all day.

Do they think I've not heard the whispered conversations that stop when I approach, not seen the pointing fingers and knowing nods, or felt the judgment from people I've known since I was a kid?

Even my skin's not *that* fucking thick.

Ironically, most don't care about my one-night stand, but are only interested because Etta's niece got it on with a Ford and they're questioning my loyalty. But Etta gave Wyatt two points of approval, and if that's good enough for me, it damn well should be good enough for everyone else.

From the kitchen window, Tayvious calls out, "I'd like to know how big his dick is! But only if he's open to some switch hitting. Otherwise, keep that shit to yourself so I'm not stricken with jealousy. I see the way you're walking!"

Charlene pipes up: "Honey-baby, you can tell me all those details so I can live vicariously through you."

I sigh, my fire flaming out in resignation. I might've shut down Pork and Beans, but more than just Tayvious and Charlene look mighty interested in actually hearing the story of last night.

I need to handle this, one and done.

"You nosy assholes, listen and listen good," I declare, staring lasers around the room. "I'm here to get your beer and food, ring you out, and if you're lucky, I'll feel good enough to beat a few of you at pool later. Other than that, my business is just that . . . mine. I will not be answering questions about Wyatt, or me, or Wyatt and me."

"Not even for me?" a voice behind me says.

I can hear the tease in the question and whirl, ready to unleash new fury on whoever is daring to challenge me. But instead of a regular who's found enough balls to speak, I find myself looking into a gorgeous pair of blue eyes that are dancing with laughter.

"Wyatt."

Chapter 16

Wyatt

It's barely a whisper, the way she says my name. But seeing Hazel turn around, the anger in her eyes drawing me in before it melts when she realizes who she's talking to, is the sexiest thing I've ever seen. And the twinkle that grows in her eyes, a twinkle of good humor, is even better.

But that's only because it was dark last night and I couldn't clearly see her face as she came in my arms.

"So, you willing to answer a question from me?" I repeat, and her smirk grows, curling at the edges of her lips and making me feel all sorts of things.

"That depends on what you want to know," Hazel says sassily. "Or if we're just going on a ranking scale. You know, one to ten."

Puss N Boots is jam-packed with people, all eyes locked on us, but it feels like it's only Hazel and me. I step closer to her, until we're toe to toe and she's looking up at me. I cup her jaw in my hands, tracing her cheekbones with my thumbs.

"You're beyond any ranking scale," I tell her quietly, looking directly into those soulful eyes. "But I do want to know if I can kiss you again."

Her smile is answer enough. I run my thumb across her soft lips, leaning in. I pause, drawing in the scent of her perfume, tasting her breath on my tongue before she comes the last half inch, and I feel her lips again.

The kiss is heady, soft and sweet at first. I want it that way just to prove a point, not to anyone watching—the whole bar's faded into obscurity in my mind. No, this is to prove to myself that last night wasn't a fluke. But a heartbeat later, we quickly ignite.

I feel her press into me, my arms going to her narrow waist as Hazel wraps her arms around me and I feel her lift to her toes, hungry for more. I move my hands to her hips, encouraging her up.

In a single bounce, she leaps, her legs encircling my waist, and I cup her jeans-covered ass. She responds by shoving her tongue into my mouth and I growl, meeting her aggressiveness with my own.

Dimly, in the background, I hear the crowd break out in hoots and hollers, someone yelling, "Hell yeah, Hazel! Ride that boy!"

Another voice yells, "Always figured her for a Chevy lover, but I guess she's a Ford girl!"

Laughter commences, but I don't care. Not when I can feel the heat from Hazel's core against my belly through our clothes and she's kissing me like she can't get enough. I pull back, on the edge of tossing her to the nearest flat surface, like one of her beloved pool tables. But I don't want to give the patrons that much of a show, so I force myself to turn the kiss into more of a sweet peck. Trying to cool us down by degrees, I rub my nose along hers, and up close, her smile is sweet. "Hi."

"Hey there, yourself." She slides down my body, and though she steps back only a few inches, I feel the loss of her. "What are you doing here?" she asks, her nose crinkling cutely.

You are all I've thought about all day. But of course, I can't say that, so I downplay it. "Well, I was craving one of Tayvious's life-changing burgers. And I really wanted to see you."

She looks surprised but pleased. "Then let's get you a table. Come on."

She grabs my hand, dragging me to an already occupied table. The two guys there look amused by Hazel, seemingly not reading that her mood has shifted in the few steps their way.

When she gets there, her voice has gone from the sweet flirtiness she offered me to that of a lioness ready to rip heads off. "Alright, Pork and Beans, time's up. Move it."

She taps the tabletop to emphasize her point, and the two guys chuckle. One says, "Yeah right."

The other one backhands his buddy's arm, still laughing. "We ain't going nowhere. But fine, bring us a pitcher of beer."

He waves Hazel off dismissively, and I have to fight back a laugh when Hazel slams the table with the side of her fist hard enough to make the bowl of peanuts spill and both men jump in surprise. "No. You had your chance, but you've been hogging my table for a solid hour without ordering. Now, scoot over to the bar if you want that beer."

I bite my tongue, wanting to back her up but knowing she doesn't need my help. Still, I offer a glare to the two guys.

"What's it gonna be, fellas?"

Seeming to find sense, they shove off from the table and stomp through the other occupied tables like a small herd of buffalo. Hazel gives the table a quick swipe with the cloth at her waist and turns to me with a smile. "Seems we have an available table right here."

"Is your hand okay?" I ask quietly as I sit down and Charlene appears at Hazel's side.

"Psssh, that wasn't nothing but a little love tap," Charlene answers. "You should see the dent she put on the side of the old cash register one time."

"Oh."

"Char," Hazel says, "you don't need to make me sound like a hothead."

"Psshaw," she says to Hazel, "you are who you are." To me, she says, "I ordered you a Fat Pussy burger and a beer. I remembered that's what you wanted last time."

Hazel clears her throat and says sharply, "Thanks, Charlene."

Unbothered, Charlene shrugs and says with a wink, "You can't blame a girl for trying."

But she's smiling happily as she walks off, leaving us alone. I look at Hazel, my brows furrowed. "Not sure about that friend of yours."

Hazel looks over her shoulder, her eyes following Charlene as she works the room. "She's good. She's checking my tables for me so I can hang out here a minute longer. But I do need to make my rounds. I've been distracted for a bit."

She doesn't sound the least bit upset about that, which makes me feel warm inside. I get even warmer when she leans forward and places a quick smacking kiss to my lips before walking away. But not before I see the happy smile on her lips and bright sparkles in her eyes.

She knows I'm going to be sticking around for the rest of her shift. And ideally, after that too.

I sit back, enjoying the view as I watch Hazel work the room. The way she interacts with everyone, leaving them smiling with her special brand of sass, snark, and sweetness, is amazing. She's got the whole room in the palm of her hand, even without tonight's attention-grabbing activities.

"You hush, Tom Simmons, before Helen hears you talkin'!" she says at one point, earning huge laughter from one table of older gentlemen. "Besides, he don't need no hints!"

I'm tempted to go ask the old codger what hints he might have for me when a plate is set down in front of me. I expect it to be Charlene making another flirty appearance, but when I drag my eyes from Hazel, I see another remarkably beautiful woman. Etta Livingston.

Politely, I give her a nod. "Thanks for the burger and beer."

Etta doesn't pull out a knife, so I guess that's a good sign. "No problem. Though you might want to wave at the kitchen window. Tay Tay put a little extra love in your Fat Pussy tonight."

I glance toward the window and see Tayvious's wide white smile. I answer with a smile of my own and add a head nod of appreciation, hoping the "extra love" isn't spittle . . . or some other kind of bodily fluid.

In the split second it took to thank Tayvious, Etta has made herself at home, sitting on the stool across from me and munching on one of my fries. Well, I guess they are her fries, too, at least until I pay my bill. "Help yourself."

"Seems we need to have a little chitchat, you and me." She grabs another fry, using it to point at each of us.

"Is that so?" I ask as calmly as possible, snatching up my own fry. "Is this the part where you tell me that if I hurt Hazel, you'll have my balls in the fryer before the next sunrise?"

Etta laughs harder than I expect, her eyes watering. "God no. She doesn't need me to threaten you, and that would get me in trouble with the health department. I ain't risking my Puss for your testicles. Besides, she told me this morning that it was casual, didn't mean anything."

I flinch before I can hide the reaction, and I realize how out of practice I am at staying stoic. Etta sees it, knowing the unspoken truth. "I see. Well, she also said it was awesome, if that soothes your pretty ego a bit."

She looks at me expectantly, and I take a deep breath. "It does." I glance down at my fries, silently offering another. "Guess we've all got egos."

"Perhaps."

I pick up another fry myself and set it back down. "So, if we don't need to talk about me and Hazel, what do we need to talk about?"

I ask the question to open the door, but I already know the answer. If Etta doesn't want to talk about Hazel, she wants to talk about Uncle Jed.

Etta leans in, her eyes sharp. "What do you know about this subdivision thing?"

Not quite the part about Uncle Jed I was thinking, but I'm not surprised by her question either. "I guess we're diving right into the deep end?"

"If you were expecting Lifetime movie–style questions, you got a lot to learn about me," Etta says with a chuckle. "And I've never been much on beating around the bush."

"That definitely runs in the family," I tell her, and Etta beams, taking it for the compliment it is. "So I won't either. I didn't know anything about it until I saw the billboard on the way into town. Since then, all I know is that Jed is up to his usual shit, looking out for number one."

Etta shakes her head. "It's more than that. He's going to destroy Cold Springs. Look around here, what do you see?"

I do as she instructs, noticing the patrons of the establishment and forcing myself to not stare at Hazel the whole time. "Uh, bunch of people eating burgers, drinking beer, playing pool and darts."

Etta reaches across the table and smacks me in the back of the head in a *very* Cold Springs maneuver. "Deeper than the superficial, Ford."

I growl but take a deeper look. "Working-class folks. Lots of blue collar, couple of geezers . . . all Cold Springs natives."

"This is an endangered species, Wyatt," Etta says. "It's a community that looks out for each other, takes care of each other. But Jed would destroy this if he could."

"What do you mean?"

Her sigh is heavy with their history, fresh as if it happened yesterday. I've heard the stories, both Jed's version, which makes him out to be the wronged party, and the likely more accurate rumors around town that paint him in a much less favorable light.

"I need you to understand, this is not about the shit that went down between us. I told you, no Lifetime movies here."

She pins me with a hard glare that demands a response, so I nod and pick up my burger, not wanting it to get cold, and dig in while she starts her story.

"Okay, so a few years back, Jed started mouthing about this big plan he had. He was gonna buy land cheap, develop it, and then sell at a huge profit. I mean, that's business, that's what he does. But he wasn't talking about buying land that was for sale, or even offering money to folks who might be interested in selling. Because people who want to sell usually have some idea what their land is worth. No, he wanted to score the land at bargain-basement prices. That's where Mayor Bill comes in."

I finish my bite, asking, "My dad?"

I'm not sure I want to know what Etta's talking about. Uncle Jed is rotten to the core, unsalvageable. But Dad? I've had problems with him, but he's not as bad as Jed. Surely, I didn't miss that. And I couldn't have . . . caused it, could I?

Some of my inner thoughts must show on my face, because Etta gives me a pitying smile.

"Take a drink, baby," she says quietly. "You're gonna need it."

I don't give it a second thought, just pick up my beer and throw half of it back in one gulp. Slamming it onto the table, I nod that I'm ready.

"Jed found land he liked on the edge of town, where he can create his own ready-made world of cookie-cutter houses. Problem was, there were people who owned the land, and they didn't want to sell. Not that he even asked them." She sneers, her thoughts about my uncle abundantly clear. "No, he was sneaky, got the city council to pass some property tax rate hikes. At the time, nobody noticed because they didn't seem to actually affect anyone. They were about single-family home rates for an area that is all zoned as farmland. Nobody saw Jed's long game."

A sick realization comes to me as I start to put snippets of previous conversations together, but I let Etta tell it her way. She shakes her head in disappointment, but it seems to be directed at herself more than anything. "That was, until there was a proposal to change the zoning, making the farms into single-family sites, which will then be under the umbrella of the new rates. You gotta understand, those folks are barely scraping by as it is. If the zoning changes or their taxes go up, they'll literally lose their homes, their farms . . . to Jed, who will build his subdivision."

The scheme sounds exactly like Jed, so I'm not surprised at his puppet mastering something like this, but I mentally play out the angles.

"What does Dad get out of it?" I ask. "He's already pissed off half of town, something I never thought he'd do."

"The new subdivision is going to be hundreds of houses, all at the higher tax rate. New voters who'll be more than happy to elect the guy who got them their new home built. Then those assessments will make the surrounding area go up in value, pushing even more of those kind into town and our kind out, and so on and so on. Cold Springs revenue will go through the roof, but at what cost?" She doesn't wait for me to answer but fills in herself: "The people. People who've lived here for decades will be forced out. It's already happening too."

I look around the room, realizing what she meant about an endangered community. "How?"

"Businesses through downtown are getting hit because Jed owns a bunch of the commercial buildings. He's raising rates on his leases, bragging to everyone that we're going to be rolling in dough soon. But nobody can afford it now. A few places have already had to close. If, and that's a big *if*, he gets his way, he's going to basically own the town—the subdivision, downtown, and of course, your dad."

She goes silent, eyeing me thoughtfully while I process everything she's told me. But she's left out one important piece. Finally, I speak up. "What do you need from me?"

Etta smiles. "Quick on the uptake, aren't ya? I'm not just telling tales to listen to myself talk. You're a Ford, but I get the feeling you're not like Jed. I thought maybe you could talk some sense into your uncle, or your dad. That is, if you give a damn about Cold Springs. Or the people here." She cuts her eyes to the side, and when I follow her gaze, I find Hazel. "She said you were only here for the wedding, probably leaving soon. That the case?"

She's not talking about whatever this shit is with my uncle anymore. Despite her earlier statement that she wasn't going to get involved with Hazel and me, she's asking my intentions.

"I hadn't made any plans when I came, just wanted to be here for my brother," I admit, showing more of my heart to her than I typically would. "I wanted to come in, toast, and leave."

"And now?" she presses.

"Haven't made any plans on leaving yet either," I confess. Her right eyebrow lifts in disappointment . . . that I might be leaving or that I might stay, I'm not sure. And though this is the first real conversation I've ever had with her, I can feel the weight of her expectations dropping onto my shoulders. Like everyone else in this town, she wants something from me and only cares about my last name.

Except Hazel. She likes you in spite of your name and doesn't want anything more from you than a good fuck.

I bristle at the idea that Hazel is nothing more than that. But I painfully remind myself that I know better. I can't stay here, shouldn't be here.

A good fuck is all you need too.

Maybe. But is that all I *want*?

"Look," I continue, "if you'd asked me two weeks ago what I'd be doing tonight, I'd have told you that I'd be doing the same thing I do every night—cracking a beer after a long day of work and sitting on my ass alone at home. No offense, but after a day in the woodshop, I don't really need to pay extra for beer I can store in my own fridge. But somehow, I came back to Cold Springs, something I didn't want to do, for one of the few people I give a shit about, my brother. Seeing him happy has already made this trip down memory lane worth it."

Etta nods, but I hold up a finger. "As for Hazel? She's an unexpected surprise, one I'd like to continue exploring. But all this shit with my family? I walked away from it for a reason, and I don't know if I want to get involved. Even if I did, Jed and Dad wouldn't listen to me. I'm the ungrateful son of a bitch who walked out and barely deserve the family name any longer."

Etta hums. "Black sheep or not, you stay around and 'continue exploring' as you say, you're gonna get mixed up in it. Can't be helped when you're a Ford, even if you barely deserve the name."

"You say that differently than they would."

"I know. But sticking around will only make it harder for Hazel when you go, because we both know . . . you're gonna leave. And she'll be here, watching Cold Springs fall apart with your name carved in the ruins."

She draws a work-worn finger across the tabletop, writing out *Ford*.

Well, shit. Talk about pulling no punches. Etta Livingston is brutally harsh and bluntly honest. No wonder Jed left her. He's not man enough to handle her. He needs soft ego stroking and a woman who defers to him in all ways.

I think about my Aunt Chrissy, Jed's wife, whose main job seems to be staying in trophy-wife condition, and try to find a single similarity with Etta, but there simply are none. I don't know how Jed and Etta could've ever been a thing, except that Etta was probably as beautiful as Hazel, thirty or so years ago.

Still, it's plain as day that they'd be a match made in hell.

Or maybe she wasn't this way until she had her heart broken . . . by a Ford. Is Etta saying I'll do the same to Hazel?

"You think I should go now?"

Etta rolls her eyes, and if she could, I think she'd slap me in the back of the head again. "No, asshole. I'm saying to stay and handle your shit. Quit running away like a scared kid."

"I'm not a kid," I tell her coldly. "And I don't appreciate being told what to do."

She doesn't back down, smirking. "Seems I've hit a nerve. Is that what your daddy did? Or what he still tries to do?"

She's right, on all accounts. But the person who treated me most like a stupid kid was Jed. So I don't answer.

Instead, I give her a guarded look and return to eating my almost-gone burger as though we haven't been talking at all. The burger is cold, and despite its deliciousness, it sits like sand in my mouth and I have to force it down.

"Fine then." She stands up but pauses at the side of the table to get the last word in. "Do whatever the hell you want, but remember that there are people here who do give a damn, Hazel included. And we could really use your help. We're trying to save this whole town from Jed. Help us. Help *her*."

Without waiting for my reply, she leaves. I watch her go, but after a few steps, I look for Hazel instead. She's dropping a round of drinks off at a table full of couples who look like they're enjoying a night out while the kids are home with babysitters.

They're all laughing at something Hazel's said, and when she turns to walk away, her smile is bright and real. I scan the rest of the restaurant, seeing people eating and drinking and playing, all having a good time together.

Is this what Jed wants to ruin?

And for what? Money?

The idea disgusts me so much I push my mostly empty plate away.

A few minutes later, Hazel completes her rounds and comes back to my table. "Judging by the deep groove between your eyebrows and the super-frowny face, Aunt Etta was her usual, charming self? Whatever she said I said, ignore it." She waves a hand dramatically. "She makes up stuff all the time, nearly a compulsive liar."

She's trying to cheer me up, so I force a smile to my face. "Etta said you told her last night was awesome. That a lie?"

Her blush is all the answer I need. "Well, I might've said that." She winks teasingly, but she's searching my face with perceptive eyes. "Look, whatever Etta said . . . seriously, forget it. I'm off in ten minutes. How about if we play a game or two, just hang out for a bit?"

I consider saying no, not because I don't want to spend time with Hazel. I do, so much. But she comes with a whole different set of expectations, ones I'm not sure I can live up to. The alternative is worse, though, so I nod.

"Yeah, that sounds fun. You got that ridiculous pink pool cue with you?"

She gives me a very insulted look, although she's grinning in her eyes. "Of course. Joan of Arc lives here, locked up safe and sound next to Etta's stick in the office."

I grab her hand, bringing it up for a kiss along her knuckles. "Go get it and I'll meet you by the tables."

A table clears as we approach, and I ask, "Eight ball?"

Hazel nods and I quickly rack the balls.

She chalks her cue and breaks, dropping a solid, the three, and the game is on. Any fantasies of her taking it easy on me because of last night evaporate on her next shot, a twin-rail bouncer that pockets the six.

Thankfully, I do get a chance when her shot on the two barely misses the side pocket. Hazel's good, leaving me without much of an angle on anything, but with a lucky shot, I'm able to put both the fifteen and the ten into their pockets.

"That was bullshit," Hazel grumbles but, at the same time, smiles a little.

"Just watch," I reply, but while I sink the fourteen, I also scratch.

"Fuck!" I hiss, stepping back. "Your shot."

Hazel chuckles, and I feel like it's the chuckle of a killer. I might not get another chance at the game. I try to watch the table, but it's distracting to watch Hazel caress her cue, bending over the table, and drawing her hand back to—

"Hey, big brother."

I jump, trying not to yell as Wren sneaks up and surprises me. "Wren!"

She grins, knowing she caught me staring at Hazel. "Fancy finding you here."

I scoff. "You knew I'd be here. But I am surprised to see you in here."

"Winston's brought me here once or twice before. He says it's a safe space from Dad and Uncle Jed." Wren waves at Etta behind the bar, who flashes a thumbs-up in return.

I gape in shock. "That woman damn near gutted me like a fish a few minutes ago, but with you . . . she's all 'hey baby, how's your momma'n'em'?"

"She giving you a hard time about the subdivision?" Wren asks, and I nod. "Not really surprised. She's asked Winston and I about it. Winston's a brick, of course, but I told her the truth. I've got about as much stroke with Dad and Jed as Ryan Seacrest."

"She accepted that?" I ask. "Or did you get the VIP stare?"

Wren laughs. "Etta knows where I stand. I might not be able to stop Jed, but I can do my part. Hell, I brought coffee to the last protest."

"You. Protest," I repeat, and Wren nods. "Nope, can't see it. Doesn't compute."

Wren smiles wryly. "Why? I care about this town too."

That she does, maybe more than me. Maybe I've underestimated my little sister. "What's your take on the whole thing then?"

"This is exponentially worse than Jed's usual assholery, a lot worse," Wren says. "I shot my shot with Dad, more than once. I've talked with him about it until I'm blue in the face, but he ignores me. And don't even get me started on Jed."

I sigh, knowing what she means. "So why does everyone think I can do something about it?"

"Hope springs eternal? Return of the heir? Some pearl of wisdom like that?" she says, and I scoff.

"Pearls before swine is more like it."

Wren tilts her head. "Maybe, just maybe, they're desperate. Or maybe they figure you're the *one* Ford with enough strength and enough balls to stand up and do your own thing once, and hope you'll do it again. Maybe, just maybe . . . you're their only hope."

I growl and cross my arms over my chest, turning my attention to Hazel, who's running the solids and joking around with the couple at the next table.

I appreciate the lightness she brings to everything. I want more of it, not all this heavy shit everyone else hits me with. I feel alive with Hazel, even if it makes me consider uncomfortable things, like what I might do to spend more time with her.

Fine, maybe like Wren said . . . I could do something.

"Well?" Wren asks, and I look over.

"Well, what?"

"I know that look, Wyatt," Wren says. "You had that same look right before . . . right before you took off. It's your thinking look."

"Ah . . . well . . ."

"And that's game!" Hazel says, standing up and grinning in victory. "Ooof, at least you got two!"

I shake my head. "Two out of three!"

"Pssh, sit down, scrub!" Hazel says. "You gotta get in line, someone already called next."

I look, and sure enough, there's a pair of quarters already sitting on the end of the table, along with a reed-thin guy of about fifty-five with

Lauren Landish

a cue in his hand. "Sorry, young man, but this young lady and I have been going back and forth for, what, six months now?"

I sit down on the stool next to Wren, giving the man a friendly wave. "You go ahead, Mr. Irsing."

It's funny, watching my old science teacher and Hazel play for money. And I have to give him credit, Mr. Irsing keeps it close. But as the eight ball drops into the pocket, he shakes his head in sportsmanlike disappointment.

"Hazel, you made two weeks of practice utterly useless," Irsing says, reaching into his wallet and taking out a twenty-dollar bill. "Honestly."

"I wouldn't say that," Hazel says, taking the cash. "You're getting better. Keep it up, and I bet I'll be handing this back to you before too long."

"I doubt that very much, young lady. Now, I do believe Mr. Ford here wants his rematch. Take it to 'im."

Chapter 17

HAZEL

Wyatt's truck is right behind me as I make the last turn, the dirt of what passes as my driveway making a rumble beneath my tires. No going back now. Not that there really was after the way the grapevine was buzzing over the wedding.

Wyatt parks next to me, his truck huge next to Nessa. He gets out, looking at the outside of the house. "Nice."

"Want to come in?" I ask, and Wyatt's smile tells me the answer. My hand is remarkably steady as I open the front door, letting him in.

"*Bawk!* Welcome home, bitch!"

"The fuck?" Wyatt snarls in surprise as I snort laughter.

"Uh-oh."

Wyatt's still confused. "What the hell is that?"

I flip the light switch and Lester appears on his perch, squawking.

"Wyatt, this is Lester," I explain. "Parrot and sailor all in one."

"I see," Wyatt says, eyeing Lester. "He's a good home security system, I bet."

"The best," I assure him while crossing over to Lester. "Come on, buddy. It's bedtime for birds."

"Lester wanna watch!" Lester says, whistling a pretty decent "bow-chicka-wow-wow" that makes me blush and Wyatt chuckle. But when I hold out my arm, Lester flies over obediently, letting me tuck him in his cage and get his cover set up.

"Got your water . . . a midnight snack . . . your curtains," I tell him as I get it all set. "You're good to go. Good night, Lester."

"Night-night!" he says before starting his fake-snoring routine.

I make sure his curtain's set and turn around to see Wyatt looking around the rest of the living room.

"You have a nice place."

"It belonged to my grandmother first," I reply, wondering what Wyatt sees. "I know it's nothing like your house, but my Gran loved it."

Wyatt shakes his head, putting his hands in his pockets. "I would never compare the two. Your home looks warm and full of life."

"And your family home?" I ask curiously, and Wyatt shrugs, though I can tell he's thinking of an answer.

"Historical."

It's a telling no-tell, but I want to know more than just his personal issues with his family. Or maybe I want to know them in a different way. "What about your place in Newport?"

Wyatt shifts, looking uncomfortable, but answers, "It's not like my family home at all. It's more of a shack that's attached to my workshop out on the edge of the woods."

I laugh disbelievingly. "You make it sound rustic, but I bet it's fancier than that."

Wyatt shrugs. "It's more about function. And the land was cheap."

The honesty in his words makes me like him that much more. He's different than I expect at every turn. "Then my thirty-year-old couch should be fine for you to make yourself comfortable while I take a quick shower," I reply, taking a melodramatic sniff of myself. "I smell like fries, sweat, and pool chalk."

Why did I say that? It's true, but there's no sense in highlighting the fact that I've been working all day and smell like a donkey's ass end.

Wyatt looks at the couch and nods. "Sure, but one thing first . . ."

He takes my hand and pulls me into him, aligning our bodies. He lowers his mouth to my ear and growls, "Maybe I like the way you smell." He places a soft kiss right below my ear, inhaling deeply. "The way you taste." Another kiss to my neck. "The way you feel."

He traces a fingertip along my collarbone, and a shiver runs down my spine. Thoughts flood my mind, and part of me wants to slow step Wyatt down the hall and into my bedroom, but I really do need a shower. And probably should shove some dirty clothes in the hamper before Wyatt's in there or he's going to think I'm a complete slob.

I groan, pulling away slightly. "I gotta shower . . . for real."

He lets me go slowly, reluctantly. In response I press my palm to his chest, begging him to give me this moment. He steps back and lowers to the couch, his elbows on his knees and eyes burning. "I'll be here."

I walk backward down the hall and into my bedroom, where I quickly strip and throw my dirty clothes into the hamper along with the small pile that didn't quite make it the previous couple of days. I'd do more, but a little bit of me still worries that Wyatt's going to disappear while I'm back here.

Quickly, I hop in the shower and suds up. I've got the showerhead on massage, and the hot water works the knots out of my muscles, but along with it, my energy is equally sapped. Frankly, as much as I want Wyatt, I can barely keep my knees from giving out as I dry off.

Realizing my body has needs beyond the sexual, I pull on my favorite comfy pj's, flannel pants and a long-sleeved shirt, which are soft but cute. I give my room one last look, wondering whether Wyatt is going to be able to see it in the state I'm in right now. I hope so . . . I don't bring men home, ever. And despite my exhaustion, I want to spend as much time as possible with him. Whether that's with a repeat of last night's amazingness or simply lying down with his strong arms around me as we drift off.

As I make my way back to the living room, I see Wyatt still sitting on the couch, his eyes immediately finding me. But I get the feeling he's been looking around, learning everything he can about me. I feel vulnerable, exposed, and move toward him slowly. "Find anything that has you running for the hills yet?"

"Well, those flannel check pants are about the only thing," he teases lightly. "Thankfully, I'm pretty hard to scare."

"I'm gonna try real hard to not take that as a challenge." Bantering with him is perking me up a tiny bit.

Wyatt scoots over, patting the couch. "Come here." Gratefully, I sit down next to him, and he brushes my hair over my shoulder. "Are you trying to scare me off?"

I shake my head, wanting to lean against him but instead sagging against the cushions. "Not exactly . . ."

"But?"

I look up at the ceiling, unwilling to meet his eyes for this confession. "But I'm reminding myself that you're leaving soon," I say honestly. I know I sound like one of those women who gets a little dick and becomes a stage-five clinger, something I am not. "It's . . . difficult."

Wyatt hums, still stroking my hair. "I haven't made any plans one way or another."

I don't want to do this, don't want him making promises he won't keep. So I don't ask for any. "Tell me about your life in Newport."

Wyatt thinks for a moment, then lifts an arm, and I accept his invitation, leaning against him and relishing the comfort of his strength and warmth. "Like I said, I've got a place attached to my woodshop. It's not much, but it's got what I need—room to work, trails out the back where I can go into the actual woods to hike, pick up interesting chunks of wood from time to time for carving bits, and room to relax."

I smile, liking the sound of it. "What do you do—like, for fun?"

"Wood," he says, chuckling. "I can do a bit of everything, really. I've restored antiques, did a family's stair banister, some in-home cabinetry work in the early days. But mostly what I do now are authentic traditional-method custom pieces, everything from furniture to antique reproduction millwork. I do an occasional art piece just for fun. That's what I use the stuff I find in the woods for."

I trace the length of his fingers, noting the rough calluses. There're scars, too, the evidence of mistakes and lessons learned. "If I'd only seen you in your tux at the wedding, I never would've thought you . . ." I trail off, not sure how to explain without being rude.

Wyatt finishes for me. "You would've thought I was just like my family. Work with my mouth more than my hands?"

I nod, ashamed.

"It's okay," Wyatt assures me, capturing my fingers in his and holding them in his strong yet gentle grip. "I was like them for a long time. Being here, I realize that . . . I've changed. Or maybe I never was like them, and that's why I left in the first place."

I shift against him, leaning into him more. In response, I feel Wyatt twist, rearranging himself so that my back almost lies against his chest, his right leg pulled up on the couch to give me room. It's intimate in a whole new way.

"Why did you leave?" I ask, laying my head against his shoulder.

Wyatt is quiet for a moment, and I think I've pushed too far. But his arms tighten around my shoulders, and I feel him inhale, his nose buried in my hair, and he answers. "I was in college. Young, stupid, having too much fun fucking off, like a lot of college kids. One long weekend, I came home for a visit. Jed took me out to lunch, said he wanted to hear about how things were going. It was fine at first. Hell, I was enjoying bragging about how well I was doing in classes, the friends I'd made, and the parties I was going to. And then he started talking about my future. He had it all planned out—my major, a list of people he wanted me to network with, how I was going to work for him after graduation. I laughed at him. I didn't know what I wanted to do, but I was sure it had nothing to do with him. And then he explained that he'd gotten me into that college because my grades certainly hadn't. It pissed me off, and then he revealed that he was paying for it, not my dad. He said he'd never had kids of his own, but he had me just the same, and he owned me. Not that I was family, not that I was like his kid. But that he *owned* me."

I wince, turning my head to see the anger in his face. "That's awful. What'd you do?"

"What I should have done was throw a punch right to his smug smirk, but I was so shocked, I waited, talked to Dad," Wyatt says. "I thought he'd support me, but instead, he was annoyed. According to him, Jed was paying for school as a gift, and I shouldn't be rude about his kind gesture. He told me I didn't know what I wanted to do anyway, so what was the harm in getting the business degree Jed wanted me to get? 'It'll be good no matter what you do,' he said. But that wasn't the point. He didn't get that Jed didn't see us as family, but as things, servants . . . or worse."

I shiver, and Wyatt squeezes me comfortingly, his arms around me warm and strong. He understands what he's saying, and knows that it sucks . . . but that I want to hear it. "Dad just didn't see it, didn't believe that being beholden to Jed would be bad. He figured it was family, and family is everything. I think Dad truly thought Jed was doing it out of real generosity, like he cared about us the way Dad always did for him. I wanted to believe that, too, even though my gut was telling me something else entirely. So I went back to school, finished the semester, telling myself it'd be okay. But the next time I came home, Jed wanted to know what progress I'd made—not my grades but in the connections. I was such a dumbass. I told him I wasn't going to be used like some trained monkey to do his bidding. We fought, and I fought with Dad. Hell, Dad and Jed fought, about the only time I've seen them actually fight. That was it for me. I dropped out of school, left home, left Cold

Springs, and went to hide." He goes quiet for a moment before I feel him shaking his head. "I was such a dumbass, thinking I was making some grand, rebellious gesture. I spent two years fucking about with wood simply because I liked woodshop in high school, and it was . . . it was pure. I could put everything aside and just meditate on the wood."

"I get that."

"I was still licking the wounds of my ego when Jed showed up, told me I would never amount to anything without him. After that, I got a job working for a carpenter who was willing to train me even though I had no idea what I was doing and was basically a spoiled brat. But I practiced and worked. I got better and better. I've got a successful business now."

He sounds proud of himself, for making himself into something no one else thought he could. I'm proud for him. "Good for you. Double birds to Jed Ford, the asshole."

I hold up my middle fingers to the ceiling, imagining it has Jed Ford's face on it or, even better, that he's actually right in front of me so I could tell him exactly what I think about him taking advantage of Wyatt. He was just a kid, with his whole future ahead of him, and Jed wanted to steal that.

Wyatt laughs quietly, and I feel his chest vibrate against my back, his arms tightening around my chest. "Yeah, that'd be cool. How about you, with Etta and your mom? You work with your family."

I hum thoughtfully. "No, it's a lot different for me. Truth is, I never considered anything else. I never planned to leave Cold Springs for college or dreamed I'd be something crazy like an astronaut. Even as a little girl, I'd sit right here on this couch and tell Gran that I was going to work at the restaurant and the bakery when I was old enough. She'd laugh and tell me I might have to pick one. But I started working for both of them as soon as I could, and here I am. We are family, but we treat each other right. There's bitching and name-calling sometimes, and there's Lester, of course. But I know they'd do anything for me. And vice versa."

"Even Lester?" Wyatt teases softly, and I chuckle, nodding.

"He's a trained home-protection attack parrot," I assure Wyatt. "He's got a black belt in bird-jitsu."

Wyatt sighs wistfully. "You're fortunate."

"I am," I admit. "I'm happy here, with my life. It might not be a lot to some people, but it's enough for me."

I look around my home, still filled with memories of Gran but equally mine now, with my own knickknacks and things. I work for Mom and Aunt Etta, jobs I got because of our relationships, but ones I keep because I'm damn good at them. I honestly enjoy my simple existence of work, pool, family, and friends.

Even Lester, though I won't tell him that or he'd repeat it until the day I die. I can hear him now: *"Bawk! You love me, you weally wuv me!"*

A yawn I've been fighting back demands release, and Wyatt laughs as I cover my wide-stretched mouth with my hands. "Sorry."

"Don't be," Wyatt says. "You're a very busy woman."

"I'm not *that* tired," I protest, but he kisses the top of my head.

"You need some rest, Miss Working Two Jobs," Wyatt says. "It means you're human."

"Basically three," I correct him. "I made as much playing pool a few nights ago as I did waiting tables all day. Hell of a lot more fun, too, but not nearly as important as helping Etta."

I feel the thread of tension shoot through him and hate that my good relationship with my family only amplifies the bad one he has with his dad and uncle. "Three, then. Glad I didn't play you for cash," he says after a moment. "I should tuck you in."

"Not getting off this couch unless you're in bed with me," I tell him firmly but quietly. "It's too late to drive home."

Talk about a piss-poor excuse. But the truth is, feeling Wyatt here with me, the way he's holding me, strong but at the same time willing to be emotionally vulnerable and share himself with me . . . things have changed.

Last night, I could tell myself it was just lust, attraction, and the fantastical romance of a wedding. I mean, Wyatt is a gorgeous man. But this is something different now. Wyatt led a seemingly charmed life, but he's got trust issues from a betrayal by the people who should never have wronged him. When a man doesn't trust easily, it means something when he shares his baggage. I know that, and I want to be someone who doesn't let him down. I'll carry those heavy suitcases of drama on my strong shoulders with him, letting him take a break from them, if only for a little while.

"One promise," Wyatt says in my ear. "We don't need to . . ."

"I know," I tell him.

He gives me a gentle push to help guide me up, and I lead him to my bedroom, where Wyatt strips down to his T-shirt and underwear. I let him pull back the covers, arranging myself best so that he can join me, tucking us both in as he spoons up against me.

It's glorious. His warmth surrounds me, his chest pressed to my back and his hand splayed on the bare skin of my belly beneath my shirt. I wiggle my hips, arching my back to entice him.

"Hazel," he says warningly.

I yawn, even as I place his hand on my breast encouragingly. "I am tired, but I . . ."

My voice falters. I don't want to remind either of us that he's going to leave, not after everything we shared tonight. But I also don't want to waste this time with him.

He understands without me saying a word. Instead, his hand cups my breast as his lips find my neck, kissing and nibbling up to my ear. The hand trapped under my neck twists to reach down, stroking my nipples as his tongue licks my ear.

"Mmmm," I whimper softly, pressing back against him. "Wyatt . . ."

"This isn't for me," he whispers. "I don't want to hurt you."

I don't think he realizes the layers of what he says, but it hits me hard. So when his free hand traces down my stomach, my knees part as he runs his fingers over my panties, stroking me through the slick nylon I put on after my shower.

"So soft," he whispers, his fingers moving up and down over my lips so gently it makes electricity crackle through my nerves. "So beautiful."

"Wyatt," I whimper again, and he slides my panties aside to dip his fingers into my wet honey. There are no more words, nothing but the sound of his fingers slipping in and out of me as his thumb strokes my clit in slow, soft circles, his other hand pinching and tugging lightly on my nipples.

I can feel him bulging against my ass, but he never moves his hips, holding me secure in his arms as his thumb speeds up until my orgasm breaks and I freeze, gasping and crying out softly. I'm 100 percent safe in his arms, and he stops, holding me close as he lets me ride it out.

When it's over I'm boneless, sagging in his arms. Slowly, Wyatt withdraws his fingers, lifting them to his mouth and licking them clean.

"What about you?" I ask, feeling him still hard against the cleft of my ass.

"Told you," he says, humming happily even though I'm the one who came. "This was about you."

I think I argue, but maybe not as I drift off to sleep.

⁂

The music's soft, coming from everywhere and nowhere at once. The sunlight filters through the trees, illuminating me as I look down at my dress.

My wedding dress. It's nothing fancy, nothing like what Avery wore, but that's okay. If anything, it's better, because it's meant for me. The ceremony's perfect for me too. There's only a small group. Mom, of course, Aunt Etta with Lester on her shoulder, the minister, myself . . .

*And Wyatt. Under the draping branches of the willow tree we're gath-
ered under, he holds my hands, his smile wide and happy.*

*"Everything about you was wrong—you were the wrong bridesmaid,
you lived in the wrong town, and you had all these wrong assumptions
about me. But somehow, you and I were meant to be together, today and
forever, right here in our hometown. And that is right. I love you, Hazel
Sullivan."*

*I blink away the tears, speechless for once in my life. Finally, I find
words, not the traditional vows, but ones from my heart . . .*

*"I was wrong. About everything. But most of all, about you. You're
more than I ever dreamed, and I've never been so happy to be wrong. Yeah,
I'll admit it . . . this one time, so listen close . . . I was wrong. I love you,
William Wyatt Ford the third."*

I startle awake, the dark night still surrounding us. Wyatt is asleep
but must sense my movement because he pulls me in, cuddling me.
We've moved, and he's on his back, but instinctively I curl into him,
laying my head on his shoulder to stare at his profile in the moonlit
darkness. He's beautiful, inside and out.

My dream tickles at the edges of my brain, feeling surprisingly
warm.

I've heard that dreams are the brain's way of processing the minu-
tiae of daily life, but it's an imprecise process. Like the time I ate cotton
candy at the zoo and dreamed of hippos dressed in fluffy pink candy
tutus doing ballet through the water. Your brain takes the information of
the day and doodles with it, making funky collages of the whole thing.

So it would make sense that getting closer to Wyatt on the tail of
Avery's wedding is probably what made my brain put that little mov-
ie-style love scene together. I shouldn't read more into it. It doesn't
mean anything.

Even so, as I fall asleep, I hope my brain cues up a sequel, or maybe
an encore performance. Because if I remember right . . . Wyatt wasn't
wearing pants in my dream.

Chapter 18

WYATT

Home. It's a strange thought, because my parents' house hasn't been home in what feels like forever. For a long time, I vowed that I'd never consider this place home again, and that if it burned down, I'd come back only to piss on the ashes.

But walking in after being at Hazel's makes it feel even less so. There's no warmth, no desire to curl up and relax. It's just walls surrounding people who happen to be related to one another.

Okay, that might be a bit harsh. I do care about Wren, Winston, Mom, and fine . . . even Dad. But it's a different kind of care. More than anything, I worry about my sister, hope for my brother . . . and my parents are more complicated.

It's a contrast between us and the lengths Hazel's family go to take care of each other. I'm quite sure that if I were to hurt Hazel's feelings, her mother and aunt know quite a few places my body would never be discovered.

"Bill, is that you?" Mom's voice comes from the back living room, and I freeze in my tracks.

For a telling moment, I consider dodging her, and glance up the stairs at the escape they offer, but ultimately call back, "No, Mom. It's me."

I regret my response approximately two seconds later, when I walk in to see Mom holding court. There's a group of women politely perched on the edges of chairs and couches, matching books with mugs of coffee in front of them. Going by the matching covers, it seems I've walked in on book club time. Mr. Puddles is lying on the rug in a beam of sunlight, watching the tray of veggies that looks to be untouched.

"Didn't realize you had company, Mom."

I can see the eager, curious looks of the women, and Mom beams. "Oh, it's fine! Come in and let me show you off a bit." She closes her book, using a notepad as a bookmark, and waves me in.

Begrudgingly, I take a few steps into the shitshow circus. "Reading anything interesting?" I say, trying to keep the focus off me.

A woman holds up her copy of a self-help bestseller and explains, "It's for our book club."

Another teases, "Don't you dare think us boring, though. We've read some spicier things too."

"I'm sure," I agree, praying she doesn't spell out their group thoughts on any bodice-ripper or ass-smacking romances. Some of these women are eligible for AARP. I don't need to know if they want handprints on their asses.

"This one is good," Mom says, and I pay attention to hopefully get these images out of my head. "My favorite quote so far is"— she closes her eyes—"'Restore your spirit by authentically representing yourself. You are reinvented each day by the priorities you focus on.'" She opens her eyes and smiles. The group hums along in agreement, virtually saying *amen* to the quote.

I blink, letting that sink in. It sounds like a bunch of word-salad bullshit if I'm being honest, but if it helps Mom, I'm not going to point out how much it smells. "What's the priority for today then?" I ask, playing along. "You know, priorities and such?"

Mom levels her eyes at me. "You are."

Her blunt answer surprises me. "Me? Mom . . ."

She shakes her head, and I swear this group of women just morphed into the Spanish Inquisition. "Don't Mom me. This is the first time you've been home in years, and I want it to happen more often. Anything I can do to make it happen, I'll darn well do."

She glares at me, and every woman nods along with her. Me against the tide, or maybe a firing squad, judging by the looks I'm getting? I could turn and walk away, dismissing her interference, especially when this group of society-sucking biddies just doesn't understand. But the pain lurking in Mom's eyes gives me pause.

I sigh and sit down in the chair next to her. "I'm sorry for not coming home sooner. I've missed you."

"Awww," the women coo.

The admission softens Mom's ire. "I've missed you too." Tears threaten to spill, and more like her usual self, she daintily pats at them as she says, "And now, Winston is married and moving out. Wren will be next."

"My Alex too."

"Brayden and Brylie too."

I roll my eyes at the women's whines and tell them all, "You make it sound like we're abandoning you."

"No, you're all doing what you should," Mom says, wringing her hands. "I know it might not seem like it, but I'm proud of you, Wyatt."

Those are words I never expected to hear, or at least, not from my family.

"Don't look so surprised," Mom continues, giving me a reproachful look. "You left with no plan, no safety net, and I worried. Oh, how I worried."

One of the women murmurs, "It's what moms do."

"But I shouldn't have. You did well, thriving and creating a new you." Mom smiles. "I see you, the new you. And I like him very much."

I don't really know what to say. This just went from awkward to humiliating. "Uh, thanks?"

"So," Mom says primly, "tell me about you."

"Mom . . ." She gives me a sharp look, and resigned, I figure out what to say. "I have my own business, my own place, both of which I enjoy."

One of the women leans forward, greedy for more. "Friends? Girlfriends? A grand-dog for your mother, for goodness' sakes?"

"No, no, and no," I answer in rapid-fire fashion. "But I'm happy."

Mom wants to argue, I can see that, but she doesn't. I'm not sure if it's in deference to me or to save face in front of the women. Instead, her eyes lower, and I think she's looking at her self-help book. Fidgeting with the edge of her notepad, she says quietly, "That's what I want—you to be happy. I just wish it was here . . . with us."

What to say? Finally, I decide to offer up some truth. "It's not all bad here. I'll give you that." Her eyes lift to mine, hopefully. "I'll come back to visit, I promise. Maybe you and Wren could even come to Newport?"

She claps her hands happily, clearly wanting to be part of my life still. "I would love that, honey. Maybe when things are less busy here?"

Busy? I don't think that's what's keeping Mom here, worried each day. That would be Dad. But she's not going to say that in front of everyone. That would ruin the appearance of everything being fine. *Just fine.*

But I won't hurt her now by pointing that out. "Sure. That'd be great."

Back to polite niceties, the same as always.

A few of the women sniffle. "It works. Just like the book said. Priorities really do restore your spirit," a blonde says, her hands over her chest and eyes looking teary.

Biting my tongue at their dramatics, I nod blankly. "With that, I'll leave you to your book club. I need to . . ." I trail off, almost having said I need to take a shower, but that would open the door to even more questions. "Prepare for my day."

It's enough, and I escape unscathed, hurrying upstairs to my room. After getting cleaned up, and using the warm spray of the shower to relieve the churning in my balls that I've felt since last night . . . I actually feel more or less human. Still, I haven't blown my load that fast since about three weeks after I discovered what jacking off meant.

I go back downstairs quietly, praying I'm not called to court again with the Mom Squad. Taking the long way around, I head out the front door and jump back in my truck, going slowly down the driveway when a yellow blur beside me catches my eye. I take my foot off the gas as the blur starts barking . . . loudly.

I brake and open the door. "Mr. Puddles . . . ssshhh!" He freezes, his tail wagging in the air and his chin near the ground, ready to play. "Fine, come on, boy." He yips once more and bolts for the truck. I sit back to give him space and he hops inside, climbing over my lap to the passenger seat like he always rides shotgun.

Then again, maybe he does.

I tell Mr. Puddles, "I don't know where we're going. I just needed to get out of there so I can think. That good with you?"

Mr. Puddles barks in answer, and I assume agreement. It's not quite "What's that, Lassie? Timmy fell down the well?" but I get the message.

"Good, let's go."

I drive into town, no real destination in mind. But I need to get my mind clear. As the blacktop rolls under my tires, everything that's happened since I got home runs through my mind . . . Winston and Avery, Mom and Dad, Hazel . . . Hazel . . . Hazel.

I get all the way downtown, and as I pass by City Hall, I see protesters with signs again: NO REZONE. SAVE OUR TOWN. FUCK FORD. And a few others.

I read them all, and it feels more real than it did when I first arrived. These people are yelling and marching around to protect not only land, but like Etta said, their way of life in Cold Springs.

Just beyond the protesters I see a billboard, Uncle Jed's cowboy-hat-topped, too-white smiling face . . . and a freshly spray-painted dick going into his mouth. Enough is enough. I need to see this potential subdivision for myself.

Hanging a left, I drive out of town, toward the land where Jed wants to build. As I do, I watch as the houses change, from the authentic historical brick builds of old-old Cold Springs, to the wood-frame and vinyl-sided homes that were built in the generation before I was born, to the prebuilt cookie cutters . . . and then manufactured homes with the occasional sprinkle of a beat-up wooden structure.

But despite the diminishing fanciness of the buildings, I see the pride and effort that people out here have. I see the effort that's been put into the farmland, the way every row has been harvested or planted carefully. I see the pastures with horses, donkeys, and cattle. The fences might not be perfectly strung with nice, fresh barbed wire—in fact, quite a few of the sections look worse for wear—but each section is mended with something, even if it's nothing more than what appears to be slender pines that have been dragged from the woods.

Still, for all the hard work and effort, I see the signs proving life has been harder than it should be for the residents. I see the rusted gates, so old that I doubt anyone knows where the key to the lock is, if it'd even open. I see the trash casually dumped in the drainage ditch that runs alongside the two-lane road, escapees from the backs of pickup trucks or tossed from windows on the way to the county dump.

But just because it's not pristine McMansions doesn't make it any less valuable. It doesn't give others the right to come in and basically steal it out from underneath the rightful landowners. I see how they want to live their lives, and how hard they're trying to hang on to the little they've got.

Jed would destroy them without a second thought. That much I know for certain. I decide to take a play from Wren's rule book, and with a smirk of evil delight, I drive back into downtown.

"Come on, Mr. Puddles," I tell the grinning goldendoodle as I pull into a parking spot outside a coffee shop near the protesters. "Let's get you a pup cup."

He barks and follows me out of the truck, trotting along at my side. He's well trained, waiting patiently outside the door as I go into a coffee shop to get supplies, including Mr. Puddles's small cup of whipped cream. But once he sees the fluffy goodness, he's impatient, so I stop and let him lick the cup clean, and once he's happy, I take the trays of coffees from the barista.

"Thanks," I tell her. Reaching into my pocket, I take out a twenty and stick it in the tip jar, earning a smile. Walking out, Mr. Puddles stays right by my side as I walk up the street to the protests. As I approach, I see wary looks.

"That's Wyatt Ford, right?"

"Yeah, Bill's boy."

"Ain't he . . . ?"

"I don't know. His sister—"

"And he's been hanging around Hazel—"

"Who'd like a coffee?" I ask, interrupting the questions and holding up the tray. "I promise, they're hot and fresh and from just down the street. My sister, Wren, says she does this from time to time?"

There're still wary looks, but Mr. Puddles is so friendly looking that I think he helps thaw the protesters, and soon the tray's empty. "So . . . whatcha here for?" an old man asks. He sips his coffee, nodding. "Nice."

"My brother's wedding," I answer, even though it's not what he wants to know.

My answer helps, though, and I hang out with the protesters. Some of them talk because I've given out coffee, some because Mr. Puddles is pretty much a cuddlebug who draws attention and snuggles constantly, and some because they want to fill me in on their point of view.

"My family's land ain't much," one man says as we walk back and forth along the sidewalk. "Fifty cows ain't going to make no man rich.

But my daddy taught me to hunt on that land. He's buried under the old oak tree, right next to my mama. And someday, I might be there too. And now Jed Ford wants to raze that all down so some damn fool can what? Park his Mercedes on top of my daddy's grave? Hell no!"

That's not the only story that I hear. These people, whether it's the farmer who raised three sons on his land to the old man who just wants to be able to retire in peace after spending his whole life working in a steel mill up north, they have their reasons.

So I walk with them, learning their tales. Mr. Puddles is the life of the party, too, getting head pats and belly scratches from all before lying down on the sidewalk to watch the activity.

Or he does for a few minutes before he falls asleep right in the middle of the circle, sort of marking the center of the protest line. That's fine by me . . . because for now I'm walking.

"Hey," I ask one of the protesters. "You have an extra sign?"

"Just one that says 'Fuck You, Ford,'" the guy replies uneasily. "Um . . . but I'll swap if you want to carry one?"

"Nah," I tell him with a laugh. "Gimme that sign. I'm fine with it."

Chapter 19

Hazel

"You are not gonna believe the shit I'm seeing with my own two eye-balls," Jesse says in my ear as I fumble with my phone and my hairbrush at the same time. Seriously, I should have pulled my hair back last night . . . or maybe let Wyatt do it for me.

I bet he'd tug on my hair just right.

"What? Your eyebrows separated by actual space instead of blend-ing into one stripe of bushy unibrow?"

"Funny," Jesse says snarkily. "I don't know, maybe I shouldn't tell you where your boy, Wyatt, is at right now? Or what he's up to."

I shouldn't ask. It's not like I have any rights to him. If he's sitting at a restaurant with someone else, even Rachel, that's his prerogative. Or if he's packing up his truck and heading out of town, that's also not my business. But damned if I don't want to know.

"What?" I ask tellingly. "Where?"

Jesse laughs. "That's what I figured. I'm downtown, filing a permit for a gig my crew's doing, and who do I see but Mr. William Wyatt Ford the third sitting in a folding camping chair, sipping coffee from a paper cup, a big ol' poster saying 'Fuck You, Ford' propped against his knees. Now, I don't think he was advertising his services, was he?"

Jesse's description is enough to make me realize . . . "He's talking to the protesters?"

"Nope," Jesse says, "he's chanting right along with them. Got his dog there by his side, wagging his tail and everything."

I must've misheard. There's no way. But . . . "He's . . . what?"

"That's what I said."

Holy shit. "I'll be right there." I almost hang up, but right before I do, I remember to say, "Thanks, Jesse!"

⚜

"Bye, Lester! Don't destroy anything while I'm gone!" I call as I run out the door less than ten minutes later, my makeup done but my hair a lost cause that I threw up into a messy bun for some semblance of being presentable.

I hear him call back, "Bawk! Bye, bitch!"

Nessa whines as I speed into town. She's not used to being pushed faster than fifty-five, but she doesn't sputter as she gives it all she's got. I pull into a parking spot by the coffee shop and climb out, virtually running for the square where the protesters usually set up.

I can almost feel the heels of my sneakers skidding to a stop when I see them and realize Jesse wasn't kidding. There's Wyatt, no longer sitting, but marching back and forth along the sidewalk with a sign that does indeed say **FUCK YOU, FORD** in big, bold letters. He looks sexy as fuck in worn jeans, a Henley shirt with the sleeves pushed up to show his ropy forearms, and dirty boots.

I'd bet this is his usual attire when he's at home in his workshop. I haven't been able to picture it, used to seeing him in his fancy suit for the wedding or the nicer casual wear he's worn into the restaurant, but now?

Oh, I can see it. I can nearly smell the sawdust and linseed oil on him in my imagination, and it's giving me a serious case of girl-wood.

Slowly, not to interrupt or break the spell of whatever I'm watching, I approach, wanting to observe him. By sticking to his blind side, I'm able to get close enough to watch him stop and start talking to a shopper: ". . . and these folks, they've got lives. Family connections. We can talk all we want about there's other places they could move to, but those places aren't *home*, you know?"

He hands the shopper a flyer and picks up his sign again. I decide it's my time to approach. "Never would've believed it if I didn't see it with my own eyes," I tease. "You've crossed over to the Dark Side."

Wyatt turns and I watch his smile grow when he sees me, at first delighted and then heated. "Can I talk to you about the petition to prevent rezoning in Cold Springs?"

If the guys who call about my car's extended warranty asked me like that—with an undercurrent of pure sex—Nessa would be the most warrantied vehicle in existence. Thankfully, only Wyatt has taken this particular approach.

"Ever heard the expression 'I'm a sure thing'?" I reply, biting my lip and flirting back just as heavily. "I'd use it here except I already signed."

"As long as you *support* the cause."

I lick the corner of my mouth, grinning. "Oh, I'm *real* supportive." I hold my hands out, palms up and rising and lowering like I'm holding a Slinky . . . or something decidedly more delicate. "I make sure I support just right."

Wyatt nearly tosses his poster to one of the other protesters and pulls me off to the side so we can talk privately. Or as private as it gets when you're nose to nose with a Ford on a downtown sidewalk. "You know what you're doing to me?"

I cock an eyebrow, still playing just a bit. "You sound like quite the passionate convert. What magic spell did Etta put you under last night?" I run a finger down his chest and feel him take a breath beneath my touch. "Or was there other magic involved?"

But Wyatt frowns. "More like a hex. She can be quite bewitching. It made me think, and today, I went for a drive out to the proposed subdivision site. Came to one conclusion: Jed's got to be stopped," he says earnestly, running a hand through his hair restlessly. "So I just . . . did the first thing I could think of."

I agree wholeheartedly, and hearing those words come out of his mouth is like a shot of caffeine straight to my ovaries. I pop up to my toes so I can kiss the absolute stuffing out of him, my hands cupping his cheeks so hard that he probably looks like a chipmunk, especially when I feel his smile. I drop back to my feet, and he laughs.

"What was that for?"

"For being you. Exactly as you are."

Wyatt scoffs lightly. "Can't say many people have told me that."

I shrug, not caring what other people think. "Well, they're dumbasses who don't know you like I do."

I slip my hand into his and pull him back toward the group. Wyatt pauses, giving me a concerned look. "Where are we going?"

"To work." I hold my free hand out and get Wyatt's Fuck You, Ford sign back.

Holding hands, we each take a corner of the posterboard, becoming a two-person parade. More and more people join us, and together, we get louder and louder. One of the women creates a funny chant about Jed, and we shout it as we march along the sidewalk.

Well, it's funny to me . . .

"Stop Jed, the cockhead!" I shout at the top of my lungs, stomping along with the rhythm, and Wyatt does the same beside me.

Even Mr. Puddles gets in on the marching, practically leading the whole parade.

Word starts to spread that something special is happening today, something beyond the typical protest. I don't know what prompted the change from the usual rally, but this is louder, bigger, and crazier than ever before.

"We need music!" someone calls out, and within minutes a phone is hooked up to their truck's speakers, doors open and modified Johnny Cash pouring out over downtown as someone sings "A Boy Named Jed."

The whole group laughs as the improv lyricist includes lines such as "Seems I had to live with my great shame, the gals would giggle hearin' my name. The guys would laugh and I'd hang my head, over my two-inch penis as a boy named Jed."

"He's not going to like that one," I tell Wyatt, who's laughing and cheering the lyricist on. "You think he'll call people in to break this up?"

"Nah," Wyatt assures me. "He'll be embarrassed, but he thinks these people are just a speed bump. He's too arrogant to see the truth."

"What's that?" I ask, and he looks around. "Wyatt?"

"This isn't a protest . . . This is the start of a movement," he says. "Look."

I look where he's pointing, and I see Sue-Ellen's granddaughter, who's the Cold Springs High band drum major, leading a good portion of the band toward the music truck, instruments in hand. When "A Boy Named Jed" finishes, the band takes over, the drums and horns a great addition that gets even more attention.

"Sue-Ellen!" I call, seeing her. "Did you do that?"

"Damn right!" Sue-Ellen says, grinning. "We're going to make sure everyone hears our voices!"

Sue-Ellen designates herself the de facto emcee of this street party–slash-protest, commandeering the improv singer's microphone to lead our ragtag crew. With the band tooting along with her, she sings in a leather-lunged voice, "*Ford!* Huah! Good God! What is he good for?"

I look at Wyatt and grin, and we both join in, chanting, "Absolutely nothin'!" Someone starts stomp-dancing to it, and soon, I can feel what Wyatt means.

To the untrained eye, it's a party in the street, with some protesting thrown in. The chanting to songs, the dance-like stomping, and the signs waving as we move as one.

But for all the fun and games—because, oh yeah, people are bumping a beach ball along overhead—this is serious business. And people know it. Whether it's the music that's being chosen, lots of protest songs, some country music, one iteration of "We're Not Gonna Take It," and the band doing a very good "Sunday Bloody Sunday," there's a clear thread running through all this.

We're pissed.

We're unified.

And we're not backing down.

As it gets later in the day, people start to leave the offices downtown. I can see the shocked glances as the suited professionals see our group. A few pause to talk, and some even join in, knowing that this isn't about suits or work boots. This is about right and wrong.

When the city council members leave their courthouse offices, a fresh surge of energy shoots through the crowd.

"Hey, ho! Why you got *bone* for Jed's *rezone?*" we yell directly at the city council members, letting them know that their constituents are well aware of who's driving the rezoning push, and being in Jed's pocket is not in their best interest.

That's all well and good, and might even be successful at swaying a council member or two, until Bill Ford steps out into the setting sunlight.

He stands on the steps of the courthouse, his hands balling at his hips as he surveys the scene. But nothing matches the look on his face when Wyatt gets up into the bed of the pickup truck and takes the microphone in hand, leading the chants for a minute before passing it back to Sue-Ellen.

Honestly, Bill Ford looks like he's about to burst a blood vessel. But I care more about Wyatt's reaction as he sets his shoulders wide and thrusts his fist in the air, ready to take on the world and his family. The protesters see it, too, looking between the elder Ford and the younger, locked in a battle as old as time.

Finally, Bill Ford finds his voice and raises his hand, shouting, "We need to keep these streets clear. You're creating a potential hazard by blocking the street. Move along."

He sounds like a pompous ass, and though he's got everyone's attention, no one is actually listening. They're rolling their eyes and chuckling to themselves. Until he threatens, "If necessary, I will call the police to clear the street."

"Seriously?" someone next to me hisses.

"I can't go to jail. I'm too cute for that," someone else says.

An idea comes to me like a bolt of brilliant lightning. "Let's move to the Puss N Boots. We can use it as a headquarters to plan our next steps."

Aunt Etta won't mind. Hell, she'll be excited about the influx of business and supportive of the cause. I'm pretty sure she's been out here protesting, too, when she's had time, which isn't nearly often enough.

Sue-Ellen nods. "To Puss N Boots!" she shouts into the microphone. The implication that this isn't over is bold and ballsy, but Bill doesn't react, nor does he spare a single glance for Wyatt as he descends the stairs and walks past the group of protesters.

Right up until he spies Mr. Puddles, who's fallen asleep on a bench from all the walking. Sounding hurt, Bill says, "Come on, boy. Let's go home." Mr. Puddles whines and comes over to sit at Wyatt's side.

But after a head pat for the loyalty, Wyatt tells the sleepy dog, "Go on, Mr. Puddles. Get dinner. Go home with Dad."

The dog licks Wyatt's hand and then obediently trots off after Bill.

"You okay?" I ask, worried. "That was a hell of a confrontation."

Wyatt turns to me, his beautiful eyes hard as marbles. "Fine. Let's go."

When he takes my hand this time, he grips me a bit too tightly, but I squeeze back reassuringly to let him know that whatever happens, he's not alone as he deals with his family.

Chapter 20

WYATT

Hazel and I march along with the other protesters, making our way to Puss N Boots. As we march, Sue-Ellen yells into the microphone a bit nonsensically, "Hell no, we won't go!"

I think someone's had a few too many memories of the Vietnam days, or maybe too many movies. Finally, someone pulls the microphone away from her to tell her, "We're literally leaving, Sue-Ellen."

She blinks, blank-faced, and then tries again, going back to her earlier chant: "Stop Jed, the cockhead!"

That works, and everyone joins in.

I agree, but right now, I'm more flummoxed by Dad. What the hell is he doing?

Threatening people with the police for making their wishes heard?

Is that what being a mayor is about to him these days? Because that sure as hell isn't what fills my memories.

We barge into Puss N Boots with all the grace and manners of feral hogs. Etta comes out from behind the bar to meet us, hands on her hips and a frown on her face. "What in the h-e-double hockey sticks is going on here?"

Hazel lets go of my hand and pushes her way to the front of the crowd, one hand waving in the air as she goes. "It's me, Aunt Etta. I brought everyone over here because Mayor Ford threatened to call the cops on us."

That changes Etta's tune, her eyes lighting with delighted fire. "For what? Did y'all burn the courthouse down or something?"

"Of course not. Protesting the rezoning. Loudly," Hazel explains.

She points back at the assembled group as Sue-Ellen starts up the party again. "Stop Jed, the cockhead!"

Etta bursts out in laughter, nearly doubling over as she slaps her thighs. "*Holy shiiit*, that's the best thing I've ever heard. Might need to change my window sign to that." She looks around with a smile and tells us, "Well, come on in then. Tayvious!"

He's already peering through the window, watching the show. "Yep, Boss Lady?"

"You'd best get that fryer a-poppin'. Fries all night, don't stop till I tell ya to."

Tayvious flashes a thumbs-up, rolling his shoulders. "Heard."

Etta, just as loudly as Sue-Ellen even without the microphone, says, "If you ain't against the rezoning, you'd best get out now. We're having a meeting!"

No one moves, only eyes looking around at each other to see if anyone's going to leave. When no one does, Etta spins and walks back behind the bar.

I think that's the end of it until Charlene steps forward, popping her gum. "Alright, listen and listen good, Hazel Sullivan. You'd best get your apron on and get to helping me or I will tell everyone in town about the time you . . ."

Hazel cuts her off, to my pique. "I'm getting it. Keep your trap shut. You're not the only one who knows the tea." She's threatening her friend, but when she turns around and comes back to me, she's smiling. "I gotta go. But thank you . . ."

"For what?" I ask, and Hazel takes my hand.

"For this." She looks left and right at the townspeople around us. "For staying, and . . . for this." She wraps her arms around my neck and kisses me fiercely. I grab her ass and kiss her back, my lips hard against hers.

There's a lot that might need to be said, but now is not the time.

"We'll figure it out."

I'm about to kiss her again when Charlene yells, "Hazel! I don't wait on my little hellions, who I love more than life itself, so I'm damn sure not waiting on you, honey-baby."

"That's my cue!" Hazel says, and with that, she's gone.

Sue-Ellen finds a chair, but instead of sitting, she stands on it, looming over everyone. "It's been a while since I've organized a revolution, but I remember the good stuff."

Um, what? Is she serious about being a revolutionary before? Honestly, I can see it. Sue-Ellen probably led some flower-crown-wearing hippies back in her day, calling out "make love, not war" as loudly as she's been chanting today.

Etta comes over to join us, asking, "What's the game plan?"

Sue-Ellen tells her, "That's what we need to figure out."

She climbs down and they continue talking, the various townspeople adding ideas here and there. Apparently, Sue-Ellen is the original proposer of the petition, but a presentation of signed disagreement with the rezoning at the hearing isn't nearly enough for this mob now. They begin brainstorming, Etta writing everyone's various ideas on a chalkboard.

I stay off to the back, my attention centered on Hazel. She's in her element, delivering baskets of fries and pitchers of beer and water around the room with smiles as she chats with people, reassuring them that everything's going to be okay. I watch her, mesmerized by her every movement, every word I can hear.

Etta and Sue-Ellen are midargument with Fred, one of the other protesters I met today, when the door opens. A pair of uniformed officers strut in, looking around shrewdly.

Charlene must've been an amazing actress in a former life, because she clicks on instantly, sashaying her way toward the officer in front and placing her arm through his elbow, though he didn't offer it.

"Well, hello there, Officer Milson. It's been way too long since you've come in to see me. Should I take offense to that?" She gives him puppy-dog eyes, her lower lip puffed out in a pout.

Officer Milson smiles, charmed by her flirting. "Nah, Charlene. No offense intended, just been busy is all."

Charlene walks her fingers up his bicep. "Well, okay then. As long as you promise that we can get busy sometime too. A girl needs a chicken-fried steak and a two-dollar margarita every now and again, just as much as a guy like you needs a night out. Or a night in."

Her wink has more innuendo than a Jason Derulo song, and Officer Milson is eating it up, right out of the palm of Charlene's hand. In fact, he takes her hand and places a polite kiss to the back of it. Still, I take a moment to check, and yeah, he's not wearing a wedding ring.

Good . . . although I really should have never doubted Charlene.

"Sorry to cut this short, babe, but I'm here on official city business tonight," Milson says, letting go of her hand.

"Sure thing, honey-baby. What business you got?" Charlene asks, clearly still trying to stall things. "Need a rush-order Fat Pussy to get you through your shift?"

Officer Milson looks like he wants to taste those words on Charlene's freshly glossed lips, but instead he asks, "Etta around?"

"Um, depends on why you're asking."

She's a good employee, but an even better friend, and I think she'd sneak Etta out the back door while holding off Officer Milson, despite their obvious history, if the situation warranted it.

Milson gets it, too, and pats her gently on the shoulder. "I understand. We all got jobs to do." Louder, he says, "Hey, Etta?"

His voice grabs the attention of everyone in Puss N Boots, especially Etta. "Hey, Robbie! What are you boys doing here?"

"That's Officer Milson tonight," he corrects Etta gently, who's making her way through the crowd toward the officers.

She smiles, warm and sharp as a hot knife through butter. "Well, considering I knew your mama before she even got married, much less had you, and I remember you with that cute little snaggletooth smile you used to have, I reckon I'll stick with Robbie. Unless you'd like to skip out on the friends and family discount next time you come in for dinner?"

Ooh, that's a threat if ever I heard one, even if a 50 percent discount on a ten-dollar dinner doesn't seem all that serious.

"Now, Etta, no need to get mad like that," Milson says with as much chagrin as a cop on duty can muster. "I'm just here on police business, so it only seems right."

Etta dips her chin in deference, though I feel certain she's never deferred to a single thing in her entire life.

"Thank you. Now, Etta—"

She holds up her palm. "I believe you meant to say Ms. Livingston, Officer Milson."

Oooh. You say *potato*, I say *poh-tah-toe*, and you better believe it isn't nearly the same thing for them to request using formal names. Milson sighs heavily, the muscle in his jaw working furiously as he becomes more businesslike. "Fine. Ms. Livingston, we got a report of some criminal mischief here tonight and wanted to see if everything is okay . . ."

He looks around pointedly, taking special note of the bulleted list on the chalkboard scoreboard that says "Suck it, Jed" at the top.

The list has exciting ideas that've been discussed tonight:

1. Expose family secrets?
(I assured everyone there were none.)

2. Does he have a sex tape?
(Etta handled that one, saying yes, but that she deleted it long ago because she didn't want *her* sex tape to get out. Understandable, but also . . . ew.)

3. Possible archeological burial ground?
(Sue-Ellen suggested that one as a way to stop Jed on the zoning front instead of a personal attack, but as far as anyone knows, there are no mass grave sites in the area. And while that's a good thing if we ever undergo a zombie apocalypse, right now, it's one less useful idea.)

Etta follows his gaze, then declares, "Nope, no mischief here. Or at least, no more than usual. We're getting ready to start our pool tournament is all."

Milson's brows rise disbelievingly. "Pool tournament?"

I didn't even see him here, but from out of nowhere, Roddy interrupts to corroborate Etta's story. "Yep, we're settling on brackets. Winner gets to play Hazel for twenty bucks. And bragging rights, of course."

Well, hell, I certainly wouldn't have expected Roddy to come to Etta's aid, nor to use Hazel as the details of his lie, but here he is, doing just that. Milson laughs, grinning at Roddy. "You think you got a shot against Hazel? I heard she wiped the floor with you last time and you got your panties all in a twist."

He's playing along with the story, giving me hope that maybe he's not all bad either. But he did come here with some ridiculous story of criminal mischief. So it's with a mix of curiosity and frustration that I ask, "Who made that report tonight, Officer?"

Officer Milson looks to me and, for the first time, realizes that there's a Ford here, at what is obviously a Jed Ford protest meeting despite the tournament cover story. "Well, that's usually confidential. Anonymous tip, you know." He winks, quick and small, letting me know that he's just trying to keep things civil while not getting his ass in a sling at the station. "But sometimes it's helpful to get quarreling parties together, see if an understanding can be worked out for the good of keeping the peace."

Etta's down with that, I can tell. And she wants things to be peaceful, too, so she says, "For sure, that's completely understandable. I'd totally be open to some mediation with whoever's sticking their nose in my legal and privately owned small business events."

Then again, that was pure acid. Sarcasm, thy name is a country woman whose livelihood is being threatened. Milson notes it too. "Well, I'll be sure to let Mr. Hancock know that. If he's agreeable as well, we'll get the two of you set down around a table to talk things out."

Etta grins. "Thank you, Robbie."

"No problem." Quieter, he says, "You think me and Marcus could get burgers to go?"

Etta reaches up, pinching the adult officer on the cheek as though he's an adorable two-year-old who shit on the toilet for the first time. "Sure thing. On the house this one time."

Releasing her squeeze, she pats his cheek twice, each of them more of a slap than a love tap, and calls out to Tayvious. "Two Fat Pussies to go. And, Charlene, can you grab these fine boys a couple of brownies too? Marcus is looking a might thin."

Quicker than ever, Tayvious has the two burgers ready and sets the Styrofoam boxes in the window. "Bye, Marcus. You be safe out there on these dangerous streets, Daddy."

Marcus blushes despite his brown skin and walks toward the bar to grab the to-go order. "Hey, Tay. Thanks for dinner."

Tayvious's eyes gleam. "You know it's gonna be *goood*. I put my foot in it every time, but I put a little extra love in yours." He kisses two fingers and rubs them on the lid of the Styrofoam box suggestively.

I really need to pay attention to things more, it seems. Cold Springs is a regular soap opera.

Charlene grabs the box from under Tayvious's affection with a scowl. "No way. If I ain't getting any dick, neither are you." Turning to Marcus, she shoves the to-go boxes and two plastic-wrapped brownies his way. "Bye now."

The two officers leave but take the urgency of the protest meeting with them. Seeing that nobody's going to get their head busted, but also that there's not going to be any kicking ass and taking names tonight, they simmer down to a lot of talk and not much else. Sue-Ellen yawns, and says, "It's past my bedtime, so I think I'll head on home."

A few others agree and start to gather their things, packing up to leave.

Roddy catches Hazel as she walks by and says, "I know the tournament was a stupid story, but we could play? No bets. Just for fun. I swear I'll be good."

Hazel's eyes find mine, and she holds up a finger to Roddy before coming my way. She steps between my knees, putting her arms over my shoulders. "You wanna hang out a bit? Or we could go back to my place?"

I lean in, putting my forehead to hers to keep the conversation between us. "I think I'm going to head home tonight. I bet Dad'll be waiting to rip me a new one. Either way, might as well get it over with." Hazel's worry makes tiny lines appear beside her eyes. I see them only because we're so close. I reach up to smooth them away. "It'll be okay. I can handle him."

She swallows and then confesses, "I'm afraid he's going to run you off. If you're gonna leave, can you . . . can you at least let me know first?"

"I'm not going anywhere," I promise.

She searches my eyes, hers flicking left and right as she measures the invisible, unspoken timeline of my words. "It's okay. I always knew you'd go home eventually. But I want to know you're okay. Otherwise,

I'm going to storm your house and probably beat the tar out of your dad." She tries to laugh, but it's so forced, it gets stuck in her throat.

"I'll let you know," I amend, giving her the vow she wants, though I truly have no plans of going anywhere. Not when damn near the whole town came out tonight to stand up to my family.

Not when Hazel is here.

She nods and steps back, turning in the space between my legs to throw an arm around my shoulder. With a forced smile, she calls out, "Okay, pool tournament's on. Who'm I beating first?"

Roddy raises his hand, volunteering. "You want me to get your cue for you?"

Hazel points a sharp finger his way, back to her normal level of sass and boss. "Don't you touch Joan of Arc."

"I'll get her," Etta offers.

People begin to tease Roddy, and despite the assertion that it's a friendly game, bets are being placed, all on Hazel—how many shots it'll take her to win, how many games she'll win before Roddy quits, how fast she can clear the table, and on and on. But she stays with me, her arm resting on my shoulders. It's a quiet declaration . . . who she's with.

I appreciate it. "Your fans await," I tease, squeezing her hip. "Do yourself proud."

She runs her fingers through my hair, her smile melting. "I'm not going to kiss you because that would feel too much like goodbye."

I swallow thickly, knowing what she means. "How about I'll see you tomorrow?"

She nods, unconvinced, and walks away, toward the pool tables. She looks back once, her eyes saying all the things she wouldn't. A lot of me wants to ignore what I need to do and cross the crowded room, pull her back into my arms, and kiss her so hard she'll never doubt me. Instead, I get up and make a quiet exit once I see that she's doing what she does best . . . owning the pool table.

The drive home is fast, or maybe it just seems that way. I step inside with steel in my spine, ready for anything. Instead, I find a quiet house. I look into the living room, expecting Dad to be on the couch, waiting in the dark. But then a figure appears in the doorway to the kitchen.

"Wyatt? Be quiet, please. Your father is asleep, and we really shouldn't wake him."

"Leo?" I ask, so surprised I forget to whisper.

In the shadows, I see an arm lift toward a face, and Leo nods. "Yes. Shh."

The kitchen light flicks on, too bright in the darkness, and I wince. Leo looks like he's aged a decade in a day, and he waves me down before gesturing me forward. "Come on. I'll make you a cup of coffee."

I go into the kitchen with Leo, thankful that my greeting is from him and not Dad, until Leo begins to tell me what's been going on here tonight while I was at Puss N Boots . . .

Chapter 21

WYATT

Wren opens my door without knocking, slipping through the small crack she's created before shutting it behind her. My glare of displeasure is wasted as she presses her ear to the door, completely ignoring me.

"What are you doing, Wren?"

In response, she holds up a finger, telling me to wait, though she's the one barging into my room, interrupting my midmorning attempt at research, trying to find any way to stop Jed.

Wren must not hear anything through the door because, after a moment, she turns. "Coast is clear. For now. But we should get out of here."

She walks over to my duffel bag, digging around to grab clothes, and hisses, "Move it or we're going to be late." She throws clothes at me as she finds what she's looking for . . . T-shirt, jeans, socks, boxers.

The T-shirt hits me in the face because I wasn't prepared, but I catch the jeans and socks, and by the time she finds my boxers, I've gathered my brain enough to say, "Those are dirty. Clean ones are in the dresser."

She drops the boxers like they've morphed into a venomous snake that's going to bite her, muttering something that sounds suspiciously like, "I'm going to need hand sanitizer, hot water, and bleach to get the jizz off my hands."

I laugh. "There's no jizz on them. I take 'em off first. Might be a bit of piss, though. Shaking it just doesn't get every drop, you know?"

"Oh my god! Disgusting!" Wren snaps, recoiling in horror while wiping her hand on her jeans. I laugh again, and she whisper-shouts, "Shh! How can you joke at a time like this?"

"Time like what?" I ask suspiciously.

She moves to the dresser, opening various drawers until she finds what she wants and throwing me clean clothes this time. "I heard about the protest. Good job, by the way. But Dad and Jed were plotting all evening, so we need to go. Like right now."

That's enough to get me up and moving. "What? When I got home, Leo said Mom was on the phone all evening, getting more and more worried about Dad not coming home after work or picking up her calls. And that Dad eventually came home drunk and passed out again. I knew he was mad about the protest, but what are they up to?"

"I'll tell you on the way," Wren says with a shake of her head.

I slip into the bathroom to get dressed, brush my teeth, and run wet fingers through my hair. I catch a glimpse of myself in the mirror and realize that for the first time in a long time, I have fire in my eyes.

My life in Newport is calm and serene by design, and I appreciate every moment of that. But some things are worth disrupting the peace.

"Alright, I'm ready," I tell Wren as I come back into my bedroom.

She's sitting on the edge of my bed, looking at my computer screen approvingly. Thank God it was research, though it would've served her nosy ass right to find some crazy porn instead.

She places a finger to her lips. "Down the back stairs, out the dining room window, and around the house. We'll take my car."

I still don't know what I'm getting into with Wren, but she's got a head start on me this morning, considering I was having zero luck in finding some magical wand to wave and stop Jed, so I'm on board with her plan.

We tiptoe down the hall and follow the path she suggested, successfully rolling down the driveway in Wren's quiet Tesla.

Still, she looks behind her several times until we're out of Cold Springs.

Finally, I ask, "You think Dad's going to send the cops after you? Pull you over the way he had them come into Puss N Boots last night?"

Wren shrugs. "At this point, I don't know. He's in bad shape, Wyatt. Leo's right: Dad did come home drunk, but he didn't pass out right away. I heard him in his office, muttering to himself and ranting. He's pissed."

"Yeah, I could tell by the stone-cold look he gave me when he saw me with the protesters."

Wren takes her eyes from the road long enough to look at me carefully. "Well, you did basically stand up and give him a big giant 'fuck you' moment."

"Wasn't my intent. I just needed him to realize the people he's hurting aren't alone."

Wren nods, and sighs. "Yeah. Well, he's not mad at you. Okay, maybe a bit," she corrects. "But he's mad at Jed. And furious with himself."

"I thought they were plotting together? That's what you said."

"They are, but that doesn't mean Dad's happy about it," Wren says, her voice tight. "He's in over his head, big-time, and I think he's starting to realize it."

Her sigh is heavy with the weight she's been shouldering. Dad might not expect the same things from Wren as he always has from Winston and me, but that doesn't mean she didn't expect them from herself. And with me gone and Winston working with Jed, she's been the one at home, helping Mom deal with Dad's spiral.

"I'm sorry I left you to handle all this," I tell her quietly.

"You're here now. That's what matters," Wren says before looking side eye at me. "You are here, right? Not going to disappear on us again?"

The question is so similar to Hazel's last night that it hits the same spot, making the pain double. But I choose my words carefully. "I haven't made plans to go back to Newport. I'm here to see this through, and then . . . I don't know."

She glances at me, hope blooming in her eyes. "Good enough for now."

She pulls up to the airport, parking on the sidewalk, and grabs her phone, making quick work of sending a text. A moment later, Winston and Avery come out the automated doors, wheeling a suitcase each.

I get out of the car to help them put the luggage in the trunk, confused at why they're back from their honeymoon so early. They're not scheduled to return until next week. "Uh, hey, guys."

Winston glares at me. "Seriously? 'Hey, guys'?" he mocks me. "That's all you've got?"

"What?"

I look from Winston to Avery, whose eyes are bloodshot and purple smudged, so I don't see it coming when my brother steps in close enough to send an uppercut into my gut.

I wheeze, bending in half. "What. The. Fuck?"

Winston leans down, growling, "I was on my honeymoon, asshole."

Avery takes his arm, soothing my brother as she pulls him away from me. "It's okay. We'll go on a trip another time. I want to check on Grandpa Joe anyway."

Winston grunts and grabs both suitcases, tossing them into the trunk angrily.

Straightening up, I look to Wren and repeat, "What the fuck?"

Wren forces a plastic smile, ignoring my question. "Well, now that the gang's all here, let's get going. Um, Avery . . . you want to go to your place?"

Avery smiles sweetly and nods. "Yeah, you three can talk and I'll make Grandpa Joe's favorite cowboy cookies for everyone."

We climb in the car, and I start to ask Winston what the hell crawled up his ass and died, but Wren cuts me off. "Not yet. Let's do that all at once. First, I want to hear about the short honeymoon you did have."

Winston lifts his chin, meeting Wren's eyes in the rearview mirror, but then looks out the window.

Avery answers instead, telling us about the beach outside their villa, and the seals that would come right up onshore. "We had fresh seafood every day, and if we tossed the fish, the seals would catch it. I clapped for them, and then they started clapping back for themselves too. It was basically the most adorable thing ever."

Wren gives Avery a small, but genuine, smile. "Sounds like it," she answers, but she's glancing in the mirror at Winston and keeping her eye on me at the same time. Considering what's just happened, she's probably worried we're going to start beating the hell out of each other.

And while I definitely don't like my brother putting one in my ribs . . . I'm going to let it slide until I know more about what the hell's going on.

Wren pulls up to what must be Avery's house. It's a cottage-style place that looks small from the outside. I'd guess two bedrooms at most, but it's well cared for, solid and strong, with a recent white paint job with beige trim.

The inside's just as neat as the outside, with worn but clean and well-cared-for hardwood floors, walls that are the same light green as the trim, and furniture that's clean but just this side of needing retirement.

And Grandpa Joe, who's sitting in a gray fabric recliner and looking spry as ever. "Well now, don't tell me I went and forgot a whole week!" he says as Avery goes over to give him a kiss on the cheek. "If I did, you might need to check my drawers. I probably dropped a deuce or two I'm not noticing!"

"No, we came back early," Avery says with a smile. "And you look great, Grandpa Joe. I hope you don't mind I came with . . . well, guests."

"Guests?" Joe says, then grins. "Look like family to me. You look good, Winston."

"Thanks, Joe."

"Wren, pretty as ever," Joe says before his eyes go to me and I can see him lick his lips, looking for my name most likely.

"Wyatt, sir," I remind him, offering a hand. "Remember me from the wedding?"

Joe grins, and shakes. "Yeah I do, you're the one that forgot how to escort a pretty young lady down the aisle and thought it was an all-you-can-eat buffet, pick the one you want."

"Um, well . . ." He's not wrong, but I look to Avery for backup, not wanting to explain myself to Joe. He sees the move and takes full advantage of my imbalance and leans forward, dropping the feet of his recliner.

"How's that working out for you? Our Hazel is a might bit . . ." He pauses, tapping his temple as he searches for the word.

"Amazing?" I suggest after a moment, strongly implying he should choose his next words carefully.

Grandpa Joe laughs. "I was going for *headstrong* and *mouthy*, but I think *amazing* works just fine." He smiles and I feel like I received some degree of approval from Grandpa Joe.

Avery is quick to take the win, and beams. "Grandpa, can I put *The Price Is Right* on for you while I make some cookies? The Fords need to have a little family chitchat."

"I reckon you can, but make sure you don't turn the TV up too loud," Grandpa Joe says before dropping a wink. "I want to be able to eavesdrop from my recliner."

Avery rolls her eyes, helping Grandpa Joe get set up just the way he likes. His home health aide shows up just as she brings out a mug of warm milk and assures us that she'll keep an eye on Joe while discreetly keeping her earbuds in, listening to her own program on her phone.

Assured as we can be, we sit down at Avery's kitchen table, silent until she gets back and starts pulling out ingredients to bake. Wren decides to take the lead. "Okay, let's start from the beginning. Wyatt, you go first. Tell us about your day yesterday and how you ended up at the biggest protest in Cold Springs history."

I'm surprised, and ask, "That wasn't the usual?"

Wren snorts. "No, the protests are typically a bunch of folks sitting in folding chairs and waving signs. There's more action at the Episcopal Church dog show. Definitely no music festivals and mini-parades downtown that are only missing clowns on stilts and floats with people throwing candy."

Huh. I hadn't really thought about how big the protest had gotten. It'd felt like everyone had a common cause and was letting their thoughts be known, especially when Dad came out, but I guess it makes sense that the protests would amp up the closer we get to the hearing.

I explain about driving out to the subdivision site, feeling compelled to go back to the protesters, and how things grew organically from there. I gloss over a few things, but tell Wren and Winston about Dad coming out, marching to Puss N Boots, and everyone planning. I wrap up with going home to Leo saying Mom was on the phone all night and Dad came home drunk and passed out.

"I can fill in the gaps on some of that," Winston says, sounding a lot calmer than he was at the airport. "Dad went to Jed's, and they were arguing about what to do. They're worried about the hearing, and that's the pivot point that sets the whole next phase off. It'll determine whether this project is a success from the beginning."

"How do you know that?" I ask, and Winston gives me a stern look.

"Because they called me, I'd like to point out again, on my honeymoon. The first call came while I was about to enjoy a private hot tub with my new wife wearing the swimsuit she bought specifically for our trip."

His anger makes perfect sense now. I shake my head, and yeah, I feel a little ashamed. Not by what I did, but the timing? Yeah, that sucks. "Fuck! I'm sorry, man. Sorry, Avery."

Winston grinds his teeth for a moment. My brother must have a colossal case of blue balls at this point, but eventually he lets it go with a nod.

"I'll let you have that punch for free then," I add, and Winston snorts.

"As if you'd be able to give me a receipt for it."

That's my brother, and I grin. "We both know I would have tried. And succeeded. But nah, let's just let it go. Honeymoons should be sacred."

The image of Winston on his honeymoon, romancing his new bride, only to be interrupted by Dad and Jed's bitching, roils my stomach. It's not my fault exactly, but apparently me being at the protest was a match to the gasoline that started yesterday's dumpster fire.

"What are they going to do?" Wren asks, eager to move on. "Dad and Jed?"

"They talked about making the hearing private, but they think the townspeople will storm the meeting," Winston says, turning back to business. "Or making the votes private, but there are bylaws about that. Basically, anything that's a secret vote by the council has no force of law, is what Dad says. So I think their main plan is to run Wyatt out of town."

"Me?" I ask, stunned. "Why?"

Winston frowns sadly. "Because, like you warned me, I'm already in their pocket, and Wren isn't going to change the outcome. But you might. You were the one standing up in the back of a pickup truck thrusting his fist in the air."

Weight crashes onto my shoulders—responsibility, expectations, involvement in something so big and important that I don't want to mess with it. A part of me wants to run back to Newport, settle back into my easy life, where I have to worry about only myself and my customers.

But this is important.

Too many people depend on this, on maintaining Cold Springs, on this community, as Etta called it.

I won't abandon them now. "What are we going to do?"

"First thing you're gonna do," Avery says as she brings over a small plate laden with heavenly-smelling sweetness, "is eat a cookie. No good decisions were ever made on an empty stomach."

I don't think many revolutions have been planned over cookies, either, but they are delicious, and help as we talk and talk about everything we know about Jed, the subdivision, and the land.

"What about your thing at Puss N Boots?" Winston asks. "What happened?"

"Nothing particularly helpful," I admit, frustrated. "They suggested blackmailing Jed over family secrets or sex tapes. Both voted down because there are none. At least not since Etta deleted her tape."

I pause to make a disgusted face, which is echoed by Winston, Wren, and Avery. From the living room, Grandpa Joe shouts, "Hell, even I wouldn't watch that, and I'm pretty hard up for porn these days. Etta, she's a pretty thing. But Jed, he'd likely make my pecker shrivel up and fall off."

I laugh, but try to push it down when Avery shouts, "Grandpa Joe! Nobody wants to hear about your wiener!"

Trying to distract from Grandpa Joe's fairly accurate, and funny, commentary, I say, "The other suggestion was checking to see if the land is an ancient cemetery. But as far as I know, we're not living in a live-action version of *Poltergeist*."

Wren adds, "A corpse army might be worth considering . . . if they're on our side."

Grandpa Joe calls out from the living room, "You young 'uns talking about the farms outside town again? Man, we used to go out there all the time, hide out in the barns, and get drunk as a skunk on moonshine. Why, I remember this one time, we plucked a whole row of Abel's cabbages and were wearing them as fig-leaf briefs to cover our ding-a-lings. But one gust of wind and the girls would lose theirs because they couldn't hold three leaves at a time." He chuckles but it turns into a cough.

Winston shakes his head, squeezing the bridge of his nose in annoyance as he mutters, "Beach, water, sunshine, my bride by my side. But noooo . . ."

"Sorry again," I tell him, placing a comforting hand on his shoulder. I highly suspect I'm going to need to do this about a thousand more times . . . maybe pay for a second honeymoon for them, somehow.

Winston shrugs me off, looking up from beneath his brows. "It's not your fault. This is what I signed up for, unfortunately."

Guilt washes over me. Winston might be the one who agreed to work for Jed, but if I'd been here, I could've steered him a different way. I could've protected him. But I left, and now here we are—on the verge of our family imploding and taking Cold Springs with it.

"We'll figure something out. We have to," I tell my siblings.

Chapter 22

HAZEL

I wrap up the last batch of Stud Muffins, one of Mom's recipes that includes oats, apples, and cinnamon, and put them in the walk-in fridge. On the rare occasion Mom doesn't sell out of every last crumb, she offers the leftovers for half-price the next day or donates them to the local police or fire department.

These will definitely not be going to the police department after Officer Milson showed up at Puss N Boots last night, whipping his power trip around. I roll my eyes, admitting to myself that he wasn't that bad, only doing his job. But I'm still not taking the department any muffins, and that's my prerogative.

The bell over the door jingles, and I call out, "Be with you in a second."

"Take your time, sweetie," a male voice answers.

I wipe my hands on my apron and walk out front to greet the customer. "Welcome to the Bakery Box. How can I . . ." My voice falters when I see who's come into the bakery today—Jed Ford. "Um, help you?"

He looks exactly like the billboards, his cowboy hat oversize, his smile ruler straight and paper white, and his blue eyes shrewd. He's also never set foot in Mom's bakery, avoiding it like the plague the same way he does Puss N Boots. Something tells me this is not a welcome-wagon inaugural visit.

"Hello, Miss Sullivan."

Then again, I'm no paper lily, wilting at the first sign of trouble. "Hello, Mr. Ford. What can I get for you?"

I'm trying my best to stick to the script of a bakery employee, even though there is a laundry list of things I want to say to him. Top of the list is, "Fuck you and the high horse you think you ride around town on," and getting less polite from there.

"Oh, I thought I'd come by and get a few treats"—he pats his belly, though his eyes haven't so much as glanced at the case full of baked goods—"and see if I could speak to your mom for a moment."

Ah . . . and here I thought we'd dance more before he got to business. "I can help with one of those at least—the treats. As for Mom, she's not here right now. Can I tell her what you're wanting to talk about?"

Jed shrugs casually. "Nothing important. Just need to go over her new lease agreement. There are a few details I want her to see, like the rent."

I narrow my eyes, catching his drift easily because it's long been the talk of the town how Jed's raising rents on the buildings he owns. So far, Mom has avoided it, and I wonder why she's had a target placed on her back now.

But I know. She's paying the price for yesterday, probably with a bonus fee tacked on because I, Etta's niece, dared to fraternize with a Ford.

"I see. Well, I'll be sure as shit to pass that little message along." There's no sugar in my voice anymore. Customer Service Hazel has exited the building, leaving it to Killer Hazel and her resting bitch face. "Did you actually want to buy something, or were you just coming in to deliver threats today?"

"Excuse me, young lady?" Jed sneers. Looking me up and down, he mutters, "I should have expected."

My bitch face is no longer resting, but active as hell. I'm glaring, snarling, and my head is on a swivel as I tell him, "One, you are not excused. Two, I am neither young, nor a lady. So cupcake, cookie, or the door?"

He lifts his chin, a small smirk teasing at the corner of his lips as though he's enjoying this. "Then I reckon I'd best take a dozen cupcakes. The girls in the office will sure appreciate them."

I should bite my tongue, but I can't stop myself, even though I know I'm only going to make this situation worse—for myself and, ultimately, for Mom. "Girls? I didn't realize you were hiring children now. I thought Maggie was your assistant? She's gotta be pushing fifty nowadays. Hell, even her daughter is a full-grown woman, with a baby girl of her own."

He chuckles as though I'm joking. I'm not. Everything about Jed Ford sets me on edge—he's entitled, misogynistic, narcissistic, and sneaky, and he lies to suit himself. An all-around oxygen thief of a human being with charming wrapping, like a rotten apple in a Tiffany-blue box.

"Oh, I didn't mean nothing by that. I take care of all my girls."

He's baiting his hook with the best worm he can think of, reminding me about how he "took care" of Aunt Etta.

"Mm-hmm," I hum snidely. I won't give him the benefit of more.

"Speaking of my girls, make sure to tell your mom about the rental agreement. It needs to be signed soon, or else . . ." He looks around the bakery nonchalantly, but there's nothing casual about the way his eyes measure the space, as though he's got plans of his own for it.

"Or else?" I echo.

"Well, I reckon I'd have to get a new tenant." His grin is pure evil, showcasing how much delight he takes in playing the Big Man to both small business owners and a "girl" like me.

I want to cat-scratch that smile right off his face, leave him with scars as deep as the ones he left on Aunt Etta's heart and he's trying to mark Cold Springs with. But attacking him physically will only get me another visit from Officer Milson, and I have no doubt that Jed would press charges. So, I go at him with my best asset—my mouth.

"You keep raising rent, and you're going to hit the tipping point where everyone's forced to close. You'll be left with empty buildings and zero rent, holding your ass and wondering where you went wrong."

Surprised that some "working girl" like me might have even the smallest amount of economic sense, he blinks once, twice, before his entire face begins turning red. His shoulders climb up near his ears as he waves a hand at the space around us. "Won't be no problem getting tenants when business is booming from the new residents. Gonna be a whole new Cold Springs soon."

"*If* the rezoning passes, you mean," I correct him.

"I mean *when* the rezoning passes."

The air conditioner in the bakery doesn't kick on, but it's suddenly ice cold in the space between Jed and me. He scowls at me, his eyes promising all sorts of consequences to this chat between us.

And though I'll have to apologize to Mom for setting proverbial fire to her lease agreement, I don't back down, answering Jed's stare with threats of my own as I cross my arms over my chest and defiantly glare right back.

Finally, Jed speaks. "That spectacle yesterday sure was something. Guess Wyatt being there got everybody fired up."

I don't respond, don't so much as move a muscle.

"It sure would be a shame for the town, or a sweet girl like you, to hitch your wagon to someone who's gonna leave."

"He's not leaving." I say it as though it's a fact, even though I don't know if it's true. Wyatt promised only that he'd tell me before he left. But he has a life in Newport, one he'll eventually go back to, but not right now. Not when he was protesting downtown yesterday, and actively involved in figuring out ways to stop Jed last night. I'm sure of that much at least.

And what about staying for you? a quiet voice in my head asks.

I can't focus on that right now. I won't be that selfish when Cold Springs needs him. Once we figure out the zoning and have the town hearing, then I can concentrate on Wyatt and me.

If there's such a thing as "Wyatt and me" then.

Jed chuckles as though he can read my mind. "Sweetie, that's what boys like him do. Leave when they don't get their way."

I have to smile at that because that doesn't sound like Wyatt at all. He might've left Cold Springs, but it wasn't a toddler temper tantrum—stomping away like Jed makes it sound. Not at all. Wyatt left because he wanted to be in control of his own destiny.

And that's the thing Jed fears most—someone outside his control. So I'm able to smile, unfazed. "We'll see."

I close the box of cupcakes I've been prepping, and push them across the counter. "Here's your cupcakes. Tell Maggie I put her favorite Buttery Nipple one in there just for her. It's the one with the tan caramel areola on top of creamy butterscotch schnapps frosting."

As I hoped, Jed looks scandalized, but he does grab the box and throw a twenty on the counter. "Keep the change."

I ignore the fact that a dozen cupcakes is more than twenty bucks, ready for this to be over with. Jed walks out and the jingle of the bell chimes again. I don't breathe until I see him climb into his jacked-up truck in the parking space out front and pull away.

"Shiiit," I say to myself. "I hate that fucker with every cell in my body. Even the mitochondria are powered up with pure octane hatred."

The adrenaline is starting to wear off, though, leaving me shaky and on edge.

Still, like the good daughter I am, I call Mom, who's upstairs sleeping off this morning's two a.m. start time.

"Is the kitchen on fire?" she mumbles groggily.

"No, but Jed Ford came by to talk about your rent."

"That motherfucking . . ." The following litany of curses would make a marine drill sergeant blush, I'm sure, but it's so mumbled, I can't understand her. By the sounds of things, she's up and getting dressed, though.

"I'll see you down here in a minute," I say, and she hums an agreement before hanging up.

Running through my encounter with Jed serves only to amp up Mom's anger. "How dare he?" she rants as she paces the kitchen floor, out of sight of the front windows. "Can he even do that?"

I shrug, not knowing the details of her lease agreement.

"What are we going to do?" I ask her, hoping she has a better idea than I do because mine basically involves castrating Jed and force-feeding him his own dick until he chokes.

"First, I'm calling the lawyer that reviewed my contract in the first place. Second, we've got to kick his legs out from underneath him." I must look excited at the idea because Mom frowns. "Not literally, although I'd sure like to."

"Damn."

She seems happily lost in the idea for a moment, but then explains, "All his business predictions are based on the subdivision. He thinks the residents there are going to create this massive profit for us, and that some of those people are going to want to open new businesses too. All leading to higher rents for him. Conversely, no subdivision means no new customers, and no new businesses. If that were the case, we'd have a better negotiating position as existing tenants in good standing. And third, I need to bake."

She starts grabbing bowls and ingredients, and I know to get out of her way. Baking is Mom's happy place 99 percent of the time, and everything she makes is filled with love. That other 1 percent is her way of coping with anger, and fury-infused baked goods have a whole different process. A much messier one.

"Whatcha making?"

"Kiss My Butt Blossoms. Sugar cookies as white as my ass, with chocolate kisses in the middle. And I'm going to bless each and every one of them with the hope that Jed gets what's coming to him."

"Do you want some help?" I offer.

"No, leave me to my baking. But maybe see if Wyatt has any ideas to stop Jed."

"Wyatt?" I question, even though I was already planning on filling him in on his uncle's shenanigans.

Mom stops her furious mixing to pin me with a look. "Jed's nervous about Wyatt. I don't know why, but he is. Coming here? Telling you he's leaving? That's about using you to get at Wyatt. Jed mentioning the protest yesterday? Wyatt."

I nod, though I don't know what it could be. If Wyatt had any real dirt on Jed, I think he would've already shared it.

"Yessiree, leave me to bake and call my lawyer, and you see if there's any way to stop Jed."

Assignment given, she turns back to her baking, dismissing me, until she freezes. Pointing with a wooden spoon, she warns, "Hazel . . . stop him without literally breaking his legs. I can't run this place with you in prison, understand?"

I place my hand over my heart, touched. "Oh, Mom, you do care. But why are you assuming I'd get caught?"

⁂

Can you meet me at my place?

My fingers shake until I get Wyatt's reply text, with a winking emoji.

Am I a booty call?

Wiseass.

No, but now I'm rethinking that. Remind me to not hop on your dick as soon as you walk in. I need to talk to you.

"We need to talk" is not usually followed by dick hopping, so maybe we should do that first? Dick, then talk.

Jed came by the bakery.

If there's anything that'll throw cold water on Wyatt's balls, that's it.

I'll be there in ten minutes.

True to his word, Wyatt is in my driveway when I get there, and his truck is covered in dust, so he must've sped like a demon down the dirt roads. He's leaning up against the side with his arms crossed, his face thunderous. He doesn't even wait for me to put Nessa in park before he's ripping the door open. He reaches in, unbuckling me while I turn the car off, and pulls me out.

His face scours mine, his fingers dancing over my jaw, down my arms, to grip my hips. "Are you okay?"

I look up at him, amused and captivated by his attention to checking over every inch of me. "What? He didn't attack me. He's not that kind of monster. But he threatened the bakery, and reminded me . . ." I look down, not wanting to show how much Jed's words affected me.

Wyatt isn't fucking around, though, and forces my chin back up with a strong hand. "Reminded you of what?" he says through gritted teeth.

"That you're leaving. That Cold Springs, and me, shouldn't get attached to you because you'll leave."

His eyes flick left and right, diving into mine so deeply that I can't hide anything from him—not my fears, and definitely not my hopes. Not even the selfishness at my center that wants Wyatt to stay for me.

His hands soften as he cups my face, and I can feel the roughness of his fingertips against my cheeks. He traces my bottom lip with his thumb and chips away at the inches between us slowly. When I can just feel the graze of his lips against mine, he growls, "I'm not going anywhere, Hazel."

The kiss is possessive, him claiming my mouth as his, and me returning the claim with a sharp nip to his lip. He hisses and picks me up. Automatically, my legs go around his waist, and his hands find the globes of my ass. The front door is unlocked—no one ever bothers with deadbolts out here—and Wyatt goes through it, heading straight for my bedroom.

Lester flies around us. "Bawk! Lester's a good boy! Lester want cookie!"

Wyatt grunts as Lester lands on my shoulder, his beak right up near our kiss. "I want a cookie, too, dude. Quit cockblocking."

"Cockblocking. Cockblocking. Cawwwkblawwwking," Lester drawls out. I'd be upset except that he already knows that word.

Trying to get Lester to leave us alone, I tell him, "I'll get you a cookie in a bit, Lester. Mama needs a minute alone."

"Hazel needs to shiiit. Phew-whee!" he sings, flying back down the hall to the living room.

I sigh, sure the mood is ruined by my damn bird talking about my bodily functions. But Wyatt doesn't slow down, tossing me to my bed and shutting the door behind us with a kick. "Take your clothes off, Hazel. I'm gonna mark you all over, so that you remember . . . I'm not going anywhere."

He reaches behind his neck and pulls his shirt over his head. I'm dumbstruck by his abs, losing count at two even though there are several more bumps leading down to the waistband of his jeans. I just can't find the mental capacity to do something as unnecessary as count when he looks so good.

"Now, Hazel," he repeats.

My mom didn't raise no fool. I start wiggling around like a worm in the sun, trying to strip as fast as possible. Just as I get my jeans down and off my legs, Wyatt's on me, his lips crushing mine as he presses me into the mattress.

"Open up," he orders, kissing down my body. I barely have a chance to let my knees part before he's kissing the inside of my thighs roughly, almost biting the soft skin before literally ripping my panties off. The sting of the fabric on my hips makes me gasp, but that gasp is only matched when he buries his tongue inside me.

"Fuck!" I cry out, my hips jerking as he sucks on my tender skin. Normally, I might opt for slow and delicate, teased and pleased. Wyatt is having none of that. It feels like he's writing his name on my core with his tongue.

And my god is my body responding. I jerk, almost coming as he slides his middle two fingers deep inside me, stretching me open.

His tongue lashes at my clit, his fingers pumping hard and deep, and when Wyatt reaches up to pinch my nipple, I go insane. In seconds, I'm thrashing on the bed, my hands balled into tight fists in the sheets as my hips buck.

Wyatt growls, the sexiest sound I've ever heard, and his two fingers stroke once again on that spot inside, unchaining me. I come hard, gasping breathlessly as he flicks his tongue over my clit again and again.

Finally, I sag back, my chest heaving as Wyatt lifts his head from between my legs, grinning wolfishly. He knows that he just made me come in what feels like record time and intensity, and he's proud of himself.

But what he doesn't know is that now I'm ready to claim him just as much as he claimed me. "If you," I get out between pants, "don't get that cock up here in three seconds, you're going to be beating off for the rest of your days."

Wyatt's grin melts, replaced with raw hunger, and he climbs back up my body, sliding off to kneel next to my face. The look on his face says he thinks he's in control, but as I cup his balls, rolling the heavy orbs in my hand while turning to my side, I know the truth. I smile lazily as I run my tongue around the head of his cock.

His body galvanizes, and I can feel the power I have over him as I suck him deeper into my mouth. Even with him there, kneeling above me, I'm the one claiming him now, in full control, teasing and torturing him with my slow lips and lashing tongue.

I want him tortured. I want him to understand that he's mine . . . that as much as he wants to own me, I want to own him.

I want to write my name on his heart.

"H . . . Hazel," he gasps as I take him into my throat. I don't speed up; instead I tug on his sack lightly, making him grunt as I hold him, literally, in the palm of my hand. Finally, my nose is buried in the soft tufts of hair at his base, and I look up at him with my eyes full of unsaid words. I stay right there, on the edge of gagging, as long as I can, and then slowly I begin bobbing back and forth on his cock until I can taste the sweet drops of precum on my tongue.

I'm tempted to have more, but my body knows what it really wants. I flick my tongue in his slit before lying back and opening my arms to him. He comes down to me, and again we kiss. He thrusts his hands into my hair, lifting and supporting my head to take the kiss deeper.

It's not as feral as it was at first, but we're not being gentle either. We're nipping, biting, and laying sucking kisses everywhere . . . I'm going to look like I got in a fight with a Hoover and the vacuum won tomorrow, but damned if I care. Not when my nipples are red from his sucking, my pussy is pulsing with want, and my skin is covered with goose bumps, sensitive to his every touch. The bruising of hickeys might be the most obvious way he's marking me, but there is so much more, so many other ways Wyatt is claiming my body.

With a shift of his hips, I feel him at my entrance, his eyes dark with want. Without saying anything, I wrap my legs around his waist. I score my fingers down his back and he hisses, arching into my touch, and then his hips buck, and he enters me to the hilt in one motion.

I know we've had sex before, but the way Wyatt fills me to capacity and then some takes my breath away. He's rock hard and insistent as he pins me to the mattress, his hips pulling back just enough to give him space to pound into me.

All I can do is hold on, my body rocked as my headboard bangs into the wall, the force of his thrusts shaking the whole bed. We buck, hips grinding and slapping, my clit bumping against his body with every stroke.

In the background, I can hear Lester squawking up a storm, proba- bly startled by the sounds of the crazy humans in the bedroom. I don't care—all I care about is the feeling of Wyatt inside me, on top of me, claiming me.

"Not . . . going . . . anywhere!" Wyatt grunts, emphasizing his words with punishing thrusts, and I feel him swell. His words trigger me and I come again, the spasms setting him off, and he comes inside me. "Damn it, Haze . . . squeeze me like that. Fucking . . . pussy vise."

I hold him, not letting him go even after he's spent, his body sag- ging with exhaustion as he tries not to crush me.

I pull him down, feeling the ache and sweat of my tired, well-fucked body, and wanting him to melt into me, knowing that I can handle it. In my bones, I feel the truth of his words . . . He's not going anywhere. He'll be right here, in my heart, no matter where he physically goes.

Even if it's back to Newport, to his life. He'll be here, the same way I'll be there, because if he does leave, he'll be taking a piece of me with him.

My heart.

Chapter 23

WYATT

The room is absolutely buzzing, the whole town piled into the too-small space at the courthouse. I'm standing at the back with Hazel, watching over everyone. Despite my sudden status as a figurehead for the protest, I'm not trying to take center stage.

Meanwhile, Dad is sitting at the center of the platform behind a small podium, Mom and Wren are sitting together toward the front, and Jed is standing along the side wall.

It should make it seem like he's less important, but quite the opposite. From his vantage point, it's as though he's silently pulling the strings connecting everything. In a way, I guess he is, because most of the council is alternating looking at the paper in front of them and then looking at Jed.

Rinse, repeat.

There is also a small group of people sitting in the front row, their suited backs straight, jaws tight, and an air of stuffy arrogance surrounding them. I don't know who they are, but I've never seen them around town.

Were they at Winston's wedding, maybe?

I'm not sure, but one thing Dad taught me over the years is how to deduce who the most important person in the room is. And my gut says it's the guy in the middle of the small group. He's the only one garnering Jed's attention, and that's telling.

The hum grows as various people talk about possible outcomes of tonight's votes. Mostly, they seem to be some combination of fearful and outraged. Scared of what the future of Cold Springs holds if the rezoning passes, and angry at the prospect of what the city council and mayor are doing under the guise of "leadership."

Hazel squeezes my hand, and I look over. Her brows lift in question, silently asking if I'm okay, and I squeeze back, reassuring her.

Etta comes through the open door and stands near us. "Couldn't get us a seat?"

Hazel shakes her head and talks out of the side of her mouth, not taking her eyes off the crowd. "We were early, but so was the whole town."

I lean over, whispering in Etta's ear, "Better to stand up. I don't want to get lost in the crowd and only be able to see the back of Jed's head. I want to see Dad's face when he leads this vote, stare him down as he sells his soul."

Etta tilts her head, looking at me approvingly. "Ooh, they say the apple doesn't fall far from the tree, but you fell, rolled away, and started a whole new orchard of your own. You, my boy, are nothing like your uncle."

That's nothing like the previous conversation I had with Etta, where she called me a kid and scolded me for not handling my business. It warms me inside.

"Thank you."

I look at Dad, noting the purple smudges under his eyes, and as though he feels my gaze, he finds me. I can't read the expression there. He seems almost . . . vacant? I remember what Wren said about Dad realizing he's in over his head with Jed, and want to feel some small degree of empathy, but when he calls the meeting to order, I push that down. Despite any doubts he has, he's leading the charge here, and while Jed has no allegiance to anyone but himself, Dad is supposed to represent the town's best interest. A duty he's failing on miserably.

"First up, old business. Mrs. Capshaw?"

"Yes," Mrs. Capshaw, a middle-aged woman in lululemon and a "Chaos Coordinator" sweatshirt, says. She pulls out a stack of papers, and someone in the crowd groans. I guess she's a regular. "For three months, the council has done nothing as the Circle K out on the highway continues to advertise energy drinks. Numerous health experts, including Dr. Oz himself, have come out against these poisons in a can, but now the advertising is . . . salacious!"

Sighs fill the audience, and Karen Hicks, one of the council members, speaks up. "Mrs. Capshaw, what do you mean?"

"The poster outside the Circle K is now trying to push 'Butt Banging Berry' flavor drinks! They're encouraging our children to engage in . . . that!"

I snort, I can't help it, but I'm definitely not the only one. "Sounds like someone needs to be butt banged, if you ask me," I whisper, and Hazel snickers. But I wasn't quiet enough apparently, because Etta backhands my bicep and gives me a harsh glare. But an instant later, she's fighting off laughter too.

"Mrs. Capshaw, while we understand your concerns," Dad says, "we heard you last month and the month before that. And as we've told you . . . that is not in our purview. You need to speak with the Food and Drug Administration, or maybe your congressperson. But the Circle K isn't even within city limits."

She sits down with a huff, crossing her arms over her chest so that the only visible part reads "Chaos," which seems appropriate. "I'll be back."

"I'm sure you will. Now, new business?"

A cacophony of voices fills the room, almost all of them wanting to talk about the rezoning plan.

"My taxes—"

"Where the hell am I gonna hunt come fall?"

"I'll tell you what you can rezone . . ."

"Lining your pockets—"

Some of the comments are funny, some are ridiculous, but most are just angry and pissed off. Most of the people here feel one overwhelming thing: they're not being listened to by the very people they elected to do just that.

As the roar continues, Hazel whispers, "I thought you said Winston was coming? I know Avery told me she scheduled an aide for Grandpa Joe."

I look at my watch, noting that Winston is now twenty minutes late. Since returning from his honeymoon, he's been working on analyzing every angle of the subdivision plan. Maybe it was the honeymoon phone call, or maybe it was the meeting at Avery's house, but he's no longer sitting on the fence on this.

Still, he's between a rock and a hard place, professionally responsible for the success of the project, but personally wanting to stop it from going forward. I've been helping, researching the way the initial property tax law was passed, but since I'm not a tax attorney, I haven't found anything suspicious there.

Then I tried looking into Jed, but he's as slick as always. Nothing illegal, just an asshole. As far as I can find, he's not even cheating on Aunt Chrissy, which is something I've always assumed based on his history.

I check the door, which hasn't moved, and tell Hazel, "He should be here."

Finally, the council gets some semblance of order, and a line forms behind the microphone. The cavalcade of comments goes on for a long time, person after person having their turn behind the microphone.

Sue-Ellen even waves around the petition before reading off every single signature. All this in an attempt to persuade council members to vote one way or the other.

Well, no one is speaking in favor of the rezoning, but Jed's presence is felt all the same.

Finally, the door opens silently, and Winston comes in, turning around to hold the door for Avery and Grandpa Joe. Avery helps Joe to the back row of chairs, where he taps on the leg of the aisle seat with his cane, making the guy sitting there move so he can sit down.

Once he's settled, Avery comes to stand with Winston next to me. "Grandpa Joe refused to stay home," she explains, "so it took us a while to come to an 'agreement.'" She uses her fingers to make air quotes.

Grandpa Joe turns around and hisses, "You mean it took too damn long for you to give in and help me to the car. We missed most of the hearing now."

Avery rolls her eyes, used to Joe's grumpiness, and he turns back around, grousing and muttering to himself.

Now that Winston is here, I ask, "Find anything?"

"Yeah, but . . ." Winston says, before pausing.

I cut my eyes to him hard. "But what? Can it stop this shitshow?"

Winston looks to Avery, obviously having already talked about this with her. She nods encouragingly. Before Winston can give me a clue about what he's discovered, Dad speaks. "If there's nothing further, we'll hold the vote."

I push Winston forward, and he stumbles over his own feet but recovers quickly enough to glare at me. Holding his hand up, he says, "Excuse me, may I speak?"

Dad's eyes narrow sharply, and Jed takes a step forward, his jaw tight.

Winston ignores both silent orders to stop and steps up to the microphone. "My name is Winston Ford. Full disclosure seems prudent, so Mayor Bill Ford is my father, and I work for Jed Ford as lead architect."

He scans the table full of council members, several of whom smile back, likely thinking they know what side of the issue Winston is on. But out of the corner of my eye, I see Jed's face . . . and he knows.

"It's been my role to oversee the Springdale Ranch subdivision, from inception to design, and depending on tonight's vote, potentially to actualization. I feel it is necessary for all parties to have complete information so that you can make the important decision you're tasked with tonight."

I whisper to myself, "Get on with it, Winston."

At my side, Avery bumps me with her elbow. "This is hard for him. He's torpedoing his career over this."

"What did he find out?" I whisper, keeping my eyes on Winston.

"It doesn't matter," Avery explains. "Just by getting up there against Jed, he's done."

I wonder if she knows about Jed paying for the wedding, and how much of a hold Jed has over Winston because of that. But now isn't the time to have that discussion.

"You're being asked to vote on a rezoning proposal for land just outside city limits of Cold Springs, making this area single-family use, which will have consequences for the farms currently located there," Winston continues. "They will no longer be legally able to farm, which is their current livelihood. Adding in the previous property tax changes, the expected end result is that these families will be unable to afford the properties. At that point, Jed intends to purchase this land as the site for Springdale Ranch."

He pauses, letting that sink in. It's the first time anyone from Jed's company has officially, and on the record, spelled out their intentions so succinctly.

"In researching the land in question, it was up to me to do a full analysis—"

Jed interrupts him, snapping, "Winston!"

Winston's head jerks to the left so that he's looking at Jed, the same way everyone in the room does. We all see Jed's anger rising, and the small shake of his head. That alone is telling that Winston has information Jed doesn't want made public.

Dad clears his throat, the microphone amplifying the sound. "Why don't we take a short break. We can reconvene in fifteen minutes?"

But Winston says sharply, "No. I don't need a break."

Dad looks at Jed uncertainly.

Winston takes advantage to press on. "This land has been farmed for generations and has a history." Jed inhales sharply, but Winston forges on. "A long and varied one."

I have no idea what he's talking about, his dry delivery not doing him any favors. I've never heard my typically trash-talking brother's professional voice, and it's surprisingly trustworthy. I believe that if he feels he's sharing important information, he most definitely is.

He glances back, his eyes asking if I get what he's saying, but I'm missing something Winston needs me to see.

"Help him," Avery whispers.

I step forward before I know I'm doing it, making my way to Winston's side. Dad's eyes narrow, his tone concerned as he says, "Wyatt?"

I'm still working it out, so speaking slowly, I say, "It's important to preserve Cold Springs, especially the history—"

Winston nods, and I know I'm on the right track, but he has to give us more information. He's the one with the research, but I will stand by his side in support.

"Which is . . ."

Winston picks up the sentence: "In rereviewing the property analysis, I recently discovered that the section of property at 812 Bellsy has a small carriage house. It was once a hideout for Beauford and Mildred Craft."

Someone in the back yells out, "Who the hell is that?"

I know this, remember it from a book I read for school once.

"Beauford and Mildred Craft were a married couple who escaped slavery in the eighteen forties by what became known as the Underground Railroad. They fled for their freedom from Georgia to Boston, and later England. Their story inspired and encouraged many."

Winston nods excitedly, probably thinking that I would be the least likely to actually know something of historical relevance. But I know this story.

"Exactly," he says. "And while the Crafts might not be as historically famous as some others, it's important to consider preservation before we make any moves that would lead to the destruction of our town's history."

Jed blurts out, "Nobody gives a shit about some old, falling-down barn."

An elderly woman stands up, leaning on the chair in front of her for support. "I do. It's my barn. That carriage house is where my favorite horse was born, it's where I hid when the Prohibition police would search for my daddy's moonshine, and it's where I store my old car now, on account I can't drive no more. And that it was part of the Underground Railroad too? You can't tear it down! Especially not for some cookie-cutter houses and Johnny-come-lately strangers that don't give a damn about Cold Springs."

Jed scoffs, and several of the council members are looking at each other like they don't care about some old lady's storage shed. I need to remind them about what's at stake here.

"If we destroy what made Cold Springs special, we'll be destroying Cold Springs. I move that we petition the state to make the carriage house a historical site, an important place in our town from the days of Beauford and Mildred Craft to today, when it's Ms. . . . I'm sorry, what's your name?"

The old lady smiles, holding her skirt out daintily, though I doubt she can bow at her age. "Mrs. Eugenia Hackwood, but you can call me Geni."

Her left eye twitches, and I'm not sure whether it's supposed to be a wink or an involuntary tic. Either way, I smile back warmly. "From the days of the Crafts to Mrs. Eugenia Hackwood."

Wren stands up, declaring in a loud voice, "I second that motion."

Dad stands, too, his face pale. "Members of the public can't make motions, nor second them. Tonight's hearing is about rezoning."

He sits back down, straightening his tie and likely wishing he could control this meeting and his family as easily. But it's not over yet. Etta calls out from the back of the room, "We might not be able to make a motion, but anyone sitting up there at that fancy table sure can. By the way, on a completely unrelated note . . . Councilman Hancock, I sure do appreciate you sending Officer Milson over to see me. He mentioned we could sit down to some mediation if necessary to work out your criminal-mischief concerns. You want me to bring your favorite Fat Pussy double bacon, extra mayo burger with fries to that meeting? Because you sure as shit aren't welcome at Puss N Boots no more."

She raises a brow, looking cunningly wicked.

I see why when a woman stands up, pissed off. "Harold! You are on a diet for your cholesterol! You can't eat things like that."

Hancock looks sick to his stomach, as if he's regretting both getting on Etta's bad side after the protest and hiding his dietary habits from his wife. Or maybe it's from eating all that extra mayo?

Hancock holds Etta's eye as he raises his hand. "I move that we petition the state to declare the carriage house of 812 Bellsy a historical site."

Etta nods, agreeing to wipe away Harold's sins, and the woman who's been taking minutes the whole meeting pops off with, "Noted!"

Councilwoman Jackson raises her hand. "Seconded."

The secretary adds, "Motion on the floor. Mayor, we'll need to vote on this matter before opening another for a vote."

Dad looks unsure what to do, but he knows the rules of council meetings, having presided over them for years. He stands, looking to his left and avoiding Jed's harsh glare. "Council member Patterson, what say you?"

Mr. Patterson seems less than happy about being the first to vote, setting his pen down and interlacing his fingers in front of him. He looks at the crowd, most of whom lean forward eagerly, and then to Dad. "In favor of the motion. Yes."

A small pattering of excitement sounds out, little squeals of hope as people grasp hands. Down the row the vote goes, and by the end, it's tied four–four. Dad, as mayor and head of the council, will be the deciding vote.

The air's thick, heavy with expectation. Me, I'm hopeful that Dad gets his head out of Jed's ass and does the right thing.

Meanwhile, Jed's grinning like it's a sure thing. He's got this sewed up, by his math.

Dad leans forward and clears his throat. "Aye."

It's just one word, but it sets off an explosion of celebration that has the whole council chambers rocking and rolling louder than the street protest a few days ago. People are hugging, crying, and someone even spins Mrs. Hackwood around gently.

Meanwhile, Jed looks like he's about to have a fit. His face is brick red, and he stares at his brother, then me, then Winston, then back to Dad.

After a minute, Dad raps his gavel to quiet everyone. "Everyone, order please. There's another proposal on the agenda that requires a vote."

The crowd quiets as everyone realizes we might be celebrating prematurely. Sure, petitioning the state might stop Jed from buying some of the property . . . but could the council still go through with the rezoning?

In theory, the subdivision could have a historical carriage house in the middle of the green space, probably with a big, garish sign donated by Jed Ford.

"Don't do this, Dad," I whisper, and I can feel Hazel slip her hand into mine as Dad speaks again.

"I need someone to make the motion."

This time it's Mr. Patterson who brings the rezoning issue to the table, seconded by one of Jed's allies, Mr. Norton. Dad nods and speaks into the microphone. "The council shall vote. Council member Patterson?"

"Nay. Keep the land the way it is."

I inhale, as Dad looks at Mr. Norton. "Council member Norton?"

Norton's been Jed's buddy for years, and I'm sure Jed has felt secure in Norton's vote for months, if not longer. But Norton knows where his bread is buttered here, and leans forward to declare into his microphone, "Nay."

It breaks the dam, and by the time the vote comes around to Dad, the matter is decided. His *nay* makes it unanimous against rezoning.

Jed is furious at his brother's betrayal, shouting over the din, "We had this planned out. What the hell?"

Etta laughs and calls out joyously, "Fuck you, Jed!"

Aunt Chrissy stands up, dutifully going to Jed's side. "Etta, you're only fighting against Jed because you're a bitter old hag from losing him. You should've left town when he left you. Nobody would've missed you a lick." She looks up at Jed as if he's her savior and hero.

Etta waves the insult away, saying, "I gave up caring for that blowhard a long time ago. I thank my lucky stars every day that I didn't marry him and got to spend my mama's last years by her side."

Chrissy snorts. "Yeah right. You've always been jealous of me."

Oh, I don't think my aunt knows what she's done, but judging by the hard look in Etta's eyes, it's game on and she's got some things she's been dying to say. Bruises and broken bones heal, but I suspect an insult from Etta will fester in your soul.

"You traded truly living for a life of ease a long time ago, and nobody wants your fancy car and big house, least of all me, because everyone can see how empty and lonely it really is."

Chrissy pales, looking around at all the faces watching the drama play out before them. This has been a long time coming between the two former best friends. And Etta's not done. "You got exactly what you deserved. And I got a happy life, with my own business, friends, and family, and without having to get on my knees for a short dick like Jed."

Chrissy huffs in shock, nervously fluffing her salon-blonde hair, and looking at Jed. "Do something."

But Jed is completely oblivious to the argument between his wife and former fiancée. All his attention is focused on whatever he's angrily snarling at Dad.

"Argh!" Chrissy growls, not having a comeback to all that hard truth, and she whirls and stomps out of the room alone.

Etta takes a heaving breath, her hand to her chest as she smiles faintly. "Damn, that felt good to say out loud."

On some level, I feel bad for Chrissy. She is stuck with Uncle Jed, after all, but on the other hand, she made her bed, reveled in it, and threw it in Etta's face at every opportunity, so it's only fair that she gets a bit of that ugliness in return.

I hear my name and look over my shoulder, finding Hazel making her way toward us in the crowd and pulling Avery along behind her. My line of sight is broken for a moment by the suited businesspeople from the front row leaving. Jed is chasing after them, talking hurriedly. I think I hear him say, "This isn't over." But the head guy doesn't look like he believes that for a second.

Turning to Winston, I ask, "Who are the suits?"

Winston grimaces, probably mentally already writing up his résumé. "Investors. Jed's got a lot tied up in this already. They're not going to be happy."

I watch Jed, who for the first time looks uncertain about something. "Is it wrong that I hope they ream him a new one? I want someone to take Jed down a few pegs."

Winston snorts. "I think you already did."

I wrap my arm around his shoulders, letting my brother know that he's still got an ally. "I think we did."

Hazel clears her throat and I turn to her, hugging her tightly as I admit that "we" is getting bigger by the moment. And she's definitely part of it. She hugs me back, and I feel more than hear her laugh. "That was awesome. You were like a one-two punch to his 'nads that he didn't see coming. Blind nut punch."

I grin, pushing her hair behind her ear and falling a little more in love with her craziness. Next to us, Avery and Winston are also embracing, and she says, "I'm proud of you, honey."

His wife's support seems to bolster Winston, because he kisses Avery warmly, stroking her hair. "I promise I'll make the honeymoon thing up."

The crowd is milling around, unsure what to do now that we've succeeded until Etta yells, "Victory party at Puss N Boots!"

Now that's a plan.

Chapter 24

Hazel

As we get to Puss N Boots, Avery gets Grandpa Joe set up at a table with Mom and Etta, who is entertaining him with fiery banter before he can even get his cane out of the way of the crowd. I'm not sure who is going to win if Etta and Joe start telling dirty jokes, but Mom will be a fair and impartial judge if the need arises.

People sit at the various tables, chatting and catching up, and a few people claim the dartboard and pool tables, starting friendly games.

As soon as Charlene sees the crowd, she climbs on the bar. "Listen up!" she yells, waiting for the hum to die down. When it doesn't happen fast enough, she places her fingers in her mouth and whistles loudly. That gets everyone's attention instantly.

"Listen! There're too many people in here for me to run around like a chicken with my head cut off, so there will be no waitressing tonight. If you want something, you'd best bring your happy ass up to the bar to order. And you can take it back to your table yourself. The only place I'm going is Tay Tay's window, the cash register, and the bathroom because the good Lord knows I can't go more than an hour without needing to piss after my babies did a number on my bladder. Understand?"

A buzz of agreement works through the group, and they go back to talking among themselves.

"Good. Now, who's next?" Charlene asks, hopping down from the bar.

I go behind the bar to make drinks for our table, and check in with Charlene. "Want me to grab my apron?"

She shakes her head, giving me a grateful smile. "Not for now. I'm okay as long as everybody does what I say. And if they don't, I guess they'll go hungry, now won't they?" She draws an invisible tear down her cheek with a finger, feigning sadness.

I laugh at her attitude and slip a twenty into her apron despite getting my own drinks. Charlene grabs my hand, stopping me. "Thanks, Hazel."

I squeeze her hand, understanding that this crowd has the potential to stress her out, but also to tip her enough to make her entire month in a few hours.

"Let me know if you change your mind. All tips are yours either way," I promise. I gather up the handles of the beer mugs, able to carry five in each hand but luckily not needing that many for our little group.

Wyatt's legs are stretched out, making him look about ten feet tall and sexy as hell as he looks over to his brother. "Did you know about the historical thing all along?"

"No, I was going through the files over and over," Winston says, accepting a beer from me. "I hoped to find something, but when I did, Jed came into the office. He knew something was up, so I flat-out asked him about it, just to be sure he knew, and he totally did. He didn't care, told me to keep my mouth shut. He actually said, and I quote, 'You owe me.' And that was when I knew exactly what I had to do."

Wyatt takes his own beer, shaking his head sadly. "I'm sorry, man. What're you going to do now? Because I'm pretty sure Jed is already working on your termination papers."

"Get a new job, I guess," he says with a shrug he can't possibly fully feel yet. "I can be an architect for another developer or freelance maybe?"

"What about the wedding expenses?" Wyatt asks as he sits up, silently pulling me into his lap. I'm confused what they're talking about but don't interrupt the moment the brothers are having.

Winston smirks cockily. "What about them?"

"He's going to hold them over your head," Wyatt says, and across the table, Avery does a double take. Obviously, she didn't know either.

But Winston laughs as he pats Avery's hand soothingly. "He can try. Seriously, what the fuck can he do at this point? He said he wanted to 'give' it to us, and now he has. It's all paid for and done. I didn't ask him to and he didn't loan the money to me. As far as I'm concerned, we'll send him a very nice thank-you note, and call it good."

"Well . . . maybe we'll return the food processor he gave us," Avery quips, grinning.

"No way," Winston snaps. "That thing has thirteen speeds. Thir-teen."

We all laugh, and Wren joins us, coming back from the bathroom.

"What'd I miss?" she asks, taking a beer and sitting down.

Wyatt suddenly backhands Winston's arm, making Wren laugh. "Holy fuck, man! You're right. It's no big deal once it's done, and Jed can only hold it over you if you let him. Maybe my way of coping wasn't the best option, though I'm not sure I would've been able to take on Jed the way you just did when I was younger. I'm proud of you, bro."

Winston looks surprised but pleased by the praise from Wyatt. "Proud of you too."

"What about me?" Wren demands. "Someone needs to be proud of me!"

Winston and Wyatt look at each other and then back to her. "Definitely proud of you," Wyatt says.

"And scared to death too," Winston finishes.

Wren preens. "As it should be."

Jesse joins us, throwing his hat into the conversation, apparently overhearing enough to tell Wren, "You don't look too scary to me."

Wren pins him with an icy glare. "Have we met?"

Jesse looks mock hurt, pouting. "At the wedding? You thought I was one of the caterers?"

Wren cringes. "Oh yeah, sorry again."

"Jesse Sullivan, Hazel's brother," he says, offering his hand.

Wren shakes. "Wren Ford."

Jesse smirks in that hot-boy way, leaning in as though confiding when he says, "I know, sweetie. Everyone knows who you are."

Wren doesn't look sure whether she likes that or not, but Jesse captures her in conversation. That's probably not a good idea, mostly for Jesse's sake, because Wren is way out of his league, but if he wants to shoot his shot, I won't cockblock him.

I turn to my man, running my fingers through his hair. "You want to get out of here?"

Wyatt sighs, his thumb tracing along the back of my hand. I know his answer before he speaks, and a pit opens up in my belly. "I feel like I need to go home and check on Dad. I'm afraid he'll have drunk himself unconscious again after that shitcircus."

Not as bad as I feared, not as good as I hoped. I'll take it. "I understand. Go, take care of your family."

"I'll go with you," Winston says, starting to get up, but Wyatt holds out a hand.

"Enjoy the evening with your bride. I got this, whether it's blame or credit, though we both know which it's going to be."

Wren, still involved with whatever Jesse is saying, pauses to throw over her shoulder, "I'm not volunteering. I've done my daughterly duty more times than any woman should. If anyone has to see Dad in his undershirt and BVDs tonight, it should be you."

That decided, Wyatt kisses me thoroughly, definitely lifting my spirits, fist bumps Winston, and heads toward the door after telling him to watch over Wren. As if she needs protection from my brother. On second thought . . . I narrow my eyes, staring at Jesse and Wren shrewdly. I'll be looking out for both of them.

On the other hand, I hate seeing Wyatt leave with the wedding over and the hearing done. I feel like our time is short, and I know my heart is going to break into a million pieces if he goes.

Chapter 25

WYATT

My worries that the house would be a mess or possibly even burning down when I get back are eased as I pull up and see that the lights are on, no windows are broken, and things are quiet when I close the door on my truck.

A bit too quiet, and I suspect Mom's upstairs as I go inside and find Dad in his office, stone sober but looking like he could use a drink.

"Dad."

He looks up, his thumb tracing the stitching of the leather chair in a repetitive pattern that feels like he's been doing it for a while. "If you could answer one thing for me. What were you thinking?"

He's not raging, more confused than anything else. Calmly, I sit down on the leather couch, propping my elbows on my knees. "Jed had to be stopped. For Cold Springs' sake and the people who live here, which is something you should've been thinking too."

Dad gets up and paces around the room, his usually tidy hair standing on end from his hands. "I know!"

I'm confused at his outburst. "You know what? That Jed needed to be stopped? Then why didn't you?"

"I couldn't." Dad stops and shakes his head, his eyes unseeing, as if he's looking into the past. "It happened so fast. He was talking about how we'd usher in the next phase of Cold Springs, and how good the growth and progress would be for everyone. It sounded like a legacy I could be proud of. He conveniently left out the farms and families, and I'm ashamed to say that once I found out, it seemed like they could just move, you know? For the greater good?"

"He's good like that. Master manipulator extraordinaire."

Dad snorts. "You can say that again." He's quiet for a moment, contemplative, and then meets my eyes. "I'm sorry I didn't believe you before."

I lean forward more, tilting my head. "You do now?"

Dad nods. "He made paying for your schooling seem like a kind thing for an uncle to do. And a business degree is generic enough to help no matter what you wanted to do. I didn't see the long game, not then and not now. Until it was too late."

"He came to see me after I left. Told me I would never amount to anything without him."

Dad flinches, his eyes beseeching me. "I didn't know he did that. Didn't know where you were or I would've come."

I believe him. He might not have come in with apologies the way he is now, but if he knew I was only a short drive away, he would've tried to talk me into coming back. In the long run, I'm glad he didn't, though, because I'm better for it, having had enough distance to recognize and appreciate the things I did learn from Dad. And also realize that maybe my leaving everything and everyone behind was a bit of an overreaction, like setting fire to the whole house when there was just one spider.

"Jed was wrong. I didn't need him," I tell Dad, standing up. "I'd already had a role model, already seen what a good man did, and knew success wasn't achieved with threats and manipulations."

Dad's shoulders slump, and he shakes his head at my comment. "Thank you for that, but I'm not sure I qualify as a good role model these days."

It feels weird putting my hands on my father's shoulders, giving him a pep talk . . . but that's what I do now, looking into his eyes. "You made a mistake. It happens. The truth of your character will be in how you recover from that, how you make amends, how you serve Cold Springs. You said you wanted to leave a legacy, but don't you see? You already have."

"Pretty sure *Ford* is synonymous with *asshole*," Dad says, still dejected. "Probably in the dictionary and everything. Not quite the history I wanted."

I shrug a shoulder dismissively. "Nah, just Jed Ford. Bill Ford has always been a good man, a good leader, a good father. Even if he's a bit blind to his brother's shortcomings."

Dad chuckles and gives me a hug. "Definitely got twenty-twenty now."

I pat him on the back. Everything's not okay between us. There's a lot of years of hurt and anger to sift through, but it's a start we can build on. Most importantly, one I want to build on again. Not only because it's what I should do, some family expectation of the son forgiving the father, but because I want to.

Dad steps back after a moment and looks out the window. "How's Winston doing?"

I shake my head, grinning. "Surprisingly great. He feels good about doing the right thing, and when I asked about the wedding expenses, he was chill about it. Said that was a gift, and he feels no obligation to follow Jed into the fires of hell because of it."

Dad blinks several times, letting that sink in. "Wow. I'm impressed."

"Me too. I should've thought about that with my college degree." I laugh, not regretting dropping out of school when my business is doing so well. I learned from the School of Life. "Guess you did something right."

I'm talking about Winston, but Dad gives me a knowing look. "Hopefully more than one thing."

"What's Jed going to do?"

Dad sighs. "I'm sure he has a backup plan, and a backup for the backup. He'll probably just pick up the plans and move them to a different site, hopefully outside of Cold Springs."

He could be right, and the smack on the ass might do Jed some good. But Jed's not who I'm worried about. "What about you?"

He shrugs. "Don't really know. I've been thinking that I've done my service to Cold Springs for a lot of years. I've done a lot of good, but tonight showed me one thing clearly. It's a changed game, and I'm not strong enough to handle it. I'm not saying I'm ready to retire tomorrow, but public service might not be it for me anymore. I think it's time to lower my stress levels, maybe do a little day-trading, and spend some time with my grandkids soon."

I hold my hands up, shaking them to wave off that energy. "Have to talk to Avery and Winston about that."

"We'll see . . ." More seriously, he asks, "What are you going to do?"

There's really only one answer that makes sense. "Talk to Hazel. I don't know other than that."

Dad nods. "That sounds like a good idea."

We look at each other for a moment, saying so much but also leaving so much unsaid. I appreciate that he's not trying to plan things for me anymore, but rather is letting me lead with no expectation of what I'm going to do. And also, I can see that he was simply trying to do what was best for me before, and that, as my dad, he had a life of knowledge and experience I was rejecting by thinking I knew everything. This is a first for us, meeting as adults with thoughts, plans, and ideas of our own that are equally important and valid.

"I think I'll head up to bed," Dad says after a moment. "Your mother was exhausted after all the excitement tonight. As much as I've put her through lately, she deserves a good night's rest."

"She's been worried about you."

He sighs. "I've been worried about me too. But I feel better now than I have in ages. I've got some apologizing and making up to do with her too."

I wish I could leave it there, but there's one more issue we need to discuss. "Dad, about that . . . do you need some help? There are programs—"

He cuts me off. "Thank you. Truly. But I'm okay, or I will be. I've been trying to escape this situation, or pretend it didn't exist. Now that it's handled, and I can look at the future with a clearer conscious, I don't need that crutch." I give him a look of uncertainty. "If not, I promise to talk to someone about it—Mom, one of you kids, or a professional."

That helps me feel better, or it's at least a start in the right direction.

Dad and I walk to the doorway, where I give him another look. "Good night, Dad."

He turns, and suddenly hugs me, harder than ever before. "Thank you, son."

It's not an instant fix, but things feel more right between us than they have in a long time. Dad leaves, and in the quiet, I enjoy the feeling of relief that rises within me. Dad wasn't so far gone after all, just a bit lost. But he can find his way back to his true self, the man who inspired me as a child, whom I looked up to as a role model. If anyone can do it, he can.

I take a seat to gather myself, and Mr. Puddles comes trotting in, jumping up on the couch and putting his head in my lap. Chuckling, I reach down and scratch him in his favorite spot, just on the edge of his jaw. "Yeah, it's good to be home, buddy. I've missed you too."

Chapter 26

HAZEL

The knock at my front door is no surprise. I heard Wyatt and his truck coming down the drive.

But Lester acts surprised, ruffling his feathers and jumping up to his perch when it comes. "Bawk! Who's at my door?"

"Oh hush, Lester, you know who it is," I shush him, not adding that I've been staring out the window for any sign of Wyatt and Lester asked me who I was looking for when my "pretty bird" was right here.

Wyatt said he was going to talk to his dad, but I wasn't sure if that would send him to my door needing comfort. Or if he'd collapse into bed after the big night.

Or leave town?

I try to ignore the little voice in my head suggesting that.

My stomach twists as I force myself off the couch and to the door. God knows, I want to see him, but I'm scared he's coming to say goodbye. This moment, with us on opposite sides of the door, might be the last possible happiness I have.

"I know you're standing right there. Open the door, Hazel." The demand in his voice . . . Is that desire for me or desire to get this over with and head back to Newport?

But damn my heart, I can't help it. I open the door, and Wyatt steps in, opening his mouth to say something when Lester interrupts us. "Bawk! Booty call, booty call, booty call!"

"Lester!" I growl, trying not to cry for some damn reason. "Shut up, birdbrain."

Wyatt lifts my chin, searching my eyes. "What's wrong?"

I force a smile, blinking back the tears. "Nothing. You did it, you stopped Jed, saved Cold Springs. I'm happy about that . . ."

"But?"

His quiet, soft demand of a question pierces the little bits of armor I've been able to put up. "But . . ."

I look at him, begging him with my eyes to understand. He reaches up, cupping my cheek in a lover's caress. "I told you I'd tell you if I was leaving."

I nod, feeling stupid for becoming one of those women who asks "what are we" so soon. Nonetheless, I need answers. "I know you did."

"And have I said anything about leaving?" Wyatt asks, his thumb brushing my cheekbone and a smile forming on his lips.

"Don't you dare laugh at me, William Wyatt Ford the third!" I warn, pushing at his chest. If I can't cry, I can rage, and rage I will.

He doesn't give an inch and, in fact, pulls me in, putting us chest to chest and talking right in my face. "Have I. Said anything. About Newport or going back?"

"No," I admit. "Damn you."

He just smiles more, and hope blooms fast and fierce, but I'm trying my best to hold back the tidal wave rushing through me. He's had issues with people putting expectations on him, and I don't want to be another person doing that, but damned if my heart isn't doing it anyway.

Stay, stay, stay . . . It beats, so loudly I wonder if he can hear it.

Wyatt takes a deep breath, inhaling my scent and whispering in my ear, "That's because I'm not leaving. I'm staying here. With you. If you want me to."

Why does he sound like he's questioning that? I obviously want to throw him in my bed, chain him up, and never let him leave. Not in a *Misery* sort of way, but in an "I love you" way. Probably a bit soon to scare the hell out of him with that, though, so I shut myself up the best way possible . . . by kissing Wyatt.

It's not the classic "I love you" kiss, all soft and violins playing and one of us lifting a heel as our toes curl. No, it's hotter, deeper, more passionate . . . but all the same it's totally authentic, and when he pulls back, he's grinning. "So . . . that's a yes?"

I murmur against his lips, "You're really going to stay?"

He growls against my neck, his voice so deep I can feel the vibration. "Not going anywhere unless you are."

I start pulling him down the hallway, kissing as we go. "I'm going to the bedroom. You coming?"

"I sure fucking hope so."

I pause, a thought breaking through the rush of want pulsing through me. "I'm glad, but why?"

Wyatt grins, smoothing the worried furrow between my brows. "Because you're here, Hazel. And I love you."

I freeze, near certain that I'm having auditory hallucinations, because there is no way Wyatt Ford just told me that he loves me.

Oh hell, is this a dream?

Maybe I fell asleep on the couch, staring out the window, watching for Wyatt, and he's not even really here? If I wake up with a crick in my neck, alone with Lester, and none of this is real, I am going to be so pissed.

I need to be sure, so I pinch Wyatt's nipple, twisting it a little.

He slaps my hand away, barking out, "Ouch. What the hell? Warn me before introducing that shit."

He's real. He's here. He loves me. He's glaring at me like I've lost my mind.

"I love you too."

And then I'm kissing him again, or maybe he's kissing me? Either way, the words ignite the feelings rushing through us, and once again, I'm blown away by the passion Wyatt holds just below the surface, keeping a tight control on his hunger.

But he releases it for me, moving us the rest of the way down the hall to the bedroom.

Lester squawks, but neither Wyatt nor I pay attention as we close the door, eyes totally on each other. As one, we take off our clothes, shirt for shirt and jeans for jeans. Wyatt's eyes burn as I push my panties down, standing in front of him fully, totally nude and vulnerable.

But I've never felt safer.

"How do you want me?" I ask, reaching out and taking his cock in my hand. He's leaking precum in less than a stroke, and I relish the velvety steel in my hand. God, he's just right for me, just right for filling my pussy . . . and my heart.

"I've been staring at your ass since the day we met," Wyatt says, his look dark with promise.

"Is that so?" I ask, turning around and shaking my hips back and forth. I sashay to the bed, bending over and waiting for him. I'm expecting heat, torrid intensity . . . but instead, Wyatt steals my heart again with a feather-soft kiss on my shoulder.

"I want you, I love you," he whispers, his hand trailing down my spine and over the curve of my ass.

His fingers find my folds, stroking and massaging me as I moan, melting into his touch. He lies over me, his chest to my back, and I turn, kissing him over my shoulder. He takes his time prepping me, stretching me until I'm desperate for him. Even still, the feeling of his cock spreading me open from behind takes the very breath from my lungs.

I push back into his stroke and make our hips clap together. "Mmmm . . . love me hard, baby."

He does. Each stroke of his cock inside me lights up my body; each time my ass smacks hard against his taut hips and stomach, I gasp, wanting more . . . more . . . more.

I want Wyatt.

All of him.

His fingers dig into my waist. His other hand is wrapped in my hair to pull me in closer as he speeds up. The muscles of his legs are tight as he pours all his strength and passion into our joining.

I push back, giving every inch of myself, until, in a frozen heart-beat of pleasure that feels like it lasts an eternity, we peak together, and Wyatt's essence explodes deep inside my body as I fall apart in his grasp.

After we clean up, we collapse into my bed, my head resting on his chest. I listen to the thrum of his heartbeat, reassured with every deep throb. It's steady and sure, in contrast with mine, which is racing with excitement.

"Oh my god, Mom and Etta are gonna flip their shit."

Wyatt chuckles, his abs rolling sexily. "Could we not talk about them while we're naked? It's kind of a buzzkill."

I lift up the blanket, peeking at the goods, and then look up at him with innocent eyes. "Doesn't seem to be affecting you too much. Unless . . ." I flip over, propping up on an elbow, and mock-accuse, "You have a thing for them!"

Wyatt rolls his eyes and grabs my hips, pulling me astride him. "I have a thing for you. Always. Anywhere. But naked, I'd rather talk about anything but family."

I nod, more than happy with that. "Deal. On the topic of family, what are we going to do?"

"Right now? I'm hoping to recover for a few more minutes and then bury myself in you again," Wyatt says in a soft, sexy growl. "After that? I'd like to take you to dinner and then let you beat me at a game of pool."

I frown, looking up at him. "Let me? I'll wipe the table with you and we both know it."

After all, pool is serious business. But Wyatt ignores my entirely not-humble brag to continue on with his plans. "And after that? I would love to take you to Newport, show you my workshop."

"Newport?" I echo, a little worried. Cold Springs is my home.

"With you, Hazel. Temporarily," Wyatt says, relieving me. "I'm not going anywhere without you, but it would be nice to get a few things. I only packed for the wedding when I came, and I'd like to get some clothes and some of my tools."

Before I can agree, the door in the kitchen opens and Etta calls out, "Getchur clothes on, kids! I wanna hear what happened with Mayor Ford. Your mama's already on her way, too, bringing some Slutty Brownies. Told her that seemed appropriate given your current position."

While she talks, I can hear her opening and closing cabinets, helping herself to plates and forks to get ready for Mom's arrival. Thankfully, Etta doesn't open the bedroom door, which allows me to sigh dramatically and look up at Wyatt. "Your place is out in the middle of nowhere, right? No parents, no siblings, just the two of us?"

He pushes a lock of my messy hair behind my ear. "Just you and me."

"Can we leave now?" I ask eagerly.

He pops me on the ass playfully, grinning. "After we talk to your family."

I groan but agree. "Fine. Let's get dressed then. I don't trust Etta not to come in here to try to get a peek at your dick." Getting up, I yell, "Aunt Etta, I hate you right now."

"Love you, too, baby!"

From the living room, Lester calls out, "Bawk! Cockblock, cockblock, cawwwkblawwwk."

At the kitchen table, Mom and Aunt Etta look at Wyatt and me with barely concealed grins. They might as well be singing, "We know you had sexxx!"

Yeah, that's not awkward at all with your mother and pseudo-mother figure.

And when I take a bite of a Slutty Brownie Mom brought, I can't help but moan obscenely. "Ermagawd, Mom. These are sooo gud."

Mom sips her coffee with a smile of appreciation. "How'd everything go with your dad, Wyatt?"

He swallows his own bite of brownie, somehow not making any vulgar noises, and answers, "Surprisingly well. We've got some work to do, but I think we're in a good place to restart things. And Dad wants to fix the damage he's done with this whole subdivision thing. He never wanted to destroy Cold Springs or its community." He looks to Etta, who nods agreeably before glee washes over her.

"And Jed?" Etta asks, looking like she wants to hear that he's nursing his wounds in a pit somewhere. Preferably with acid dripping onto them.

Wyatt shrugs. "I think he likes being a big fish in a small pond, and Dad said he probably has a plan B, or more accurately, a site B, for the subdivision. Somewhere outside Cold Springs, which makes sense to me, but he'll have to get funds. According to Winston, those people in suits at the hearing were investors, and they walked out pretty angry."

Mom asks quietly, "Is it wrong if I hope the contract he signed with them is ironclad in their favor?"

Uh-oh, that doesn't sound good. "Did you hear back from the lawyer about your lease?"

Mom's nod is resigned. "Yes. The bad news is, Jed can change my rent because the term of the lease is up. It's part of the renegotiation, fair and square."

Etta adds eagerly, "Tell 'em the good news."

Mom's grin is pure devilment as she says, "I'm going to have to raise prices across the board, just a little. Probably twenty-five cents on everything. I'm going to call it a Jed Ford Fee."

Etta laughs. "Hell, it'll bug him more to have the menu redone with every item listing the price plus a Jed Ford Fee. Bad publicity will irritate him more than anything. I can't wait!"

Wyatt laughs. "You women are evil. I love it."

I can't help but smile happily. Most men, hell, most people, would be terrified of the crazy ideas we come up with and run for the hills. But Wyatt not only isn't scared, he approves and laughs along with us.

Aunt Etta leans my way, talking behind her hand, but keeping her typical volume so that everyone can hear the "secret" she's sharing with me. "I like this one, even if his last name is Ford and he's kin to Jed." She fakes spitting on my clean floor as she says Jed's name, and I suspect that's going to be a new habit.

I look at Wyatt, who's grinning easily as he eats, and tell Etta, "I like him too. Maybe one day, he'll make me a Ford too." I wink and Wyatt chokes on his brownie.

Mom and Etta laugh loudly. "Good job, girl. You gotta keep them on their toes."

"She definitely does that," Wyatt agrees. "Wouldn't have it any other way."

Epilogue

WYATT

This morning was like most others, with Lester scaring the shit out me. He must have escaped from his cage, and he's decided my morning wood is a mighty fine place to perch to wake up Hazel, and though I've switched to sleeping in boxers, it hasn't deterred him in the slightest. You think an alarm clock is bad, try bird claws on your dick. He's also taken to mimicking Hazel's sounds of pleasure with eerie accuracy, which is not welcome in the slightest when I come in from my workshop out back and have that split-second thought of *what the fuck is she doing?* and then find a mouthy bird, not my woman jilling off.

But today, despite its start, is not any other day. It's a beautiful afternoon, the sun shining over the field behind Hazel's house. Well, our house, I guess, since I've been living here almost a year. But honestly, my real home is the steel-framed workshop out back that's the new home of Ford Fine Carpentry.

And the house will always be Hazel's—her family's homestead passed through generations. One day, I hope she passes it on to our children. Maybe a daughter just like her mama?

The thought brings a smile to my face. That joy only grows when I see Mom and Dad. They're doing well since Dad retired as mayor of

Cold Springs, regularly doing yoga together, and starting their own book club for just the two of them. Sometimes their choices of literature surprise me, but hey, who am I to judge?

They walk down the makeshift aisle, which is mostly a section of grass framed with flower-filled vases, to sit in the front row of the small gathering of people, which notably does not contain Uncle Jed and Aunt Chrissy. We sent invitations, to be polite, but didn't even get an RSVP.

So be it. We still see them around town here and there, and Jed's still the largest contractor in the area, employing the bulk of the construction crews, but rest assured, every project and permit with his name attached is given extra attention at city hall. He still hasn't found a new site for Springdale Ranch, but I'm sure he hasn't given up on looking.

Next to Mom and Dad are Winston, Avery, and Wren.

Winston started his own private architecture firm, saying he learned how *not* to do business from the worst, and he's doing great things with it, already designing custom homes and a few commercial buildings well outside Cold Springs' city limits. But so far, his favorite project has been a renovation of the town library. Francine Lockewood specifically asked for Winston to do the design, a kind of olive branch to our family after she took over as mayor. But there were no hard feelings between Dad and her. In fact, Dad wished her well and promised to help with anything she needed, including the annual book drive for the town's new lending libraries, which she happily accepted.

Avery is due with their first child any day now. They're going to name him Joe after Avery's grandpa. And though I wouldn't tell Avery this, we've got a secret pool going on what baby Joe's first word is going to be based on Grandpa Joe's influence. My money's on *frank and beans*, though Hazel's got a decent shot at winning with *bullshit*. Either way, little Joe will lay his head in the custom, one-of-a-kind crib I made especially for him. Avery cried when I presented it to her and Winston at their baby shower, and I think Mom and Dad finally understand that what I do is art. My medium is simply wood.

Wren is doing . . . whatever it is Wren does. She's always busy, that much I know, but she keeps her life pretty close to the vest and we respect that. I suspect she's seeing Jesse, because I swear I've smelled sawdust on her and she would never deign to come into my woodshop, but so far, I can't prove it. If it's something important to her, she'll let us know.

Then I see Hazel. She is stunning, her white dress billowing in the slight wind and her dark hair pulled up. Her smile grows with each step as she walks toward me, her mom at her side. When they reach me, Daisy gives Hazel's hand to me and then leans in to kiss my cheek. Loud enough for only Hazel and me to hear, Daisy says, "She's your problem now."

Hazel's jaw drops in shock. "Mom!"

Daisy laughs and winks at her daughter before going to sit down.

The ceremony is beautiful and simple, just the way Hazel dreamed. Hell, this whole thing was put together with pride, some elbow grease, and Hazel's skillful negotiation tricks.

When it's my turn to speak vows, I speak from the heart. "You might've been the wrong bridesmaid, but you are . . . without a doubt . . . the right bride. And I can't wait to spend forever at your side. I love you, Hazel."

She smiles, though tears are threatening to spill over. "I love you, too, Wyatt. Even if you are a Ford."

She pauses, and right on cue, Etta stage-whispers, "Fucking Ford." Everyone laughs, even Dad.

Moments and a kiss later, Hazel Sullivan becomes my wife, Hazel Ann Ford. But it's merely a formality—she's been mine for a long time, and I've been hers. We merely sealed the promises we've made to each other with a kiss, our first as husband and wife.

We raise our entwined hands in celebration, and the small group cheers and claps. We walk down the aisle, but Hazel turns around at the end, right before we pass the fence into the yard. "Alright, everyone, let's go to Puss N Boots to party. Mom's got cake set up, Tayvious made his famous chili, and I've got twenty bucks that says me and Joan of Arc can whip any of your asses at pool."

That's my Hazel. So wrong, but just right.

ABOUT THE AUTHOR

Wall Street Journal, USA Today, Washington Post, and #1 Amazon best-selling author Lauren Landish welcomes you into a world of rock-hard abs and chiseled smiles. Her sexy contemporary romances—including her wildly successful Bennett Boys Ranch books, the Truth or Dare series, and the Big Fat Fake series—have garnered a legion of praise from her readers. When Lauren isn't plotting ways to introduce readers to their next sexy-as-hell book boyfriend, she's deep in her writing cave and furiously tapping away on her keyboard, crafting scenes that would make even a hardened sailor blush.

For all the updates and news on her upcoming books (not to mention a whole lotta hunks), visit her website at www.LaurenLandish. com or follow her on TikTok (@laurenlandish), Instagram (@Lauren_ Landish), and Facebook (@Lauren.Landish).